SCOTT FREE

ALSO BY JOHN GILSTRAP

Nathan's Run
At All Costs
Even Steven

SCOTT
FREE

a novel

JOHN
GILSTRAP

ATRIA BOOKS

New York London Toronto Sydney Singapore

ATRIA BOOKS

1230 Avenue of the Americas
New York, NY 10020

Library of Congress Control Number: 2002105799

ISBN: 0-671-78686-5

First Atria Books hardcover printing February 2003

10 9 8 7 6 5 4 3 2 1

ATRIA BOOKS is a trademark of Simon & Schuster, Inc.

For information regarding special discounts for bulk purchases,
please contact Simon & Schuster Special Sales at 1-800-456-6798
or business@simonandschuster.com

Designed by Jaime Putorti

Printed in the U.S.A.

In memory of the thousands of innocents who went to work on September 11, 2001, never knowing it was their last day.

With special thanks to the hundreds of firefighters and police officers whom I suspect did know, but went to work anyway. Words cannot capture the breadth of their sacrifice, any more than they can express the depth of our gratitude.

God bless you all.

ACKNOWLEDGMENTS

Always and forever, the first nod and heartfelt thanks go to my family. Joy and Chris, you are the reason why every day is beautiful—even the cloudy ones. I love you so much.

In the pages that follow, you'll discover that Scott O'Toole has a passion for heavy metal music. If he enjoyed the works of Beethoven or Britten or even Stravinsky, my research would have been easy— certainly less painful. As it is, the assault to my ears was rendered far easier through consultation with students of the Governor's School for Humanities and Visual and Performing Arts, class of 2000, conducted at the University of Richmond. Greg, Hailey, Max and Craig, thanks a million. (And remember, Max, Scott had blue hair long before you did.)

I'm an east-coaster who happens to love the western mountain ranges. If I got some of the little details wrong, my apologies to the residents of Utah. For the details I got right, I owe thanks to Dot Jackson. On the techie side of things, Brian Drake of Outfitter Satellites taught Scott and me everything we know about satellite phones. My dear friend and fellow author John Ramsey Miller put me in touch with my newfound weapons expert, Bill Grist. Thanks to all.

Thanks also to Linda Shorb at October Country Muzzleloading, Inc., for her patient assistance in helping me to understand the workings of modern day flintlocks. As it turns out, that particular subplot never materialized, but I'd be remiss not to acknowledge the kindness.

Then there's the backstage crew that just keeps me going: Jeff Deaver, who provides counsel that no one else can; Sandy Berthelsen, number-one fan and supporter; Duffy Ward, M.D., medical (and outdoor) consultant, walking buddy and good friend; and Joe, the aging black lab who makes my office a little warmer every day.

In the pages that follow, I paint a portrait of literary agents that is none too complimentary. This is fiction, folks. The reality is, without my own agents, Molly Friedrich and Matthew Snyder, I'd be lost in this business. Thank you both for all you do.

The people at Atria Books and Pocket Books work very hard to make my stories more compelling, and to put them into the hands of readers. Thanks to Judith Curr, Tracy Behar, Louise Burke, and especially to George Lucas. Thanks also to the dedicated professionals at Michael Joseph, my U.K. publisher, with special nods to Tom Weldon and Rowland White.

DAY ONE

1

THE CESSNA DANCED all over the sky.

The pilot shouted to Scott over the engine noise, "Everything's gonna be just fine. The storm's just a little heavier than I'd anticipated."

A little heavier. As in, the walls of the Grand Canyon are a little steep.

The pilot tried to put the best face on it. "Forget it. In ninety minutes, our ears'll be bleeding from the music."

Scott shot him a look. "You told me ninety minutes a half hour ago."

The pilot tossed a tense shrug. "Like I said, the storm's worse than I thought."

Metallica was appearing at the Delta Center in Salt Lake City, and the pilot—a ski patroller named Cody Jamieson—had somehow scared up two tickets from a couple of college kids who'd let the blizzard intimidate them. Nobody in their right minds would risk getting stranded on the back roads of the Wasatch in weather like this.

For Cody, however, road conditions were irrelevant. He had his very own airplane—a twenty-five-year-old high-wing job that he'd picked up for a song and maintained himself in a little corner of the hangar at SkyTop's private airstrip. The idea was to fly out of the storm, then beat its arrival in Salt Lake City. If they ended up stranded after the concert, Cody knew some people at BYU who'd put them both up in a heartbeat.

It seemed like a good idea at the time.

The aircraft lurched violently, the worst bump yet, knocking Cody's flying charts onto Scott's lap. "Air currents," he explained before Scott could ask.

This whole thing was beginning to feel stupid. They'd met less than a week ago while Cody was writing Scott up for skiing out of control on Widow Maker. It turned out that the ticket was little more than a warning, but Scott had gone off like a bomb anyway. He was the only skier *in* control, for crying out loud. It was a matter of principle. He'd thrown down his poles and his hat, kicked off his skis, and was ready to fight it out. "Why don't you write up those assholes for doing two miles an hour on a black diamond slope?"

Cody ignored the challenge and asked him what he played.

"What?"

The ski patroller nodded toward Scott's head. "The hair. I figure you've got to be part of a band."

Scott's bushy crop of blue hair had earned him the nickname Smurf from his soccer teammates. "Guitar," he said, caught off guard by the randomness of it. "Lead guitar." Just like that, the acrimony evaporated.

At twenty-one, Cody was five years Scott's senior, and also a guitarist—heavy metal all the way. A first-year member of the patrol, the guy was anxious to find somebody to jam with, and Scott put him to shame. As payment for impromptu lessons, Cody introduced his new buddy to the gang, giving him the chance to slug down illegal beers and participate in the ski patrollers' late-night snowmobile races. Best of all, it gave Scott a reason to spend as much time as possible away from his mom. They dubbed him their mascot, and thanks to the nod from Cody, they treated him like a full-fledged member of the crowd—almost more a member than Cody, who, as a rookie, was the brunt of unrelenting teasing and practical jokes.

So, when the Metallica tickets became available, Cody chose Scott.

But this snowstorm crap was more than he'd bargained for.

Rodeo cowboys enjoyed smoother rides. "Do you have any idea what you're doing up here?" Scott shouted.

The question drew a nervous glance. "I know enough to find the airport and set us down."

"Then how come we're still in the air?"

"I think the winds blew us a little off course," Cody admitted.

Something in his tone sparked a note of terror. "Does that mean you don't know where we are?"

"It means I know reasonably well where I am. If I could just get a quick peek at the ground, it would help a lot."

The reality hit Scott like a slap. The only way to catch a glimpse of the ground was to get closer to it, and here in the mountains, that was a good way to get snatched out of the sky by a rock. "Why don't you call on the radio? They'll look at your spot on the radar screen and tell you where you are." Scott had seen enough movies to know how this sort of thing worked.

Cody Jamieson seemed not to hear the question. When Scott repeated it, he snapped, "I don't have a transponder, okay? They can't see me on their screen."

"Well, call in a Mayday, then."

Again, Cody seemed not to hear.

"Cody?"

"The radio doesn't work."

"*What?*"

Cody didn't bother to repeat himself.

Scott's head swam with the utter stupidity of it all. He was in the company of a moron, but he swallowed his anger. Never piss off the only guy who knows how to fly the plane. "Can you at least turn up the heat?" he asked. "I'm freezing."

This time, he didn't even expect an answer. He pulled the headphones from his Discman over his knit cap, hit Play, and cranked up the volume. That done, he pulled his seat belt tighter, donned his gloves, and tried not to think about the approaching wave of air sickness.

With his eyes closed, he tried to become a part of the music, to forget about the danger. The Stones CD was one he'd stolen from his dad's collection—not his first choice for facing death, but he wasn't about to go fishing for something new. As he tried to concentrate on the power and complexity of Keith Richards's guitar licks, Scott did his best to ignore the slamming beat of his heart.

Cody Jamieson's terrified shriek cut through the music like a razor through flesh. Scott snapped his eyes open and started yelling, too, even before he saw the obstacle that loomed up out of the darkness ahead of them.

By the time he realized it was a tree, they'd already hit it.

SHERRY CARRIGAN O'TOOLE sat in the far corner of the White Peaks Lounge. She thought of it as the power spot—the one from which she could take in the entire room with a single glance. The place was packed, despite the $9.00 price tag on the drinks, and the atmosphere positively vibrated with news of the blizzard. Sherry gleaned from her targeted eavesdropping that as good as the slopes had been these past couple of days, another foot or two of fresh powder would make this the vacation of a lifetime. Add the presence of the president of the United States, who had already proclaimed SkyTop Village to be his family's longtime favorite vacation spot, and the tongue-waggers could barely contain their enthusiasm.

Whoop-de-freaking-doo.

In the forty-five minutes that Sherry had been waiting for Larry to show up, she'd been hit on twice, once by a ski patroller who looked like the Marlboro Man, and the second time by a guy in his sixties who must have had a lot of money, because guys that ugly always had a lot of money. On a different day, she might have been complimented by the attention, but not today. This whole trip had been a disaster from the very start. Brandon had Scotty so thoroughly brainwashed that she'd never had a chance to break through to the boy.

In fact, at the close of their fifth day in skiers' paradise (and Sherry's personal hell), they were further apart than when they'd arrived. How was that for gratitude? Here, she'd negotiated him a week off from school, footed the bill for him to spend a week in the place he'd always dreamed of going, and he copped an attitude because she didn't want to ski. Like that was some big surprise? She'd *never* liked to ski.

For the better part of a week, then, they'd barely seen each other, their interaction limited mostly to breakfasts on the heels of his late-night returns, his breath smelling of beer. Night before last, she could have sworn that he purposely breathed on her to get a rise. Nice try. She'd be damned if she was going to play the queen-bitch role that ex-hubby Brandon had assigned to her. If Scotty wanted to experiment with underage drinking, then she couldn't think of a bet-ter, safer place for him to test his wings.

She took a long pull on her second cosmopolitan, noting that Carmella, her server-this-evening, was watching. Sherry signaled for one more.

The White Peaks Lounge was a room that didn't know what it wanted to be when it grew up. Built in the 1930s in the rustic style of the lodge itself, it seemed to be trying to attract a younger crowd. Unfortunately, the small cocktail tables and chrome-and-leather sling chairs didn't make the place look modern so much as it gave the impression of a retro yard sale.

For the last five minutes, she'd been matching avoided glances with a balding, forty-something guy sporting a cast on his arm. Every time she felt the heat of his gaze, she'd look up in time to see him looking someplace else. That kind of adolescent crap drove Sherry crazy. If they wanted to make a pass, then they should just have the balls to take their shot and get the rejection over with quickly.

Oh, shit, here he comes.

Armed with what had to be his third martini, the guy spun him-self off his barstool and sauntered her way. Unlike so many of the other orthopedic victims she'd seen these past five days, this guy had an athletic look that told her he'd earned his injury doing something daring. As he approached, the eye contact held, and she greeted his smile with one of her own. Maybe rejection wasn't in his future after all.

"Excuse me," he said, gesturing to the empty seat. "Is this taken?" His smile was liquid from the booze.

Sherry gave him her coyest smile. "I've been saving it for my assistant, but he seems to be running a little late."

Mr. Charming pulled out the chair. "May I?"

Sherry shrugged.

"My name is Bernard Caplan. People call me Bernie." He extended his hand across the table and Sherry took it.

Why did that name ring a bell? "Pleased to meet you. I'm—"

"You're Sherry Carrigan O'Toole," Bernie said.

Sherry felt herself blush. *Ah, a fan* . . .

"I've read your books. You caught me staring from over there, and rather than be mysterious, I thought I'd come on over and meet you personally."

Sherry did her fawning-fan giggle. "I'm so happy you did. And what did you do to your arm?"

Bernie made a face that said the injury didn't mean a thing. "Some beginner idiot on Dark Passage rammed me from behind yesterday. Broke my wrist. You know, I catch you on the radio from time to time."

This time, the giggle was real. Handsome, athletic and a fan. This had real possibilities.

"Do you recognize *my* name, by chance?" Bernie asked.

Sherry's eyes narrowed as she churned Bernard Caplan through her memory banks. Something was there, all right. Something so close . . .

"That's okay if you don't," Bernie said with a dismissive wave. "It's actually *Doctor* Bernie Caplan, and I'm the chief of psychiatric medicine at the University of Virginia."

Something changed behind Bernie's eyes, and as it did, Sherry felt her stomach flip.

"I saw you here, and I thought to myself, 'When will I get another chance like this?' So, here I am." Just like that, with the precision that only a mental health practitioner can muster, all the humor evaporated from Dr. Bernard Caplan's face. "I wanted you to know that I think your brand of moralizing pop psychology does more harm to more people on a daily basis than all the world's missed diagnoses combined. In the past year alone, I've treated two teenaged girls who were depressed to the point of self-destruction because they could not meet the minimum standards of perfection you laid out in *The Mirror's Not the Problem.*"

Sherry felt the muscles of her chest and abdomen tighten, preparing for battle. "That's 'minimum goals to strive for,' " she corrected. "And *Mirror* sold nearly a million copies in hardcover."

Bernie smiled. The real one wasn't nearly as attractive as the one he used to lure her off her guard. "You say that as if it's something to be proud of. Millions of people are duped every day by charlatans."

"Now listen here—"

"There's no need to get defensive," Bernie said, showing his palms. "I just saw you here relaxing, having a good time, and I thought I'd share with you what you've put a real doctor through since you became the self-help quack-of-the-day."

A shadow fell across the table. "Is there something wrong here?" Finally, Larry had arrived. Six feet tall if he really stretched, and a hundred-fifty pounds on his fattest day, Larry Chinn's entire life was ruled by Sherry O'Toole and *Gentlemen's Quarterly*, not necessarily in that order. With his close-cropped, spiky bleached hair and tiny granny glasses, he was the poster child for closeted gays. Tonight, he wore chalet chic—blue jeans and a turtleneck, with a cotton sweater tossed over his shoulders—and, sensing the tension at the table, he tried his best to look intimidating.

"I think that Mr. Caplan was just leaving," Sherry said. She got the honorific wrong on purpose.

Caplan assessed Larry with a single condescending glance. "Indeed I was," he said. "But just remember, Sherry, one day the public will wake up to your nonsense, and you'll have to deal with your peers again." He stood. "When that day comes, I'll be waiting for you."

Now it was Sherry's turn to be smug. "Dream on, Caplan," she said. "If I decided to retire tomorrow, my great-grandchildren wouldn't know how to spend the money I've made."

Caplan raised his glass in a mock toast. "Until the malpractice suits," he said.

Larry watched him walk back to the bar, then slid into his place. "Is that true?" he asked.

"What? About malpractice?"

"No, about your grandchildren not being able to spend all the money you've made."

Sherry scowled. "Of course not." Then the scowl turned into a grin. "That'll happen in two more books."

Larry nodded at the dregs in Sherry's glass. "How far behind am I?"

"Two." Then, as if on cue, Carmella reappeared, a new drink balanced on her tray. "Soon to be three."

Larry ordered a White Russian ("heavy on the Russian, light on the white"), and finally they were alone in the crowd.

"I suppose you're wondering why I wanted you here," Sherry said.

"I only hope that it's for a long string of clichéd openings like, 'I suppose you're wondering why I wanted you here.' Want to know my sign?"

Sherry made a face that looked like a snarl. She leaned into the table and Larry joined her. "Have you been to the phone booth that they have the nerve to call a bookstore?" she asked.

"Actually, no. And given the fact that we're at one of the top five ski resorts in North America, with some of the finest powder I've ever seen, I can't imagine why."

Sherry was in no mood for irony. "They only have three of my books," she said. "Actually, to be more precise, they only have three copies of one book—*Mirror*—and that's only in paperback. There's not a single copy of *Mirror II*. Do you know how embarrassing that is? My seminar is in two days, and they've only laid in three paperbacks."

Larry looked at her like she'd sprouted leaves. "Sherry, do they carry *any* hardcovers?"

Sherry took a sip of her cosmo. "I don't know."

"Well, if the store is as small as you say, they probably don't."

"What about *It's All in Your Smile* or *The Microwave Mom?*" Sherry protested. "They're both in paperback, and neither of them are in the store."

Larry sighed deeply and looked over his shoulder to check on the progress of his drink. "Have you thought about taking a skiing lesson? I mean, my God, Sherry, you need a little life here."

"I don't participate in sports where gravity and trees combine as mortal enemies."

Larry laughed. "Why are you here? Why take a seminar gig at a ski resort if you hate skiing?"

"You know damn well why."

Larry rolled his eyes. "Right. Brandon and Scott. God forbid they have fun together. You know, there's something really twisted in all that."

"What's twisted," she said, "is that 'Team Bachelor' crap. Makes me sick."

Sherry tried her best to show a flash of anger, but she knew Larry wouldn't buy it. They'd known each other too long, gone through too many adventures together. No one fully understood her relationship with Larry—Sherry wasn't entirely sure she understood it herself— but he was the one person who understood her. She called him her assistant mostly because the world frowned on the notion of paid companions. Half of the professional publishing world assumed that they were lovers, and the other half assumed that they were both gay. Sherry honestly didn't give a shit.

"Well, it'd be one thing if you trumped Brandon in doing something you actually enjoyed, but as it is now, who's laughing harder, know what I mean?"

Sherry sighed. "I know exactly what you mean." She took another sip of her drink, just as the White Russian arrived for Larry. "I'm not a total bitch, you know. I did actually hope that maybe Scotty and I could get to know each other a little better. But I never see him."

"That's because he's *skiing*, Sherry. Ski resort. Skiing. Do you see the link?"

Sherry laughed in spite of herself. "Well, during the day, sure. But I don't even see him in the evenings. God knows what he's been eating."

"He's sixteen. He hates the world."

Sherry thought about that. Adolescence was defined all over the world by rebellion. It was the same in every culture, every race, every religion. She'd heard some interesting theories that it was true in every species. Sometimes she wondered if teenagers didn't in fact *become* a different species for a while.

She checked her watch. "Tonight, for example," she said. "The last thing we said to each other as he was on his way out to the slopes was, let's meet for dinner. He was supposed to call me, or at least leave a message at the chalet, but no. Not a word." She saw Larry's eyes shift. "What?"

"Excuse me?"

"You know something."

He made a face like she was crazy, but he squirmed in his chair. "I know a lot of things."

Sherry wasn't buying it. "You wear a guilty conscience like a badge, Larry. Let me hear it."

"I told Scott I wouldn't say anything," he hedged. Way to hold out till the end.

"Larry."

He sighed. "He went to Salt Lake City."

Sherry's jaw dropped. "He *what?*"

Larry squirmed some more. "There's a concert there. He went with some ski patrol guy he met. Nice guy. I did a couple of runs with both of them."

Sherry couldn't believe she was hearing this. "Have you looked at the weather out there? How on earth are they going to drive to Salt Lake City?"

More squirming. "They're, um, not driving, actually. His friend is a private pilot. He owns his own plane."

This time, Sherry's rage was real. "Jesus, Larry, how long have you known about this?"

Her anger surprised him. "Since this morning."

"And you didn't say anything?"

"What was I going to say?"

"Oh, I don't know, something like, 'Hey, Sherry, your son has lost his mind.' My God, they're *flying* in this weather?"

Larry dismissed her with a wave as he took another sip of his drink. "Will you relax? If it wasn't safe, they wouldn't let them take off in the first place."

2

THE SENSATION OF PAIN was unlike anything that Scott had ever felt. His whole body seemed to vibrate with a sharp, bright-white agony that made him feel as if he were ready to explode. A full-body toothache. It was that sharp. That hot.

It was so quiet. After the horrific noise of the crash, the grinding and twisting of metal and the screams that might have been his own, the silence terrified him.

"Cody?" He could barely hear himself. "Cody?" He said it louder this time, but the night still returned only silence.

The feeling of disorientation was overwhelming—huge pressure in his head and his belly, yet the unmistakable sensation that he was floating. He had no idea how long he'd been here. His mind played an image of him climbing out of a hole in his brain. As he pulled himself closer to the rim, the pain blossomed. Bitter cold pressed in around him, explaining the sensation of a million needles in his skin.

Hypothermia!

His mind fired the thought like a rifle bullet, launching him to a new level of alertness. These temperatures played for keeps; on a night like this, a few hours could mean eternity in a box.

Scott O'Toole had no intention of dying tonight.

Why couldn't he move? He considered for a moment that he might be paralyzed, but the pain and the cold ruled that out. He wasn't breathing right, either. The pressure in his head. The pain in his belly.

Oh, my God, I'm upside down.

"You there, Scott?" The voice came from so close by that Scott wondered for a second if he wasn't just thinking out loud.

He jerked his head to the left to see Cody Jamieson's silhouette hovering just inches from his own. A jet black splotch against the lighter black background, the pilot's hair stood straight on end.

"Dude, I'm fucked, man," Cody said.

Scott didn't like the fatalistic tone. "Hey, we're alive, right? That's a good first step."

"No, dude, I mean I'm really fucked up. I can't feel anything below like my chest."

Scott's gut tightened at the thought, but he sensed that this was a time to keep things light. "Count your blessings. I can feel every damn thing, and it all hurts. What the hell happened?"

"You've heard of flying at treetop level, haven't you?" Cody forced a chuckle, which became a wheezing, gagging cough. "I taste blood, dude."

"Probably just cut your lip."

Cody coughed again, and as he did, the whole world seemed to move around Scott. It was a swaying motion, back and forth. And then everything shifted. For a second, he thought they were falling, but then it all settled down again. The movement caused a new sound to gurgle out of Cody, half moan and half wail.

"What? What is it?" Scott yelled.

"Oh, man, I am so righteously fucked."

"We need a light," Scott said. "I can't see a thing."

Cody's shadow moved in the darkness. A hand motioned lazily toward the bulkhead behind Scott and to the right. "Check the wall there. There should be a flashlight mounted to a charger there."

Scott strained to turn, but this disorientation was killing him. Left, right, up, down, none of them had any meaning. And why couldn't he move?

The seat belt.

Of course! He was still strapped into his seat! That explained the pressure and the biting pain in his gut, too. The seat belt was cutting him in half. Until he got that undone, he wasn't moving anywhere to recover anything.

But first, it was time to do an inventory. Maybe he was hurt, too, but just hadn't figured it out yet. His head felt fuzzy, and he was almost certain it was bleeding, but as he gingerly explored his scalp with his fingertips, it seemed that his brains were all tucked in where they belonged. There on his forehead, though, right at his widow's peak, a nasty gash flashed a jolt of pain when he touched it. Yeah, he was bleeding, all right. He moved his shoulders next, and then his back, as best as he could in his current position. Everything felt stiff, but nothing felt terribly wrong until he worked his way down to his right ankle. He moved it, and the joint screamed. It felt as if his foot were jammed into something—or better yet, *between* two some-things.

Shit, that's what I need. A broken ankle out in the middle of nowhere.

Actually, he'd broken his ankle before—last year, in fact, during the final soccer tournament against the Madison Warhawks—and this didn't feel as bad as that. His toes wiggled inside his boot without pain, and when he moved his knee, it didn't feel like the top of his head was coming off. *That* was what a broken ankle felt like. This just felt like a pinned ankle. In his mind, he re-created the look of the cockpit's floorboards and determined that he must somehow have gotten himself tangled up in the rudder pedals. If he could just ease his foot a little to the left . . .

There! He felt it move. It hurt like hell, but what did he expect, leveraging bone against steel? The more he pulled, the more he felt his boot move. Okay, at least it was definitely not broken. Let's hear a hip-hip-hurrah for that little blessing.

Finally, his leg was free; but as his boot pulled away from its restraint, Scott dropped completely away from his seat, the strap across his lap now bearing his full weight. The pressure drove the air from his lungs and squished his guts. It was choking him. Didn't he read some-where that you could die simply by the act of hanging upside down for too long? Something about blood pressure in the brain.

As his eyes adjusted to the darkness, some of the shadows began to make sense to him. Through the puffs of gray that were his breath, he could make out the outline of the windshield, and the post where it joined the side of the fuselage, but the rest was all forest and snow. And Cody Jamieson's dangling head.

"You still awake, Cody?"

The pilot groaned again. His breathing had become juicy—a sound like the last pull through a straw.

"You'll be okay," Scott said. "You just watch. We'll be out of here in no time." *Even if we don't know where here is,* he didn't say. A thousand things needed to be done, and first on the list was getting himself out of his seat. Once he had his feet on the ground, he could start thinking through everything else. But he was upside down! The instant he unlatched the belt, he was going to drop on his head, which was already throbbing quite nicely, thank you very much. He used his gloved hands to explore the area over (under?) his head and found that he could just barely reach the top of the cockpit—maybe a two-foot drop. Not so bad.

Okay, this was it. Holding his left arm over his head to absorb the impact, he found the seat belt buckle with his right. One . . . Two . . . Three! He lifted the clasp with his fingertips, and instantly, he dropped like an anvil, catching most of the impact on his neck and shoulders.

Cody Jamieson howled as the aircraft trembled under the impact. The howl became a scream as the plane shifted again, this time taking on a bizarre yawing motion that Scott might have written off to dizziness from his head injury. Outside, a gust of wind pelted them, and the yawing and the screaming got even worse.

Scott needed that flashlight. Sprawled flat on the ceiling now, he could just make out a blinking red light, barely bigger than a pinhead, but bright as a lighthouse in the near total darkness. The flashlight on his Uncle Jim's boat had a beacon just like it, working all the time, with or without power, always visible in an emergency.

The plane shifted again, and he froze. Something about this wasn't right. And when he put the pieces of the puzzle together, his heart nearly froze in his chest. "No, it can't be," he told himself aloud. "Tell me we're not."

Suddenly petrified to move at all, Scott stretched out as far as his arms would allow to pull the light from its charger. It came free with a click. The dim beam might as well have been a klieg light, instantly transforming pitch black to blinding white. It took Scott all of three seconds to assess the severity of his nightmare, and one more to wish he'd never found the light.

He'd never seen so much snow. It swirled everywhere, inside the aircraft and out, driven by winds that somehow grew colder as Scott could see them blow. The windows on the Cessna were all gone now, and beyond them, the snow fell in thick clouds among the twisted and broken limbs of trees.

Wincing against his fear of what he might find, Scott inched toward the opening and dared a peek down at the ground, which was every inch of fifty feet below.

BACK IN THE CHALET, Sherry worked one phone while Larry worked the other.

"I understand that the airport is closed," she said to somebody named Angela at the airport in Salt Lake City. "You've already told me that. What I want to know is, whether a plane has landed there."

"No, ma'am, there have been no landings," Angela said. "No takeoffs, either. That's what happens when you close an airport."

Sherry wanted to smack her. "Are there other airports, then? Municipal fields where someone might land a small private plane?"

"Dozens of them, but they're all closed, too. Is someone over-due? Is that why you're so distraught?"

Interesting question, Sherry thought. "Can you hang on just one second?" She covered the mouthpiece and turned to Larry. "What have you found out?"

Larry hung up his receiver. "Not a thing. Apparently, the airfield here is unmanned. People can take off and land as they please. There's no radio communication, nothing."

Sherry sighed. "So, what do I tell these people? Is he missing, or isn't he?"

"It gets worse. I haven't even been able to find anybody to verify that this Cody guy's plane is missing. Maybe he keeps it someplace else."

Anger was beginning to trump Sherry's fear. "So, for all we know, Scotty's really at somebody's room, getting laid or drinking beer." She turned back to Angela. "Listen, thanks for your help," she said, and then she hung up. She headed toward the wet bar that separated the enormous living room from the enormous kitchen. "You want a drink?"

"Sherry, you have to do something, here," Larry said, moving to block her passage. "You can't just assume that he's out getting his rocks off, if in fact he's out there lost in a snowstorm."

She faked left, then moved right to get around him. It was time to switch to scotch. "I've been thinking about this," she said. "Scott is lazy and he's full of attitude, but he's not stupid. He wouldn't take off in a little airplane in this weather."

"For Metallica? Who are you kidding?"

Sherry poured three fingers and downed half of it on the first gulp. "I just don't want to press the panic button."

Larry saw something in her expression that caused him to scowl. Suddenly, he sensed that they weren't talking only about Scott anymore. "Say what's on your mind, Sher."

Sherry inhaled loudly and let it go as a sigh. How could she put this and not seem harsh? "If Sherry Carrigan O'Toole goes shouting from the rooftops that her son is missing, and then he turns up drunk somewhere, the tabloids will eat it up. I'll look like a fool."

Larry looked at her like she was crazy. "The *tabloids?* Jesus, Sherry, you've never been in a tabloid. You're an author, for chrissakes, not a movie star."

"I'm a television personality, too."

Larry threw his hands in the air. "I don't believe we're talking about this. He's your *son.* Want to see yourself get torn apart by the press? Let the word leak out that you knew there was a chance he went missing but refused to say anything. They'll hang you in effigy, and I'll carry the rope!"

Sherry clasped the sides of her head with her open palms. She hated stress, and she hated making decisions quickly. "You know who's going to have a field day with this, don't you? Brandon. God, I can hear him now."

"Sherry!"

Larry couldn't possibly see the world through her eyes. This whole thing was Brandon's fault to begin with. If he hadn't made the divorce such a damn war, then she wouldn't have to constantly up the ante. How else could she hope to overcome the lock those two had on each other? Team Bachelor. Why not just settle for Super Dad and Scott the Wonder Boy? Brandon had always resented her career and her money, always looked down his nose at her because she didn't have time for Little League and soccer and brownie-making. She could already hear his condescending tone and see his supercilious sneer as he confronted her on this one, as if it were her fault that Scotty had wandered off.

"I know you think I'm crazy, Larry, but I really think we need some data before we mobilize the cavalry."

"Well, what do you want to do?" Larry checked his watch. "It's almost seven o'clock."

Sherry thought about it, and the more she turned it over in her mind, the less she believed that Scott was really in any jeopardy. "Let's first verify that the plane is missing."

"How? I just told you—"

Sherry waved him off. "You've been talking to the wrong people. For what they charge paying customers to stay here, I bet I can get resort management to find out anything I want to know." She picked up the portable phone again and started to dial, then stopped after three digits to stare at the buttons. The reality of it hit her all at once, and her breath escaped her throat in a gasp. "Oh, my God," she said. "Scotty might be dead."

Larry hurried toward her to lend comfort, his arms wide, prepared to envelop her in a hug. "Oh Sherry . . ." When he was still five feet away, he stopped abruptly and ducked as Sherry hurled the phone at him, missing his head by inches.

"Why didn't you tell me he was going up in an airplane?" she shrieked.

• • •

CODY JAMIESON WAS INDEED righteously fucked. A sliver of broken tree about the size of a two-by-four had skewered him through the belly, entering dead center at what looked to be the base of his rib cage, and exiting through the back of his seat. Scott gasped as his flashlight beam found the damage, and he quickly looked away.

"I'm gonna die, aren't I?" Cody asked. There was a resolution to his voice that Scott found unnerving.

"Nah, you're gonna be fine."

"You're a fuckin' liar, dude. And not a very good one. Anyone ever tell you that?" Again, he faked a chuckle, and again, his body—and the plane—shook from his wracking cough. "The freaky thing is, it doesn't hurt. I mean, I can feel with my hands where the spear goes in, but it must have done something to fuck up my spine, so it's like I'm touching somebody else, know what I mean?"

No, Scott didn't know what he meant. And he didn't want to. He wanted to know nothing at all about what it felt like to die. He didn't want to hear about bright lights, or angels or any of that crap. Right now, all he wanted to know was how in the hell he was going to get out of this tree without getting killed himself.

Think, Scott, think.

"Just promise me you won't pull this thing out, okay?" Cody said. "If I judge things right, the pressure from the wood is about the only thing keeping me from bleeding to death."

"We're up in a tree," Scott said, daring another look out the window and over the edge. "*Way* up in a tree."

"Thinking of leaving me here, are you?"

A blast of wind howled like a train whistle through the evergreen boughs, rolling the plane a good five or ten degrees. Cody and Scott both yelled as debris slid across the ceiling and out into the vastness of the night.

Yeah, Scott was thinking of leaving him; but even as he did, his conscience burned. If Scott saved himself, Cody would die. It was that simple. Never in his life had Scott ever read a story or seen a movie where the good guy leaves another good guy to bleed to—

The plane pitched again, more violently this time. "Oh, God,

Scott!" Cody shrieked. "Oh God, help me! It's hurting! Aw, fuck, oh, Jesus, it's hurting!" His words came in a rush as the aircraft continued to pivot in its cradle.

Scott didn't know what to do. As the whole world shifted around him, and debris tumbled everywhere, he scrambled for something to grab hold of. The pilot's unspeakable screams drove him even faster. The flashlight tumbled from his hands as he grabbed for something solid enough to hold his weight, and as the beam swept past Cody Jamieson's face, Scott caught the shutter-flash glimpse of a shimmering gout of blood lurching from the pilot's nose and mouth.

Now, the screams all came from Scott. Something cracked, with the sound of a pistol shot, and then the plane was falling. It was a hesitant, slow-motion fall, twisting and tumbling on all axes at once as branches and pieces of wreckage slammed into him from all directions. It was all shadows and noise and pain. He saw only varying shades of blackness, dark black against light black, and it all revolved at a speed that seemed too slow for the noise and debris it generated.

Through the confusion, Scott saw a rectangle of charcoal gray. His brain saw it as a window, and his body reacted without him even thinking. A tree limb would hold his 145 pounds a hell of a lot more easily than it would hold the wreckage of an airplane. As the rectangle passed, he dove for it, and just like that, he was out in the bitter cold, tumbling on his own through the limbs and branches, desperately reaching into the blackness for something to hold on to. He managed to snag a big branch in the crook of his elbow, his legs bicycling in the air. The odor of Christmas trees filled his head as the Cessna fell farther and farther away. Finally, the noise of the impacts stopped.

And then he was alone.

3

BRANDON O'TOOLE PRESSED THE BUTTON to lower the garage door, and dragged himself through the mud room into the family room. It was nearly ten o'clock, and it had been one hell of a day. He could barely focus his eyes as he sifted the mail. Junk, junk and more junk. Somewhere in this world there was a master mailing list, and when he found where it was located, he swore to God he'd burn the place down himself.

He missed Scott. For crying out loud, the kid had only been gone for five days, yet it felt like a month. He'd spent a week away lots of times—every summer for camp. What was it about this week that made it seem so impossibly long?

No Ph.D. required to answer that one.

The SkyTop trip was classic Sherry. She *hated* skiing. The whole time they were married, she'd refused to go, even though Brandon's status as a volunteer ski patroller got them free lift tickets at any of the nearby resorts in Virginia or Pennsylvania. Skiing was what the *guys* did for fun, and it drove Sherry nuts. This was her most despicable move yet. Not just skiing, but skiing at SkyTop Village—for Brandon's money, the most beautiful spot on earth. He'd made the mistake of mentioning his intention to take Scott there one day, and Sherry had beaten him to it.

Look up "controlling bitch" in the dictionary, and there's a picture of Sherry. For an entire week, Scott would be treated to a nonstop litany of what an asshole his father was. Who'd be bitter about such a thing as that?

What had he ever seen in Sherry? He often questioned himself about that, and as best he could tell, it was something akin to a lucrative business arrangement. She had her Ph.D. in psych with enough of her own personal problems to keep three practitioners in business, and he had his career at Federal Research, and together, they'd be able to live a great life, sustained by really great sex.

And for ten years, it worked; until Scott stopped being the obedient little boy she so enjoyed parading in front of her patients as the poster child for good parenting, and he started experimenting with adolescent attitudes. *Okay, Mom* became *in a minute,* and *sure* became *why,* and suddenly, the great Sherry Carrigan O'Toole, celebrated author of *The Mirror's Not the Problem,* found herself foundering in the same rocky waters where her patients' ships had so often run aground.

It was all Brandon's fault, of course; it had nothing to do with her own neurotic obsession with her only child's quest for excellence, or the fact that she'd never had time to counsel *him.* As the son of a famous author—she'd been on *Oprah,* after all—Scott had no need for such things. Apparently, if it hadn't been for Brandon's insistence that the boy attend *public* school and associate with people whose parents weren't as neurotic as she, then Scott would have had the decency to repress the normal struggles of childhood. Overnight, it seemed, the men in Sherry's life became giant boils on her butt.

They conspired against her, don't you know, intentionally putting the jelly or the milk on the wrong shelf in the fridge, and allowing dirty socks to touch the floor instead of making it all the way to the hamper. And God knows Scott's soccer and basketball seasons were keeping her from fulfilling the contract on her second book.

A few weeks on the *Times* list means a lot of dough, easily trumping Brandon's hundred seventy grand a year, and money made Sherry Carrigan O'Toole queen of the roost, leaving Brandon and Scott as mere servants to the court. At first, these bizarre changes in his wife bugged him. For months, they bugged him. Then one day, without fanfare or any single event he could point to, he realized that he just didn't give a shit anymore.

He suggested they get a divorce and she said okay. Really, that's all there was to it. They sold their house in Great Falls, and Brandon moved to a four-bedroom split-level in Fairfax, while Sherry bought a showplace in Georgetown, an address commensurate with her new-found ego. That Scott would live with Brandon was a foregone conclusion; none of them even questioned it.

Until the attorneys got involved, and Sherry suddenly discovered her long-lost maternal instincts. She sued for sole custody initially, but then the thought of actually winning must have frightened her, because within a week, she'd changed it to joint custody.

Child-sharing, Brandon called it. Like job-sharing, or ride-sharing. All about Sherry's convenience, without a lot of consideration for what's best for Scott. Brandon refused.

No, he declared, it would be sole custody with visitation rights, and he, Brandon, would be primary custodian. Twenty-eight thousand dollars in legal fees later, it all boiled down to this: If Brandon relinquished rights to their marital stock investments—about $3 million—Sherry would go along with his custodial demands, provided her child support payments would never exceed $1,500 a month, even during the college years. Brandon signed the papers without two seconds' negotiation.

For the price of a Georgetown showplace, Sherry O'Toole had sold her son. If Brandon hadn't been so ecstatic, he might have felt sorry for her.

So, Brandon and Scott became Team Bachelor, and they'd gotten by pretty damned well these past six years. Granted, they ate a lot more frozen dinners than they probably should, but they ate most of them together, and Brandon would bet bucks against buttons that he knew more about his kid's friends and activities than ninety percent of the two-parent families on the block. Brandon worried sometimes what would happen in another two years when he found the nest empty. Who was he going to talk to? How was he going to stay plugged in to what was going on in the community? How was he going to deal with the loneliness?

Thank God it was only a week. Meanwhile, if he really needed a reminder of his son's presence, he needed only to look around the family room. As Brandon crossed to the kitchen, it took real effort not to step on some bit of mess that Scott had left behind: two pairs of socks that he could see, three pairs of shoes and a week's worth of dishes and glasses. For all their strength and bonding, Team Bachelor shared not a whit of housekeeping talent. Brandon was a borderline slob in his own right, but Scott made Oscar Madison look like Martha Stewart. The boy was a mess-making machine, and totally oblivious to it.

Of course, Brandon could have just cleaned it all up himself, but what was the point in that? Team Bachelor succeeded because of their commitment to cooperative independence. Long-term survival depended on each pulling his own weight. As it was, Scott's vision of the universe held himself at the center of everything, with all the world's resources focused solely on his personal needs. The less Brandon did to promote the fantasy, the better.

He put the mail on the counter under the telephone, noting with a sigh the blinking red 8 on the answering machine. Knowing that none of the messages were for him, he pushed the button and went about the business of nuking himself a Lean Cuisine. Chicken Teriyaki. What the hell, maybe he'd nuke two.

The first message featured Scott's just-a-friend-not-a-girlfriend-even-though-I-spend-my-life-on-the-phone-with-her buddy, Rachel. She wanted to make sure that he had a nice trip, and that he knew she was thinking about him. Oh, and she really hoped that he'd use the trip as a means to learn to get along with Sherry.

The second message was from one of Scott's band buddies at Robinson High School announcing a change in the rehearsal schedule.

Three and four were more words of encouragement from Rachel, first apologizing for meddling in Scott's relationship with his mother, because she knew how tough a time he had with that sometimes, chased fifteen minutes later by a double-reversal, in which she apologized for apologizing.

Brandon had to laugh. That girl could burn up more tape than a recording studio.

The final four messages were all hang-ups, the time stamps for which were fifteen minutes apart.

How odd. Punching the time into the microwave, Brandon tossed the empty box into the trash compactor, then scrolled through the caller ID to see that the hang-ups were all from the same number—the Fairfax County Police Department. He scowled.

The digital countdown on the microwave had just cleared 2:00 when Brandon picked up the phone to call the number back. He'd pressed only the first two digits when someone mistook the knocker on the front door for a battering ram, hammering hard enough to make Brandon jump out of his shoes.

"I have a doorbell, you moron," he muttered, replacing the receiver on its hook and heading toward the foyer. He'd made it halfway when they hammered on the door again. "I'm coming!" Brandon shouted. "Jesus, do you think I missed it the first time?"

A quick look out the peephole revealed the image of a freezing cop, the fur collar on his nylon jacket nearly touching the furry ear flaps of his Elmer Fudd hat. Brandon pulled open the door.

Actually, there were two men out there. The one he hadn't seen through the peephole was a priest of some sort. Or maybe a chaplain. He wore a clerical collar. Brandon felt all the air rush out of his lungs.

"Mr. O'Toole?" the police officer asked.

Brandon nodded. "Yes. Brandon O'Toole. That's me. What's wrong?"

"I'm Officer Hoptman. This is Father Scannell." With an uneasy glance, the cop deferred the rest to the priest, who inquired, "May we come in?"

Brandon quickly stepped out of the way, ushering them into the foyer. "Tell me what's wrong." He said the words as a demand, but his head screamed for them to apologize for frightening him. He wanted to hear a sentence that began, *Everybody's going to be okay, but . . .*

Hoptman winced as he said very softly, "I'm afraid we have bad news for you, sir."

SCOTT FELL THE LAST TEN FEET, landing on his back. Snowflakes kissed his upturned face. He choked on one as he drew in a deep breath, and his cough shot a jet of white vapor toward the sky. Rolling first to his side, he struggled up to his knees, and for the first time got a real glimpse of his surroundings. Down here, there was more light; the world was still a dim black-and-white television picture, but at least the shapes had definable form.

Behind him and to his left, the wreckage at the base of the trees made a soft popping sound, casting an instant of bright light, like a camera strobe, bright enough for him to see his shadow against the snow. He could barely make out the twisted pieces of aluminum and steel that had once been their Cessna. "Cody!" he called. "Cody, are you here?" Sooner or later, he'd have to check to make sure, but Scott didn't entertain even a moment's doubt that the pilot was dead. For the time being, he'd settle for recovering his dropped flashlight. There it was, over there by another tree, still on and casting a beam straight up into the air.

The snow was nearly hip-deep out here, and as he forced his legs to piston their way through, his ankle protested with shots of pain that reached all the way to his knee. That the ground below the snow was uneven and treacherous made it all the worse.

The wreckage sputtered again, and now that he was closer, the arc revealed a glimpse of the devastation. The plane rested nose-down, with the cockpit either crushed flat or buried, but either way invisible. Behind that, the passenger compartment and tail were twisted like a discarded toy. The right wing was nowhere to be seen, but the left one looked pretty much intact. Scott's breathing faltered as he took it all in. He had no business being alive at all.

Armed with his flashlight, Scott waded back to the wreckage to check on Cody. This couldn't be happening to him. Two hours ago, he was sneaking across the SkyTop airfield, looking forward to a night of heavy metal nirvana, and now, here he was in the middle of absolute nowhere, waiting to look at a dead friend. A part of Scott told him that he should be feeling some remorse for all this, some sadness for Cody's death, and maybe that would come, but for the time being, he was just pissed. This was supposed to be a concert night, dammit, not a plane crash night. And when it was all over, he was supposed to be asleep in a warm bed, and maybe a little hung-over in the morning. Now, when it was all over . . .

Actually, he didn't want to think about that.

He reached the body before he reached the airplane. What he saw made him gasp and turn away. Apparently, the fall through the trees had yanked the spear out of Cody's body, because now it was gone. Where it once protruded through his parka, Scott could now see a lump of entrails about the size of his fist. Cody just lay there in the snow, steaming and staining the whiteness red.

"Oh, my God," he breathed.

Until that very instant, none of it was real. Oh, the fear was real, and the cold was real and the pain was real, but not the death. Cody's mouth gaped, and his eyes stared straight into the void. Snowflakes were already accumulating on his eyeballs. In another twenty minutes, they'd be invisible. In two hours, the body would be completely concealed.

In a few more hours after that, if the storm continued at this pace, the entire crash site would be covered. According to his watch, they were closing in on 9:30, and the temperature seemed to be dropping as fast as the snowflakes. Scott felt his heart rate triple as he realized that of the two of them, Cody Jamieson may well have been the lucky one. Better to die quickly than to suffer the slow death of hypothermia.

Scott recalled the mountain survival class he'd attended last year with his dad, and the words of the instructor, Sven What's-his-name, rang clear in his head. *Everybody worries about starvation in the wilderness. But in the winter wilderness, your number one priority must be shelter. Food and water are luxuries to be secured later. At night, when the temperatures hover at zero or below, death can come in hours.*

Scott remembered thinking that the class was lame—he'd gone because of the free skiing in the afternoons—but he'd taken notes any-way because there would be a test at the end, and Scott *always* took notes for tests. Once he'd written something down, it was burned into his brain forever. Mr. Forbes, his guidance counselor, told him that his recall was as close to a photographic memory as he'd ever seen.

Pulling himself away from Cody Jamieson's remains, Scott tried to organize his thoughts. It was time to listen to Sven.

Problem was, when Scott and his dad had built their shelters in class, they'd worked in daylight on a sunny afternoon with shovels and two-person teams. Here, he faced the prospect of working alone at night in the swirling snow without tools. Just how in the hell was he supposed to do that?

"SO, YOU DON'T ACTUALLY KNOW that they crashed," Brandon summarized, grasping for anything that looked like hope. They sat in the living room, in front of the dark fireplace, Brandon in the middle of one sofa, his visitors on the sofa facing him.

Officer Hoptman's sigh betrayed frustration. "Mr. O'Toole, sir, I don't know anything firsthand. All I know is what we heard from the Utah State Police. Apparently, your son and a friend took off from the ski resort to attend a concert, and they never arrived."

"And what was the friend's name again?"

Hoptman paged backward in his notes. "Jamieson. Cody Jamieson. I'm sorry that I don't have more solid details, but this is coming to me twice filtered. Your wife filed the initial missing person's report—"

"My ex-wife," Brandon corrected.

"Okay, your ex-wife, then. And even there, things are a little fuzzy. They assume that they flew, mainly because the plane belonging to Cody Jamieson is missing from the airport. Plus, there are some witnesses who heard one or both of them talking—"

"How long, then? Before we have harder details, I mean?"

Brandon knew these people had no answers, but it was as if he somehow needed to direct the discussion. As his visitors searched for something to say, Brandon zeroed in on Father Scannell. Of the two men before him, the priest seemed the most willing to answer questions. "So, what happens next, Father?"

At sixtyish, Father Scannell looked more like a tennis player than a priest, his leathery skin testament to many hours in the sun. He wore his white hair closely cropped with a part so sharp that it looked sculpted. But it was the priest's eyes that captured Brandon and wouldn't let him go. A shade of blue that he'd never seen before, the eyes were at once piercing and sad, windows to a soul that had absorbed and absolved more than its share of sin. Scannell spoke with those eyes, and right now they offered only sympathy and kindness. Brandon wanted none of it. Terror blossomed in his gut like a poisonous black flower. Clamping his jaw tight and pursing his lips, he cocked his head to the side as his vision blurred.

"We can pray," the priest said softly.

The quiver in Brandon's gut turned to pain. There had to be more than that. Praying was the last resort, what you did when all options were gone. You prayed for the dead.

For the first time, he saw what they saw: A plane crash at night, in the mountains, in winter. In Utah. Brandon drew a huge breath through his mouth, and held it, hoping to stop his head from spinning. "He's not dead," he whispered. "My son is not dead."

"Pray with me, Mr. O'Toole."

"He's not dead!" This time, his voice showed strength that the rest of his body didn't possess.

"Then we'll pray for God to protect them and keep them safe."

"Scott is not dead. He *can't* be dead."

Father Scannell held out his hand, and Brandon looked at it for a long moment before grasping it. Then the priest offered his other hand to Officer Hoptman, who closed the circle. Brandon watched, dumbstruck, as they bowed their heads.

"Heavenly Father, in the name of your Son and the Blessed Virgin, we ask you to intercede at this critical hour. To protect Scott O'Toole from harm, and to guide him to safety. We beseech you to open his heart to your love and your guidance. . . ."

Don't let him be dead, Brandon thought. *Let him be healthy and unhurt. Let this all be a miserable dream or a terrible mistake.*

If what these people said were true, Brandon would know it. The cosmos could not continue its normal rhythm while his son was in mortal danger. It just wasn't possible.

Praying was not the answer. It couldn't hurt, but it wasn't anybody's solution. Brandon needed to take real action, concrete action. He needed to do something that would directly affect the outcome of this nightmare, without intercession from third parties, God notwith-standing. There had to be something. Someone he could call. Some action he could take.

"How do they go about locating lost aircraft?" he asked, inter-rupting Father Scannell's prayer.

The priest looked startled. "Excuse me?"

"Not you, Father." Brandon's tone sounded more abrupt than he'd intended. "Officer Hoptman, how do they locate lost aircraft?"

The young police officer looked suddenly confused, caught off guard. "I don't know, sir. I've never actually participated in something like that."

Brandon nodded. That seemed reasonable. Aircraft don't fall out of the sky every day. "Who do I need to call to find out?"

"I'm afraid I don't know that, either."

"Would your supervisor know?"

Hoptman shrugged. "Maybe. I guess. Listen, Mr. O'Toole, these are things that I think can—"

"There's a phone on the wall around there in the kitchen. Do me a favor and call your supervisor and give me a jump start on this thing, will you?"

Hoptman and Scannell exchanged confused glances. "I don't understand, sir," the officer said. "A jump start on what?"

"On finding my son."

Scannell sighed deeply and leaned forward, his elbows on his thighs. "Look, Mr. O'Toole, at times like these the tendency is to reject bad news. It's only human. But I really must say—"

"Save it, Father," Brandon interrupted. He didn't care that it came out harshly. "I know what the chances of survival out there are, okay? I'm a ski patroller myself. But you know what? Scott has camped his whole life. Just last year, we took a winter survival class together." He turned to Hoptman. "Do you think anyone out there knows that?"

The officer didn't answer, obviously assuming the question to be rhetorical. He seemed startled when he realized otherwise. "No, sir, I suppose not."

"Don't you think we should tell them, then? Whoever *they* are?"

Hoptman nodded.

"Did I mention that there's a phone in the kitchen?"

The cop knew his cue when he heard it, and he rose quickly from the sofa and disappeared.

"Please don't expect the unreasonable," Father Scannell warned.

Brandon eyed the priest narrowly. The man meant well, but he didn't understand. Not Scott and certainly not Brandon. "Isn't that what prayers are all about, Father?"

4

THE MAN WHO CALLED HIMSELF TEDDY wasn't much of a talker by
nature, but tonight the role required it, so he just chatted along as if
he'd forgotten how to breathe. In the past five hours, he'd covered
music, food, movies, religion and politics—the latter only after listening carefully to what his new friend thought about the issues. No
sense unnecessarily pissing people off. For a while there, back in the
truck stop, he was worried that he might be laying it on a little too
thick, but in retrospect he should have known better. Some people
were just too friendly for their own good.

But ultimately, when the heavens dumped this much snow, only
the weather made the A-list for discussion. Would they close the
interstates or wouldn't they? How many New York skiers would turn
up frozen to death in the morning? One particularly animated discussion among the truckers was the ethical reasonableness of pushing stranded four-wheelers off the road when they were stupid
enough to drive in powder that was deeper than their axles were
high.

The truck stop banter required the patience of a fisherman. Fact
was, if Teddy hadn't hooked a ride with someone—if he'd gotten
stranded there—his careful planning could have unraveled very
quickly. He could have found solace in the fact that the cops had far
more important things to do on a night like this than trace the tags on
his car, but it wasn't impossible, and as a man who stayed alive by

controlling risk, he'd wanted to be back on the road as quickly as possible. The idea was to abandon the car at the truck stop and catch a ride under the auspices of having hitchhiked this far. Tomorrow was his mother's eightieth birthday, don't you know, and he was coming home to her as a surprise.

Teddy's mother had had more eightieth birthdays than McDonald's has fries.

One guy in particular had looked like he might be a strong candidate. He sat in a far corner and made eye contact periodically, but every time Teddy had offered a smile, the other guy looked away. Teddy didn't like that. He'd considered for a moment that maybe the guy was watching him—that he knew more than he should—but the very idea seemed preposterous. Still, one could never be too careful. Teddy had decided to make the first move if the stranger didn't approach soon. All the professionalism in the world couldn't crush irrational paranoia completely.

The stranger in the booth became irrelevant, though, the instant that Maurice Hertzberger waddled in. Clearly a regular, Maurice chatted it up with the waitress who, by pure happenstance, seated the newcomer in the booth directly across the aisle from Teddy, who continued on with the small talk. He tossed off a casual how-ya-doin', which led to the where-ya-froms and within ten minutes, Teddy had received an invitation to move his place setting over to Maurice's table. That's when the conversation turned to the eightieth birthday. Damn this weather, though. It would be a bitch finding a ride.

Right on cue, Maurice had made his offer and Teddy had his chauffeur. Thus began the five hours of endless chatter.

"The roads are getting worse by the minute," Maurice observed for at least the dozenth time. In profile, his huge belly made his arms look too short to steer.

"You're doin' great by me," Teddy replied. Thanks to a theatrical fat suit he'd picked up on an Internet auction for about seventy bucks, people would remember Teddy as a full-figured fellow himself. The suit added a good fifty pounds to his appearance, and the bushy beard concealed his lean features well enough to not raise casual suspicion. "You must drive this route a lot."

"Actually, no. Salt Lake is my usual run, but I don't take this route. Certainly not in this weather." Maurice reached across and playfully slapped his passenger on the arm. "This one's for you and your mom."

Teddy appeared moved. Acting was part of his job description, too. "Are you serious? I didn't expect you to go out of your way."

Maurice waved him off. "Oh, hell, I don't mind. Night like this, it's kinda nice to have the company, know what I mean?"

Teddy returned the playful slap, only his probably left a bruise. "Maurice, that is so nice of you. I really am very touched." In the blessed silence that followed, Teddy watched in his peripheral vision as the driver rubbed the spot on his arm.

The quiet endured for only thirty seconds. "You sure you don't want to call home or something?" Maurice asked. "You're welcome to use my cell phone."

"No, that's all right. Thank you."

"You sure?" Maurice tried again, this time thrusting a matchbook-size cell phone at his guest. "Your mom must be worried sick."

"She's not expecting me," Teddy explained. "And even if she was, she doesn't have a phone."

Maurice recoiled at the thought. "No kidding? She doesn't have a phone? How come?"

This was actually kind of fun. New territory to be explored. "She thinks they're the work of the devil," he said with a hearty laugh. Then, in his best old-lady voice he added, "I've been on this planet since nineteen and twenty-three and never once saw the need for a telephone. Somebody wants to talk to me they can damn well come to my door and talk to my face." *That sounded pretty good,* he thought.

Maurice chuckled. "But what about emergencies? What if she gets sick?"

Teddy laughed, maybe a little too heartily. "You don't know Mama. Never been sick a day in her life. I always figured the germs were afraid of her."

Maurice enjoyed that one, too. His boisterous laugh jostled the cab. At the rate they were traveling, Teddy figured they had another forty-five minutes to share. Maybe an hour.

ARAPAHO COUNTY POLICE CHIEF Barry Whitestone listened to the bad news and gently placed the telephone receiver back in its cradle. Out in the squad room, beyond the glass panels that defined the walls of his office, six officers stared hopefully at him, then looked away when they saw his expression. Some nights, nothing went right.

He pushed his wooden desk chair back on its casters, and headed for the door to make it official.

"Is it as bad as you look, boss?" asked Jesse Tingle. At twenty-seven, Jesse was the second-oldest cop on his staff, and at that, he got carded at every restaurant.

"From every angle you can think of," Barry replied. He helped himself to a seat on the front corner of an empty desk. "With the storm blowing the way it is, nobody will put a plane in the air, and the weather service says this is all we'll see for the next thirty-six hours."

"What about ground teams?" asked Charlotte Eberly, the department's token nod to equal opportunity for women.

Barry shook his head. "Don't know where to send them, and even if we did, who'd go out in this? I alerted Burt Hostings, and he says he can have his search and rescue troops assembled within two hours of getting our call."

"If the roads are open," Jesse cautioned.

"Exactly," Barry agreed. "If the roads are open. And who wants to cover my bets for that happening?"

Charlotte shook her head, totally baffled. "Such craziness. What were they doing up there in the first place?"

"The pilot was twenty-one and stupid," Barry said.

Charlotte looked at him like he smelled bad. "Aren't *you* Mr. Sensitive."

"Hey, it was Metallica, for God's sake. Cut him a break." This entry into the conversation came from James Alexander. Blue-black, and built like the linebacker he'd been all through college, James had a voice that made the ground tremble.

Barry arched an eyebrow. "You a heavy-metal fan, James?"

James smiled. "Helps me digest my watermelon. I read in the *Denver Post* that this is their tour to end all tours. Tickets are scalping for a thousand bucks a pop."

"The hell you doin' reading the *Denver Post?*" Jesse wanted to know. Even if he'd seen James's Phi Beta Kappa key, he wouldn't have known what it was.

"Denver, New York, Washington and L.A.," James said. "I read all four."

"Every *day?*"

James laughed. "Only Denver on the weekends. That make you feel better? All that Sunday supplement crap makes me feel guilty about all the trees I'm killing." Then, to Whitestone, "So we're not gonna do anything tonight about the crash?"

"We can pray and think pleasant thoughts. Unless you've got better ideas."

"They're dead," James said. "If they weren't when they hit the ground, then they sure as hell are now."

"Don't be so sure," Barry cautioned. "I got a message from the . . ." He rummaged through his pockets looking for the slip of paper where he'd jotted the note. ". . . the Fairfax County Police Department in Virginia, where one of the fathers lives. Dad wanted us to know that his boy—the youngest victim, Scott O'Toole—has had winter wilderness survival training."

"That's bullshit," James blurted. "How old is he?"

"Sixteen, I think. Maybe fifteen. I don't remember."

"Well, it's bullshit."

This drew an incredulous laugh from the chief. "Why is it bullshit?"

"Because no sixteen-year-old can keep himself alive in the mountains during a snowstorm. Lord Almighty, it's near zero degrees out there."

"Everywhere I turn, I'm surrounded by optimism," Charlotte mocked.

"It's not about optimism," James argued. "It's about pragmatism. Reality."

"So you say, 'write them off and assume they're dead?' Sounds to me like you're in the wrong line of work."

Jesse intervened with hands outstretched, as if he were stopping traffic. "Easy, guys." To Barry: "What about tomorrow?"

The chief shook his head. "I think the Air Force'll be able to get somebody up over the storm to listen for their locator beacon, but a rescue will depend on the weather. The Civil Air Patrol will be scrambled to head up that part of the search."

This triggered a disdainful snort from James.

"What now?" Charlotte wanted to know.

"The Civil Air Patrol? You ever seen the Civil Air Patrol?"

Charlotte made a motion with her shoulders that might have been a shrug.

"I've seen them around my little brother's high school. They're kids. Air Force wanna-bes whose voices haven't changed yet."

Looking shocked, Charlotte turned to Barry for confirmation.

The chief half nodded. "They're really an Air Force auxiliary, and yeah, the high school kids—cadets, they call them—do a lot of the leg work. But the commanders are all active duty or retired military."

"Am I the only one thinking about the movie *Taps*?" Jesse asked.

"I don't believe that," Charlotte said. "Who are all those people swarming all over crash scenes on the news?"

"We're not talking a 747 here," Barry explained. "This was a little Cessna with two people on board. The Civil Air Patrol has jurisdiction over the search. That's just the way it is."

"Unless you're an ex-president's kid," James added. "When he crashed, they dispatched the whole friggin' Navy."

Barry rolled his eyes. Why was everyone on edge tonight? "And the two incidents are exactly alike," he scoffed. "Except for those little details like (a) it was a president's kid, and (b) it was over water in stable weather."

"Typical of those assholes in Washington," James said, but Barry cut him off.

"James, that's it. You've got your speech-making face on, and I'm too tired."

"I got a question," Jesse said, "speaking of Washington assholes.

How much crap do I gotta take from that Secret Service prick, Sanders? I don't say hello to that guy without he starts giving me directions."

Barry smiled wearily. "Take the crap he gives you, multiply it times five and welcome to my world."

"Who gives him the authority?"

"He's the head of the president's security detail, Jesse. As long as the First Skier is in our backyard, I guess Sanders gets to call his own shots."

"I don't like him," Jesse said.

James laughed. "Well, I think you ought to write a letter."

Charlotte turned to the chief. "Did we ever make a decision about search and rescue?"

"I think we decided to wait," Barry said. "For tonight, those two kids—if they're still alive—are just going to have to make do. Like I said, prayers and good thoughts are always welcome."

BY TWO IN THE MORNING, Scott was all but spent. Working in the dark to conserve battery power, the effort to build his shelter had left him exhausted. For nearly four hours, he'd been using a hand-size piece of wreckage as his shovel, trying to dig a hole big enough to shelter him from the biting wind and deadly temperature, but it wasn't going well. The wind kept undoing everything he did. His shoulders ached and he felt dizzy from the exertion. He had a hard time catching his breath.

He tried to grunt his way through it, the way he'd grunted his way through countless soccer games when he thought that his body had nothing left to give, but this time was different. No matter how aggressively he gulped at the air, it seemed that his lungs couldn't get enough, and the effort of it all left him feeling progressively worse; sick to his stomach with a pounding headache.

But there was no stopping. Not in this game. To stop was to die. His efforts had produced a hole in the snow. Two holes, really; one straight down about two feet, and then another that extended off of that one three feet horizontally. Maybe he should call it a tunnel— the shortest tunnel ever built, leading to nowhere. And because he'd deposited the excavated snow back up on the surface, creating a little dome, he'd been able to carve out enough height to make the space maybe three feet high on the inside. He'd covered the floor with spruce boughs he'd dragged over from the ground surrounding the wrecked airplane.

He was sweating like a pig. He should have taken off his coat, or maybe his sweater or turtleneck to keep from soaking them, but now he worried that it was too late. If he exposed the wet fabric to the elements now it would freeze for sure, and then he'd be in a world of hurt. Tomorrow, maybe the sun would come out and he could dry his stuff. Meanwhile, he had to hope that the extra $300 he'd paid for his high-tech parka would pay off and the material would wick away the perspiration as advertised.

Numb, and barely able to stand, he dug the flashlight out of his coat pocket and dared a quick look at his handiwork. The shelter had a lot wrong with it. It looked nothing like the well-engineered example that Sven had built, or even like the one he'd constructed with his dad's assistance. The flat ceiling was bound to drip water on him, and the flat floor would keep it colder than it needed to be, but for the time being, it would have to do. It was all he had in him.

Bedtime. Collapse time. But first he had to piss. Stuffing the flashlight back into his pocket, Scott traipsed across the crash site to face a tree. He calculated the wind direction and did what he had to do.

In the fifteen seconds that his hands were exposed to empty his bladder, the flesh on his fingers felt frozen. He knew better than to try managing a zipper and two layers of underwear with his gloves on, but by the time he tucked himself away and zipped back up again, he could barely feel his fingertips. It would take an hour for them to warm up again, he was sure.

"Jesus, it's cold." As he snugged his collar up as tightly as it would go, his spine launched a shiver. He pulled his wool cap even farther over his ears.

He turned to head back, and stopped dead. Where was the shelter? Panic gripped him as he scanned the black and white landscape. It had to be there. He'd just built it, for heaven's sake! So, where was it?

It all looked the same. Snow was snow and trees were trees, and he'd walked around the crash site so much that his footprints were of no help guiding him.

"Okay, Scott, don't be stupid. It's here." Yanking the light from his pocket, he hurried back to the twisted airplane to get his bearings. The shelter was off to the left side of the wreckage, that much he knew. That meant it had to be straight ahead of him somewhere. Maybe straight ahead and a little off to the left.

Sven's words came back to him. *At night, up, down, left, right, they can have no meaning. All there is, is snow. People die of exposure just yards from their tent because they were unable to find their way.*

No way.

No way was he going to freeze to death—not after he'd invested all that time and every dram of energy into building the damn shelter. No way in hell. It had to be here.

And it was. Not in the spot where he'd projected it to be, but close. From this angle, the mound wasn't that big, and the doorway looked barely bigger than a footprint. But he'd found it, and he was safe, and the instant he was out of the wind, the temperature seemed to warm by fifty degrees.

Scott retracted his arms from his sleeves—gloves and all—and hugged himself inside his coat. He lay on his side, his knees drawn up to his chest, and he fell asleep.

He dreamed of dying in the woods.

5

"YOU CAN STOP at the crest of the hill over there," Teddy said, pointing to a wide spot on the two-lane road.

Maurice shot him a look. "Where?"

"There, just on the side of the road."

"But there's nothing there."

Teddy laughed again. He'd laughed more tonight than he had in a year and he was sick to death of it. "You'll see when you get there. There's a little road. That's the way to Mama's place."

Seemingly against his better judgment, Maurice downshifted the rig and brought it to a gentle halt at exactly the spot Teddy had indicated. "That's a road?"

"That's what we call it." He extended his hand. "I surely do appreciate the ride." Snow and cold swirled into the cab as Teddy opened the door.

Maurice didn't like this one bit. "Teddy, I feel terrible just leaving you in the middle of the road like this."

Teddy shook his head and smiled. "Just a short hike down that lane and I'm home, buddy."

Maurice opened his mouth to argue, then abandoned the effort. "Suit yourself," he said. "Just be careful."

Teddy acknowledged him with a nod and gathered up his travel gear. He started to climb out then stopped. "Hey, I have something for you," Teddy said, holding up a finger. Slinging his backpack from his shoulder to the ground, Teddy pulled his glove off with his teeth and rummaged through his things, pulling out a pint bottle of clear liquid before putting everything back together. "Are you a drinking man?" he asked.

Maurice smiled and patted his enormous stomach. "I've been known to take a sip or two."

Teddy handed him the bottle. "Here, then, have this."

Maurice laughed. "What is this, moonshine?"

"I guess. That's what it looks like to me. A guy gave it to me in my travels, but I don't really partake. I'd like you to have it."

Maurice looked at him skeptically. "I don't know . . ."

"Please," Teddy said. "Otherwise I'll just pour it out. Be careful with it, though. You probably don't want to be driving this big rig with that stuff in your veins."

"Why, thank you kindly," Maurice said, accepting the bottle and slipping it into his pocket. "I'm staying just up the road a piece. Maybe this'll help me sleep." Suddenly, he seemed anxious to be moving again.

Teddy smiled. "Thanks again, Maurice. I really appreciate the kindness." With that, he swung the door closed and waited on the shoulder, waving as the rig pulled away.

There was indeed a house at the end of the lane, but Teddy had never visited it. He never needed to. The owner was an old moonshiner and hermit named Pembroke. For the tidy sum of $200 a month, Pembroke allowed Teddy to store a dirt bike and a snowmobile on his property, housed in a shed that was so carefully camouflaged that sometimes even Teddy had a hard time finding it. His arrangement with Pembroke was simple: Teddy sent the cash monthly to Pembroke's post office box, and the old man never asked any questions.

Of course, Pembroke would never associate the name Teddy with the man who sent him the money every month. That man was known as Kevin Clavan, who just happened to be the same man who people in town knew as Isaac DeHaven.

In this weather, he didn't even bother to try the electric starter on the snowmobile. After four pulls and a little adjustment on the choke, it fired right up.

• • •

SHERRY STARTED TO POUR another scotch, but Larry snatched the bottle from her. And then the glass. "Not tonight," he started.

"Give that back," Sherry protested. "You're not my mother."

Larry fired what little had made the glass down his own throat, then headed toward the kitchen with the bottle. "Maybe not, but I'm your keeper, and tonight, you need to keep your head right."

"Larry! I'm in a crisis."

He pivoted to face her, his hands on his hips. "Yes, I know. And we've established that it's my fault. I've offered profuse apologies, none of which have been accepted, and now you want to get hammered to make it all go away. I'm not going to let that happen. Brandon has called three times, and sooner or later you're going to have to talk to him. If you slur your words, he'll go ballistic."

Sherry recoiled at the thought. "I do not slur my words."

Larry spun and resumed his strut to the kitchen. "Oh, that's right. I keep forgetting that the sky is green in your world."

The phone rang.

"Do you think Scotty is okay?" Sherry asked, laying her head on the arm of the sofa.

"No, I don't think he's okay. I think he's been in a plane crash." The phone rang again. "Are you going to get that?"

Sherry draped her forearm over her eyes. "No. I know it's Brandon, and I don't want to deal with him right now." She heard him make his exasperated growling sound as he picked up the receiver in the middle of the third ring.

"Sherry, it's for you," he said. Then, under his breath, "Gee, imagine that, this being your chalet and all. It's Audrey Lewis."

Now, that got her attention. Sherry sat up straight. "Are you sure it's not Brandon?"

Larry stared at her through the opening that separated the kitchen from the dining room. "Am I sure? Let's see, I think I can probably tell the difference between your ex-hubby and your agent."

Actually, it wasn't as easy as it might seem. A teetotaling health freak in reality, Audrey had the voice of a Camel-smoking barmaid and the chops of a prizefighter. The world of New York publishing lived in fear of crossing her, and her clients had the bank accounts to prove it.

Sherry reached across the coffee table for the portable phone. "What does she want?"

Larry tapped his lips with his forefinger. "Mmm, to talk to you, maybe?"

"You're such an asshole."

"Oh, cut me till I bleed, why don't you?" Larry rolled his eyes and made himself busy in the kitchen.

Sherry brought the phone to her ear. "Hello? Audrey?"

"Oh, my God, Sherry, I just heard. How are you?"

"Not well," Sherry said, her voice cracking. "I'm terrified."

"I can only imagine," Audrey said. "Have you heard any news at all?"

"Only that they're reasonably sure that he and this Jamieson kid tried to fly into the storm, and now no one's heard from them. From what they tell me, no one even tracked them on radar. I don't know . . ." She stopped for a second. "Wait a minute. How do you know about this?"

Audrey sighed. "Brandon called me. Look, Sherry, you have to talk to him."

"No. I don't need his shit. Not tonight. I don't need his speeches."

"He's worried about his son, Sherry."

"*His* son," Sherry repeated. The phrase brought real pain. "It's always *his* son. Brandon's son. You know, he's my son, too."

"Have you been drinking?"

That was it. "Why does everyone think I'm drunk?"

"Because you're not making sense! Jesus, it's not a parenting competition."

"Where Brandon's involved, it's always a parenting competition," Sherry growled.

Team fucking Bachelor. Where was the cute nickname for *her* relationship with Scotty? Nowhere, because Brandon had never left room for there to be one. He wanted Sherry to be June Cleaver, and she wanted to build her career. Was that so difficult for everybody to understand? Certainly, Brandon was smart enough and twenty-first-century enough to understand. While they were married, he'd pretended to do just that. Then in the divorce depositions, he'd turned it all against her. Such was the magnitude of his jealousy for her success that he used her ambition—the very ambition that had paid for the Mercedes he drove and the sprawling estate he lived in—as evidence that she was an inattentive mother. Asshole. Well, two could play at that game, as he'd found out when she put the bank account into play. "You want custody?" she'd challenged through her lawyer. "Then just give me everything else."

Sherry had trumped the bastard at his own game. Brandon had climbed so high on his high horse that he couldn't possibly say no. It was the perfect trap. Even her lawyer couldn't believe he'd fallen for it. Sometimes, it was just too easy.

But with her victory came Brandon's unending access to her baby boy's brain, the ability to spin every confrontation in his own favor. Well, two could play at that game as well. For eighteen months, Brandon had promised Scotty a trip to SkyTop, yet he'd never delivered. Cue Super Mom for another delicious victory.

"You can't shut him out of this, Sherry," Audrey pressed. "I just talked to him. He's out of his mind with worry."

"And I suppose he claims this whole thing is somehow my fault."

"To tell you the truth, we didn't get that far. He asked me to ask you to talk to him. And if that didn't work, he asked me to get some details to pass along."

Sherry sighed deeply. "Let him call the police if he wants details."

A long moment of silence passed as Audrey regrouped. Finally, she said, "Listen, Sherry, you know I don't like to get involved in personal matters where I don't belong . . ."

Uh-oh, Sherry thought. Something bad was coming.

". . . but I'm going to butt in just this once. I mean, I know you're worried out of your mind, and I hope you know that I'm praying for only the best outcome to all of this—"

"Get to it, Audrey." As she spoke, Sherry grabbed up a fistful of peanuts from the bowl on the coffee table and threw them at the kitchen pass-through to get Larry's attention. When she had his eye, she motioned for him to pick up the extension. She never even heard the click as he lifted the receiver.

"Well, all right, I'll just be blunt. The thing of it is, you have to be a little careful how you handle yourself these next few days."

"Careful?" Sherry looked to Larry and got a shrug in return.

"Yes, careful. A lot of people have invested time and money in developing a certain air of expertise around you. Since you make your living helping other people cope with their problems, there's a certain decorum that's going to be expected as you deal with your own."

Sherry made a growling noise of her own. "Oh, for God's sake—"

"I'm sorry, Sherry, but you have a vindictive streak that can really do you some harm if you aren't careful."

Sherry shot a can-you-believe-this look to Larry. Yes, he could. Anger began to boil.

"You're getting pissed," Audrey said. "I can hear it in your breathing pattern. All I'm trying to tell you is, right now is exactly the wrong time to reignite your war with Brandon. Just play nice, okay? If you can't do it because it's the right thing to do morally, then do it because you can use the good press."

Good press? Something flashed in Sherry's head, and she drew her feet up under her on the sofa. "Audrey, I know you. It's almost four in the morning in New York, yet instead of sleeping, you're here on the phone with me. You're hatching something."

Audrey gave a nervous chuckle. "Please understand that I'm not trying to exploit the situation here—"

Larry groaned, "Oh, God."

"I'm *not*. But let's face it. There's a valuable news story here. An opportunity for women all over the country to witness how America's favorite shrink deals with stress."

Larry shook his head vehemently and covered the mouthpiece with his hand. "Hang up and run away," he said.

"Way to be stealthy, Larry," Audrey mocked. "I heard every word. And you can hang up anytime you want, Sherry. But I'm telling you—and I'll say again that I hope to God that Sammy comes home just fine—"

"Scotty," Larry corrected.

"It *is* four in the morning," Audrey snapped. "Scotty, then. Forgive me. Anyway, I don't see how a little free publicity—if handled gently and with a lot of care—is going to have any negative impact on him; but it sure as hell can have a positive impact on you. Is that so wrong?"

"What do you have in mind?" Sherry asked, earning a glare.

"In the short term? Maybe an appearance on the *Today* show. I happen to know that there's an NBC producer vacationing there in SkyTop with you, and she owes me a favor. I bet I can get you on tomorrow morning. Um, make that *this* morning. Actually, I've already talked to her. With the president being there and all, there are certainly enough camera and sound people."

"Absolutely not," Larry said.

The response startled Sherry. "Why not?"

"They go live at seven, eastern time. That's three hours from now. You'll look like last night's hors d'oeuvres."

"It's not a beauty contest, Larry," Audrey protested. "It's not even a book tour, though God knows the sales of the *Mirror* series have been slipping. She's a worried mother, for Christ's sake. She's supposed to look like she hasn't had any sleep. Honestly, Sherry, Molly Bartholomew is a sweetheart. She's the producer I was telling you about. She won't let you go on the air if you're hideous."

Oh, now, that was reassuring. "Okay," Sherry said. "Do it."

"Excellent," Audrey said. "Now, I want to talk to you about a book idea I had."

"Jesus, Audrey." This time, Sherry and Larry said it together.

"What? Is it so wrong to pursue unique opportunities while they're hot? I think Baker Publishing would jump on the chance to publish this story. Rich Czabo recently moved there, and I thought, if I could lock him in early, it would probably be good for a solid six figures."

"No," Sherry said.

"Why?"

"We're talking about my son, Audrey."

"We are not. We're talking about you. It's just so high-concept. 'The counselor needs assistance.' "

Sherry could hear the finger-quotes as she uttered that last phrase. "It's unseemly."

"It's horrifying," Larry said.

"How is it horrifying? Jesus, everybody wants to know how celebrities deal with stress. It's a natural."

"No, Audrey," Sherry repeated. "And I'll say it again, in case you didn't get it the first time. No. Good God, I'd look like a ghoul."

"No one would have to know," Audrey pressed. "We could put a complete embargo on the story."

"I'm hanging up, Audrey. Call this Bartholomew lady and tell her we're a go in the morning."

"Okay," Audrey said. Sherry envisioned her as wired on thirty cups of coffee. "And I'll let you know what Rich Czabo says about the book."

"Audrey!" The line was dead.

"She's Satan incarnate," Larry said as he wandered back in from the kitchen.

"She's made me a fortune, Larry."

He stopped in his tracks, placed a hand on his hip. "I'm sorry, have you not read *Faust?*"

She flipped him off.

"This television thing is a mistake," Larry warned.

"Oh, for heaven's sake."

"Roll your eyes all you want. People are going to see you on television within a few hours of Scott's disappearance, and they're going to draw all the wrong conclusions."

"What wrong conclusions?"

"Exactly the same conclusions they would have drawn about a book: that you're exploiting this whole thing for publicity. With all due respect, my dear, you don't do 'caring nurturer' very well. Your strong suit has always been 'in-your-face preacher.' "

Sherry recoiled. "I'm insulted."

"Well, forgive me, then." Larry headed for the foyer. "You pay me for my opinions, and I give them to you."

"Is that what I pay you for?"

Larry opened the door and paused before leaving. "I don't know what the hell you pay me for. But in deference to the generous check, just please take my advice and be careful."

Sherry glanced at the clock and panic gripped her. "Oh, my God, look at the time. I've got to get a couple of hours' sleep."

"I'll give you a wake-up call at five-thirty," Larry said.

"And then another one ten minutes later, in case I fall back to sleep!" Before she could finish, the door was already closed. She had no idea whether he heard her.

6

THERE'D NEVER BE A WAY for Brandon to thank Jim Lundgren adequately for his help.

After working the phones for an hour, trying to find an airline that was still launching planes this late at night, he'd finally realized the hopelessness of his efforts. Noise restrictions forbade any commercial liftoffs after 9:00 P.M. As a last resort, he'd called Lundgren, president of Federal Research—Brandon's employer for the past eighteen years—with the express purpose of stepping way out of line. "My son's been in a plane crash out in Utah," Brandon explained to the groggy executive. "I can't find a flight to get me out there, and I—"

"Take my jet," Lundgren offered, without missing a beat, and without hearing the rest. The Gulfstream was a perk reserved only for the top dog, and no one—*no one*—else was permitted to use it. "I'll call the pilots right now and have them meet you. You know how to get to Manassas Airport?"

He didn't but he said he did. That's what maps were for. "I can't thank you enough for this," he'd said.

Lundgren replied with a huff. "Now we're both wasting time. Keep me informed, take as long as it takes. Don't even think about the plant. Mary and I will keep you in our prayers."

Now, as the posh Gulfstream cut through the night on the way to Salt Lake City, Brandon tried to determine his next move. An obsessive planner, he visualized problems as giant knots, even the most hopeless of which could be untied if you just turned it over enough times. A tug here and there, action and reaction. To Brandon, that was what problem-solving was all about.

Sitting in the luscious leather chair with his seat belt loosely fastened across his lap, he closed his eyes and tried to find the thread that would lead to Scott's rescue. He had no idea where to begin. He didn't know the players, he didn't really know the situation, and now that he thought about it, he didn't even know where Arapaho County was, precisely.

Even more basic than that, he didn't even know what he hoped to accomplish out there. What could he possibly contribute to the search effort? Surely prayers offered from Virginia carried just as much weight with God as prayers launched from Utah, and beyond that, what did he have to offer? Would he even be welcome?

Probably not. He didn't care. His goal here was simple: He wanted his son back. He left for Utah alone to return to Virginia with Scott at his side.

Maybe he could help with the search. At the very least, he could be another set of eyes combing the terrain. Would that satisfy him? Suppose another team found his boy, and Brandon was off traipsing through a different search grid? Was he ready for that?

And what if they found the wreckage, only to discover that . . . well, that it was bad news? The worst news? Suppose Brandon himself was the one to find it? Was he ready for *that?* Is that how he wanted the final memories of Scott to be burned into his brain? A grotesque image of a dismembered corpse tried to form itself in his mind, but Brandon opened his eyes before it took shape.

"He's alive," he said to the empty cabin. "I know he is." And don't bother asking how he knew. He just did.

But what if he wasn't alive? Worse yet, what if Scott were dead and that reckless asshole of a pilot who killed him were still alive? Of all the possibilities, that was the scenario that Brandon had the hardest time wrapping his mind around.

He knew how people were going to react to this accident. All they were going to see were the impossible odds, and no matter what

Brandon said, they were likely going to dismiss his words as the blind optimism of a frightened father. It was human nature to think that way, just as he always assumed that missing kids on the news would ultimately turn up dead. It was just the way things happened.

But not this time. Brandon would talk himself hoarse to convince everyone involved in the search that Scott was still alive. He was a strong boy, an experienced camper. A winter survival course graduate. If anyone could prevail against the odds, it would be Scott.

Brandon's job was to make damn sure that no one gave up on him.

The clock was his enemy now, the one element that showed no mercy, ticking endlessly forward. Closer to the end. Closer to death.

He's not dead!

But he had to be hurt, didn't he? A person can't just fall from the sky and not be hurt. But how badly? Concussion? Broken leg? Broken *back?* Brandon's mind tapped into the horror of lying paralyzed in the snow, slowly freezing to death, or worse yet, burning.

Oh, my God.

No! He couldn't think this way. He couldn't allow it. Pessimism was an unaffordable luxury. Negativism need not apply. Still, the most horrible images lurked just outside the door, waiting for his defenses to weaken.

Scott's life was Brandon's life. They were a pair. Team Bachelor. And while the boy was strong enough and smart enough to plod through life without his old man, Brandon knew with absolute certainty that he himself couldn't make the trip alone.

He didn't possess that kind of strength.

DAY TWO

7

SHERRY SAT IN A HARDBACK CHAIR, in front of a six-by-six-foot-square wall emblazoned with the familiar peacock logo. The sign on the door out in the hallway read PRESS ROOM, but the place was really a ballroom that had been hijacked by the press corps for the duration of the president's visit to SkyTop. A dozen such minisets lined the perimeter of the room, one for each of the networks and cable stations, plus a dozen others from around the world, with logos Sherry didn't recognize. In the far corner, toward the front, sat a familiar blue lectern with its two microphones. Somebody just needed to add the presidential seal, and the lectern would become the set for a presidential press conference.

Security had been tight but not impossible as she'd reported in for her interview. When she asked why, she learned that the First Skier, as the press had dubbed the president, had no plans to do anything but ski until the Founder's Day address later in the week. They assured her, however, that if the time came when POTUS wanted to address the nation, an impenetrable security net would materialize in an instant.

As it turned out, when Audrey had referred to Molly Bartholomew as a friend, she'd overstated the relationship by about twelve thousand percent. "Sworn enemy who didn't have the clout to argue" was far more accurate. It turned out that Audrey's real friend was Molly's boss in New York, who'd yanked Molly away from a planned day off in order to accommodate this interview. They'd scheduled it for the eight o'clock hour in New York, after they'd discussed all the hard news for the day, but before they'd turned to the latest fashion trends.

As a camera moved into place in front of her, and two floodlights became supernovas, Sherry tried to sit motionless as Molly threaded a microphone under Sherry's sweater and another technician jammed an earpiece into her right ear.

"Here's the deal," Molly explained. "They're trying out a new news anchor this morning. His name is Brock, and try not to laugh when you say it. Anyway, he's going to be asking you these questions"—she handed Sherry a sheaf of papers—"during the bottom of the hour news break. Look into the camera when you answer and try not to shout."

"I've done television before," Sherry said. "Are we going to be live?"

"Absolutely. And if you do a good job, it'll probably be broadcast all day at the news breaks and on CNBC." The producer made a point of looking Sherry squarely in the eye as she added, "This is news, not *Frasier,* okay? Nobody yells 'cut' if you screw up, so try to get it right."

Sherry nodded and looked down at her notes. At first glance, she didn't see anything too difficult. It was mostly about emotion. How was she holding up under the stress? Did she think that the authorities were acting quickly enough? Are there things about her son that the world should know?

With the microphone finally clipped to the collar of Sherry's turtleneck, Molly took a call on her cell phone. "Hello? Yeah? Shit."

Sherry's heart rate doubled. "What?"

Molly held up a finger and listened for a moment more. "Okay, yeah, we can be ready." To Sherry, she said, "Change in plans. They want to go live in one minute, as soon as they come out of the break."

Instantly, Sherry's mind went blank.

"Don't look so scared, Mrs. O'Toole. I wrote the questions and they're all softballs."

"It's Dr. O'Toole," Sherry corrected.

Molly rolled her eyes and smiled. "Quiet on the set, please." She donned a headset with a boom mike and stepped behind the camera, disappearing in the glare of the lights.

After a brief pause where nothing seemed to move, Sherry's earpiece popped to life, and she was listening to the *Today* show. A satiny smooth voice was in the process of introducing the segment when Molly's voice boomed, "Okay, Doc, stand by. We're ready to go in five, four, three . . ."

SCOTT FELT LIKE HE'D BEEN BEATEN. Every muscle, every joint screamed a dissonant chorus, with his ankle playing the role of lead singer in the newest boy band, Scott O'Toole and the Agonies.

But at least he'd lived through the night. What were the chances of that? How about a thousand to one? Nobody would have touched that bet. Stack a night of sure hypothermia on top of surviving a plane crash, and you might as well hand over your dollar to the lottery.

According to his wristwatch, it was nearly eight in the morning. He'd slept for a solid six hours—about what he got at home during school. During the night, though, his shelter seemed to have shrunk. It was like being in a grave.

That was the thought that drove him back outside.

The rescuers would come today. He knew it as surely as he knew his name. He'd never held much hope that people would come looking for him last night, not with the storm raging the way it had been. Now that it was daylight, though, even though the snow continued to fall, he figured that the search teams would find the margin of safety they'd need to do their jobs. He expected them to come by air, but he'd say yes to a dog sled if that was all they had to offer. He was ready to be warm again.

Outside the shelter now, Scott surveyed his surroundings, wincing against injuries he swore to God he didn't have last night. His neck and his back hurt, his fingers throbbed, and his ankle hurt all the way up to his knee. That didn't even count the six thousand bruises that had to be covering every inch of flesh beneath his clothes.

"I feel like I yelled 'redneck' in a biker bar," he mused aloud. The image made him smile, and even the smile hurt.

Everything looked so much smaller in the daytime. Distances that had seemed impossibly far last night now showed themselves for what they really were. The whole crash site, including the wrecked Cessna and the pitiful shelter Scott had built didn't cover a circle more than a hundred feet in diameter. Last night, he'd have sworn that it was twice that large. Maybe more. That's what happened when every step through the deep snow yielded such little distance.

Even the twisted remains of the airplane itself seemed smaller. The unrelenting snowfall had blunted every edge and rounded every corner. If he hadn't known that wreckage lay under all that powder, he'd have thought maybe it was a strange rock outcropping. Okay, a *very* strange outcropping with flashes of blue and red paint.

Still, if he'd just been wandering by this spot, not expecting to find anything, he wasn't at all sure he'd have seen it.

The thought froze his insides.

Standing there in the hip-deep snow, he arched his back and looked straight up. Through the swirling snow, the lead-colored sky appeared only as tiny patches of gray, peeking through an unrelenting canopy of frosted green, the arms of countless towering firs stretching forever toward the sky.

Oh, my God, we're invisible.

He could hardly see the wreckage from the ground, for crying out loud—from close enough to spit on it. How the hell could anyone see them from the air? What were these trees, a hundred years old? Five hundred? God only knew how many secrets they'd concealed from the air.

Stop it, he commanded himself. *You're panicking.*

Damn straight, I'm panicking. Facts were facts, and no lies he told himself were going to thin out these trees.

Maybe they're all torn up from the crash.

That was always a possibility, wasn't it? When something as big as an airplane falls through the canopy, it would have to leave a hell of a mark, wouldn't it? Broken branches and shattered wood. It'd have to do at least that much damage, right? Up above, from an angle that was invisible to him, there had to be a clear sign of damage that would draw the rescuers' eyes to his location. That was his ray of hope.

The snow.

His stomach knotted even tighter as he lifted his face again, craning his neck to watch the gray specks against the gray sky. It hadn't let up a bit all night. Whatever damage might have been visible on a clear sunny day was now completely obscured by an even blanket of white. Nobody would be able to see a thing.

So, what was he supposed to do? Just wait? What was the point of that? Wait for what?

For rescue. It's what everyone who'd ever written or spoken a word about being lost in the woods had said: You stay put and wait for the rescuers.

Who couldn't see you.

In the snow.

When you were freezing to death. And hungry.

Yes, that's what everybody said. He remembered Sven telling the class how important it was to decide ahead of time what your response to an emergency was going to be, so that when it finally happened, you'd be prepared to respond. *Commit yourself to doing the sensible thing,* he had said. *And never back away from that commitment, no matter how tempting the alternatives might be.* For all Scott knew, a whole battalion of rescuers was just minutes away.

But what if they weren't?

For the first time since last night, Scott felt the claws of real fear kneading his insides. Would he freeze before he starved, or vice versa? And after he was dead, was there even a remote chance that someone might find his body and give it a decent burial?

He wondered what it would feel like in that last moment. Did you really understand that you were dying, or did it sort of sneak up on you and sucker punch you into the Great Beyond? Would he go to heaven, or had all that cussing and talking back and jerking off sentenced him to hell instead?

"All right, stop it!" he commanded aloud. "Just stop it." He gave his head a hard shake and punched himself in the chest. Sven had warned the class about panic. It was the first session, as Scott recalled, and the grizzled Scandinavian was addressing the psychology of the stranded victim. And Scott had taken notes.

"You are scared," he'd said, through whatever accent that was. "You are all alone in a strange environment, and you are scared to death. What is going to happen? Will you survive? If you don't, what will it feel like to die? Will it hurt? Will you know when that last minute arrives?" As he'd asked these questions, he'd paced slowly around the room, making eye contact with each of the dozen or so students, of which Scott had been the youngest by at least five years. Sven had zeroed in on the boy, his piercing eyes blasting all the way through to the back of his head.

"Well, it's natural to be scared," he went on, as if addressing Scott individually. "It's good to be scared. Healthy, even, because fear makes us all more aware. It sharpens our senses and makes us better survivors. But . . ."

Sven paused here and leaned in very close to Scott and he'd lowered his voice nearly to a whisper.

"But *panic* kills. This is when the fear switches from its rightful place in your gut and spreads like a cancer to your brain. Panic comes when fear is all that's left in here." He'd poked Scott in the chest . . . "And here." . . . another poke, between his eyes. "You worry only about death—not how to live, mind you, but about when you'll die. You visualize death, and when you do, you give up on life. *That,* young man, is the moment when your fate is sealed."

Jesus Christ, it's like he'd had a crystal ball tuned to Scott's future. How had he known so precisely? Scott trembled from the chill these memories triggered. As creepy as Sven had seemed, he clearly knew his stuff. When you're cold and wet, and the snow falls without end, and you realize that the odds are bad at best, it's so easy just to give up, to stop fighting. And when that happens, what's left? It's not like you could just sit down and take a break; you couldn't hit the Pause button and go get a snack or switch game cartridges.

Scott understood now what Sven had been trying to say: Unless you plan to live, and work on the assumption that you're going to come out of the experience alive, then you might as well kill yourself early and get it over with.

"There's a way to do this," Scott said, and hearing the words, he actually believed them. "There's always a way." All he had to do was figure out what it was.

So, what was first?

He needed a better shelter, for sure. Last night's hole in the ground had kept him alive, but not much more.

What about food? Scott was a decent fisherman from a rowboat on a calm lake, and he'd read the stuff in Sven's handbook about setting traps for small animals, but who was he kidding? He didn't know jack about baiting traps, even if he'd had the tools and materials to build one.

So, what *about* food? He couldn't go without forever, and he was already pretty damned hungry. Yesterday at SkyTop, he'd barely taken time to scarf down a quick burger before heading back out to the slopes. He hadn't come to SkyTop to eat, he'd come to ski. Since then, dinner and breakfast had passed him by, and as lunchtime loomed, his belly was aching pretty badly.

Out of nowhere, Scott remembered his seventh grade history teacher, Mrs. Fesson, with her turkey neck and her yellow eyes, reveling in her macabre stories of cannibalism at the hands of the Donner party and the soccer team that crashed in South America.

"Would you?" she'd asked. "If it were the only means to survive, would you eat the flesh of another human being?"

As an academic exercise, it had seemed so simple. Of course he would. Humans were animals just like everyone else. Why shouldn't their bodies be put to good use? Not every day, of course—not in a supermarket, for crying out loud—but in an emergency, for the good of everyone else, what would be wrong with consuming their flesh? Scott had gotten an A that day for his classroom participation, and a comment after class from Mrs. Fesson that it was nice to have him contributing *constructively* for a change.

Yeah, well, what seemed so obvious and easy in the classroom was way far out of the question in the real world, when a friend lay dead over by the wreckage. He'd never be that hungry. Ever. No matter what.

He didn't have a fire to cook it on anyway.

Fire! God, would that solve a thousand problems or what? He'd have warmth, a place to cook and a signal for his rescuers, all in one package. The survival trifecta. All he needed was a dry place in the middle of the snow, an ax to cut wood and something to light it with. More likely than encountering flying pigs, he supposed, but just barely.

There was just so much to do! Sure, a signal of some sort was important—probably more important than food, despite his rumbling gut—but all of it would have to wait for the shelter. As if to drive the point home, God launched a blast of wind through the trees that cut through him like a scythe, and turned the crash site into a swirling white cloud.

This time, he'd build the shelter the way Sven had taught him, but first he needed some decent tools. Digging with that stupid chunk of metal had left him exhausted, with precious little to show for the effort.

His eyes turned to the plane. When you fly in the winter, in a place like Utah, wouldn't you need a shovel on board?

Sure you would. All Scott had to do was go back to the wreckage and find it.

Past Cody Jamieson's body.

It lay just where he'd left it, though not as thoroughly covered as he had hoped. He could still make out the human form under the snow frosting, and his nose still poked through the surface, dark gray against the stark white. There he was, just so much frozen meat. The thought made Scott feel ill.

Take a look, he told himself. *Screw up one time and that'll be you.* So much meat for the freezer.

God had brought him this far. Scott was personally responsible for the rest.

8

BACK EAST, when Barry Whitestone was first earning his chops as a Maryland State Police officer, it had always been the full moon that brought out the crazies. Call it superstition if you want, but when he looked back on his first twenty-five years of police work—and even as far back as 'Nam—when you stacked up all the bizarre incidents he'd been involved with, most of them happened when the man in the moon was smiling brightest.

Out here in God's country, it was a snowfall. The harder it blew, the wilder the calls became. Domestic battery, drunk skiers, suicides, you name it. The chances of something deeply weird happening were directly proportional to the speed of the wind and the depth of the snow. Last night it was a private plane dropping out of the sky, this morning it was a dead trucker at the Broken Arrow Motor Lodge.

Not any trucker, mind you. Oh, no, that would be too easy. This was a five-hundred-pounder. Died in the bathtub. James Alexander was already there when Whitestone arrived, standing with his fists on his hips in the doorway to the bathroom, watching the paramedics do their thing.

"How dead is he?" Whitestone asked.

Deputy Alexander stepped aside to let his boss have a peek. "Why don't the big ones ever die in bed?"

Whitestone stepped halfway into the white tile room to behold a very large naked man stuffed into a very small bathtub. And to answer his own question, the man was *very* dead.

"Does he have a name?"

James looked at a wallet he'd forgotten he was holding. "This is Maurice Hertzberger. Independent trucker, lives—*lived*—in Concordia, Kansas. The maid found him this morning. She doesn't know whether to seek counseling or turn him into a lamp. Either way, you're gonna need dynamite to get him outta that tub."

Whitestone laughed. "Aren't you in rare form this morning."

"It's the blizzard, man. I got too much Jamaican blood in my veins for this winter shit."

Barry took the wallet with him as he wandered back into the main room. "Rather be hangin' back in the 'hood, Deputy?"

It was Alexander's turn to laugh. His "hood" was a twelve-acre tract of family-owned land in the Hamptons—unless you counted their eighteenth-floor apartment in Manhattan's west fifties or the four-acre spread in West Palm. "I just don't like it this cold," he said.

"Well, James, you should have studied the map more carefully when you moved out here. The mountains and the altitude should have been a clue. You know, you being a cop and all."

As Barry spoke, he helped himself to Maurice Hertzberger's personal effects, rummaging for nothing in particular. "Do you have any reason to suspect that this visitor to our fair county died of anything unnatural?"

"I think he was murdered," James replied, and the comment drew a startled response. "I mean, look at the guy. Young, the picture of health, obviously worked out regularly. Does he look like somebody who might, oh, I don't know, drop dead from a stroke?"

Whitestone made a clucking noise and shook his head. "Such cynicism from such a young man. Makes me worry for your soul, James. Makes me worry for your soul."

Chief Whitestone liked James Alexander. Of all the cops he'd hired over the years—and that was a *lot* of cops—James was one of the most promising. In a county that tended to attract two personality types—dimmer bulbs who weren't good enough to get on the force in Denver or Salt Lake, or power-mad fascists who saw the uniform as an excuse to play with guns—James Alexander was one of the rare breed of sharp-witted Gen-Xers who took the job for all the right reasons. If he had a fault, it was his directness, but only because it was interpreted by many of his coworkers as a chip on his shoulder.

"What's this over here?" James asked, pointing to a pint bottle on the nightstand, three-quarters filled with clear liquid.

Barry was closest. "I know what it looks like," he said, picking it up and unscrewing the cap. He took a sniff and recoiled. "Yep, that's what I thought. This, young deputy, is moonshine. Just like my dear departed granddaddy used to make."

Alexander cocked his head, took it from him. "You're serious?"

"About it being shine, or about my granddaddy making it?"

James shrugged. "Okay." He took a whiff. "God, that's awful."

"I'm serious on both counts. I grew up on the Eastern Shore of Maryland. A little town called Easton. There were only two kinds of people there, ones who built stills and ones who busted them up. Let's just say there's apt to be more lawmen among my successors than there are among my ancestors." He watched with amusement as James struggled with his curiosity.

"Before you take a sip, you might want to look at Maurice again."

James looked surprised. "You think he was poisoned?"

"No, I think he stroked out, just like you said. On the other hand . . ." He decided to let James draw his own conclusion.

"Maybe I'll send this to the state police lab for testing," James said.

"I think maybe that's a good idea."

BRANDON O'TOOLE HAD BEEN expecting a bigger show. In his mind, he'd built this picture of a hundred men, most in military uniforms, swarming around wall-size maps, coordinating the search efforts over field phones and walkie-talkies. The movie in his mind was a big-budget thriller, with a makeshift command center set up on the tarmac of the local airport, or maybe the National Guard Armory.

What he found instead was the Arapaho County Police Department, located in the center of the ten blocks that defined Eagle Feather, Utah. A cross between a West Virginia mining town and a dilapidated set for cheesy westerns, Eagle Feather showed all the life signs of a corpse. What few trucks remained on the streets—there were no sedans or compact cars—were buried under four feet of snow. All but Brandon's rental Cherokee, that is, and the massive Humvee sporting a blue-and-red light bar on the roof and a badge decal on the door.

He did his best to park legally, and hovered his hand over the ignition for a moment, wondering whether or not he should keep it running, if only for the heater. Doubt disappeared, however, the instant he considered how few gas stations were likely to be open in the middle of a storm such as this.

Opening the door and sliding out into the snow, he was reminded for the thousandth time how foolish he'd been to dress for a Virginia winter while traveling to Utah. Blue jeans and a zippered jacket just didn't cut it out here, and neither did the ankle-high Rockports that he wore on his feet. A hat wouldn't have been a bad idea, either. His bald spot had never felt so huge.

As Brandon walked over the buried parking blocks toward the elevated sidewalk, he noted how different the snow was out here. Back east, snow was so heavy that a waist-deep accumulation would have been virtually impossible to walk through. Here, though, the dry flakes just breezed out of his way.

With a different sign on the door, the police station might just as easily have been a barber shop or an insurance office. It sat adjacent to a Gallagher's Shoe Repair, in the corner spot. Just another storefront among storefronts, occupying three demised spaces. Glass windows in the front gave it away as not the first occupant the developer had in mind when he built the place—back in, say, 1945.

Someone had obviously made a valiant effort to scrape the sidewalks clean, but as the wind blew yet another snow devil down the street, Brandon understood why the job had been abandoned.

A little bell pinged as Brandon pulled on the glass door and stepped into the foyer. It pinged again as the door closed behind him. From the inside, the place looked every bit the police station that it was. Opposite the front door, running parallel to the window, a concrete-block wall spanned the entire width of the place, with a steel door in the center and a teller window of sorts on the far left, where someone clearly was supposed to be stationed behind the bulletproof glass, but was AWOL for the time being. They'd made an effort to fancy the place up with fake flowers on veneered tables next to Western-style plastic furniture, but at the end of the day, it still looked like a police station, and no amount of paint-by-numbers pictures of boots and spurs could change that.

Brandon made his way to the teller window and thumbed the silver Ring Bell For Service button. Somewhere beyond the concrete and Lexan, he heard an electronic buzz, and thirty seconds later, a tall, scrawny guy in his twenties appeared in the window carrying a steaming cup. He wore a black wool sweater with padded shoulders and elbows, a silver badge over his left breast and a name tag over his right, which read Tingle.

"Howdy," the man said, displaying a grin full of perfectly aligned teeth. "What can I do for you?"

As much out of habit as anything else, Brandon produced a business card from his pants pocket and slid it through the slot in the window. "My name is Brandon O'Toole. Are you the man in charge here?"

Tingle scowled as he read the card and shook his head. "No, sir, that'd be Chief Whitestone, and he's not here right now. You a salesman or something?"

Brandon felt his ears flush. That had been a test, and this goober had failed. "No, my son was on that airplane that crashed yesterday."

Jesse Tingle's face lit up instantly with recognition. "Oh, shit" slipped out before he had a chance to stop it, and he became instantly apologetic. "I'm so sorry, sir. I should have recognized the name. Please, step on inside and I'll see if I can get the chief on the radio." He reached under the counter and the lock on the steel door buzzed. The regulars, Brandon saw, could use the glowing keypad next to the door to let themselves in.

Brandon pulled on the handle and stepped into a clutter of desks and filing cabinets, on which every possible surface was concealed by stacks of paper. Of the eight desks he could see, only three were occupied, and each occupant watched their visitor with combined suspicion and curiosity while Tingle scurried toward a glass-walled office in the rear corner. Before he got there, though, the door pinged again, and a few seconds later, in walked the man who had to be the boss.

Whitestone doffed his jacket, a curious expression on his face. He wore the same black sweater and shiny badge, only where Tingle's badge was silver, the chief's was gold. Pushing fifty, this new man carried himself with athletic grace as he strode toward Brandon. Of average height and weight, he'd seen more sun than his dermatologist would approve of, but on him, the leathery skin gave him a cowboy ruggedness. He had the look of a man who could be intimidating as hell when he wanted to be.

Jesse made his pitch from across the room. "Chief Whitestone, this man is Bradley O'Toole. He's—"

"It's Brandon," he corrected. "And I'm—"

"You've come a long way, Mr. O'Toole," Whitestone said. As he closed to within ten feet, he led with his outstretched hand. "I'm Barry Whitestone, police chief around here. Welcome to Eagle Feather." It was like shaking hands with stone. "You must be worried sick." He ushered Brandon toward his office with a sweep of his arm. "Please, come on back and I'll catch you up on what we know."

Brandon made no secret about watching the people who watched him, returning their curious glances with hard stares. If his gaze made them uncomfortable, so much the better. What the hell were they doing in the office anyway, when his son was freezing out there somewhere?

Whitestone paused at the door and allowed Brandon to enter the tiny office first.

From behind, Jesse Tingle asked, "Can I get you something to drink? Hawaiian Punch?"

Brandon scowled. "Excuse me?"

Whitestone chuckled. "How about a cup of coffee? I have a pot brewing in my office, twenty-four–seven."

Confused, Brandon nodded. "Coffee, please."

Whitestone closed the door and gestured to a wooden chair. "Welcome to Utah," he said. "The Mormon capital of the world. Not many coffee drinkers among the locals." He walked to an ancient Mr. Coffee that perched precariously on a bookshelf. "Cream? Sugar?"

"Both, please." Brandon settled himself into the hardback chair. Whoever wrote the budgets for Arapaho County clearly didn't care much about the aesthetics of the police chief's personal office space. Wood for the chairs, gray metal for everything else.

The chief presented Brandon with a steaming cup. "You're from back east, right?"

"Virginia. About fifteen miles west of D.C."

Whitestone set his own cup on his desk and sat heavily, folding his hands on the blotter. "Nice area. I was stationed at Fort Belvoir for two years back when I was young and stupid." Clearly, he wanted to make this as lighthearted as he could, but Brandon was having none of it. The chief sighed. "Okay, well, actually, your wife summed it up pretty well this morning."

"My wife?"

"On the morning news. You didn't see her?"

Brandon groaned against the headache that had begun to gather behind his eyes. "No, to tell you the truth, Chief, I spend as little time as possible watching, listening to or sharing oxygen with my *ex*-wife."

Whitestone made a curious face, but he didn't pursue the point. "Well, here's the long and the short of it. We don't know much more now than we did twelve hours ago. The Cessna carrying your son and his friend apparently left around five o'clock last night, on their way to Salt Lake City. To our knowledge, they never arrived, and we presume that they have crashed."

He'd never get used to hearing the words spoken aloud. "But you know where they are, right?"

"I can't imagine how difficult this must be for you, Mr. O'Toole," the chief said.

"Call me Brandon, please. I asked you if you know where the plane went down."

Whitestone signaled the answer with a sigh. "Well, we'd like to think so. I mean, we know they started at SkyTop around four-thirty or five and presume they headed for the main airport in Salt Lake

City, but the fact is they never filed a flight plan, so we don't know anything for sure."

"But, we know generally," Brandon prompted. "Assuming that they were headed where they said. And frankly, where else would they go?"

"Like I said, I hope we do. With this storm blowing, though, we haven't had a chance till this morning to actually go out looking for them."

Brandon pressed harder. "But if you know point A and you know point B, and you know how long they were in the air, then you must have a decent idea where the wreckage would be. Hell, when the Kennedy kid crashed a couple of years ago, they were able to pinpoint a spot in the ocean just from radar."

Whitestone's face grew even darker. "Unfortunately, that was New York and Boston. This is Utah. Because your son's plane was flying outside the normal flight paths, no one was paying too much attention. They had no transponder, so they were difficult to track. In the middle of a storm like that, it's my understanding that it's easy for a small plane to get lost in the ground clutter. Mind you, this is information I've only learned myself in the past few hours. As for plotting them on a map, that's what we're hoping to do. But it was damned windy out there last night. It could be . . . Well, there's certainly plenty of hope that we'll find them right where they're supposed to be."

While the chief's words said hope, Brandon noted that everything else projected the opposite. "Isn't there some sort of locator beacon on the plane?"

This time, Whitestone knew that his words would hurt. "Not this aircraft, no. Frankly, to be compliant with FAA regulations, it should have. Unfortunately, it appears that Cody Jamieson wasn't always a rule-follower."

"Jesus Christ," Brandon spat. "If that son of a bitch survived, I swear to God I'll kill him myself. So, you're telling me we're looking for a needle in a haystack."

"I'm not sure I'd characterize it quite that way—"

"Don't bullshit me, goddammit!" Brandon boomed, and then he backed off right away. "I'm sorry."

Whitestone shook it off. "No need. You've got to be frazzled. How did you get here, anyway? The airports are closed, and so are the roads."

Brandon shrugged. "You'll have to talk to the pilot about the airport, but those barricades don't really close a road. They just provide an extra obstacle. Besides, nothing performs like a rental car. So, tell me about your search efforts so far. You have crews hiking up into the mountains?"

"Where would I send them to? Like I said, we don't know—"

"What about airplanes?"

"The Air National Guard has provided an airplane to monitor radio frequencies for distress calls, but for the time being—"

"I meant *search* planes."

Whitestone set his jaw. "Please, Mr. O'Toole. Brandon. I know what you'd like to see out there, but until the weather breaks, there are limits to what we can do."

"And for right now, the best you can do is sit around with your thumb up your ass?"

Whitestone's eyes went hot. "We're doing what we can," he said at length. "Out here, Mother Nature calls more shots than we do. If that looks to you like we're sitting on our thumbs, I'm sorry. The weather's supposed to clear this afternoon."

Brandon wanted to break something. Time was their most lethal enemy, next to the weather, and Chief Whitestone was telling him that his team of rescuers—if, indeed there even was such a team—didn't have the balls to face down either one. "You're giving up, then?"

Whitestone shook his head. "God, no. First chance we get, we'll be all over that mountain looking for them. Search and rescue is a dangerous business in the best of circumstances, and we're all willing to stretch the odds to make a save. But we can't do an air search until the weather dies down, and it just doesn't make sense to send ground teams in to wander aimlessly. Surely you understand that."

"What I don't understand is, why this Jamieson kid has more balls than your entire police department. He was a reckless idiot, but at least he had the courage to try something."

Whitestone's eyes burned hotter. "Mr. O'Toole, I want you to do us both a favor, okay? Never mistake bravado for bravery. Foolishness for guts. With all respect, your son and Cody Jamieson did a stupid, stupid thing. And nobody on my staff wants to duplicate their stupidity. I'm sure that hurts, but it's just the way it is."

Brandon heard the air rush out of his lungs as the news sank in, and for a moment, he wondered if he'd be able to take a breath at all.

"Are you all right?" Whitestone rose from his chair and reached across the desk to place his hand atop Brandon's. "I'm sorry if that was too much detail. I thought . . . You impressed me as someone who appreciated bluntness."

Brandon inhaled deeply and held it for a second. "I just get so angry—" He cut himself off. Whitestone was a cop, not a psychologist. Brandon would deal with his anger on his own time. "I appreciate your candor—your bluntness, as you say. I want to know every little detail."

Whitestone watched the other man carefully for a long moment before lowering himself back into his seat. "This needn't be all down time," he said, reaching into his desk drawer for a pad of yellow legal paper. "Tell me about your son. Do you have any recent pictures?"

Brandon pulled his wallet out of his back pocket and opened it, grateful to be doing something useful. He found Scott's school picture and handed it over. "This is about two years old—eighth grade, I think. He's sixteen now and he's grown about six inches since then, but hasn't gained an ounce." Long and thin, the boy in the photo stared at the camera with his head cocked, a crooked grin exposing perfect teeth. The blue eyes showed a serious side, too, giving the impression that maybe he knew a few more secrets than he should.

"Handsome boy," Whitestone said. "Would I recognize him from this photo?"

Brandon nodded. "I think so, yes. Except for the goatee that only he can see. Oh, and his hair is blue now."

That brought the chief's eyes up. "Excuse me?"

Brandon smiled. "Closer to purple, actually. The kids on his soccer team call him Smurf."

Whitestone laughed. "Artist or musician?"

"Sounds like the voice of experience."

"I've got a thirteen-year-old drummer at home. I lost the earring battle two years ago, but haven't faced the hair war yet."

Brandon made a dismissive motion with his hands. "I don't even fight it. I think he's up to three earrings—maybe it's four. I know there's two in at least one ear. I figure what the hell? It's his money and he's on the honor roll every quarter." He laughed as he recalled the day Scott broached the hair issue. "It's a look, he tells me, for his band. He's lead guitar, and features himself to be the next Kirk Hammett."

"Ah, heavy metal. I get a headache just thinking about it."

"Scott's actually pretty good," Brandon said. "And if you can't listen to the Stones, then Metallica ain't a bad substitute. Anyway, I made him wait six months on the hair, and when he still wanted it, I said okay."

Whitestone seemed genuinely intrigued. "Is it permanent?"

"As permanent as any dye, I suppose. I mean they had to bleach it down to white before turning it blue. Now, ask me if I'm washing blue-stained pillowcases every week. The answer is yes."

The chief shook his head. "And I thought I was daring by wearing a ponytail halfway to my ass."

God, wasn't that the truth? Brandon thought back to the screaming matches he'd had with his own father over the length of his hair. A career Navy aviator and an Academy grad, his father knew only one hairstyle—high-and-tight—and saw the hippie movement as a bunch of Communist sissy-boys. When young and rebellious Brandon had refused to get a haircut, his father had produced a straight razor and threatened to take care of it himself. Only the intervention of his mom saved the boy from a bloodbath, but from that day on, his dad introduced the boy as "my daughter, Brandon." They never spoke again, his father and he, after that day with the razor. Eight months later, nearly to the day, a surface-to-air missile reduced Lieutenant Commander Curtis O'Toole to so much humidity over the skies of Hanoi.

Brandon dedicated his life to avoiding the same mistakes with his own son. Sitting there in Barry Whitestone's office, his brain flashed images of the morning when Scott was maybe three hours old and they made eye contact for the first time; not just the squirmy look-at-all-the-new-stuff gaze that he'd seen earlier, but that real, bonding, I-trust-you-with-my-life stare. It came with a smile, and Brandon realized in that instant that all the times when he *thought* he'd fallen in love had just been poor imitations of the real thing.

Under different circumstances, the long silence that filled the chief's office might have felt uncomfortable, but this one didn't. Here, two fathers sat together, one of them facing down a nightmare, and the other wondering how he would cope in similar circumstances. Life shouldn't be as fragile as this, Brandon thought. It shouldn't be permitted that years of hard work and attention and wonderful times could be wiped out so quickly. Thousands of people logged millions of hours in the sky every year. Why should it be Scott who added a notch to the statistics? Why not a kid who was less deserving of an easy, happy life?

Brandon felt pressure building behind his eyes as he pondered these things. Sometimes life was so damned unfair that he couldn't stand it. But he wouldn't lose control. Not here, and certainly not in front of a stranger. If he gave up hope, then so would everyone else. And there *was* hope, dammit. Plenty of it.

When he glanced up at the chief, Whitestone at first looked away, but then tentatively returned his gaze. "He's alive, you know," Brandon said, pleased that his voice still sounded strong.

Whitestone set his jaw, nodded. "And we'll find him."

9

WHAT CODY JAMIESON LACKED in flying skills he made up for in preparedness. Scott had struck the jackpot on tools. The Cessna had a full complement, including the Holy Grail du jour: a three-foot, folding G.I. shovel just like the ones he'd seen in countless war movies. In addition, the toolbox, whose latch miraculously had not even sprung during the impact, contained screwdrivers, a hammer and a socket set. So, if the occasion arose for him to, say, mount a ceiling fan out here, he was all set.

All morning long, Scott had been dreading the task of digging a larger shelter, wondering the whole time how he was going to get this super-powdery fluff to pack down tight enough to make good walls. The answer, he'd decided, was simply to dig deeper, but he didn't know if he had enough strength left to do that.

That's when he noticed the severed right wing resting at the base of a towering pine, and the brainstorm hit: why dig when you can build? Sven was the first to encourage his students to take obvious shortcuts, particularly when it came to building shelters, making use of ground cover or natural formations. Caves, he'd said, were a particularly fine choice. With the wing, he could build his own cave. Digging was simple when you didn't have to worry about the ceiling collapsing.

Invoking the lesson he'd learned last night, Scott removed his parka and turtleneck and hung them up on protruding pieces of wreckage, opting to work only in his long-sleeve undershirt. Even at that, he was sweating by the time he was done.

Using his new shovel, Scott first dug a foxhole, down as close to the forest floor as he could get, and then he placed the overburden up around the edge of the hole until the rim was about as high as his chin. With that done, he built himself a little shelf to sleep on, remembering from his class that the coldest air would settle to the lowest spot of any enclosure. Next, he lined the entire hole with the softest, most pliable pine boughs he could find. Insulation was king out here. If Sven had said it once, he'd said it a thousand times.

The final step in Scott's construction project was to drag the severed wing over the top of his creation, giving himself a solid roof, which he reinforced with a good three feet of insulating snow, packing it down as tightly as the dry powder would allow. By the time he was done, the shelter was nearly big enough to stand in, and at least as big as any two-man tent you'd buy at the sporting goods store. As more snow fell, the shelter's insulation properties would only improve. As a final test, he lay down on his handiwork and smiled. Call it skill or call it luck, but his first-ever shelter-from-scratch was actually *comfortable.* For the door, he utilized the right-hand cockpit door, which he removed with the help of the hammer and screwdriver from the tool kit.

Sometimes, it's the little things that make you want to dance or belt out a war whoop. Scott had remembered, and he'd performed, and the result was a hell of a lot better, even, than what he and his dad had put together for the class. Maybe it wasn't all a lost cause, after all. Maybe he could actually pull this thing off. Wouldn't that be a kick?

As he pulled his sweater and parka back on, Scott forced himself to return to his mental checklist. What was he forgetting? He had short-term survival taken care of. Sort of. He had shelter. Now he needed food and water. Eating snow was not an option, even though it intuitively seemed like a solution to thirst. Sven had made the point repeatedly: frozen liquids cooled you from the inside out, thus inviting hypothermia. As for food, well, he didn't have an immediate answer for that, either. That left him with the remaining priority of rescue.

He'd read *Lord of the Flies* and he'd seen *Cast Away,* so he knew even without dredging up the lessons from his survival class that he needed to focus his energy on building a fire. Problem was, Ralph and Piggy and Tom Hanks all found themselves on overheated islands. How the hell was he supposed to get things to burn in the snow? Even if he had matches (which he didn't), how would he sustain the flame once it ignited? Seemed to Scott that even if he got something to catch, it would put itself out as the ground around it melted.

Hell of a thing to leave out of the lecture, Sven.

One thing at a time. Find a source of fire, and then worry about keeping it burning. He'd been all through Cody Jamieson's pockets, and found nothing remotely resembling a match. Or flint and steel or even two sticks to rub together. American Cancer Society be damned, why didn't people smoke anymore?

There had to be a way. There's always a way; you just have to look at things from a different angle. Kind of like those find-the-word puzzles where turning the sheet upside down sometimes made things more obvious.

Scott hiked back to the wreckage for another look. The arcing from the night before had stopped, so he figured that the battery had died. Not that he'd know how to convert electricity to fire anyway. Seemed to him that as they were taking off, he remembered seeing a box about the size of an automobile first aid kit, marked Emergency in red letters, attached to the bulkhead just behind the pilot's seat.

That's what he was looking for. Surely, whoever manufactured an emergency kit for airplanes must have foreseen the possibility of a crash, and the need to signal somebody. That only made sense. With any luck at all, the emergency kit would be manufactured out of the same stuff that they made black boxes out of for airliners.

Snow hadn't accumulated much inside the cockpit, thanks to the smallness of the openings, and the compartment's orientation away from the wind. The place was a mess of papers and scattered debris, though, among which he found another flashlight, a dog-eared topographical map that he figured might come in handy, and there, wedged under a piece of the backseat, the emergency kit. He carried it back outside and sat in the snow to open it.

The kit was bigger than he'd remembered, maybe eight inches by twelve inches, and about three inches deep. Inside, he found some bandages, and a sheathed survival knife not unlike the one he remembered from his father's collection of Vietnam stuff. (Scott figured that the knife must have been a personal addition to the kit from Cody; the knife by itself was worth more than everything else combined.)

Nestled in the bottom of the kit, wrapped in its own little Baggie, was the best discovery of the day: a flare gun. Smaller than the ones he'd seen in movies, the Day-Glo-orange pistol came with its own instruction sheet, which explained that the manufacturer had preloaded it with a single flare. He read through the rest of the instructions, finding nothing beyond the obvious. Huge block letters across the bottom of the sheet warned: KEEP OUT OF REACH OF CHILDREN.

He found other flares as well—fusees, they were called, and they looked just like the ones that cops set out at the scene of auto accidents. So, there was his source of fire. His matches. Things were looking up.

Stuffing the flare gun into his coat pocket, he carried the fusees back to the shelter and placed them on his sleeping shelf, on top of the greenery, on what he hoped would be a dry spot. Then it was back outside to give some thought to making a signal fire.

SITTING AROUND THE POLICE STATION twiddling body parts was going to drive Brandon over the edge, in all likelihood bringing the chief and his staff tumbling behind him. With the weather this bad, nothing could happen. He couldn't do anything to change that, and neither could the police. Having him sit there waiting for nothing just made everybody uncomfortable.

Every hour or so, on the regular news updates, Brandon caught glimpses of rebroadcast segments of Sherry's appearance on the *Today* show. She could barely contain herself, she was so upset. She had no idea that Scotty—Scott *hated* to be called that—had even met this Cody Jamieson person, let alone decided to take a trip with him. For a while, she never even reported him missing, because she'd just figured he was out with the other teenagers, doing whatever it was teenagers did when they got together. From there, the interviewer took Sherry through what little was known about the search efforts, and he left her with his prayers for a speedy and happy resolution to this terribly stressful time, before moving on to a commercial for diapers.

The time had come for Brandon to confront her face-to-face. He wasn't sure what he wanted to glean from the meeting, but he knew that it had to happen. Pretty Boy Brock never quite got around to the questions he wanted to ask.

He snagged the tourist bus for a ride up to SkyTop. By the time he arrived at Sherry's mansion on the mount, he felt like he'd been for a ride in a clothes dryer. The driver kept the heater set at a constant 300 degrees, and with chains on the back tires, the converted school bus rode like a stagecoach with square wheels.

As he'd expected, it was Larry Chinn who answered his knock. "Oh, my God," he breathed, clearly startled. "It's you."

Brandon stepped past him into the foyer without waiting for an invitation. "Hi, Larry." Inside, the place was a palace, bigger than most wealthy people's year-round homes. Open stairs rose from his right, climbing the front wall and leading to a bridge spanning the massive two-plus-story vaulted great room. Straight ahead, on the far side of the enormous family room with its walk-in fireplace, the wall was built entirely of glass, offering a breathtaking view of the ski slopes, and beyond them, of the craggy mountain peaks that stretched to the horizon. "You sure there's enough room in here?"

"It *is* lovely, isn't it?"

Brandon didn't give much of a damn where people fell on the sexuality spectrum, but Larry was just effeminate enough to put his teeth on edge. "Is your boss around?"

"She's sleeping." He said it in a half-whisper, as if a hand grenade in the foyer could even be heard in the sleeping wing, wherever that was.

"Wake her up. We need to talk."

Larry seemed very uncomfortable about this. "Brandon . . . um, Mr. O'Toole . . . I'm not sure if it's even appropriate—"

"Please don't piss me off, Larry. Okay? Do me that favor. Tell

Sherry that I'm here. Better yet, tell her that I'll be here until she deigns to see me."

Larry sort of hugged himself as he gaped, wondering what he should do.

"Please," Brandon whispered. "I admire your loyalty, but believe me when I tell you that you don't want to get into the middle of this one."

"I don't presume to pry where I don't belong, Mr. O'Toole, but she really has been *very* tired—"

"Yeah, I know. It's exhausting dodging phone calls before having to get up for the networks."

Larry saw something in Brandon's expression that convinced him. "I'll see what I can do."

With that, Larry hurried out of the living room and up the stairs, leaving Brandon alone in the palace. Honestly, he could think of four-star hotel lobbies that were less well-appointed. Sherry-the-bitch had pulled out all the stops to impress Scott this time around. He wondered how well it had worked.

Why couldn't she just have left well enough alone?

"Relax, Dad," Scott had told him at the front door on his way out. "Team Bachelor is safe. It's just a ski trip." In business, Brandon's friends knew him as the Ice Man—coldly calculating, with a perfect poker face. At home, he was as opaque as window glass. Scott could read him like an eye chart.

Brandon waited all of ninety seconds before heading off to explore the place.

He figured the chalet to have six bedrooms, and he found Scott's on the same level as the living room. If the blue-tinged pillowcase hadn't given it away, then the explosion of clutter certainly would have. The boy's room here was twice the size of Brandon's master bedroom at home, complete with a fireplace, a king-size bed, and a view that rivaled that of the great room. The decor was early great white hunter, with the bust of some animal over the fireplace, and a collection of bows and arrows on the wall, some of them clearly antique, but others of a space-age design. It surprised Brandon that of all the rooms Scott could have chosen as his own, he chose the one with dead animals on the walls. Then he looked next to the bed and he understood perfectly. A built-in stereo system dominated the wall, with speakers that could cause structural damage.

Sure enough, when Brandon pressed the Play button on the remote he found on the nightstand, a CD changer cued up Metallica's Black Album. Their first Black Album. The latest was undoubtedly plugged into Scott's head, courtesy of the portable player that never left his possession. As heavy metal flooded the room, he lost track of time. He sat there on the bed listening to the guitar riffs, all the while seeing Scott's fingers flying across his Gibson guitar, belting out a serviceable impression of Kirk Hammett. The sound, of course, was perfect, but Brandon had to smile as his mind's eye watched the boy work on the lead-guitar body language—the roundhouse strum, as Brandon liked to call it, and the jumps and the kneeling riffs. One day the kid would be damn good, he knew, but until he outgrew the adolescent gangliness, the physical elements of his performance would always have that comical edge.

Then again, not everyone saw his baby boy in the same light as he did. Among his fellow classmates at Robinson High School, Scott was apparently quite the babe. A hottie. Brandon had learned this little detail during back-to-school night when some girl's mother—herself single and clearly on the prowl—sought him out to share with the father the depth of the son's babehood. His hottiness. Brandon had received the news with pride and grace, and wasted no time in passing it on to the babe himself, who responded with a shade of red that one rarely saw in nature.

"Please don't say anything like that in front of my friends," he'd begged.

"I think they already know. Apparently everyone does."

"Oh, God," Scott had groaned. "You're going to, aren't you? I know you. You're going to be sitting with some parent who's bragging about their kid's SAT scores, and you're going to say, 'Yeah, but my son's a babe.'"

"But I'm proud to be the father of a babe. You should be proud to be one."

"Oh, God."

And so it had gone for a good five minutes until Scott had taken offense and left the kitchen in a huff. Leave it to teenagers to be offended by compliments.

As "Enter Sandman" ended and "Sad But True" began, Brandon found himself petting a T-shirt that Scott had left crumpled on the bed. He recognized it as one he'd bought last summer in Hilton Head, featuring a peg-legged pirate with a bandanna and an eye patch riding a shark skeleton bareback, by way of advertising a brand of surfboard wax. Scott had bought it for the picture and it had been one of his favorites ever since.

The rush of anguish came as a stab as Brandon fondled the shirt, feeling the limp softness of it between his fingers. It was a connection—a link to his son, and as he handled it, the lingering odor of Mennen anti-perspirant and Brut aftershave wafted past, sharpening the pain and driving it deeper. As the music grew louder and Kirk pounded his guitar strings, Brandon buried his face in the dirty shirt and inhaled the aroma.

He closed his eyes and squinted hard, trying to force the pain away, but it only grew sharper. How could they have put their son in the middle of all this? How could he, Brandon, have forced Scott to feel bad about a trip he had every right to treasure?

How am I going to live without him?

The tears arrived in a rush, flooding out as a wracking sob. Jesus, what had he done? What was he going to do? The desperate sadness was a knife blade—a bayonet thrust through his soul. The agony of it took Brandon's breath away, and with it, his sense of hope. Scott Christopher O'Toole lay dead or dying out there somewhere, and the last thought he'd take with him was the guilt of having disappointed the man who was in fact his single greatest fan.

Brandon buried his face deeper into the T-shirt and tried to imagine what it would have been like to have one final embrace.

"Brandon?" Sherry's voice stirred something ugly in his gut. "Brandon, where are you?" She was in the living room, and without even looking, he could see her with her hands on her hips.

Settling himself with a deep breath, Brandon wiped his eyes and stepped out of the bedroom into the hallway. Sure enough, there she was, with just the posture he'd imagined.

"Where the hell were you?" Brandon said, walking toward her.

"I was upstairs sleeping." Clearly, she'd made an effort to fix her hair, but the back still showed signs of bed head.

"I meant last night," Brandon said.

Sherry held her hands up astride her face, her fingers splayed— her ultimate sign of frustration. "I was just tired and scared, all right? I didn't want to have to deal with you. That's why I didn't answer the phone, and that's why I didn't return your calls. I'm sorry, okay?"

"*Earlier*, Sherry. Where were you earlier? When Scott was deciding to go to some concert?"

"Oh, like this is *my* fault?"

"For one week out of your busy life, you were supposed to be a *parent!* Now, where the hell were you?"

Sherry shook her head and headed back for the stairs. "I don't have to listen to this. You're delusional."

Brandon grabbed her arm and pulled her back around. "No, actually, you do have to listen to this. I want an answer."

"Get your hands off me, before I call the police."

"I've spent all day with the police," Brandon sneered. "Want me to tell you which one to talk to? How did this happen?"

Sherry yanked her arm away. "How dare you!"

"Answer the goddamn question! How does a sixteen-year-old boy manage to climb onto an airplane and fly into a snowstorm when you're here watching him?"

Her hands went back to her hips, her head cocked. "Do you really think that I'm with him every single minute of the day? Scotty's a teenager, for God's sake. In case you haven't noticed."

"His name is *Scott*, Sherry! He hates being called Scotty. And it's *because* he's a teenager that I do keep an eye on him."

"Oh, that's right, I keep forgetting that I'm dealing with the perfect father. Excuse me for not calling you for an instruction book before I left."

"Jesus, Sherry, it's not about being perfect! It's about being reasonable! Now, where the hell were you?"

"I was at breakfast, Brandon. And then I did some work. And then I had lunch and then I wrote a little more, and then, wouldn't you know it? It was time for dinner. That's where I was. Now, I suppose by your yardstick of reasonable parenting, I should have had Scotty in a playpen at arm's reach all day, but somehow, that seemed wasteful. You know, inasmuch as we're at a ski resort!"

"Where you have no business being in the first place!" Brandon boomed.

Sherry laughed that derisive little chuckle that always pushed him over the edge. "Oh, so now we get down to what's really bugging you. You're afraid of losing the parent olympics."

"I'm afraid of losing my son! To hell with you and me, Sherry. Has it dawned on you yet that our son has been in a plane crash?"

"Has it dawned on you that it's not my fault?"

Brandon swatted a lamp off its end table, and then launched the table itself with a kick. "Goddammit, Sherry, it's not even *about* you! Like most of the things that go on in the world every goddamn day, this one is not even remotely about *you!* Why can't you see that?"

"Because you keep blaming me for it! And you're paying for that lamp!"

He swatted another one just for good measure. And in that moment, he realized that he was out of control. He realized that coming to the chalet had been exactly the wrong idea, and that if he didn't walk away right this moment, he was going to hurt her. He took a step closer, and while he could see the fear in her eyes, she refused to step back.

"The depths of what you don't comprehend are truly frightening, Sherry," he said. His voice was a whisper now, and his forefinger hovered an inch from her nose. "But you listen to me very carefully. If they don't find Scott, or if they find him and he's anything but one hundred percent healthy, you're going to pay."

10

AT TEN MINUTES TO THREE, Isaac DeHaven thumbed the switch on the shortwave radio, pleased to hear the *thump* that demonstrated there was life in the speakers. Living like this in the middle of nowhere, he always enjoyed a sense of satisfaction when the equipment still worked. Repairs in the wintertime could pose a hell of a problem.

Isaac called his little piece of heaven a "cabin," but by anyone else's standards it was much more than that. Built originally as a hunting lodge back in the 1920s—and then modified a decade later to minister to the needs of the bootlegging crowd—the Flintlock Ranch was constructed entirely of logs harvested from the surrounding forests and sported close to four thousand square feet of living space. He had all the comforts he needed, with the exception of a truly efficient heating system. On days like this, even with the wood stoves stoked and the heat set on high, it was hard to bring the temperature much past sixty-five. A hell of a lot warmer than outside, to be sure, but never quite warm enough to shed his sweater and socks.

Returning last night after five days, it seemed as if the frigid weather had settled into the very foundation of the place. He threw another log onto the fire and opened the stove's damper a little more, then settled into his plush leather chair, his feet crossed on the ottoman, just inches from the blaze in the firebox.

As necessary as it was to leave the ranch from time to time, he always dreaded it, and always savored the days that followed his return. It was the solitude, as much as anything else, he thought. And in the winter, the solitude was sweeter than at any other time of the year. The grass didn't grow; it was too cold to repair fences. Winter was Isaac's time for music and books and maybe a little writing. For days on end, he might never exercise his vocal cords at all, and that was just fine with him. Life was too short to spend it talking to others.

Not when there were books to read, music to listen to. The walls of Flintlock Ranch were papered with books, thousands of volumes, stretching from floor to ceiling, wrapping the entire perimeter. Isaac read everything, from memoirs to classics to junk fiction. He knew the law as well or better than any new associate in any law firm in the nation, just as he knew disease as intimately as any fourth-year medical student. When he listened to a Mozart symphony or a Beatles album, he knew not only the music, but where it fit in the composer's total body of work. Isaac didn't actively seek out to learn these things, he just did. And with little else to clutter his mind, he retained more detail than he lost. He supposed it was just the way he was wired as a human being.

What he could not absorb in sufficient quantity to slake his interest was current news, and that, as much as anything else, was the function of his shortwave radio. On it, he could listen not only to the news of the United States, but also to that of France or Germany or Spain, or any of the other nations whose languages he spoke fluently. Inevitably, though, after just an hour or so of announcer-speak, he would feel his temper heating, his mood darkening. Then it would be time to restore the gentle silence, interrupted only by music.

Isaac DeHaven's nightmares were all noisy, filled with people he didn't know, invading his space and his mind with random commotion that accomplished nothing. The nightmares relived his days in prison: five years wasted in the company of humans who were barely more than animals, guarded by men who believed that a piece of metal pinned to a shirt somehow gave them power over others; that it relieved them of responsibility for the suffering that they inflicted on the men placed in their care.

Isaac didn't waste his time on hatred, but if he did, it was the prison guards who would feel the heat of his emotion. The nightmares were all that separated Isaac from a truly utopian existence out here in the wilderness. If they would leave him alone, then his contentment would be complete.

Isaac's brain fired a shiver before he fully comprehended why. It was the song on the radio—Andy Williams crooning "Moon River." His heart racing, Isaac checked his watch and verified the time: it was precisely 3:00. "Well, I'll be damned," he muttered.

The signal had been set up years ago. Isaac would listen to the obscure radio band every afternoon. If there was a problem, then straight-up at three o'clock, he'd hear "Moon River." So, this was a first. "Moon River" meant that Isaac had somehow screwed up, and the very thought of it baffled him. Isaac *never* made mistakes.

Then he remembered the man in the truck stop. The one who kept looking at him and then looking away. He'd sensed that something was wrong even then, but was distracted by Maurice before he could act on his suspicions.

"I *will* be damned." He said it again, because it was the only thing he could think of to say.

Isaac checked his watch again, this time to verify the date: February 25; 2/25. It would be 2:25 tomorrow morning before he would be able to pick up the coded message, and in the meantime, he'd just have to wonder. Surely it was a mistake.

Just to be on the safe side, Isaac wandered into the little study hidden behind the panel in the kitchen wall, and over to the vault. He dialed in the combination, pulled the door open and scanned the collection of weaponry. Until he had some notion of what was going on, he traded in the little .38 snub-nose that always graced his waist for an H&K 9 mm. Then, just to be sure, he slipped a full magazine into an MP5 assault rifle before closing and locking the door again.

With a deep sigh, Isaac turned off the radio, selected a Rimsky-Korsakov CD for the player and settled back into his chair.

Try as he might, mental peace would be hard to come by on this night.

•　　•　　•

SCOTT AWOKE THINKING somebody had hit him. Out of nowhere, a cramp seized his stomach, pulling his knees up to his chest. It was a deep, grinding pain that started low and spread quickly, like a kick in the balls, leaving him wondering if he might puke. He clenched his jaws against the bile that flooded up behind his tongue, willing the contents of his stomach to remain where they were. A minute later, the pain was gone, but it left him feeling weak, shaky. He needed food. Water, too, probably. He scraped a glove full of snow away from the inside wall and shoved it into his mouth. To hell with Sven and his warnings. He had to chew to make it melt, and as he swallowed, he could feel every inch of its progress down his gullet.

He closed his eyes.

Work to stay awake, Sven told him. *Sleep is a very dangerous thing.*

As he drifted off again, Scott dreamed of dying.

AIRPLANES.

Scott bolted upright, fully aware before he was fully awake. Propelled by adrenaline, he scrambled for the shelter door, pushing it open and crawling out into the snow.

The thick canopy overhead distorted the sound of the aircraft engines just enough that Scott couldn't tell where they were coming from. They could be overhead, or they could be two miles away, propellers churning the air relentlessly. As he listened, Scott's spirits soared.

"They're looking for me," he announced to the forest.

That had to be it. A passing airliner or a military plane would have jet engines; the sound of people in a hurry to get where they're going. But propellers were for cruising. For rescuing. He let out the war whoop of all war whoops.

This was it. The best moment of all. Wrap a lifetime of Christmases and birthdays into one package, throw in seventh grade, when he made straight A's all year long, and even the day he got his driver's license, and you wouldn't come close to the jubilation of this moment. His war whoop rattled the trees, and he found tears tracking down his face—hot trails on cold-numbed flesh.

Truly, they were here.

But did they know? Could they know? The trees were too thick! He needed to make it easier for them somehow. He needed to send a signal so they'd know how close he was.

So, how close was he?

He had no idea, and with only one flare in the gun, he couldn't afford to make a mistake. The sound came from everywhere. Well, everywhere but directly overhead.

Scott closed his eyes and executed a painfully slow pirouette, hoping to pinpoint the direction where the sound of engines was strongest. After two rotations, he wrote off the half of the world that lay beyond the wreckage, and concentrated instead on the half that lay beyond the new shelter. According to the compass on the zipper fob on his coat, that put it on the western half of the globe. But where? Before he started chasing after a noise, he'd better know where the hell he was going. He shuddered to remember how disoriented he'd become the night before. Never again.

He could do this. If he paid careful attention to the compass as he walked, and used the knife from the survival kit to blaze a trail, he should be able to go wherever the sound took him, and still be able to find his way back. Hell, he'd done it a thousand times on Scout trips. So what if the penalty for a mistake was a little higher? Okay, a lot higher.

He even had a map to follow: that ratty, overfolded USGS map he'd found in the cockpit. He hadn't really looked at it yet, so for all Scott knew, it was a map of Poughkeepsie, but maybe not. If he took it along, maybe he'd see some landmark that would tell him exactly where he was. Who knows? Maybe he'd break into a clearing and discover that they were right at the foot of Mount Rushmore. Okay, that would put them way off course, but still. Certainly, it couldn't hurt to take it along.

It all came back to him quickly, once he started walking. Use your compass to sight in on an object, then lock onto the object with your eyes and walk to it. When you get there, use the knife to mark it with a blaze for the return trip and take another sighting. The process was tedious as hell, but this was no time for shortcuts.

He gave himself an hour—forty minutes out and twenty minutes back; the return trip shorter because he didn't have to stop to mark blazes. Progress was slow. What looked smooth as white icing in fact hid countless rocks and dead falls. Thank God his ankle was feeling better—not perfect by a long shot, but a heck of a lot better. According to the rules for orienteering, success depended on never letting your eyes wander from the selected target, but he had to look down every now and then, just to see where he was putting his feet. If, when he looked up again, he couldn't decide whether his original target had been the tree on the right or the left, he'd have to shoot another azimuth.

He quickly learned to choose landmarks with character—something to distinguish them from all other features. A dangling branch, maybe, or an odd growth pattern. For the blaze itself, he preferred to strip a section of bark, leaving a white stripe against the dark wood of the trunk, but he was flexible. For one blaze, he'd actually tied a knot in the top of a four-foot hemlock sapling. It took more time than he could afford, but it was kind of fun.

An hour into it, he realized that his forty-minute goal had been foolhardy. His arms ached from all the cutting and hacking, and as sweat dripped down the crease between his nose and his cheek, he had to chuckle at the irony. Cold as witches' titties, and here he was breaking a sweat by walking.

The ticking clock was a problem. Not only was darkness moving closer, but he worried how long the planes would continue to buzz the air before they just gave up and went home. They'd come this far; the rest was up to him, and he still didn't know where he was going.

But the noise was closer. Maybe it was just the thinning trees, but honest to God, he swore that the sound of the engines had grown louder by half. He could almost *feel* the sound in his chest.

Breaking through a wall of spruces, the gentle slope he'd been climbing for so long grew sharply steeper. But of course. What better time to encounter a huge hill than when your legs are screaming for you to sit down? The growl of the engines drew him closer still.

Leaning into the slope, his boots started to slip. Steeper still, and now he used his hands. Soon, the terrain was more vertical than horizontal. Every muscle screamed for him to stop, but he wouldn't listen. He couldn't. After this much effort, there had to be a reward, even if it was just a level patch of ground where he could rest for a few minutes.

Finally, the crest. Blood pounded in his ears as he scaled the last twenty feet.

But the crest wasn't a crest at all; merely a high spot before a gentle downward slope through thick trees, beyond which Scott could just barely see a cliff that looked like the edge of the world. He ran toward it, and slid to a halt, inches from the edge of a vertical rock face that dropped hundreds of feet into a fog that concealed whatever lay below. The bitter wind lashed his face as he looked out into a steel gray sky, still obesely pregnant with snow. Out here, beyond the windbreak of the forest, the air seemed twenty degrees colder.

The propeller buzz seemed farther away now, completely concealed by clouds. Then the engine grew loud again. This made no sense. Maybe it was just an acoustical trick on a cloudy day; clouds did that sometimes. How many times had he heard a jet engine right overhead, only to find that it belonged to a spec way up in the sky?

He only needed one good glimpse of the airplane; good enough that they'd be able to see a flare if he fired it. Correction: *the* flare, his only one. "One shot only, Mr. O'Toole," Scott said to himself in his best Sean Connery from *The Hunt for Red October*. Assuming the flare worked, and that the pilots were watching, and they'd know what it meant when they saw it—hell, assuming Scott knew how to fire the damn thing—then this nightmare could end. He could already feel the flannel sheets against his skin. The food in his belly. Three days of nonstop sleep.

So, where was the plane?

The sound shifted to his right, and he turned his head to follow it. The aircraft refused to show itself through the fog, choosing instead to tease him from someplace just beyond his sight.

Then he saw it. Just a flicker, really; a shutter-flash peek at a black silhouette just visible through a hole in the overcast, gone as quickly as it appeared. But it seemed so far away. It might as well have been on the other side of the world. And now it was gone completely.

Shit.

He waited another two minutes before his next snapshot of the faraway craft, and then three more for the next one after that. It was orbiting a pattern that was every bit of five miles away. Maybe even more.

Shit, shit, shit, shit, shit.

Then he got it. In a burst of clear vision, he knew exactly what had happened, and the realization took his breath away. Dropping back a few yards to get himself out of the wind, Scott dug through his coat pocket for the topographical map, which he spread out on the snow, anchoring the edges with snowballs.

"SkyTop," he whispered. "SkyTop, SkyTop. Where the hell are you?" There, he found it, nearly in the middle of the map, where someone had circled it with a yellow highlighter. Cody, he supposed. His hands trembled in his gloves as he traced a line across the map from the ski resort to Salt Lake City.

Wherever he was, he figured he had to be somewhere near that line. No! That's where the plane would think he was. In reality, he should be a couple of miles to the east of that. But where? Reading the contour lines, he saw countless peaks and valleys along the eighty-mile route, but nothing that matched the gorge that he'd just seen with his eyes. With a twenty-foot contour interval—one rust-colored line on the map for every twenty-foot change in elevation—the gorge should register as a solid brown ribbon on the map, but nothing he saw even came close.

"Look for a river," he told himself. This kind of canyon could only be carved by a river.

But there *was* no river. What was he doing wrong? It shouldn't be this difficult. You had green for land, blue for water, and a smattering of other colors for everything else. Where the hell was the river?

Then, he saw it. "Oh, shit," he breathed. "Oh, no, no, no, it can't be . . ."

He snatched the map up into his fist and crawled back, until his head and shoulders cleared the ridge and he could see down into the gorge again. He found the spot on the map where the blue line of the river was flanked by his heavy contour line, and then traced that to the small section of the ribbon that ran north and south, just as this gorge did.

Scott tilted his head up and squinted through the haze. According to the map, the opposite side of the gorge should be flanked by two big peaks, the one on the right significantly taller than the one on the left. It seemed like five minutes passed before the wind cleared away enough of the fog for him to see, but when it did, and he saw that he was right, an icy fist twisted a handful of guts.

He ducked quickly back down to look at the map one more time, and then again to verify his findings with his eyes.

"Oh, my God, we're thirty miles off course." Thirty *miles!* Jesus.

Think, Scott, think. There had to be a way. The day never dawned when there wasn't hope. He could do this. He *had* to do this.

Otherwise, he was sure to die.

11

SCOTT STAYED THERE on the slope longer than he should have, triple-checking his calculations, praying that he'd screwed them up. But dammit, he never screwed up in math. How could they have wandered so far?

He tried telling himself that none of that mattered now, but the sentiment seemed hollow. Seeing that airplane so far away served to emphasize the hopelessness. And as far away as it was, its pilots probably thought they were buzzing the outermost reaches of their search area. So much for ending it all with a flare.

Scott sat there in the snow long beyond the time when his butt had grown numb from the cold. With the map put away, he turned the flare gun over in his hands. He'd been stupid to think it would be so simple.

Maybe he should shoot anyway. Shoot now and take a chance. What did he have to lose? For all he knew, this was the closest he'd ever be to rescue. What the hell? He had no food, no reasonable prospects to find any, certainly not in this weather. If he didn't take his shot now, how did he know he'd even be alive to try again tomorrow?

He had to try. Now.

But where was the plane? Where was the constant hum of its engines? Where the hell did they go?

"Scott, you're an idiot," he moaned. He'd hesitated and now he'd lost. Closing his eyes, he inhaled deeply. The freezing air hurt his sinuses.

The wave of despair blindsided him. He'd never felt so insignificant. So what if he died? Who would even know? Who would care? Oh, sure, his dad would mourn him, and his closest friends, but after a few days, what difference would it make? What difference did Scott make?

These thoughts terrified him. When the time came, he wanted his death to be a momentous event—the stuff of headlines all around the world. *Rock Star Scott O'Toole Dies in Plane Crash.* Rock stars always died in plane crashes. Well, at least he got that part right.

A crippling sadness overtook him without warning, taking his breath along with it—a great puff of white vapor lost in a white world. Who did he think he was kidding? How did he ever allow himself to believe that he could make it through this thing? Christ, he didn't even belong on the trip that stranded him here in the first place.

He never should have accepted her invitation, her gigantic *up yours* to his father. Skiing was a Team Bachelor thing; Mom had nothing to do with it. Looking back on it, Scott wondered how he could have been such a shit to a man who always treated him like a prince. If this was God's way of paying him back for hurting his dad, then the Big Guy won big time. Score it 21-zip at the half with things looking bad for the O'Toole team.

Recognizing the dark thoughts for what they were—the leading edge of panic—Scott swiped the crystallized tears from his eyes and struggled back to his feet. It was time to go back. He'd already wasted too much daylight. Night was coming and he dreaded it more profoundly than death itself. The night would bring endless hours of frigid darkness where his mind would occupy itself with terrifying thoughts of God only knew what, too numb to stay awake, but too frightened to go to sleep.

The blazes, it turned out, were a wasted effort. His outbound journey had cut a deep trench through the snow. A blind man could have found the way back. He rationalized that the way his luck was running, if he hadn't carved the blazes, then sure as hell, there'd have been some huge tornado of wind to obliterate his tracks.

Nothing had changed at the crash site. As the light began to fade, all that remained for today was to build a fire. For that, he turned to the wreckage itself. If he couldn't start a fire with gasoline, then shame on him. He could drain fuel from the tanks into a container of some sort and then light it with a fusee at just the right moment, and the column of greasy black smoke would be visible for miles.

But the timing would be important. With darkness approaching, it would be stupid to light it tonight. And having seen and smelled gasoline fires before, he knew that the smoke that made it such a great signaling device would make it impractical for any other use— like, say, keeping warm. No, he'd have to wait till he heard the approach of the engines and light it then. In a perfect world, the search planes would be attracted to the smoke, and then when they were directly overhead, he could fire his flare. Call it a plan.

His dad used to tell him that God never closes a door without opening a window. Yeah, well, the windows were a hell of a lot smaller than the doors.

Still, at the end of the millionth mood change of the day, Scott once again felt that he possessed some measure of control over his future. But he had to move quickly. Dusk approached, and he wanted to be ready the instant he heard the first sound of engines in the morning.

With just a little luck, come noon tomorrow, he'd be out of here, tucked under an electric blanket with the thermostat set to nuclear. After that, his face would be all over *Good Morning America* and *People* magazine. Maybe they'd even give him a chance to play one of his songs on the air. Would that be cool, or what? The beginning of his real career. Maybe God's window was bigger than he'd thought. All he had to do was make it through one more night.

Noon tomorrow. Nineteen hours, half of them in the freezing night—the hours when sanity and survival were their most fragile.

And the sun was falling fast. He had maybe an hour to get his signal fires set up, before he needed to be inside the shelter.

Only an hour.

• • •

BY THE TIME BRANDON RETURNED to Eagle Feather around five, patches of blue had begun to invade the matte gray sky.

Road crews had been busy. Plows had created great mountains of filthy snow on both sides of Main Street, all but obliterating the view of or from any of the storefronts. All the way down the mountain, he'd tried to get through to the chief's office on his cell phone, but with all the switchbacks, his phone couldn't hold a signal.

The slick street made him walk like an old man as he approached the elevated sidewalk, but once under the cover of the overhang, things got easier. He reached for the glass door, then deferred to a young man on his way out, clearly a local, just from the way he was dressed. "Thank you," the man said as he sidestepped quickly to free the door up for Brandon.

Brandon nodded and smiled.

"Are you Mr. O'Toole?" the stranger asked. "Scott O'Toole's father?"

Curiosity formed an uneasy mix with dread in Brandon's gut. "I am."

The man stripped the glove off his right hand and reached out. "Tommy Paul," he said. "I worked with Cody Jamieson up at SkyTop. Him and Scott hung around a lot together this past week and I got to know him. I'm really sorry to hear about all this."

Brandon shook Tommy's hand gratefully. "Thank you very much."

"He really was a good kid. Both of them were. I'll miss them."

"They're still alive," Brandon said. He tried to keep his tone easy, confident.

"Oh, yeah. Right. Well, they've certainly still got a chance, don't they?"

"A good chance. So, when did you last see Scott?"

Something changed in Tommy's demeanor—nothing huge, but Brandon suddenly had the feeling that the conversation was stretching longer than the stranger had expected. "Um, let's see. Night before last, maybe? The night before the crash."

"Tell me about it."

A switch flipped somewhere, and right away, Tommy looked uneasy as hell. "It was just, you know. Some of us were hanging around the patrol shack. Nothing big." He made a show of checking his watch. "Look, I really should be running . . ."

Brandon stepped closer and purposely softened his stance, his expression. "Tommy, relax, okay? I'm not looking for trouble—not for you or anybody else. I know that Scott likes to down a few beers when he gets a chance, and I know that he's always on the prowl for a good time. I don't approve, exactly, but I'm a realist. What we say stays between us, I promise. I'm just grateful to have some insight into his trip here."

Tommy relaxed and in time he smiled. "Then you know what we did. No drugs, I promise you that, but we did down a few brews." He started to laugh. "Cody was one crazy dude, and Scott just seemed to make him crazier. When they got jammin' on the guitars, man, it was something."

Brandon beamed.

"Knew his way around the slopes, too. Scott, I mean."

"I'm on the patrol back home," Brandon explained. "Nothing like the stuff you do up here, I'm sure, but Scott spent just about every cold weekend of his life on the slopes somewhere."

Tommy nodded. "Yeah, he mentioned something about that. Talked about you a lot, in fact. We have a tradition here called midnight snowmobiles. It's a race up Widow Maker. After he damn near ran me off the trail, he told me that you taught him that every race has only one winner. Despite the fact he nearly killed me, I had to admire the spirit."

"So he won?"

Tommy scoffed, "Hell no, he didn't win, but he didn't get hurt, either, when I rammed him into the hay bales." Brandon must have looked shocked, because Tommy quickly added, "It was all in good fun. But like he said, there's only one winner."

Brandon understood perfectly, and again, his emotions felt frazzled. He needed to break this off before he lost it. He forced a smile and shook Tommy's hand again. "Thank you very much for sharing that," he said. "It means a lot to me."

The sadness made Tommy uncomfortable. "My pleasure. Listen, if you're still in town tomorrow, we're having a little prayer service in the chapel for Cody. And Scott, too. If you want to stop by . . ."

Brandon considered that. "Let's see how the day plays itself out, okay?"

Tommy nodded. "Sure, it's your call. I just wanted you to know. Five-thirty tomorrow afternoon, after the slopes close." He tossed off a wave and was on his way.

Brandon stepped inside the station and pressed the buzzer. Jesse Tingle let him in. "Welcome back, sir. No news yet, I'm afraid."

"The place looks busy."

"Yes, sir. Now that the weather's calmed down a bit, we're beginning to get the flood of calls. Burst pipes, medical assistance, auto damage, that sort of thing. The nonemergency stuff that I guess people thought could wait for a while. All that and the president of the United States. I voted for him and now I can't wait for him to leave." He stopped, suddenly aware of how little Brandon cared about any of this. "I'm sure the chief can give you better details on your son than I can."

"Is he in?"

"Not just now. He had to run out for a few minutes, but I expect him right back. Just make yourself at home."

"Think the boss would mind if I helped myself to his coffee pot?"

Jesse winced. "I suppose it's okay if you're current on all your vaccinations."

Brandon smiled and headed for Whitestone's office. The squad room had taken on the feel of a beehive. Staffing appeared to have doubled from the morning's skeleton crew, and all of them seemed sharply focused on whatever they were doing.

In the chief's office now, he navigated his way to Mr. Coffee, found himself a clean-looking cup and helped himself to the dregs in the pot. It looked more like the tail end of an oil change than coffee, and loading it with creamer and sugar only made it taste like creamier, sweeter waste oil. He chugged the whole thing and stepped back into the squad room. All around him, deputies wandered in and out, phones rang without pause, and through it all, the air vibrated with the staccato scratching sounds of radio transmissions, most of which, to Brandon's ear, were just so much garbled static.

With all battle stations manned, Brandon found himself with nowhere to sit, until one of the friendlier faces from the morning—Charlotte Eberly, he remembered—offered him a chair in front of her desk.

"I took the last of the chief's coffee," he said. "I'll make more if you point me in the right direction."

Charlotte gave a disapproving wave. "I don't have anything to do with his sinful ways. I do my best not to pay attention."

Okaay. "Might I ask where the chief went?" Brandon asked, anxious to change the subject.

Officer Eberly had returned to whatever document she had up on her computer screen and spoke without looking. "He's on a tour of the square with the mayor."

Brandon scowled. "A tour?"

Charlotte looked up. "The Founder's Day speech," she said, but it clearly meant nothing to Brandon. "You know that the president grew up in this county, right? Well, he's the keynote at the hundredth anniversary of Founder's Day. I understand there'll be a big announce— Oh, here he is!"

Brandon turned to see Barry Whitestone striding down the center aisle between desks and he rose to intercept. "Nice tour?"

Whitestone didn't know how to interpret the question. "Let's talk in my office."

Twenty seconds later, they were in their same spots as this morning. Brandon barely waited for Whitestone's butt to hit the chair. "A *tour*, Chief? My son is out there somewhere, and the best use of your time is touring a photo op?"

Whitestone was on the feather edge of losing his temper. "Tell you what, Mr. O'Toole, why don't I find a place out back where you can rant, and then when you're done, you can come back here and we'll talk all this through."

Anger boiled in Brandon's gut. In about ten seconds, this was going to get ugly.

Whitestone leaned forward, his arms folded on the desk. "There's something you need to understand, Brandon. From the very beginning, I've promised you blunt honesty, and here's a big dose of it. Are you ready?"

Brandon glared for a moment, then nodded.

"Finding those two boys is our very top priority, but not our *only* priority. On a different day, with different weather, the air would be black with civilian and military aircraft scouring that mountain. Once they found some indication of where they were, there'd be nobody in this building but the roaches as we all headed out to save them. But this is *this* day, not a different one, and on *this* day, it's been snowing like a son of a bitch. Runways have to be plowed, and flight crews have to make it in from home. It's just not a simple task. We've got thousands of citizens in this town, tens of thousands of tourists and the leader of the free world who loves to keep a high profile."

"So, I'm supposed to just wait?"

Someone rapped lightly on the door before opening it. It was Jesse Tingle, and Whitestone held him off with a raised forefinger. "No, you're supposed to worry like hell. You're a father, it's your job. It just happens that life would be a lot easier for all of us if you would take a shot at trusting me. Yes, Jesse?"

"I'm sorry to disturb you, but there's a phone call for Mr. O'Toole. A Nadine Yodell?"

Brandon inhaled, as if to make a speech, but found himself short of words. To Jesse, he said, "Okay. Yeah, I'll take it."

Whitestone rose with Brandon, but stayed behind his desk as the deputy led his guest to a tiny cubicle that Brandon had never even noticed.

"She's on line four," Tingle said. "The one that's blinking."

Nadine was Brandon's administrative assistant back at Federal Research. She was his gatekeeper, his watchdog and one of his closest confidants. As Brandon settled into the seat and punched the extension, Jesse stayed around just long enough to make sure that he got it right.

The voice on the other end was the first thing that felt normal all day. "Hi, Mr. O'Toole, it's me. Have they found him yet?"

Hearing the question asked so directly, by such a familiar voice, brought a fresh rush of emotion. He quickly cleared his throat. "Uh, no, not yet. They're about to go out there looking for him, though. I've got a really good feeling about it."

"I'm so sorry. We all are. Everybody I've talked to today wants me to make sure I tell you that you're in their prayers."

Brandon nodded and turned away from the others in the squad room. "That's sweet of all of you. Please thank them all for me."

"It's all over the news here today, too. At Scott's high school—Robinson, right?"

"Right."

"Well, at Robinson, they apparently had a big assembly, where every student tied a yellow ribbon for him. I saw a picture of it on television. There's four thousand students there, and every surface has a yellow ribbon somewhere. It made me cry just to look at it."

Brandon clamped his jaw and shut his eyes tightly. He saw the picture in his head: thousands of students, most of them weeping with the depth of emotion that only adolescents could muster, ceremoniously tying their ribbons, and holding each other while they cried for his son.

"Anyway, it was a beautiful thing to see," Nadine continued. She seemed a little unnerved by his silence.

"I'm sure it was," Brandon whispered. He cleared his throat again, and then one more time before he felt in control. "Listen, how's the place running without me?"

"You shouldn't worry about us," she said. "Worry about you."

Mother Nadine. "Easier said than done. I feel like everybody in the world has something to do but me. I'm going nuts here. Humor me and make me feel important again."

Nadine laughed too hard. Humor in the face of disaster is tough to pull off. In five minutes, she ran down the hit list of important issues. He listened, made a few comments, and then they were done.

He hung up just in time to see the chief's door open. Whitestone beckoned with a finger.

Brandon tried to read Whitestone's expression, only to decide that the chief would have made one hell of a poker player.

Chief Whitestone stepped aside to usher Brandon into the inner sanctum. "Help yourself to a seat," he said.

"What's up?"

Whitestone gestured again to the wooden chairs, while he walked behind his desk to take a seat in his own. "Please."

Brandon sat.

"Take a look here," the chief said, spilling a topographical map across his desk. "We've had a plane in the air for about three hours today, scouring the length of this route between SkyTop and Salt Lake City." He traced an invisible line on the map with his forefinger. "Now, I'll grant you that with the time available, we were only able to do the most basic, and frankly unscientific kind of search, but I'm sorry to say that it turned up nothing."

Brandon nodded, trying his best to show no emotion. "You say you searched the line. What about the area around the line, to either side?"

Whitestone nodded, appreciating the question. "Here's how we did things: The pilots traveled this line countless times today, starting in a tight oval, and then expanding it on each pass. They were looking for any signs of a crash—wreckage, footprints, fires, signals, anything."

"Can they actually see anything from up there?"

Whitestone shrugged. "Some places yes, many places no. That's the problem we're facing here."

"So you're telling me they saw nothing at all."

Whitestone paused, looking as if he wanted to find a better way to phrase it. "Yes, I suppose that's what I'm telling you. If you take this straight line on the map, the search today covered twenty-five miles to either side of it."

A fist in Brandon's chest was using his heart as a punching bag. "But you're not finished, though, right? The search will continue through the night?"

Whitestone looked away. "No, it won't. There's more weather coming. A squall line's moving in from the west that'll be getting here right around dark, and will play havoc for the better part of the night. The good news is, tomorrow should be pretty clear, and we've received commitments from the Air Force for some help."

"Meanwhile, those kids spend a second night in the mountains."

Whitestone acknowledged the point with an imperceptible nod.

Brandon continued, "And tomorrow, when the search resumes—*if* the search resumes, because God knows we can't get people to drive through the snow—all the signs you're looking for will be just that much more buried. Did you know that Cody Jamieson's friends are already planning his memorial service?" Brandon asked.

"I heard it was a prayer service."

"Same thing. It means that the participants have lost faith in everything but divine intervention. They're writing the kids off, Chief. And so are you."

Whitestone made no response.

"It's too early to give up," Brandon pressed. "They've still got time. I know my way around cold weather survival, and I'm telling you, they've still got time."

Whitestone conceded the point. "Yes, they do. There are a lot of variables, of course. It got down to fifteen below last night, and we're expecting more of the same tonight."

"But the snow and its cloud cover will moderate the temperature," Brandon countered.

The chief nodded again. "It's still damned cold. We had a high of twenty-three down here today. Up on the mountain, who knows? But yes, assuming they dressed for the weather, and given their training, I suppose there's still time."

"As long as a week, I'd say," Brandon pressed.

For the first time, Whitestone showed real skepticism. "Not hardly. I'm sorry, but I just don't think that's possible."

"How long, then?"

Whitestone sighed. "Assuming they've made it this long, that means they've already sheltered up somewhere, so I guess it's not out of the question that they can make it through tonight as well. But we'd better find them tomorrow."

"Do you believe they're still alive?"

The chief squirmed in his chair. "Come on, Mr. O'Toole, I don't have a crystal ball. I have no way of knowing—"

"Please, Chief. It's important to me to know. Do you believe in your heart that my son is still alive?"

For a long moment, the two men just stared at each other, their gazes locked. Twice, Whitestone opened his mouth to say something, and both times he aborted the effort without making a sound. Finally, he closed his eyes. "No, sir, I don't."

12

SOMEWHERE AMONG THE THOUSANDS of tiny parts scattered in the snow, you'd think there'd be a decent-size container, but the best Scott had been able to come up with was a thermos cup. Hey, any port in a storm, right?

Now he just needed to find the gas cap. Okay, so that wasn't exactly difficult. The stenciled label, Fuel, helped a lot, as did the arrow pointing to a rectangular panel that looked remarkably like the one on his dad's car, only this one was on the wing root on the left-hand side. With the wreckage twisted the way it was, the panel faced down, such that once Scott loosened the cap, gravity should take care of the rest, posing the far greater worry that maybe he wouldn't be able to stop the flow once he'd started it. The last thing he needed was a flood of gasoline in his front yard.

So, he decided to take it slow. Working bare-handed to keep spilled fuel from soaking his gloves, he straddled the wing as if it were a horse, poised the cup under the spout and reached for the fuel cap. The fuel started to flow after a half-turn, splashing out from behind the cap like water from a shower head. The combined effect of cold and wet on his skin was like folding his hand into a nail sandwich.

It didn't smell like gasoline, though. More like kerosene, or maybe diesel fuel. When the cup was full, he retightened the cap and carefully slid to the ground. He spilled half of the fuel in the process, but truly didn't care as he moved quickly to shove his hands back into his gloves.

He decided on a spot about twenty yards from the shelter as the location for the signal fire. He knew he should probably burn it all night long, but with such a small container, it would burn out too quickly, and no way was he going to spend the entire night shuttling himself in and out of the cold to refill it. Besides, the plastic thermos cup would probably melt as it burned anyway. Plus, it had started to snow again, so the planes would be grounded. With the cup positioned where he wanted it, he shoved the fusees butt-first into the snow next to it. When he heard engines again, he'd be good to go.

And none too soon. The transition from day to dusk seemed to pass in mere moments, pulling the temperature down another ten degrees. Or, maybe that coldness he felt along his spine was merely the realization that another endless night lay ahead.

The noise from the woods startled him.

"Hello?"

It stopped at the sound of his voice, a rustling sound off to his right. Probably just the wind. *Bullshit. The wind's been blowing all day.*

He wanted to think that it was the approach of rescuers, but knew better. Rescuers have no desire to be stealthy. "Hello?" His tongue felt as if he'd licked a chalkboard.

There it was again, only this time from his left, directly opposite where it was before.

"Who's there?" This time he yelled, his voice cracking in the wind.

The third sound came from behind him, and he whirled to face unyielding forest. Scott's heart hammered a hard-rock cadence in his throat as he listened intently, wishing he hadn't left the flashlights in the shelter. As he tried to see through the cloud of blowing snow, the woods growled at him, a basso tone so deep that he more felt it than heard it.

Oh, shit! Oh shit, oh shit, oh shit . . .

More growls from his left and his right.

"Only two species of animals hunt in packs," he remembered Sven telling them. *"You've got your big cats, and you've got—"*

The wolves showed themselves one at a time, cautiously approaching from three sides, filthy and gray. Scott stopped breathing as he watched them lower their heads and inch forward one tentative step at a time. Thirty, maybe forty feet separated him from the closest animal; a distance they could close in three seconds.

"Never run," he remembered. But that's precisely what his body was screaming at him to do—run as fast and as hard as his legs would carry him. They could tear him apart standing there or tear him apart running away. Did it really make that much difference?

The animals moved with choreographed grace, each step in unison, their faces obscured by the clouds of vapor that rose from their panting jaws. He found himself somehow entranced by their eyes. What had Sven told them? Had he ever said anything about wolves? Where the hell was his photographic memory when he needed it, goddammit? He needed to . . .

What? What the *hell* was he supposed to do?

He had to scare them off. That was his only chance. He was bigger than them, after all, and smarter. Plus, they were probably scared, too. What were the chances that they had ever seen a human being before? That had to give him some kind of advantage, didn't it?

He waved his arms in a giant shooing motion. "Ha! Get out of here! Go on, git!"

The wolves jumped at the sudden motion, and looked for a moment as if they might run. Scott could almost read the curiosity in the faces of the closest two as they looked to the center wolf for a cue. That'd be the alpha dog, he reckoned, the wolf in charge, and he didn't seem startled at all.

Scott shouted again, but this time to less effect. If anything, it seemed to piss them off. Alpha lowered his head and peeled his lip back to reveal a set of teeth that better belonged on a shark. The growl deepened in pitch. He advanced. The others followed, closing in from all sides but one.

This was it. No negotiating, no bluffing, these beasts were going to attack, and Scott was flat out of options. The knife. Could he possibly be fast enough with the blade? Even if he killed one of them, the others would tear him to pieces in seconds.

Just let it be fast. Don't let it hurt too much.

The flare gun! Jesus, he still had it in his pocket! At this range, maybe it would fire with enough velocity to hurt the bastards. Maybe even kill. And he'd still have the knife left to take on a second one. As for the third, well . . .

"Oh, man, I'm so screwed . . ."

Scott's eyes locked with Alpha's as he slowly pulled the glove off his right hand and stuffed it down the front of his coat before searching his pocket for the flare gun. He fought the urge to draw down the way they did in the old cowboy flicks. Right now, his killers seemed hesitant, as if they were waiting for him to seal his own fate with the first move. The flare gun felt like a toy in his hand, all plastic, but for the metal hammer and trigger. As the stubby barrel cleared his pocket, he thumbed back the hammer.

Only Alpha moved now; the others paused and watched, as if waiting their turn to play with their new chew toy. Scott wondered if they somehow knew how terrified he was.

"Please stay away," Scott begged. He realized for the first time that he was crying. He didn't want to die. Not here, not this way. "Please just leave me alone. We don't have to do this."

Alpha cocked his head as Scott spoke, as if he could understand every word. What he heard seemed to please him. The wolf moved closer still.

And then he charged. The growl transformed to a horrid, guttural roar as he sprinted across the snow, closing with more speed than Scott ever could have imagined. The boy never had time to aim a shot, or even pull the trigger, but somehow, the gun bucked in his hand, and the air filled with the stench of burning magnesium.

The projectile caught Alpha squarely in the face, dropping the beast into the snow, amid a spray of blood, as the flare itself ricocheted off into the trees, there to sputter and dance as it burned itself out.

Startled, the other wolves turned and ran for the woods, stopping abruptly just at the edge of Scott's line of sight. As if on cue, they both turned to face him again. The growling grew more fierce, but their postures looked somehow less frightening.

"I said get out of here!" Scott yelled. "Leave me alone!"

The wolves jumped again, and even took a couple of steps back, but unless Scott could put on another show of strength, he knew they'd charge.

If only he had another flare. He pointed the empty gun as if it were loaded—as if they could tell the difference—but how long could it take before they tested his bluff? Christ, one lousy flare. Who ever heard . . .

Fusees. There they were, both of them, sitting at his feet in the snow. They could work. Still keeping the gun trained on the animals, shifting his aim from one to the other, he stooped to his haunches and slipped his hand around one of the road flares.

God, the unbearable slowness of it all. His mind screamed at him to hurry as his heart bruised itself against his breastbone.

Without their leader, the other two wolves seemed confused, but Scott knew the moment would pass. There was no masking this kind of terror, and clearly they sniffed it in the air. They started to close again.

As he went to work on the fusee, he let the empty gun fall to the snow.

The teenager's hand refused to cooperate in the cold. It felt swollen and useless on the end of his arm, and as he shifted his eyes in the rapidly dimming light to see what he was doing, he noticed that his skin was nearly as red as the flare's scarlet wrapper. The translucent cap over the striking end of the fusee came off easily in the cold, but not so the smaller, flatter cap that covered the striker. For that, Scott had to use his teeth, and the effort made his gums bleed.

Thirty feet now, and closing. One way or another, in a few seconds, this would be all over. Holding the striker in his bare fist, he pressed it against the striking end of the flare and scraped the two together, just like striking a big match. He got a spark, but no ignition.

The wolves recognized the movement as a threat and they doubled their pace. Twenty feet separated them, no more.

Scott struck again, and this time, the beasts made their move. They charged . . .

. . . And the flare flashed to life, a hissing jet of red flame that nearly disappeared in its thick cloud of smoke.

Scott held the fusee like a sword, at arm's length in his bare hand. "Ha!" he yelled. "Get outta here!" He whipped it back and forth. "Get outta here or I'll stick it in your damn eye!"

The flash of noise and light startled the beasts into aborting their charge, but this time they didn't retreat. Instead, they formed a tighter circle around him, neither more than fifteen feet away. They bared their teeth and slobbered in the snow as they feinted lunges and snapped at the air.

Scott moved like a retreating fencer, pointing his fusee first at one animal and then the other as he worked his way back toward the shelter. Twenty yards to go. Fifteen.

"Get out of here! Leave me alone, goddammit! Just leave me alone!"

But they kept up with him, step for step, never closing the distance, but never allowing it to open and inch. They were patient, these animals, and they knew their jobs. Sooner or later, Scott would make a mistake—maybe he'd trip, or he'd drop his flare—and when he did, they'd be on him in an instant.

Ten yards to the shelter, and then what? Then he'd barricade himself inside and wait for the beasts to test its strength. Sven had never mentioned anything about wolf-proofing.

Five yards to go. Scott shifted the flare from his bare hand to his glove, while he fished through his pants pocket for the survival knife. He unsnapped the safety strap with his teeth and let the scabbard drop to the snow.

Scott's entire world had transformed to a shimmering red sphere, with him in the middle, and death just barely visible as shadows at the periphery. With the shelter only inches away, he might just have a chance, but he'd be most vulnerable when he dropped to his knees to climb in, and from there it would be a test of strength and will. Would the aluminum door hold? Would they claw and chew right through the walls?

Or worst of all, would they pounce when he was still only halfway in and tear his throat out?

The animals sensed that something was about to change, and they increased the rhythm and ferocity of their feints as Scott jabbed at them with the burning fusee. They weren't buying it anymore, barely flinching. They'd assessed him, and they knew a bluff when they saw it.

Scott dropped to his knees in front of the door tunnel, and the wolf on the right made his move. This lunge was for real, all teeth and momentum and Scott met him with the flare. He felt the beast's matted fur, and then he smelled it burning at he jammed the flare into its face. Maybe its eye, maybe its mouth, he couldn't tell for sure, but the growl instantly became a yelp—a shriek, really—as it retreated into the night.

He had the seconds he needed to scramble backward, feet-first, into the shelter and pull the heavy aluminum back over the opening. Using the armrest as a handle, he pulled for all he was worth to set it in place, but the walls and floor had turned to slick ice, making it difficult to get leverage for his feet. Acrid smoke from the flare gouged at his eyes and his throat as he jammed his boot into a tiny crevice for leverage. The door was as locked as it was going to get. He stubbed out the fusee by jamming it like an enormous cigarette into the floor.

Darkness.

Silence.

Above the tympani beat of his racing heart, Scott could hear only the sound of his breath as it heaved in and out in huge gulps, wheezing in his throat, and creating great white clouds of condensation that somehow were visible even in the dark. Outside, for the longest time, he heard nothing at all, not even the whining yelp of the animal whose face he'd burned.

He could smell his own fear.

Minutes passed in the silent darkness. They were out there, waiting. Plotting. Damn smart animals, those wolves. The way they worked together, and the intensity of their eyes told Scott that they knew exactly what they were doing; that he didn't have a chance against them.

Suppose this was exactly what they wanted him to do?

The thought came out of nowhere. Suppose they were an even more clever team than he'd thought? How perfect would it be to drive him into the shelter, only to encounter a fourth wolf already inside, waiting for him?

Jesus, Scott, you're losing it. Yeah, okay, but just suppose.

I'd have seen it. No doubt about it. But *suppose.* The thought was ridiculous. First of all, they weren't that smart, and secondly, the shelter wasn't that big. There simply wasn't a place to hide.

But suppose . . .

The darkness in here bore a thick, physical presence. It had weight. He couldn't see a thing. And what you can't see can easily turn you into a corpse.

He couldn't take it anymore. Keeping one hand—his bare hand—on the door, he laid the survival knife at his knee and fumbled through the darkness with his glove, feeling for the flashlight that he knew had to be there.

The pale yellow light proved what he already knew. Still, what a relief.

They hit the door panel with the force of a linebacker, and the air filled with horrendous guttural growls as they pushed against the door and clawed at the snowy doorjamb. Scott's foot nearly slipped against the impact, but not quite. Hot breath puffed against his ear.

"No!" he shrieked. "Goddammit, no!" But his high-pitched voice only seemed to double their resolve. Again and again, they threw themselves at the door, and with each impact, Scott felt things slipping. They tore at the doorjamb as if it were a bone.

They'd finally outsmarted him. When they finally forced their way through—and they would, without a doubt—he had no retreat. He was dead, his guts ripped from his body.

"Oh, please," Scott whimpered. "Oh, please, oh, please, oh, please . . ."

And there it was. One of them broke through the snow at the edge of the door, next to Scott's left elbow. Just a paw at first, and then a snout, with jaws chewing savagely at the air.

Scott screamed. It was a little girl sound, and for a flash he wondered where it was coming from. Then he didn't care. Without thinking, Scott snatched the knife from the floor and used it like a hatchet to hack at the snout. The animal screamed as the knife bit deeply into its flesh, and when it retreated, it nearly wrenched the weapon from Scott's hand.

An instant later, it was back, snorting a crimson aerosol as it further mauled the air. Scott slashed again, a more powerful blow this time, amputating a chunk of anatomy from the bloody mess of fur and teeth. It stuck to the blade and flew across the shelter as he raised the blade for another plunge.

Then the snout was gone.

But Scott wasn't about to let himself be fooled again. *Surprise me once, shame on you . . .*

He didn't move. He sat there frozen in place, his knife hand poised for the next assault.

Again, the silence overwhelmed him. First such a cacophony, and then nothing. His heart pumped raw terror through his veins, leaving him light-headed. It roared like breaking waves in his ears.

"Come on, you assholes," he whispered. *Please make them go away.*

He heard them again. Somewhere out there beyond the walls, the wolves hissed and growled, their noises reaching that same frenzied level, but they didn't sound so close anymore.

What did that mean?

Who cared? And they were moving now. If he listened hard enough, he could hear the sounds of tearing flesh.

Then he got it: Alpha dog, once the top of the heap and now just a snack for his friends. The circle of life. One creature serving all others.

And then he shuddered when he remembered Cody Jamieson. Oh, Jesus. *I should have buried him.*

But he was frozen, right? A TV dinner for wolves. Maybe they wouldn't find him.

They did, of course, but not until well after midnight.

DAY THREE

13

THE CODE WAS DESIGNED back when Isaac DeHaven was more paranoid than he'd been in recent years. Unnecessarily complicated, it nonetheless remained relatively secure. On the first day of every month, a person he'd never met received a $5,000 wire transfer via a Swiss bank account, which received its marching orders from a bank in the Caymans. In return, the person he'd never met, yet trusted literally with his life—Isaac thought of his contact as a man and assigned him the name Sam—ran two seemingly innocuous radio stations. Twenty-four hours a day, 365 days a year, the stations were active on the amateur bands, playing a taped loop of music on one, and random Morse code transmissions on the other. By being active all the time, any potential eavesdroppers would be hard-pressed to divine the treasure from the garbage.

Isaac suspected that Sam was an errant fed who wanted to make some money on the side, but for all he knew, he was the ghost of J. Edgar Hoover himself. Frankly, none of that mattered too much. What mattered was accurate information, and Sam was filled to the brim with it.

The clock read 2:24 as Isaac rubbed his eyes and shook his head to clear it. At this hour, he worried about his foggy brain making a foolish error.

At precisely 2:25, he heard the stutter code of ten dots in a row, and then he was ready to copy. His Morse was a little rusty, so it took him several tries to jot it all down. Fifteen minutes later, when he looked down at his pad, he saw:

6789ssmqxnusejqpntqpymczamwtmabbprywrfvsgb8vmjrfvs
rttmxiabrtyutladjjfopwpabumlkdtbhgiabibmnywqbsvp
wroincxzbartfztorkmabxzasolmnbcqlvrzxxmltabqpmzxrbtoj
q7lmhplsqdvkoiimjpobabtgmnnpf9vjgdkajmprsi1234

The message would repeat itself for another forty-five minutes or so before returning to a broadcast of truly random letters and numerals that Isaac figured Sam must have programmed into some sort of computer.

He poured himself a scotch, carried the message over to his favorite chair, and settled in for the chore of decoding. The sequence 6789 marked the beginning of the message, and *1234* the end. In between, every fifth letter was the one that counted, and the sequence *ab* marked the ends of words. To decode the message itself, he needed only to move each letter ahead five places in the alphabet. Thus, the first letter of the message that counted—the *x*—was in fact a *c*. The next four letters in the message meant nothing, and then the *j* translated to an *o*.

After decoding the first two words, Isaac knew that it was the worst of all possible news. His hands trembled a bit, in fact; not so much from fear, but out of a sense of loss. What would be, would be, he knew. But he'd been hoping that the serenity would last a little longer.

Isaac didn't bother to check his work, there was no need. At worst, he might have dropped a letter or two, but what would that matter?

He tore the decoded message from its pad and read it one more time before tossing it into the fire. No, there definitely was no mistake:

"Cover blown You in danger They coming soon."

14

BRANDON O'TOOLE spent the night in jail.

Well, it had seemed like a good idea at the time. He didn't relish the thought of sleeping in Sherry's chalet, and a dozen phone calls proved that the hotels were bursting at the cornices with stranded vacationers and presidential staffers. When Whitestone offered him a holding cell for the night, he'd taken him up on it. Eagle Feather wasn't Alcatraz, after all.

But it wasn't Mayberry, either.

Brandon didn't recognize the deputy seated at the processing desk, but he seemed to have a great deal of trouble understanding the chief's explanation of why their newest guest needn't be strip-searched, could wear his own clothes and did not have to be locked into his cell. "In fact, Lester," Whitestone had said, "he's free to walk out anytime he wants to. No shooting, okay?"

He said that last part as if it were part of a child's game; as in, "no give-backs" or "no lead-offs from second." Lester nodded, but Brandon worried why Whitestone had felt the need to say it in the first place.

Oh, the details they leave out of the brochure. Nobody mentioned to Brandon that the lights stayed on all night, or that the prisoner down the hall liked to call for air strikes in his sleep, but those were things that he could live with, given the circumstances. The toilet, on the other hand, was out of the question. Deeply stained yellow-brown, it had no seat and less privacy, and he'd progressed too far in life to do his business where everyone with an inclination to watch could do just that. Thus, Brandon tested Lester's trigger finger three times during the night as his nerve-wracked digestive system made use of the main rest room out in the office area.

If he angled himself just so in the cell, he could watch Lester at work at his tiny desk. Who'd have thought that a prison guard would be a master paper airplane architect? All night long, the deputy sat at his desk folding white copier paper into intricately designed aircraft, all of which exhibited the aerodynamic properties of a brick. Lester cursed every failure, but never lost a beat pulling the next sheet off the stack, oblivious to the world so long as he was folding and tossing.

Brandon made a valiant effort at the sleeping charade until about four, at which point he just gave up. What was the point of lying there counting roaches when he could be doing something more productive? What that something was, he didn't yet know, but just about anything would be more engaging than this.

Then he got it: The airport! If the weather lifted as predicted, he could be there when they launched the searches. And even if he could be of no more assistance than he was today, then at least he'd be underfoot one step closer to the action.

This time, as Brandon left his cell, he tossed a friendly good-bye to his jailer, but Lester didn't even look up.

The road crews had done a hell of a job. If they'd been hit with this kind of storm back in northern Virginia, the schools would have been closed for a month. Here, the roads were all but clear.

That same level of attention had not been directed to the airport parking lot, however, which resembled an expert ski slope without the slope, each mogul representing a parked vehicle. Brandon smiled at the thought of some poor sap coming home from his vacation in the Bahamas only to find that his ice scraper was buried under four feet of drifted snow.

Brandon targeted a low spot between two moguls and plowed the rental into it, breathing a sigh of relief that the space was not concealing somebody's VW Bug.

No one would ever mistake the Arapaho Regional Airport as anything but the portal to a small town. Brandon saw two buildings along the side of the parking lot, pretentiously labeled as Terminal One and Terminal Two. Combined, the two structures might have been 7,000 square feet. Inside Terminal One, he saw only three counters, each bearing that sixties-era ultramodern look. The stations paralleled a carpeted wall that identified them as ticket booths for Wasatch Airlines, Jones Car Rental and, on the far right, General Aviation. All three stations were closed, as were the metal detectors and X-ray station.

Brandon didn't know what General Aviation meant, exactly, but his instincts told him that it was the desk whose future occupant would be most able to help him out.

"Can I help you, sir?"

Brandon nearly jumped out of his skin at the sound of the voice that boomed from the shadows. He whirled to see a groggy, twenty-year-old security guard standing in front of the door to what might have been a closet, his right hand hovering over the revolver strapped to his hip. "Jesus, you scared the crap out of me!" Brandon exclaimed, bringing his hand to his chest. The guard wasn't laughing. Brandon said, "Yes, you probably can. I understand they're running a search and rescue operation out of this airport, and I was wondering where I might find the people involved with that."

"You're not supposed to be here," the guard said. "The airport is closed. Won't open again till six o'clock."

Brandon checked his watch. "That's only an hour from now."

The guard confirmed the time with a glance at his own wrist. "You can't stay here," he said.

"It must be fifteen below outside," Brandon said. "I can't stay out *there*. I'll freeze to death."

The guard—Freedman, according to his name tag—clearly saw the dilemma. "What are you doing here?"

"I told you," Brandon said. He tried his best to look like the friendliest, most reasonable man in the world. "I need to talk with the search and rescue people."

"You a reporter?" Just from the way Freedman asked the question, Brandon got the sense that an affirmative answer might very well reacquaint him with Lester the jailer.

"No, I'm nobody's reporter. My son was in the plane that crashed. I was just hoping I might be able to talk to the people who are looking for him."

Instantly, everything about Freedman's demeanor changed. His scowl softened into something that looked like pity and he stepped forward to extend his hand. "Oh, man, I'm so sorry," he said. "Of course you can stay here. It's cold as—well, it's too cold outside." He hurried to pull a chair from inside the door where he'd obviously been napping and he gestured for Brandon to sit. "Can I get you anything? Something to drink?"

Brandon held up a hand and shook his head. The very thought of Hawaiian Punch at this hour turned his stomach. "No thanks. I don't need anything but directions."

The guard disappeared behind the door again and quickly came back with a second chair for himself. "Please sit down," he said, and Brandon obliged him. "I'm Brigham, by the way," he said. "Brigham Freedman. And I'm sorry for being so unfriendly before."

Brandon waved him off. "No problem. Hey, you were just doing your job, right?" *How do you know I'm not a terrorist with a good line?* Brandon didn't say.

"Thanks for understanding."

A long moment of silence hung in the air. Brandon prompted, "The search and rescue team?"

"Oh, yeah, of course. God, where's my head? Yesterday, they had a couple of the locals up in their own planes, but today, I understand that they're rolling out the Civil Air Patrol."

Brandon nodded as if he understood what that meant. "Okay, and where would I find them?"

"Well, they're all over. They're volunteers. I was a cadet back when I was in high school. A guy named Colonel Morris is in charge, and they'll be mustering over at Terminal Two in just a little bit, I suspect. In fact, Colonel Morris is over there now. I just saw him arrive about twenty minutes ago."

Brandon stood. "He's in Terminal Two, then?"

Brigham stood as well. "Yes, sir, but you're really not supposed—" He locked eyes with Brandon and gave up. "Yeah, in
Terminal Two. Just go through those doors there and follow the fence
line."

"Thank you, Brigham. I appreciate it." They shook hands again
and Brandon headed for the door.

"Sir?"

Brandon turned.

"I hope they find him."

Brandon smiled. "Don't worry. We will."

BRANDON WAS WILLING TO BET that Terminal Two never saw
commercial traffic. As he passed through the double doors, the
building's red brick façade gave way to the baby-shit–colored concrete block that Brandon had come to associate with military facili-
ties, a decorating style emulated by many buildings at his own plant.
The green tile floors bore the the look of pure efficiency that never
would have been tolerated by paying customers. Then again, it wasn't
as if the residents of Arapaho County had a lot of options to choose
from.

The first set of double doors led to a second set, and from there,
Brandon found himself in a large room littered with a dozen mis-
matched desks and chairs and telephones. Most looked as if they
hadn't been used in years, and if it weren't for their precise arrangement in rows, he might have guessed that Terminal Two was little
more than a ground-level attic.

Sounds of movement drew his attention to the left rear corner of
the terminal, where he saw a man in a green flight suit hunched over
an ancient computer screen, involved in what looked to be a game of
Free Cell. Brandon started that way, and the click of his heels on the
lineoleum alerted the man that he was not alone anymore. Startled,
the man jerked around and fixed Brandon with the glare of someone
who was annoyed to be caught in the act of relaxing.

"You must be Colonel Morris," Brandon said, noting the silver
oak leaves embroidered on the man's epaulets.

"I must indeed," the man said, rising. Around five-ten, with black hair that had just begun to gray at the temples, Morris looked to be about forty-five. He had the physique of a swimmer and the smile of an insurance salesman. "What can I do for you?"

Brandon led with his hand, which Morris accepted. "My name is Brandon O'Toole. My son is one of the people you're looking for this morning."

Morris looked instantly uncomfortable. "Oh," he said, and as he searched for more words, nothing seemed to come to mind.

"I have an unusual request," Brandon said, getting right to the point. "I spent all day yesterday down in Eagle Feather, waiting for word in the chief's office of how you guys were doing."

Morris's expression darkened even more.

"Oh, I know not much progress was made. Weather and all of that, and that's fine. Well, it's not fine, but at least I understand. Anyway, I was wondering . . . Do you have any kids?"

The question caught Morris completelty off guard. "Excuse me?"

Brandon just let the question hang there.

"Well, yeah," Morris said with a shrug. "I've got two, one in college, one just starting high school. Why?"

"Good. So, surely you can understand my circumstances. The frustration of waiting, powerless."

Morris seemed to know where this was going, and he wasn't happy. "I'm sure it must be very difficult for you. Hell, impossible for you. But if you're about to ask if you can go along—"

"Don't say no," Brandon interrupted. "Not just yet. No is too easy an answer. I want you to think about it first. I could tell you that I spent four years in the Air Force—which I did—and I could tell you that my current business is all about defense systems and such— which it is—but I know all of that is irrelevant. You've probably got standing orders not to do the very thing that I'm asking you to do, but I'm asking you to think about it really, really hard."

Morris sighed and made a pained face. It was too early in the morning to have to weigh decisions such as this. "Look, Mr. . . . ."

"O'Toole."

"Mr. O'Toole, I appreciate your situation, I really do, but you hit the nail right on the head. I'm an officer in the Air Force Reserve, and in my spare time I'm the commander of this CAP squadron, and if you've been in the military, you know that regulations rule. You also appreciate what happens when those regulations are violated. I can't just—"

Brandon held up his hands to cut Morris off. "You're about to say no, and I still don't think you've thought it all the way through. For example, the regulations say you can't have civilians in the aircraft with you, right? Isn't that what you were about to tell me?"

Morris's scowl returned. "Well, yes, but—"

"Okay, then, tell me this. What do you intend to do if you find them?"

"Excuse me?"

"Well, my son and his friend are both civilians. If you find them, and it's physically feasible to pick them up, you'd do that, right?"

Morris rolled his eyes. "Mr. O'Toole, it's not the same thing and you know it."

"I don't know anything of the sort. In fact, because you are an officer in the Air Force Reserve, and therefore an intelligent, thoughtful man, I believe that the more you think about it, the more you'll see that civilians are civilians, and that as circumstances change, so can the requirement to rigidly stand fast to the rules." Brandon was making this up as he went along.

Morris sighed again, this time a deep groan that might have been a growl. "Oh, God, Mr. O'Toole . . ."

"Call me Brandon, please." There, he'd seen it. The first crack in Morris's resolve. The argument had made a dent. "You see it, don't you? You see that I'm right."

"What I see is a father who's desperate to be a part of the effort to find his son. But there are other factors."

"Let's talk about them," Brandon said, sounding like the very essence of reasonableness. "Let's talk about the main priorities here. Certainly, I'm not a risk to your crew's safety, and I'm hardly a lawsuit risk. Besides, if you think about it—"

"Shut up," Morris barked. Brandon recoiled. "Just shut up and let me think for a second, will you? Jesus, it's too early for this."

Interesting transition, Brandon thought. Just like that, Morris had gone from off guard to back-in-control. It was time for Brandon to show that he could follow orders.

Morris returned to his desk and placed his hand on the computer mouse, moving a black eight over to a red nine and freeing up the ace of spades, which crawled its way to its spot above the rest of the animated cards. Brandon didn't know what to make of this. Surely Colonel Morris wasn't ignoring him. But it was annoying as hell to watch him lose himself in a game of cards. A good two minutes passed in silence as Morris worked to expose yet another ace, and then, without any fanfare, he swiveled back around to face Brandon.

"Where'd you come in from to be here?" he asked.

"Virginia. Just outside Washington, D.C."

"In the snow?"

"Yes, sir. A friend offered me a plane and a pilot. Good wings and brass balls."

Morris nodded, weighing things in his mind. "Please do your best not to make me regret this," he said, finally.

Brandon nodded once. "I promise."

15

SCOTT AWOKE WITH A START, unaware that he'd fallen asleep, and overwhelmed with the need to vomit. He barely made it from his butt to his knees before his insides cramped up hard, doubling him over till his nose nearly touched the frozen floor. He retched and his stomach heaved, producing only a thin line of yellow gunk that quickly spread as a stain on the shelter's floor. Two more in quick succession produced only more of the same, and by the time his guts settled down, Scott found that he was crying, and feeling stupid for it. He wiped his eyes with the sleeve of his parka.

You got nothing in you to puke up, his mind told him, and right at this moment, he wasn't sure whether the thought of food was attractive or repulsive.

As he stared at the mess he'd made, it dawned on him that he could see without a flashlight; that morning had finally arrived, ending the longest night of his life. Well, thank God for that.

The wolves' feeding frenzy had lasted for hours, producing sounds unlike anything he'd ever heard: a nightmarish cacophony of growls and barks and whimpers, punctuated with that grotesque tearing sound as meat was pulled from bone.

But they never again attempted to enter the shelter.

He crawled outside. The sun had climbed high, casting crisp black shadows against the sparkling snow cover. Marring what could have been a beautiful sight were the horrid remains of last night's feast. The unbroken blanket of snow had been churned savagely, what once was white now stained crimson. Straight ahead of the shelter's opening, great tufts of torn fur rose from the center of the largest stain—what could only be the remains of the alpha dog that he'd stunned or killed with the flare gun.

"Jesus," Scott breathed as he took in the carnage.

But the real horror, he knew, lay behind him, over at the base of the tree near the shattered cockpit. His mind screamed for him not to look, but he couldn't help himself. His head pivoted without his instruction, his eyes half-closed in anticipation of what they might see.

Cody Jamieson was gone. Like the area around Alpha, the snow had been churned and chewed, but unlike that other horrific scene, this one was still white, except for the few spots where tree bark and other debris had been tossed about.

"Thank you, God," Scott whispered, daring a glance upward. The thought flashed through his mind that he should likewise ask God for some blessing for Cody, but he couldn't think of the right words. Truth be told, he didn't want to think about it at all.

Overhead, where the sky dared to peek through the towering pines, Scott saw a welcome blue that he hoped would dull the edge of the razor-sharp cold. Last night had been a bad one, even colder than the one before, and as the morning breezes sheared the topmost dusting of flakes away from the snowpack, the ice crystals seemed to bite harder against the exposed flesh of his face.

This had to be the day. Today, he would be rescued or he would die. He'd worried about such things yesterday, yes, but he'd known that he still had time. Today, that time had expired. Today's priority had to be food. He had to find something nutritious enough to keep his stomach from heaving out what little remained to fuel his day.

But how? He had no idea. Today *had* to be the day.

Yeah, well yesterday had to be the day, too. And tomorrow, when he tried telling himself the same thing yet again, maybe he wouldn't have the strength to stand.

Stop it!

Stop what? Recognizing the truth when he saw it? Recognizing the obvious fact that the rescuers he kept fantasizing about had no idea where he was? Should he stop wondering exactly what it felt like to die, when he knew that come tomorrow morning, or the next one, or the one after that, he was just flat-out not going to wake up at all?

Scott felt the old panic returning, and this time it rushed him like a flood, moving faster than he could react and washing away his ridiculous pretense of hope. His heart rate doubled and then doubled again as he paced a ragged circle around the crash site. *I'm going to die here!* his mind screamed. *I'm going to starve, or be eaten or just slowly freeze to death.*

"Goddammit!" His shriek echoed off the trees, and the effort of it made his voice crack. This wasn't right; this wasn't the way it was supposed to be. He was sixteen years old, for Christ's sake. He was supposed to be in school today, in the warmth of history class, or English or geometry. He wasn't supposed to be out in the middle of the damn woods, wondering when his death would arrive.

How does shit like this happen in the first place? How, in the days of global positioning satellites and Internets and all that high technology, could they not be able to find a crashed airplane?

The flare! The fusee! Oh, God, he'd left the second one behind when he'd dashed for cover in the shelter! Was it still there? *Oh, please God, please God let it still be there!*

Scott scrambled through the snow, back toward the grisly stain that once was Alpha, and he fell to his knees, his hands outstretched as he clawed through the snow to find it.

It has to be here. Has to be here . . .

And there it was. The wolves had kicked it aside and partially buried it as they shredded their former boss, but the waxy red stick remained right where Scott had tossed it. Grabbing it up into his gloved hand, Scott examined it. It looked healthy enough; no obvious signs of damage.

He inhaled deeply and released a long sigh that completely enveloped his head in vapor. One thing had gone right. One in a row, the first of the day. Maybe it was the start of a trend.

Still on his knees, staring up at the sky, he started to pray silently, but then decided that maybe God needed to hear him. "I'm sorry for everything," he said softly, a part of him aware of just how stupid he must sound. "I don't know what you want to hear, but if you're angry, then I'm really sorry. But you've got to help me out of this one. I don't mean to tell you how to do your job, but—"

Above the gentle silence of the forest, just barely louder than the soft rush of the breeze, Scott could almost make out the sound of an approaching aircraft.

GIVEN MORRIS'S ARMY FLIGHT SUIT and the insignia on the epaulets, Brandon had expected the search aircraft to be more . . . military. He'd expected polished silver or olive drab; maybe something in camouflage, with muted American flags stenciled on the tail and the fuselage. Instead, he found himself the third man in a single-engine four-seater, confined to the impossibly small back bench, while Colonel Morris flew from the left front seat, and a seventeen-year-old cheerleader-type named Stacey took up space in the right seat. The high wing, supported by struts that extended from either side of the fuselage, afforded a sweeping view of the sugar-white forest, from horizon to horizon.

Brandon's neck hurt from the strain of staring at the ground through the scratched 24 x 24-inch Plexiglas window. For hours now, he'd listened silently through his headset as the flight crew chatted about the weather and about their homes and their families. Brandon had learned that Stacey was nearly certain that some young buck named Jerry was going to ask her out soon, and much to his surprise, Colonel Morris did a convincing impression of someone who cared. To Brandon, it seemed as if they purposely talked about everything but Scott—everything but the job at hand.

Today's search efforts involved four planes instead of just one, and each of the four had been assigned a segment of the same ground that had been searched the day before. According to the experts—what few of them there were—Cody Jamieson's Cessna had no business being beyond these confines, and their best chances of finding and rescuing Scott was to concentrate the search in the prescribed areas.

The preflight briefing had been conducted by a guy named

Feldman, who wore the silver eagles of a full colonel on the epaulets of a bus-driver blue uniform that had been purchased a good twenty pounds before. Well into his sixties and bald, Feldman spoke with the forcefulness of one who had conducted many such searches in the past.

"We're looking for any signs of a crash," Feldman had told the group. "Signs of burned or broken trees, debris, gouges out of the rock face, anything that might have been caused by a crashing air-plane. If you find it, or even if you think you found it, get down as low as you can and try to confirm. If, after that, you're still reasonably confident, then give a shout and we'll get a chopper and a search team down there as soon as possible."

Brandon had been impressed by the seriousness of the assem-bled searchers, especially given their average age, which to his eye was about sixteen.

Brandon didn't understand the strategy. Covering the same real estate over and over again made no sense to him. Suppose they were looking in the wrong place? How would they ever know? And if not this place, then where? It seemed painfully obvious that Cody Jamieson was clueless from the beginning. No emergency locator, no emergency call for assistance, yet the search commanders' whole strategy assumed that he was marginally on course.

Where was the logic?

Sometimes, in the absence of hard data, you had to just randomly choose a course of action and stick to it, but what if they were flat-out wrong to begin with? What then?

Two hours. That's how long they'd been cruising the same real estate, looking for the invisible. Two additional hours of cold and mis-ery for Scott. Two more hours for him to lie in pain or in fear, waiting for the rescuers who might be in the wrong place altogether.

Brandon liked the range of mountains immediately to the east. Call it intuition. Call it a hunch. Hell, call it sheer boredom from looking out the same window at the same scenery, but he felt they needed to be over there. Not here. There. And the more he thought about it, the more certain he felt.

"Hey, Colonel?" Brandon asked into his headset.

"Yessir?"

"What about those ridges over to the east? We gonna take a look over there?"

"No, sir, I don't believe so. The search plan calls for us to focus right here. They've worked out the likely flight path for the downed craft, and this is where they put it."

Brandon nodded. Made lots of sense. But the colonel was wrong. "I think we should take a look over there," he said.

Morris stiffened, glanced as Stacey. "That's really not in the game plan, Mr. O'Toole," he said, finally.

"How far is that over there?"

Morris looked, calculated in his head. "Maybe eight, ten miles."

"Is it that outrageous that a plane could wander that far off course in a snowstorm?"

"It's not outrageous, no. In fact, it's not outrageous that it might have wandered just about anywhere, but that's not how we conduct a search."

Brandon knew not to push too hard. "Seems to me, we're coming up on two days of searching the same area, and we've turned up nothing. Haven't found so much as a dent in the snow. You call that no data. I call it negative data. Maybe it's time to assume that we're looking in the wrong spot."

"You may be right, Mr. O'Toole, but I'm not in the position to make that call."

"Suppose you saw someone waving his arms outside of the search area. You'd fly over there to take a look, wouldn't you?"

"Come on, Mr. O'Toole—"

"No, no, I'm not going to tell you I saw someone waving his arms, but I will tell you that I have a very strong feeling that Scott's over there on that ridge. I can't give you anything stronger than intuition, but I'm telling you, I know my son is over there."

Brandon could hear Morris sigh into his intercom. He looked to Stacey, who shrugged and looked away.

"This is exactly why you shouldn't be here. If every pilot acted on his hunches, the search pattern would become haphazard and meaningless."

"Please." That one word just hung there in the air. Brandon could feel the weight of it himself. He could only imagine how it weighed on Morris.

Another sigh.

"Just one pass. As a favor to me."

In the final sigh, he heard Morris make two decisions at once: that he'd humor his passenger; and that said passenger was hereafter forever grounded.

The pitch of the engine noise deepened as the pilot throttled up and banked hard to the right.

SCOTT HAD BEEN WATCHING the planes all morning as they flew their oblong circles over the wrong spot, white specs against the cobalt sky, occasionally flashing like a nova as they passed through the sun's glare at just the right angles. At one point, about an hour ago, Scott found himself screaming out at the aircraft, and wildly waving his arms, as if there were even the remotest chance that they could see him. He'd cursed, he'd begged, he'd shrieked himself hoarse, but the lazy circles continued on and on.

Out of nowhere, a stomach cramp blossomed deep in his gut, doubling him over and forcing a grunt from his throat. He thought for a moment that he might puke again, but talked himself out of it. Nothing to barf up, remember? Maybe it was just the despair, but Scott swore that he felt weaker today. His hands shook more, and not just because of the cold; though God knew it was friggin' freezing.

Deep down inside, he knew that he'd begun to die. Closing in on forty-eight hours without food, and clearly no rational expectation for rescue, this was the beginning of the end.

The planes were so *close*. There *had* to be a way. There had to be—

Something changed in the sound of the airplane's engine that made his head jerk up for another look. At first, he had difficulty focusing on the little spec in the distance, but when he reacquired it, he realized that it had finally broken its monotonous circular orbit, and was headed in a new direction. It looked like it was heading out, on a course directly away from him. They must have run low on fuel.

Shielding his eyes against the brilliant sky and the piercing white of the snow, he watched as the lone airplane headed home. Oddly, as he watched, the growl of the engine grew louder.

"Oh, shit," Scott breathed. It wasn't heading home; it was coming right at him! He let out a war whoop as he jumped to his feet and waved his arms wildly over his head. "Here I am! Right here! Right here!"

He needed his fire.

Scott turned too quickly as he bolted back toward his impromptu camp and lost his footing, catching a face full of snow. It hurt, but it didn't slow him down. Jesus, this was it! Finally, he had his first good shot at a rescue. He had to light the fire, and he had maybe five minutes to do it.

By now, his tracks through the snow were plainly visible—great carved trenches. The vibrating growl of the airplane's engine filled the woods as he plowed on. He fell again, filling his nostrils with snow, but an instant later, he was back on his feet.

The engine grew louder still. Scott's arms and legs pumped wildly as he half-ran, half-stumbled past the dead fall that he'd guesstimated to be the halfway point. Scott's entire world had compressed itself into two sounds: the noise of the approaching airplane and the frantic in and out of his own breathing. Nothing else existed. Nothing else mattered. The exertions of a 100-yard dash yielded the progress of a baby's crawl. His legs and his lungs screamed at him to slow down, but his brain pushed him on and on.

There was the site! He could see it now. And there was the little cup of fuel he'd put out. Some had spilled, but even from this far away, he could see that there was enough.

If the plane wasn't overhead, it was damn close when Scott slid to a halt and again lost his footing. He could do it! There was time! Not much, but at least there was time.

His hands seemed to know exactly what to do as they snatched the fusee from its perch in the snow. He pulled the plastic cap, yanked the protective cover with his teeth and struck it like a giant match. It lit instantly, enveloping him in a cloud of acrid white smoke.

• • •

"SLOW DOWN," Brandon said into the intercom. They'd dropped their altitude to treetop level, and at this distance, the unbroken carpet of white sped by at an impossible speed.

"This is as slow as she goes without falling out of the sky," Morris replied.

If he were able, Scott would make a sign, of that Brandon was certain. A smoke column made the most sense, but it might be anything.

Scott was down there. Don't ask him how he knew, but he did. He was there.

But the white carpet yielded nothing; not even a brief glimpse into the world that lay below.

THE WOODS SHOOK with the lumbering vibration of the airplane. In Scott's mind, it could have been a hundred airplanes for all the noise it made. It was close—so, so close—maybe even on top of him already.

But there'd be time. There had to be time. This was his moment!

He touched the fusee's searing red flame to the surface of the fuel in the cup, taking care to remain a respectful distance, just in case it flashed. The flame touched the surface and . . .

. . . nothing happened.

"What?" Scott yelled. "No!" He tried again, and again. Still, nothing. "Shit!"

How could it not light? He raised the cup to his nose and recoiled from the stench of the fuel. It was the right stuff, so why wouldn't it light? He put it back on the ground and again touched the flame to the shimmering surface. The noise of the plane vibrated in his chest.

Nothing happened.

"Come on!" he yelled. "Light, goddammit!"

And it did, with a slight, nearly inaudible *woof* a pitiful orange flame appeared for just an instant over the surface of the fuel, but in the time it took for Scott to smile, the flame went out again.

"No!"

As he tried again, and again, only to see the same brief flashes of flame, the noise of the engine peaked, and through the canopy of leaves, Scott saw the giant shadow pass overhead. The sound Dopplered and began to diminish.

"No!" Scott screamed to the woods. "No! I'm here! I'm right here!"

Trembling now, and working faster than his hands could manage, he frantically waved his fusee over the top of the basin. He needed smoke, goddammit. They were here! Right here! And he couldn't get the fuel to light!

"Don't do this to me!" he yelled, and then a shiver hit him, launching itself like a torpedo from the base of his spine to his shoulders. It made him jump, an odd reflex motion that came from nowhere, and lasted only an instant.

His hand jerked, dunking the tip of the fusee into the contained puddle of fuel, extinguishing its flame forever.

16

SHERRY SAT AT THE ELABORATE fold-down desk in the living room, her fingers hovering over the keys of her laptop, waiting for the muse to arrive. She'd been like this for an hour. She never should have accepted the seminar gig. What was she thinking? Way out here in the middle of nowhere, how could she ever imagine that enough people would sign up to make it all worthwhile? The people in charge told her that it would be a packed house, but she recognized the feel of sunshine being blown up her skirt.

It was billed as an empowerment lecture, based on the principles set forth in *The Mirror's Not the Problem*. Women these days were their own worst enemies. The baggage they carried with them through life, shouldering not only the guilt of failure, but also the guilt of success, made the glass ceiling bulletproof. Good Lord, she'd delivered her speech so many times, you'd think she'd have had it memorized by now. Maybe she did. Who could know? But it was part of her routine to rewrite it in full on the day before she was due to hit the stage. That kept it all fresh.

But not when your son is missing and everybody wants something from you; not when everyone is watching to see how well you hold up under the pressure. Nobody can concentrate in conditions like that.

Sherry had instructed Larry to get her out of this thing, to persuade the conference center manager that she was too distraught to go onstage, but it didn't work. They had a contract, the manager reminded him, and people had traveled to SkyTop from all over the country to hear Sherry Carrigan O'Toole talk about her philosophies of life. They were here, and they were snowbound, and the manager was not about to deal with a revolt simply because the featured speaker was feeling worried.

"It would be one thing if the boy were dead," the manager had told Larry. "People might understand that. But just because he's missing? I don't think so. Hell, this is precisely the kind of counseling that Dr. O'Toole specializes in, isn't it?"

Sherry had had to force that last part out of Larry. He'd known that it would hurt her feelings, and bless his heart, he wanted to protect her from as much heartache as possible. So, come ten o'clock tomorrow morning, Sherry would be out there on the stage, with or without something to say.

When the phone rang, Sherry rose to answer it, just to have something else to do, but Larry beat her to it. He covered the mouthpiece with his hand. "It's Audrey," he said.

Sherry groaned, considered refusing the call, then took it anyway. "Hello, Audrey."

"I saw you on the news yesterday," Audrey said. "In fact, just about everyone in New York saw you on the news yesterday. My phone has been ringing off the hook. Has there been any news about Scotty?" She seemed proud that she'd gotten the boy's name right without stumbling over it.

"Not a thing. The weather let up some, though, so at least they're finally out searcing for him."

"Well, I hope you're taking notes," Audrey said.

"Audrey, you didn't," Sherry growled. She sensed what was coming and she looked up for Larry, only to see that he'd already picked up the extension.

"I swear to God I didn't call anyone. They called *me*. They saw you on the air, and they started falling all over themselves for the book rights."

Sherry flushed. "Did you not hear what I told you yesterday?"

"What am I supposed to do, Sher, not answer my phone? Baker's offered $500,000 for U.S. rights alone." Audrey slipped that in quickly.

Sherry gasped. *Half a million dollars?* She looked toward Larry, whose scowl turned angry. "Audrey, no. It's not right. I'm not going to make a profit from my son's misfortune. I told you no yesterday, and it's still no today."

"Be reasonable," Audrey begged. "That's a lot of money."

Larry proclaimed, "It's exploitation."

"Christ on a crutch," Audrey spat. "Does he flush the toilet for you, too?" This wasn't the first time that Larry had played angel to Audrey's devil.

"I value his advice," Sherry said. Her tone left no room for argument.

"Well, it's bad advice this time. Most people work their whole lives for a shot at this much money. Here I am handing it to you, and you're acting like I'm the bad guy."

"Have you no shame at all?" Larry asked. He was as close to shouting as he ever came. "Tell us about the escalation clause that ups the payments if they find Scott dead."

Sherry gasped.

You could almost hear Audrey turning red. "That's really offensive, Larry. How dare you? I am not exploiting a soul here, and there's no one on the planet who hopes more fervently than I that the boy turns up healthy and happy. Honest to God, from where I sit, this isn't even fundamentally about Scotty's misfortune. It's about how a mother deals with crisis."

"But the crisis is her son!" Larry shot a pleading look to Sherry. "Are you going to say something?"

Audrey didn't give her the chance. "Look, I didn't call to joust with Mister Morality, okay? This is about you, Sherry, not about him. And I'm telling you that this is a terrific deal, and that you'll shoot yourself if you don't take it. Maybe not tomorrow, or even next week, but sooner or later, when some reporter for *Field and Stream* earns three mil for the movie rights to the story *you* should have written, you're going to jump off a bridge."

Sherry sighed. "I just can't do it, Audrey."

"Because Larry says it's a bad idea? The very same Larry whose livelihood depends on your livelihood?"

Sherry shook her head. "Because it's wrong."

Now Audrey's anger was palpable. "I'm going to say something to you now that I've never said to any of my authors before, okay? And Larry, I just want you to muzzle yourself while I say it. You, too, Sherry." She paused for effect. "Yours is not the only interest in play here, okay? Rich Czabo at Baker's can use a big book, and he's been nothing but good to me. *Mirror*'s not the powerhouse that it once was, so a little publicity won't do you any harm on that front. And, Larry, before you say a word, remember that what I'm proposing doesn't approach the exploitation level of those Everest books. Those people actually died for the author to make money."

Another pause, followed by a big sigh. The wind-up for her biggest pitch. "Sherry, I'm not going to lie and tell you that I can't put a $75,000 commission to good use. Good Christ, this is like money from home. A lot of people support you, honey. You are where you are today thanks to the help of a lot of people who aren't going to understand why, all of a sudden, you don't give a shit about them anymore."

"That's not fair!" Sherry protested. "I do so give a shit. I know exactly how much I owe them for all they've done."

"Then show it. Don't walk away from the opportunity of a lifetime. And what about your fans? What about those people who pour their hearts out to you and hang on every word of advice that you give? Don't you think you owe *them* an inside peek at what you're going through? Don't you think that there are countless people out there who go through this same kind of worry—with a sick child or an injured spouse—who would gain tremendous personal comfort knowing that even famous people have to deal with worry and tragedy?"

Audrey paused for a moment to let Sherry absorb it all. She had a point, you know. People *did* depend on Sherry for advice. This wasn't just her livelihood they were talking about; it was her reputation. Didn't she in fact owe those people a little something of herself? Isn't that really what she got into the business for in the first place?

"I suppose it wouldn't really be exploiting Scott," Sherry mused.

Larry was horrified. "Sherry!"

"Exactly," Audrey said. "What you do now can't possibly have an effect on the outcome of Scotty's problems. But how you handle the crisis, and how you share it with others, well, that can help countless people to cope on their own."

Larry said, "Audrey, you're so full of shit I can smell it from here. Sherry, this is Audrey Lewis you're talking to, not Mother Teresa. There's not an altruistic bone in her body. It's all about the money. Don't let her pull you to the dark side."

"Screw you, Chinn," Audrey spat. "How dare you question my motives? And what the hell difference is it to you?"

"Her motivations don't make a difference, Larry," Sherry said. "Her point's valid either way."

"Oh, my God, you're going to do it!" Larry couldn't believe it.

"Think of Psychic Edge Books," Sherry said, referring to a tiny independent bookstore in the Bay Area of San Francisco. "They sell fifteen hundred copies of my books when I sign there. That's their big profit for the year. It's what keeps them in business. They were there for me when I was nobody."

"What are you saying?" Larry kept the phone to his ear, even as he spoke directly to her. "That it's okay to sell out your son so some bookstore can make money?"

Audrey interrupted, "Larry, shut up."

But Sherry didn't need Audrey in her corner anymore. "I'm not selling anyone out—"

"That's sure as hell what it's going to look like!"

"Only to the people who are predisposed to pounce on everything I do anyway. Audrey's right about my readers and listeners, too. What I do has an impact on *many* people's lives. Spiritually *and* financially. I'd be foolish not to recognize that."

Larry closed his eyes and shook his head, resigned to failure. "I don't believe you're doing this."

"Take the offer, Audrey," Sherry said.

• • •

SCOTT STARED AT THE DEAD FLARE, his mouth agape. What had just happened? How the hell does fuel put fire *out?* This couldn't be happening.

Oh, but it was. Happening to him: Scott O'Toole, tenth-grade geek and wanna-be guitar star. He listened as the engine noise faded and changed directions, heading back toward the ridge on the other side of the valley, and he knew that his one good chance at getting out of here had just flown away.

"Shit!" Scott screamed the word loudly enough to hurt, his voice cracking from the effort, and he heaved the dead flare like a dagger, spinning it end-over-end into the tangled mess of the woods. Anger like he'd never known boiled up from somewhere and spread like a grim shadow through his whole body. "Come back!" he shrieked, but even as the words left his sore throat, he knew they were wasted.

The damn fuel didn't light. It didn't *light!* Christ, if he'd been trying to make it not burn, it would have been like a goddamn bonfire. "Fuck you!" he spat at the blue container and he kicked it, launching an arc of brown-yellow fuel that stained the snow in a dotted line ten feet long.

Then he sank to his knees and fell back on his haunches.

Don't panic, he told himself. *Don't panic. Panic kills.* "Don't panic!"

Tears arrived from nowhere, stinging his eyes and freezing on his face. They brought with them the final hopelessness; the absolute certainty that he was going to die. Pressing his gloves to his face, he tried to make them stop, but they came anyway, in an unstoppable flood.

"I don't want to die," he sobbed. "Please come back. Please . . ."

He wanted to be strong. He wanted to be the hero, the boy who did everything right, and goddammit, he *had* done everything right. But when the plane finally came—the one moment that he'd been planning for—the goddamn fuel didn't light!.

Scott O'Toole was going to die right here in the woods, slowly, either starving or freezing his way to Heaven—*oh, please let it be Heaven*—dying just a chunk at a time. He remembered Sven's pictures of fingers and noses and ears that had been blackened by frost-bite. He remembered one particularly horrendous picture of a hiker whose nose had been amputated, leaving behind this hideous two-chambered scar that made the victim look like some monstrous pig-human hybrid.

Well, at least he wouldn't have to live with that. He might have to die with it, but he wouldn't have to live with it.

His stomach cranked again, and again he doubled over from it.

He should have tried to hike out for help yesterday, while he was still strong. What had he been thinking, blazing trails and building shelters? He should have spent the time walking. To hell with the experts who tell you to stay put. To hell with waiting for rescuers to come to you. All of that assumes that someone is on the way in the first place!

Yesterday, he had energy. Yesterday, his hands didn't shake. Today, it was already too late.

But tomorrow will be even later.

That thought startled him. At least today he could still stand, he could still think straight. Who knew about tomorrow? Tomorrow he could be dead.

So, today was the day. He was out of choices. It was walk or die. Okay, or die walking, which was sort of the same thing.

Even if he did this crazy thing and left today, it was probably too late in the afternoon for him to start. What was it already? Two? Maybe three in the afternoon? He didn't bother to check his watch. Another couple of hours and it would be dark again.

And then it would be another endless night. When the sun rose again, he'd be a whole day hungrier, a whole day closer to death. Wasn't it better to die out there, trying, than it would be to die here in the shelter, just waiting?

Before he realized that he'd even made his decision, Scott had the map out of his pocket. Man oh man, that was a lot of green and brown nothing.

He pointed to the spot on the map where he'd calculated the crash site to be, and from there, he looked for some positive sign. Surely there had to be a building around here somewhere. Surely.

Well, you'd think.

If Scott recalled correctly, the USGS maps were compiled from data gathered from aerial photographs—in this case, according to the legend at the bottom, a photograph taken ten years ago. At a scale of 1:50,000, the area illustrated on the map seemed impossibly huge.

Wait. There. What about that one?

His hand paused at a tiny cluster of four black dots along the blue line that Scott knew to be the river. *Could that be a house?* he wondered. Or a series of them? A place with a telephone? A ranger station, maybe?

It was definitely a building.

But Jesus, it was a long ways away. Using the length of his thumb to estimate the measurements of the legend, he figured the cluster of buildings to be ten miles from here. That was the bad news.

The good news was, it was *only* ten miles from here. Better than eleven, right? And a damn sight better than fifteen or twenty. Sometimes you had to force yourself to look for the bright spots.

Suppose they weren't even there anymore? Suppose they had burned down five years ago, or even last week?

Scott shook the thoughts away.

He worked the numbers in his brain. Assuming a person walks five miles an hour in normal circumstances, with the hills and the dead falls and such, plus the snow, he figured that his progress would be half that fast. Ten miles at two and a half miles per hour was only four hours. Actually, if he set off right at this very moment, he might even make it halfway before dark.

Suddenly, all of this seemed too easy. What was he forgetting? What was the one plainly stupid thing he'd forgotten to do?

A lot can go wrong in ten miles. He'd never hiked that far without a trail to follow. He had his compass, sure, but one degree over ten miles was a long way. Then there was the risk of wolves. Or grizzly bears or falling off a cliff or—

Enough! How was he going to do this?

Maybe even the compass thing wasn't such a big deal. The buildings sat right on the river. As long as he followed the river, he should be able to find the buildings. Really, it was that simple. That didn't mean he could ignore the compass and map, but it did mean that he could make faster progress through the woods. He wouldn't have to shoot a new heading every few feet the way he'd done the day before.

So, he'd head basically south, choosing the least steep route to the river, and from there just let the water be his guide. Boom. He had a plan. Part of him wanted to think it all through a little more, consider other options. This felt too easy.

In the end, he decided to think about it as he walked.

17

LONG SHADOWS PAINTED BLACK STRIPES across the blinding white roadway in front of the now-familiar police station. After seven hours aloft, Brandon had parted company with Colonel Morris on the tarmac behind Terminal Two, and with nothing else to do, headed back to Eagle Feather.

What a difference a day made. Yesterday's deserted streets were now packed with people, most dressed in the standard uniform of winter tourists: designer skiwear that looked great but left them shivering. Brandon watched these people, and as he did, he wondered which of them had children, and of the ones who did, how many had ever feared for those children's lives. Suddenly, he felt very alone, as if everyone else in the world had someone near them to care about and to nurture. No one should have to fend alone with this kind of worry. It sat like a block of ice in his belly, and with each tick of the minute hand, it grew geometrically.

His mind again conjured the image of his only child, gasping for help where no one could possibly hear.

Brandon paused as he turned the corner on Main Street, his attention drawn to the Whiteout Saloon, which loomed directly across the street. From its long, arched windows to the ornately carved doors topped with stained glass, the place looked like it had been drop-shipped directly from some back lot, where it served as the set for a nineteenth-century whorehouse. Judging from the clientele he saw passing through the doors, this was not a place where he'd be likely to find the pink drinks served in plastic cowboy boots that characterized the first choice of tourists with kids. This was a drinking establishment. Exactly what he needed.

He crossed at the corner and walked right in. Inside, the John Wayne theme continued. An ornately carved bar stretched all the way down the left-hand side of the room, every third or fourth chair occupied by someone who no doubt thought that they had real problems in their lives. Two dozen little round tables littered the rest of the room, each of them playing host to four identical bentwood chairs. As he surveyed the room, Brandon could almost see the stuntmen busting this furniture over each other's heads in the obligatory brawl scene.

He headed for the bar, choosing the most isolated seat he could find. The bartender wasted no time homing in. "What can I get for you?" Above the racks of bottles, the saloon's only anachronism—a fifteen-inch television—showed a four-wheel-drive truck plowing through a snowdrift, spraying mud and snow everywhere. The camera work told Brandon that it was probably just a commercial, although it could have just as easily been the evening news.

Something about the bartender amused Brandon. Aged somewhere between fifty and seventy, the guy had a complexion like a yellow raisin, and his voice had the deep basso tone that could only come from years of unfiltered Camels. When he glanced at the man's name tag, he couldn't help himself from laughing out loud.

"Your name really Joe?" Brandon asked.

The guy looked confused. "Yeah. Can't say anybody's ever found it funny, though."

Brandon raised his hands to ward off hard feelings. "Meant no harm. It's just that in a place like this, what name could the bartender possibly have *but* Joe?"

The bartender still didn't get it.

"Never mind. Like I said, no harm intended. You got any Glenmorangie back there?"

"Twelve year, eighteen or twenty-four?"

Like that was even a choice. If he was going to poison his body, he might as well do it in style. "Let's do the twenty-four. On the rocks."

"Eighteen's better," Joe said. No longer offended, he'd switched directly to tip-earning mode. "Smoother, I think."

Brandon nodded once. "Done. I defer to the expert."

"Saved you four bucks, too." As Joe walked away, Brandon noticed that he even had the bowlegged swagger of an old cowboy. The bartender moved with the halting efficiency of a man who hurt most of the time.

Brandon put his elbows on the bar and rested his face in his hands. Just how long did he have to go, he wondered, until someone yelled olley-olley-oxenfree and ended this nightmare? He was ready to be awake again. He was ready to wake up with a start in the morning only to find that Scott had once again slept through his alarm. He wanted to roll him out of bed and yell at him for running late.

He wanted a hug from him. And a kiss. Even at sixteen, his son still gave him a kiss good night before bed. It had been part of their routine forever, and he hoped that it never faded away. Somewhere in his own childhood, handshakes had become the only means to express affection with his father, and on the day Scott was born, Brandon had made a pledge never to make the same mistake with his own son.

He shifted on his stool and opened his eyes to find that his drink had arrived, mysteriously and silently. Joe had already retreated back to the far end, apparently reading his customer's body language, which hollered that he wanted to be left alone. The cardboard coaster stuck to the bottom of the glass as Brandon took a sip. Damn smooth, indeed. And Joe had gotten the recipe exactly right: two ice cubes, the rest scotch.

He chased the first sip with two more, then set the glass back onto the polished mahogany to wait for the alcohol to do its job. Never much of a drinker, he did enjoy the warmth it brought, the certain clarity of thought. He remembered his college days when his buddies used to go out bingeing, and about the best he could do was a buzz after a six-pack, and endless puking after the seventh beer. He'd learned early to recognize his limits.

God, that was a long time ago. Hell, this morning was a long time ago. He tried to imagine how far he'd have to roll back the clock to make the horror go away. Would it have been as simple as saying no to Sherry? If he had done that, would everything else have been just fine?

Well, maybe, but who was he to deny Scott a week away with his mother? And who the hell was she to put him in that position?

That's really what it kept coming back to. Why did that selfish bitch have to put Brandon in this situation in the first place? Did she really hate him that much? Did she really have so little regard for the relationship that he and Scott had built over the years that she had to force a wedge between them?

Yes, she hated him at least that much.

Enough to kill their only son.

Whoa! That thought came out of nowhere. Startled the hell out of him. Scott wasn't dead, dammit! He wasn't.

And even if he were, how could Brandon possibly lay the blame for a plane crash at Sherry's feet? That wasn't right.

Still, if she'd just kept to her own business, and out of theirs, then sure as hell, none of this would have happened.

"She can't even ski, for Christ's sake!"

"Excuse me?"

Brandon looked up to see Joe, a curious expression on his face. "Huh?"

"You talkin' to me?" Joe asked.

Brandon scowled. He must have spoken his last thought aloud. "Oh, no, don't mind me. I got some problems today, is all."

"Judging by the look on your face, it's gotta be a kid or a woman."

"Or both." *Jesus, where do bartenders get their psychiatry degrees?*

"Yep, I figured. You okay?"

Brandon looked at the man's eyes. They looked curiously young for a man so old. Green, the way a cat's eyes were green. When people throw out a question like that, they either want an answer, or they're just engaging in a word-reflex. Joe impressed Brandon as a straight shooter. He probably thought he wanted to know, but once he heard, he'd be sorry he asked.

"Yeah, I'm fine," Brandon said. "Or I will be."

Joe waited for a moment—a silent opportunity for Brandon to change his mind—then shuffled back to his duties.

As Brandon watched the old man cross under the television set, his eyes were drawn to the white-bread news anchors on the screen. The picture cut to the standard-issue blonde with perfect teeth, and as she spoke words that were too soft for Brandon to understand, he saw a cartoon image of a plane crash over her shoulder, and if he wasn't mistaken, he read her lips as she mouthed the phrase, "Scott O'Toole."

"Turn that up!" Brandon shouted, startling the shit out of Joe.

"What?"

"The television! Turn it up! Turn it up now!"

Rattled, Joe had to search for the remote. He found it near the beer taps, just about a microsecond before Brandon was about to launch himself across the bar. The picture had already switched to a reporter standing in front of the building Brandon recognized as Terminal Two, but this pretty-boy was already well into his monologue before the sound became audible.

". . . until sundown, but then authorities will have to suspend operations until morning. Given the weather predictions for this evening—yet another punishing snowfall—even that seems iffy."

The picture cut to the image of a dour man whom Brandon had never seen, speaking into the bulbous end of a microphone. The graphic on the bottom of the screen identified him as Fire Chief Norman Howlette. "If you don't know where to look, you're bound to have trouble finding someone. Everything's made worse by the snow cover. Truthfully, if we don't find that wreckage soon, we're going to have to make some tough decisions."

"What kind of tough decisions?" asked a voice from offscreen.

Howlette looked suddenly uncomfortable, as if he were aware of the camera for the first time. "The toughest."

"You mean to discontinue the search?"

"Oh, I don't know that we'd ever officially discontinue it, but there's a big difference between search and rescue, and search and recovery."

"And that difference is?"

Howlette scowled, clearly wishing that this parasite would go away. "The difference is, you can only rescue someone who's still alive. And, well, it's awfully cold out there."

An invisible hand squeezed Brandon's belly. He realized as he looked down at his drink, still poised for a sip in front of his mouth, that his hands were shaking. Half of it spilled before he could set it back down on the bar.

What did these people think they were doing? Who were they to even *think* about giving up? Rage blossomed as he stood and fished with trembling hands for his wallet.

From his station over by the beer taps, Joe watched, and those green eyes showed that he understood now. He understood every-thing. "Forget about it, sir. This one's on the house," he said.

Brandon cocked his head and looked strangely at the old man.

"Really," he said again. "Go fight for your boy."

BRANDON DIDN'T EVEN SLOW DOWN for the door. If it hadn't opened easily, he'd have knocked it down. He made eye contact with Jesse Tingle, and the deputy buzzed him in without questioning a thing.

As Brandon marched down the aisle through the maze of chairs and desks, all work stopped and all eyes followed him. Apparently, his rage was that obvious. He set a course for Chief Whitestone's door, and no force on earth was going to stop him. At least three of the armed officers stood at their desks.

"Is he in?" he asked Charlotte Eberly.

"Yes, but—"

"Thank you." Thank God the doorknob turned easily. Brandon threw the door inward, but caught it before it could destroy the wall.

Whitestone looked startled, then angry. "Hey!"

Brandon's door slam shook the building. "Is what I just heard on the news true?"

The chief looked away. "I haven't been watching the news —"

"Don't bullshit me. It's true, isn't it? You guys are about to give up."

Whitestone thrust out his hand like the traffic cop he no doubt once was. "Absolutely not. Who said we're about to give up?"

"Some fire chief on the news."

"Well, we're a long way from that, I assure you."

"How long?"

Chief Whitestone thought for a moment as he sat back down. "We're certainly continuing the search tomorrow. In fact, we hope to add two more airplanes."

"Unless the weather turns bad again."

The chief inhaled noisily. "Well, yes, the weather is always a consideration."

"And they're predicting more snow for tonight?"

"Yes."

"What's the plan for the day after tomorrow, then?"

Whitestone considered lying. Brandon could see it, like a neon sign on the lawman's forehead. He actually opened his mouth to do it before he shut himself down. "Tomorrow's the last day we'll be treating this mission as a search and rescue operation." There it was, right square on the nose.

Brandon helped himself to a chair. Suddenly, there was nothing to say. "But that's my son up there."

Whitestone nodded and his eyes reddened. "I know that."

"And if the weather's bad tomorrow?"

Whitestone sighed again. How was he going to explain this? "The issue, Mr. O'Toole, is one of probable survival. Our experts tell us that after tomorrow, there's just no reasonable expectation that they could . . . well, you know. We confront this same sort of issue when a boat sinks. At first, we all go balls-out to rescue all survivors, but then, mathematically, physiologically, there comes a point where it's just not possible for anyone to remain alive."

"Even if they have outdoor survival training?"

Another sigh. "Their aircraft crashed in a storm, Mr. O'Toole. They fell out of the sky."

Brandon pounded his fist on Whitestone's desk. "God*dammit!* You never believed they were alive from the beginning."

"I never led you to believe otherwise."

"How can I expect you to fight for one more day, when you believe in your own heart that it's useless?"

"I did fight for another day."

That stopped Brandon cold. "You did?"

Whitestone nodded. "That's why they're going out again tomorrow."

"Unless it snows."

"Unless it snows a *lot*. It's just the best we can do. I'm sorry."

Brandon stared. Could it possibly be that this was all there was? He nodded silently and pressed hard against the wooden arms of his chair to raise himself out of his seat.

Whitestone rose with him. "Can I . . . get you anything?"

Brandon didn't even hear him. "So, tomorrow night. Or the day after. What happens?"

The chief scowled. "I'm afraid I don't understand."

"If they're . . . not found. How will I . . . Will I ever . . ." He couldn't bring himself to form the question.

"When the snow melts and visibility gets a little better, we'll start looking again. It's hard to hide wreckage like that for too long."

"And the boys? Scott?"

"They'll be treated with the utmost dignity and respect. You have my guarantee on that."

Brandon fell silent again. He supposed that about covered it. There should have been a thousand questions, but he couldn't imagine what they were. He couldn't imagine anything, in fact.

"Let me walk you out," Barry offered.

"No," Brandon said. "Actually, I think I'd really prefer to be alone right now."

Whitestone said something sympathetic, but Brandon didn't hear it. He felt oddly separated from his body as he walked out of the police station, oblivious to the stares.

THE TINY CHAPEL SAT NESTLED among towering pines. Built to hold maybe 200 people, it sported a rectangular sanctuary with a vaulted roof, and a thirty-foot steeple on the end nearest the parking lot. It was a place of nondenominational worship, where everyone was welcome. Brandon knew this because a glass-enclosed menu board out-side the front door said so. Three stained glass windows on either side depicted scenes from the Bible, the Torah, the Koran and the Book of Mormon. The place looked like a Christmas card.

For the longest time, he sat in the parking lot, watching the little church, listening to the barely audible sounds of hymns being sung. His Jeep was one of maybe a dozen automobiles in the parking lot, among twice that many snowmobiles and countless pairs of skis, all stacked neatly in racks along what doubtless became sidewalk after the spring thaw. Stalactites of ice hung from the eaves, dangling below the thick layer of snow that blanketed the roof.

Brandon didn't know why he'd come here; it was the last place on earth he wanted to be. Those of a more religious bent than he were altogether too anxious to grease the pathway to Heaven by prema-turely presuming death. For Brandon, the real sin—the real *sacri-lege*—lay in giving up. Yet, it was so easy to do. Father Scannell, the priest who'd first broken the news of Scott's disappearance, had been ready to pronounce death even before the details were known. And now it was Whitestone. He could hear it in the chief's voice. Hell, he could hear it in his words. They would find the boys alive tomorrow, or they'd resume the search for their bones in the spring. Jesus, how could it ever come to this?

Brandon sat there for the longest time, trying to think of some-thing—*anything*—that would make things different. He longed for a sign of hope.

Maybe it had been a mistake to come out here to Utah. Maybe he'd have been better off just staying at home, waiting for the phone to ring with word of final resolution. But if it were not for him, who else would have been the cheerleader for Scott's cause? Who else would have stood in the way of the naysayers? Whitestone had already said that if it hadn't been for Brandon's pushing they'd have called off the search already.

He told himself that while it wasn't much, at least it was some-thing.

He slid out of the Jeep and pushed the door closed. The air seemed colder up here than it did down on Main Street. He pulled his collar up against it and kept his head down as he waded toward the glowing chapel. In the darkness, he couldn't tell if the snow that whirled around him was falling from the sky or merely driven by the wind. He climbed the two steps to the red wooden doors, pulled one open and stepped inside.

The turnout touched his heart. Virtually every seat was taken, all of the occupants young and vital, still dressed in their skiing attire, many still wearing their ski boots. Up at the front, beyond the altar rail, a red-faced blonde with a tight ponytail was speaking to the group from the pulpit. It was clearly a story of Cody Jamieson's antics, and while Brandon had arrived too late to catch the real gist, the congregation clearly found it funny.

Brandon stood in the back, behind the last pew, watching more than he listened. With no intention to stay more than a few minutes, he removed his gloves but not his coat.

As far as he could tell, this service was by and for the resort staff. The young man in charge seemed more a master of ceremonies than a minister, making sure that everyone who wanted one got a turn at the microphone. Brandon's mind conjured an image of what the service at Robinson High School must have been like as Scott's friends gathered to remember the good times, to say nice things.

The next speaker to take the pulpit was all of twenty-one. She had an athletic look about her that was something short of pretty, but somehow attractive, nonetheless. She brought no notes from which to speak, and she adjusted the microphone just-so before she started talking.

"I'm Sandy Masterson," she said. "I'm not really sure what I want to say, other than to remember that Cody wasn't the only one on the airplane that day. I don't know how many of you had a chance to meet Scott O'Toole, but he and Cody were friends. They seemed to have hit it off right away. I wish I knew more about him—Scott, I mean—so I could say more, but I just wanted everybody here to think about him, too. If I close my eyes, what I remember about him isn't just that wild hair . . ." A chuckle of recognition rumbled through the crowd. ". . . but also his smile."

Brandon's throat thickened as his vision blurred. Throughout the chapel, heads nodded in recognition of that smile.

"He always seemed happy to be hanging around with the patrol, and when he'd laugh, it was like this light came on in his face. I wish I knew what he liked and what he was afraid of and what he loved. I think we all wish that we had known him better, but for the time being, at least I have his smile to look at in my mind. And I like that."

Having run out of words, Sandy looked suddenly uncomfortable behind the microphone, and she sort of shrugged as she turned to make her way down the short flight of stairs leading from the pulpit.

Brandon smiled. He didn't think that anyone had noticed him standing there, and that fact made the tribute to his son all the more poignant. Suddenly, it didn't matter so much that they talked about Scott in the past tense; it didn't matter that they had given up. What did matter was that they had gotten to know the same Scott that he'd known for sixteen years, and they had paid tribute to him as the person he really was.

A new warmth filled the void in his soul as he pulled on his gloves in preparation to leave, but before he could take a step, he felt a hand on his arm. He turned to see a couple in their sixties standing so closely together that they were virtually one. Brandon knew who they were before they said a word. The sadness in their eyes told him.

"Are you Mr. O'Toole?" the man asked.

Brandon nodded. "Yes, sir, I am."

"I'm Arthur Jamieson. This is my wife, Annie. We're Cody Jamieson's parents."

Brandon pulled the glove off his right hand and greeted them both with a blank expression. He wanted to hate these people for what their son had done. He wanted to lash out at them, but seeing their agony swept those feelings away. There was a limit to how much people could hurt, and this couple was already there.

"We're so sorry," Annie Jamieson said. "There's no excuse for Cody taking the plane up in that weather. I can't imagine what you must think of him."

Brandon opened his mouth to speak, but no words would come.

"He's never done anything like this before," Arthur said. "He's always been a good boy. A responsible boy." He paused while he gathered himself. "I don't . . . I can't . . ." The old man's voice cracked and he hugged his wife closer to him.

"We're just so *sorry*," Annie said again.

"Well, I'm sorry, too," Brandon whispered. For the terrible thoughts he'd harbored for their son, for the way he'd never even thought to worry for him.

It all transpired behind the backs of the congregation, unnoticed but to a few. As Brandon and the Jamiesons stood there in silence, unsure what to say, the moment grew uncomfortable.

"We didn't mean to interrupt," Annie said, finally. "We just didn't want you to leave before we told you how sorry we are."

This time, Brandon's wan smile came easily. "I'm not going anywhere," he said. He nodded toward a nearly empty pew on the left-hand side. "There's a spot free over there. I'd be honored if you would kneel with me and pray."

DAY FOUR

18

HIS DAD WOULD BE WORRIED SICK. The thought troubled and comforted him at the same time. At a gut level, it was kind of nice to think that somebody was filling God's party line with prayers. You never knew if things like that helped, but five'll get you ten that they never did any harm.

Wading through the snow on this endless march toward who knew where, Scott imagined the look in his father's eyes as he got word of his fate, and his throat thickened. How could he have been such a shit? He hated himself for the countless times he'd used the Battle for Scott to his own benefit.

Dad liked to think of himself as an aloof, independent leader, but Scott knew that the real Brandon O'Toole was like a rudderless ship in a storm. If Scott died, the old man would just come apart. And for that, Scott felt profoundly sorry.

"I'm going to make it," he told the snow. "And I'm going to be better. I swear it."

He peeled back the soft elastic wristband on his glove and fumbled for the button to illuminate his watch. Two in the morning. How did that happen? Last time he'd checked—just a few minutes ago, he thought—it was just a few minutes after midnight. The backlit display left a green ghost on his retina after his wrist turned black again.

He wondered when the fog had rolled in, until he saw snowflakes impacting his coat sleeve. The fog was really a new storm, and now that he opened his ears, he could hear the steady hiss of flakes falling through the trees. Christ, it was already knee-deep—hip-deep in some places. How long could it possibly keep up like this?

The compass! Jesus, he hadn't checked it since . . . since the last time he checked his watch. Two hours! Holy shit, two hours was a lifetime! Where had the time gone? He must have fallen asleep while walking. Was that even possible? His brain had that dull, stupid feeling that he sometimes got after a long period of intense study for a test, or when he was trying to write a song. He felt like he wasn't a part of this world anymore.

Think, Scott, think. How much trouble was he really in?

Then he remembered. Once he'd located the river, he'd put the map away. As long as the river remained on his left, then he really couldn't go far wrong. Now that he listened carefully to the night, he could hear the water clearly. Perhaps he'd always heard it but just forgot that he was listening for it. It was the exhaustion. Had to be.

Still, he wanted to see it, just to be sure. He turned and followed the sound. Sure enough, there it was, just barely visible as a shiny black line snaking through the white cut of the riverbed. Everything would be okay.

He didn't even want to think about the two hours. He supposed that's what happened when you didn't eat for three days.

Or, maybe he was freezing to death. Goddamn that Sven. Scott kept hearing that heavily accented voice telling him about the slow death that was hypothermia: the slurred speech; the diminished mental capacity; the overpowering need to sleep. Scott remembered thinking that he must have been hypothermic nearly every night when he went to Boy Scout camp, way back when. And he was certainly hypothermic on New Year's Eve a few years ago, when his dad lost track of the time and let him stay up till four in the morning. Christ, by those symptoms, Scott had been hypothermic more times than he could count.

How were you supposed to tell the difference? He'd asked that question of Sven, who'd responded with one of his glares and said, "You judge by your surroundings. If you find yourself without shelter in the middle of winter, and you feel like you did on New Year's Eve, then you probably are in trouble."

Big help.

Scott started to laugh. Something about the absurdity of it all just struck him as funny, and as the chuckle boiled up from his gut to become a real, hearty case of the giggles, it occurred to him that laughter in the face of this kind of danger had to be yet another sign of his impending death. And that made it funnier still.

"Well, screw it," he told the night. One thing was by-God certain. Come tomorrow morning, he'd either be alive or dead.

Sometimes death is a relief to the barely living, he heard Sven say in his memory.

"And screw you, too."

The river jogged sharply to the east, a landmark obvious enough to warrant a check of the map. A glance at his watch showed him that it was 4:12 A.M. That couldn't be right. In just over thirteen hours, he'd walked only six inches on the map and he still had four inches to go.

God, he thought, *I'll never make it.*

He checked again, but nothing changed. Sighing deeply, he rested his head against a tree for just a few seconds, then snapped himself back to attention and stood. He could sleep later, for as long as he wanted to.

Maybe forever.

ISAAC DEHAVEN STOOD IN THE BACKYARD, drinking in the beauty of it all. There was no silence like the silence of a nighttime snowfall. A gorgeous spot 365 days and nights a year, the Flintlock Ranch had special charm in the winter. Perhaps it was merely the contrast between light and dark, cold and warm. He would miss it.

The terseness of last night's message weighed heavily on him. *You are in danger.* Sam didn't send such messages lightly. Damn. *Cover blown.* So, the time had come for him to leave. Moving constantly had once been such a routine part of his life that it never bothered him. Now it did.

In three days, he'd be gone. With one thing left to do, he had to stick around that long, but then it was good-bye, Utah. Three days.

Cover blown.

Well, what the hell? The storm would make it tough on everybody. As long as the snow continued to fall, and the winds continued to whip the way they were, only a fool would venture out. Nights like this had death written all over them.

In this case, they were deadlier for the hunter than they were for the hunted.

Tonight, he could afford to sleep. And most likely tomorrow. After that, sleep would be a risk; but at least his job would be done.

THE SNOW STOPPED FALLING around six. Scott didn't realize it until he stepped into a clearing and looked at the sky. He gasped at the beauty of it. Millions of stars—literally, millions of them—studded the sky in clusters and bands so dense that he wondered for a moment if they might be clouds. He'd never seen such a thing. At home, there was too much ambient light rising from the streetlights and post lights of suburbia. For the longest time, he just stood there, staring up into forever, understanding for the first time why so many pages of classical poetry were dedicated to the moon and the stars.

Soon, as the blackness lightened, turning neon pink in the east, he could feel the temperature rise, if only slightly. Under his cap, his ears and his cheeks felt brittle with the cold; his chin and his upper lip felt chapped.

Overnight, his gait had slowed to a step per second, about the most he could muster. Still, he pushed himself. To stop was to die. He made a deal with himself. All he had to do was walk on for ten more minutes. Just ten. Then, he'd renew the deal for ten more. By the time he did that just six times, he'd killed another whole hour.

One foot after the other. Just keep your head down and walk. But each step, it seemed, yielded less distance. His legs and his back screamed from the effort of every step, and below the smooth surface, rocks and sticks and saplings continually lassoed his feet, causing him to fall, always face-first, and his hands never seemed to be fast enough to catch himself effectively. He imagined that he had more snow stuffed down the front of his ski jacket than lay on the entire mountainside, but to clean it out would mean taking his gloves off for the zipper, and then putting them back on when he was done. To tell the God's honest truth, he wasn't sure he had that much energy.

By 6:30, it was snowing again, harder than before.

The riverbed had begun dropping away a long time ago, as the terrain changed from mostly downhill to mostly up. If he listened carefully, he could just hear its rushing sound, but the last time he wandered toward the noise to take a peek, he found a fifty-foot sheer cliff and he'd steered clear of it ever since.

It was nearly eight o'clock when Scott paused at the base of a long hill, looking up and wondering how he was possibly going to make it through this. "Ten minutes at a time," he told himself aloud, but his voice sounded breathy and weak, barely audible. "One step at a time."

But there'd been so many steps. Hundreds and hundreds of them. Thousands. And now, this hill rose above him for what seemed to be forever, a constant twenty-degree slope without relief.

Put your head down and walk. One step at a time. Left foot, right foot. Left foot, right foot. Good leg, bad leg. On and on forever till you die.

Sixty seconds yielded maybe twenty steps, and each one of them took the same effort as a mile at the school track. Two minutes. Three minutes. He looked behind, then looked ahead and saw that he'd barely moved.

"Please," he gasped. "The night was supposed to be the hard part. Don't take it away from me now. Just get me to the top of this hill. Just this one, and then I'll take care of the rest. Please. I need Your help."

19

FIVE MINUTES BECAME TEN, and Scott passed the halfway mark on the hill. *You gotta keep going now. It's longer to go back than to go ahead.* Yeah, but downhill was a helluva lot easier. What he wanted to do—what he *needed* to do—was sit down and rest. Maybe take a little nap. He owed himself a little rest. He could afford that much.

After the crest of the hill.

Fifteen minutes. One foot was barely clearing the other now, and he'd fallen three more times, opening a cut on his forehead. He didn't care anymore. At least the blood was warm. Until it froze.

Can't do this.

Gotta do this. He chose to look only behind him this time, to see just where he'd been, and the view of the forward progress lightened his heart, even as it pounded behind his breastbone. His lungs hurt. His head hurt. And his legs. Oh, God, his legs.

His stomach churned, too, and inexplicably, he found himself thinking of bacon. Honest to God, he swore he could smell it.

How weird was that? He didn't even *like* bacon that much. Not that he wouldn't eat a dog shit sandwich right about now if someone offered it.

But why fantasize about bacon? Why not french fries? Or a cheeseburger. McDonald's cheeseburger. Better yet, the Number Two Value Meal: two cheeseburgers with fries and a drink. Supersized. Keep your flame-broiled, have-it-your-way square hamburger patty crap and let him have the real thing. The original.

And a glass of orange juice, freshly squeezed with lots of pulp.

Left foot, right foot. Good leg, bad leg . . .

As he climbed, he kept his head down, watching his shins dig their trenches through the powder. He found his mind wandering back to a soccer game from eighth grade. He saw himself up against some tall Mexican kid who had the skills of a pro, but only three-quarters of Scott's speed. It was late in the fourth quarter, and the Mexican was making his break for the tying goal. The kid had blistered the halfbacks, and all that remained between him and the score was Ryan in the goal box and Scott, who came out of nowhere to level him. *Bam!* The kid hit the ground like a crash-test dummy. The ref gave Scott a yellow card for rough play, but it didn't matter. The ball stayed out of the box and Smurf was a hero to his teammates.

He reached the top. He couldn't believe it. He whirled to look behind him, and sure enough, there was the endless, unbroken path of his footsteps through the woods, zigging and zagging around trees and rocks. And if he focused really hard, he imagined that he could see his tracks for another half-mile beyond the base of the hill.

"Yes!" he cheered, but it came out as a raspy croak. He looked toward the sky and nodded his thanks. Only now it was time to cut another deal, maybe this time for thirty minutes instead of ten.

Ahead of him lay the down slope, equally long, but a little steeper, and not nearly as heavily treed. Beyond that, the ground flattened out and he could see the river again. He stood there at the crest of the hill for a long time, wobbling on unsteady legs as he willed himself to move on. *Come on, downhill is easier than up. Ten more minutes. That's it, just ten more minutes . . .*

But his legs wouldn't work. Suddenly, Scott knew that if he tried to take another step—if he so much as lifted one leg—the other would crumble under him. He needed to rest. God, he needed to sleep. Just a few minutes, no more. Just a ten-minute nap, and he'd be up again and refreshed. He knew he would.

You sleep, you die.

Sven's voice returned, but for the first time, Scott truly didn't care. *Fine, then, I'll die. Take me. I'm ready.*

And his knees sagged. He was done. This was his spot. This was where they'd find him, whether the searchers were human or animal. This was it, atop the last hill, at the end of the walk that killed him.

It felt good, too, propped up there against a tree, his knees drawn up nearly to his chest. If only there were a way to lie down without jamming snow into his frozen face, he swore that he could fade away and sleep forever. This dying stuff wasn't all that difficult, after all.

Bacon.

There it was again, stronger than ever. He could almost taste it. Unsure whether he'd been in his spot for a minute or an hour, Scott forced his eyes open just a crack. Something out there wasn't right. Down low like this, the world looked different, a tableau of random vertical slashes that were the trunks of towering pines, but without the visual clutter of the low-hanging branches, which were mostly at head height or above. The tree trunks stood like silent sentries, guarding the patch of ground that had been theirs for centuries.

What was that at the bottom? A line of uniformly stubby trees crossed his vision horizontally, way at the bottom of the slope, where they just almost couldn't be seen. Scott shielded his eyes and squinted even harder. What the hell was he looking at?

Jesus, it's a fence.

Of course! A fence! A man-made fence!

He'd made it. Yes! By God, he'd actually made it!

His wind-chapped lips broke and bled as they pulled back into a smile. He wasn't going to die here, after all.

Rolling to all fours, he used his tree for support as he rose to his knees, and then willed his legs to take his weight. They felt dead, as if they belonged to someone else. They were totally spent.

"This is bullshit," he told himself, and he clawed his way up the trunk until his feet were flat against the slope and his knees were locked.

Bacon. God, they're having breakfast!

The thought of food and a warm blanket drove him forward, caroming from one tree to the next as he fought to control his downhill speed. Left foot, right foot. Good leg, bad leg. He didn't care any-more. In five minutes, maybe ten, he'd be done. He'd have food in his belly, and he'd be sound asleep.

Where's the fence?

Suddenly, it was gone. How could that be? Scott stopped himself against a tree and jammed his eyes shut. He shook his head and reopened them, but still it was gone. A mirage? *Please, oh, please . . .*

He pressed on, and a few seconds later, there it was again, hiding, it turned out, behind those low-hanging branches.

He could see the house now. It was a big sprawling thing, leaking a wispy trail of smoke from its chimney, rising only a few feet before the wind wrestled it back to the ground.

Come on, God. Ten more minutes. Really. This time for real. Just ten more minutes.

Left foot, right foot. If he fell, he flat-out didn't know whether he'd be able to pick himself up.

Good leg, bad leg.

ISAAC PULLED THE PAN OFF the burner and set it aside. In the forty-odd years that he'd occupied the planet, he'd yet to stumble upon the right recipe for bacon. There was a very fine line between crispy and burnt that he'd never quite been able to nail down. The bacon and eggs were a treat for himself. His life in the near future would be a succession of hotels and flophouses, so today would be his day of self-indulgence.

Setting the pan on the counter, he reached for the tongs and he froze. Something moved out on the hill.

Isaac darted to the window. As he squinted through the snowfall, his right hand instinctively moved to his holster. This wasn't possible, was it? They wouldn't possibly move against him in this kind of weather. What would be the point? Isaac would have all the advantage.

There it was again, bouncing from tree to tree on the slope near-est the river. Only one, but where there was one, there was always another. This bozo was hardly the professional that he'd been expect-ing. He wandered like he was drunk, like he didn't give a damn who saw him.

Moving quickly now, Isaac holstered his pistol and grabbed his MP5 on the way out the door. Standing in the open, in the snow, he shouldered the weapon and peered through the scope.

What he saw surprised the hell out of him.

THANK GOD SOMEBODY WAS THERE. Scott saw a man standing in his snowy yard, his stance a little awkward, as if he were holding something on his shoulder.

Scott tried waving, but his arms were too heavy.

"Help!" he shouted, but the vocal cords didn't work either. "Please help me!"

The man was waving, too, but it wasn't a gesture of friendship as much as it seemed to be a gesture of urgency. He seemed to be yelling, but Scott couldn't decipher the words.

Scott smiled and tasted blood. He'd made it. Finally, the nightmare had ended. He'd be warm again, with food in his belly—

Was that man holding a gun?

He saw the muzzle flash and the puff of smoke. He actually had time to understand that he was dead before the bullet arrived.

THE RIFLE'S SUPPRESSED REPORT barely made it past the muzzle before it was lost to the wind. When the boy fell, Isaac couldn't believe it. It was supposed to be a warning shot, for God's sake, just close enough to get his attention.

Lowering the rifle, Isaac scanned the hillside for signs of the boy, but he was gone.

How could that be?

He stood there, riveted in place as he tried to put it together. When he raised the scope back to his eye, he clearly saw the stripe his bullet had cut in the bark of the nearby tree.

He couldn't possibly have hit him, so where did he go?

Then he understood. "Oh, shit."

FOR AN INSTANT, Scott thought that he was flying. It was a wonderful feeling of weightlessness, and he wondered if this was what it meant to die.

Then he hit the ground, his shoulder first, triggering a flailing, ass–over–tea kettle tumble that never seemed to end. It was a nightmare of impacts; head, back, knees, shoulders. Trees and sky became snow and then trees and sky again as he slid and tumbled out of control down the river side of the embankment.

When he finally hit the water, he landed back first, and he was instantly immersed. The pain of the frigid water was excruciating; he might as well have landed in boiling oil. He tried to scream, but his mouth filled with water. It raced up his nose and down his throat, and when he tried to gag, he only brought in more.

Struggling to find the surface, he kicked hard and the current coughed him up. He saw a brief flash of sky before he saw nothing more at all.

20

Somewhere in the darkness, in the far reaches of Scott's mind, a voice prattled on about something, but he couldn't quite make out what it was. A news report, maybe? The noise sounded as if it were coming from the end of a galvanized tunnel. His awareness of his pain blossomed more quickly than that of his surroundings. Everything hurt—his back, his neck, his arms and legs. *Everything*. But his stomach especially. Even through the fog, he recognized the need to eat.

His eyelids resisted his efforts to open them.

Finally, his left eye cooperated. He lay on his back in the middle of a large room, and his vision sparkled a bit on the periphery. The light in the room danced, as if from a fire. He was on somebody's sofa, buried under a thick layer of blankets. Beyond the lumps that were his feet, a fire blazed in a stone fireplace. That noise he'd heard was someone talking about the weather.

He dared move only his head, trying to figure out where he was. A living room, he supposed, rustic and a little worn down.

"So, you're alive!" boomed a voice from behind. A man stepped into his field of vision. "I was wondering there for a while."

Scott cleared his throat. "Who are you?" It was like licking sandpaper.

"You first," the man said. As his host sat on the coffee table opposite the sofa, Scott couldn't help but notice the pistol on his hip.

"You shot me," Scott said.

"Evidence to the contrary notwithstanding, eh?" The man laughed, but Scott didn't get the joke. "Who are you, son? And why are you wandering around in this weather? With blue hair."

Scott shifted his position under the blankets and felt skin against skin. He had no shirt on. As if to verify it, he pulled his arm from under the blanket and looked at it. He was naked. He shot a look to the man with the gun.

"Your clothes are drying in the other room," Isaac explained, reading the look for what it was. "I went fishing in the river and reeled in a blue teenfish." He laughed again.

Scott rattled his head, hoping to shake something into place that would make sense. Oh, yeah, the fall. The water. "You rescued me?" he croaked.

Isaac half-shrugged. "Rescue is too heroic. I sorta just snagged you as you floated by."

"Thanks." Scott buried his arm under the covers again and drew the blankets tight. He didn't know that he'd ever be warm again.

"You were going to tell me your name," Isaac prodded.

"Scott O'Toole."

The man cocked his head. "Scott O'Toole," he mused aloud. "Why does that name ring such a—" Then he got it. "Holy shit, boy, what are you doing all the way over here?"

Scott hated being this addled. Nothing this guy said made sense.

"You're one of the plane crash kids, right?"

Scott nodded.

"Well, criminy Jesus, you're supposed to be forty, fifty miles from here."

The way he said it, Scott wondered if he was supposed to apologize. "Who are you?"

"Isaac DeHaven." Isaac offered his hand, and Scott again pulled his arm from its cocoon to shake it. "How long have you been walking?"

Scott shook his head. "I don't know. I started at about three in the afternoon."

Isaac did the math. "Jesus. How far, do you know?"

"I figured it to be about ten miles. This place was the only build-ing on the map."

"What map?"

"In my pocket. Wherever my pocket is."

Isaac thought about this. "The news said there's two of you."

Scott looked away. "Not anymore." The words sounded awful, so permanent. "Do you have anything to eat?"

"What does 'not anymore' mean?"

"It means he's . . . not alive anymore." Scott didn't want those images to return.

"He's dead, then," Isaac said. "Is that what you're telling me?" The thought seemed to please him somehow.

Scott nodded. "Killed in the crash." He thought about mention-ing the wolves but decided not to.

"Too bad." The words were meant to be sympathetic, but the tone didn't quite sell them. Isaac stood abruptly and headed off, out of Scott's field of vision. "You must be starving. When was the last time you ate?"

Scott had to think about that one. As he struggled to a sitting position, he noted that Isaac was heading toward a kitchen. "Tuesday morning, I guess."

That stopped his host cold in his tracks.

"What?" Scott asked.

"This is Friday," Isaac said. Then, as if to drive the point home, "Late Friday."

Jesus. No wonder he was hungry.

"Anything in particular you'd like?"

Now there was a good question. "Got any Froot Loops?"

Isaac laughed. "No, I'm afraid not."

"How about bacon?" Scott asked, remembering. "Bacon and eggs?"

Isaac smiled. "How do you like them?"

ISAAC'S CLOTHES NEARLY FIT SCOTT. A little baggy, especially across the shoulders and chest, but serviceable. It was slow-going at first, weakness and nausea threatening each step. His muscles and joints all felt as if they'd been manufactured from melted glass.

Despite the lure of the sofa, Scott sat at the table in the kitchen to eat.

"How many eggs can you handle?" Isaac asked.

Scott answered without thinking. "Four." He quickly caught himself and added, "Please."

Isaac smiled. "How about I start you with one and we'll work up from there." He served the egg fried, over easy with two strips of bacon and a piece of toast.

In less than a minute, it was all gone and Scott handed over his plate for more. Nothing had ever tasted so good. A second egg followed, with more toast. God, it was wonderful. Isaac returned to the stove for one more, and just like that, it wasn't so wonderful anymore. In fact, it was an emergency. Scott barely made it to the sink in time to upchuck all of it. The heaving brought tears to his eyes, and the crushing disappointment made them real. When he was empty again, he felt a hand on his back, rubbing him gently between his shoulder blades.

"Too much too fast," Isaac said gently, handing him a towel.

Scott wiped his face. "But I'm *hungry.*" His legs felt wobbly.

Isaac walked with him back to his chair at the table. "This time, we'll start with some toast. Your stomach's shrunk."

It wasn't the meal he'd fantasized about, not by a long shot. But it stayed down. After four slices, he felt full. "So, now I'm a supermodel," Scott quipped. "Thank you."

Isaac smiled. "You're welcome." He gathered up the boy's plate and carried it to the sink.

"You seem like a nice guy," Scott said. "So, why did you shoot at me?"

Isaac continued to clean as he replied, "That's a long story. I'm just glad I didn't hit you."

"Were you trying to?"

Isaac took a deep breath, as if he were considering an answer, then said, "Your mother's famous, isn't she?"

Scott snorted out a chuckle. "She thinks she is. She wants to be."

"You don't approve?"

"I don't *care.* There's a difference."

Isaac acknowledged the point with an eyebrow. "Sounds like home is not the happiest place in the world."

Scott regarded his host for a long moment. Lean and clean-shaven, he had a powerful look about him, despite his unremarkable size. His hair—a military buzz cut—had a certain home-inflicted quality to it. The eyes were hard to miss, though: dark brown laser beams.

"How come you won't answer me about the shooting?" Scott pressed.

Isaac answered slowly. "Let's just say that I don't like visitors all that much."

"So, you shoot them?"

Something in Scott's expression made Isaac laugh. "Well, no, not always."

"How come you're carrying a gun now?"

"Does it make you nervous?"

Man, you'd think it would, wouldn't you? But something about Isaac's demeanor actually put Scott at ease. "More curious than nervous," he said.

Isaac finished at the sink and helped himself to the chair opposite the boy at the table. "Well, curiosity can be a dangerous thing, Scott. If I were you, I'd keep that in mind." The words sounded more like advice than a threat. "I carry the gun because I need to. Now, tell me about your mother. On the news, I keep hearing references to her being a famous author."

Scott dismissed the notion with a one-shouldered shrug. "She's a psychologist who writes books on how people should live their lives."

"And you don't like that."

"I told you, I don't care."

Isaac just waited for the rest.

"Okay, I think you should learn to live your own life before you start telling other people how to live theirs."

"She doesn't do that?"

Scott took a deep breath. "You know what? I'm tired. I don't want to talk about this."

Isaac held up his hands in surrender. "Okay, then we won't talk about it."

"Good. Thank you." Nobody moved for a long moment. "How can I get word to my dad that I'm okay?"

Isaac stood and led the way back to the living room. "Well, now, that's something of a dilemma."

"Can't we just make a phone call?"

Isaac laughed. "Maybe you need to step outside and take another look where you are. I don't have a phone. No lines run out this far."

"You've got electricity," Scott observed. "Don't they run together?"

"I've got electricity because I've got a bank of batteries out there in the shed and a windmill to recharge them. I've got running water because another windmill keeps the storage tanks full. Those flames you see on the stove don't run from underground pipes, they run from a big tank out back. This is the country, my friend." He laughed again. "In fact, you don't get a whole hell of a lot more country than we are right now."

"So, how do I tell him? I need to tell people about Cody, too."

"I guess when the storm settles down, and the roads get cleared, I can take you to a phone."

Scott thought about that. He hated like hell to think of his dad enduring any more than he had to. "I heard you talking to some-body," Scott said.

Isaac's head came around at that one. "How's that?"

"Before I completely woke up. I heard you talking to somebody. I don't remember what it was about, but I remember it just sounded like a conversation."

Busted. "That was a radio," Isaac said, finally. "Short wave. Sometimes, when I get a little loopy from the quiet, I turn it on to chat." Isaac sat in a chair near the fire and gestured to the sofa for Scott.

"Well, why can't we put out a message on the radio that I'm okay?"

Isaac sighed. He really didn't want to get into this. "You are a nosy son of a bitch, aren't you?" he said, shaking his head. He ges-tured to the sofa again. "Please, take a seat."

Scott sat.

Isaac took a long moment to collect his thoughts, then rubbed his face vigorously before beginning. "You put me in a spot."

Scott just waited for him to get to it.

"Okay, here it is. I'll tell you, and then we'll deal with what to do about it later, okay?"

The boy nodded, but something in the tone put him on edge.

"Do you know what the witness protection program is?"

The gasp escaped Scott's throat before he could stop it.

Isaac saw the recognition and nodded. "Well, there you go. A few years ago, I testified in court against some really bad people who did really bad things. I broke confidences, I tape-recorded conversations, and then I sent them to prison for the rest of their lives, plus a good chunk more." He paused for a moment, then stood. "Do you want some whiskey?"

Now *there* was a question he'd never been asked before. "Sure." Scott shrugged. "Why not?"

Isaac continued to speak as he walked to the kitchen and poured two shots of Jack Daniel's, one three times larger than the other. "These bad guys—"

"What are their names?" Scott interrupted.

"You gonna talk or you gonna listen?"

Scott sank back into the cushions.

"I'm not gonna tell you their names, and I'm not gonna tell you what they did, because that's none of your concern. All you need to know is that they and their friends promised to kill me. The operative word there is *promised.*" He paused to let the concept sink in as he brought the drinks back to the living room. "There's an open-ended contract on my head. Five hundred thousand dollars to the man who does me in."

Scott's jaw dropped.

Isaac handed him the glass. "And before you get any ideas, trust me. These are not people you want to be doing business with."

Scott vehemently shook his head. "God, no. I'd never even think—"

Isaac raised his glass. "To life." He fired half of it down in one gulp.

Scott brought the glass to his lips, sniffed it.

"Tell me this isn't your first drink," Isaac said.

Scott sort of shrugged, inexplicably embarrassed. "Well, I've had beers."

"Trust me, kid, there's only one way to do it. Fire it on back and don't let the sofa buck you off."

The boy looked at the drink for a second or two, then downed it in a single gulp. It was like drinking burning razor blades. Took his breath away.

Isaac laughed, toasted him again. "Welcome to manhood, kid." The fact that Scott couldn't make his voice work triggered another laugh. "Anyway, in return for my testimony, your parents' tax dollars gave me a new name and a nifty place to live. You're not gonna puke again, are you?"

The question caught Scott off guard. No, he wasn't going to puke, but he sure did feel warm all of a sudden. "I'm fine. What does that have to do with me getting word to my dad?"

"Press coverage. I can't afford it."

"I won't tell where I am, just that I'm safe."

"Can't afford it. This is my life, kid. I value it highly."

"So, what happens?" Scott asked. "You're just gonna keep me here forever?"

Isaac issued a giant sigh. "Well, I tell you what. That would have been a hell of a lot tougher choice a week ago than it is right now."

Scott cocked his head.

"A couple of days ago, I got word that the bad guys know where I am. My cover, as they say, is blown, which means that I've got to pull up stakes when the storm stops. I figure I can drop you someplace, and by the time you make the right phone calls, I'll be long gone."

"How did your cover get blown?"

Isaac sighed, wishing that he'd never opened Pandora's box. "I went someplace I shouldn't have gone. It was stupid, but there you go."

"Where'd you go?"

"None of your business."

Scott struggled to wrap his mind around it. It was all pretty cool when you got right down to it. "So, you, like, went to the store or something, and somebody saw you?"

Isaac's body language testified that he was ready to move on. "Something like that, yes."

"Did you know it was stupid at the time?"

"Let it go," Isaac snapped.

Scott tried to piece the puzzle together. "So, these bad guys. They know that you're here."

"That's what they tell me."

"Which means that they'll be hunting for you."

"So it seems."

"Which explains why you took a shot at me. You thought I was them."

"Exactly."

Scott paused again, waiting for the computer in his brain to plow through it all. "So, you really *were* trying to kill me?"

Isaac leaned in close. "If I'd wanted you dead, you wouldn't be here. Trust me. Sniping was one of my greatest skills before I started to squeal on people for a living. I just wanted you to know that you were in the wrong place. Then you panicked and went into the water, and I went fishing."

More thought. "So, how do you know the bad guys aren't out there right now? I mean, shouldn't you be watching for them?"

"It's a five-hundred-*thousand*-dollar contract, not five million. I don't worry a lot about them making an appearance in this weather. Not at night, anyway."

Scott let it go, his mind wandering to images of him getting caught in somebody's crossfire.

"Okay, Scott O'Toole," Isaac said, startling him. "I've come clean, so now it's your turn. Tell me about your family."

"Why?"

Isaac shrugged. "Think of it as a sign of good faith. You get to know me, so I get to know you. I assume that your parents are divorced."

Scott nodded. How did he know that?

"And that you live with your father, not your mother."

"How do you know?"

"Because of what you told me about your mother, and the fact that you only cared about getting word to your father that you're alive. No concern about telling Mom anything. I presume that you and she don't get along."

"Now *there's* an understatement," Scott snorted.

"So, why did they divorce?"

"I guess they stopped loving each other."

"They told you that?"

"Actually, I caught my mom fucking a grad student when I was ten."

Isaac nearly choked on his Jack Daniel's. "Excuse me?"

It was Scott's turn to laugh. "What can I say? Back in elementary school, we used to get off at, like, one in the afternoon on Mondays, and I guess she forgot about it. I came home and there they were." He hadn't thought about this in years. How could that be? How could he *not* have thought about it, yet have it all be so clear in his memory? He remembered the rhythmic thumping and his mother yelling, "Oh, Jesus, oh, Jesus!" And then he remembered walking into the bedroom.

"What did you do?" Isaac asked.

Scott threw off a shrug of indifference. "They saw me and they stopped." But the reality was far more complicated than that. Here in the cabin, staring at the fire, Scott saw himself jumping up on the bed, beating on the beard-and-sideburns geek with his fists while he scrambled to cover himself up. Scott had never been so angry, before or since.

"So, you told your old man and they got a divorce."

Scott shook his head. "No, I didn't. I never told him. Never. I was too ashamed."

"But he knows about it."

"Not from me, he doesn't."

"I don't believe you."

"Fine. Neither does she." How many times had she grilled him, over and over again? *You told him, didn't you?*

"Why would you keep a secret like that?"

"Because I told her I would."

Isaac didn't know quite what to make of that. "Why do you think she doesn't believe you?"

Scott genuinely didn't like this line of questioning, and he squirmed. "I don't know."

"Why do you *think?*" Isaac pressed. "You be the psychiatrist. Why wouldn't your mother believe you when you say you never told your father about her . . . about the incident?"

None of this was any of Isaac's business. Scott didn't like the way he was pushing and prodding to peek into areas of his private life. Still, it was an interesting question. Finally, he said, "I think it's because this way, she gets to blame me for everything." The room turned silent for a long time before Scott added, "Can we call it even now?"

21

BARRY WHITESTONE PICKED UP THE PHONE to call his wife. They hadn't spoken all day. Eagle Feather being the kind of community that it was, he'd grown accustomed to having lunch with her more days than not, and today, between the storm, the president, the death down at the motel and the search for the plane crash kids, he'd barely had time to think, let alone eat lunch.

He needed to talk to Janey, if only to touch base with the part of his life that was always happy. The Jamiesons had joined the O'Tooles here in town, and the whole thing was eating away at him. He'd seen plenty of grieving people in his time—parents, kids, brothers, sisters—but there was something about the intensity of Brandon O'Toole's angst in particular that resonated with Barry. Maybe it was the fact the Brandon's Scott and Barry's Tyler seemed cut so nearly from the same cloth. Maybe it was merely the man's limitless capacity for hope.

He'd just finished dialing the number when Secret Service Special Agent Ed Sanders appeared in his doorway, clearly anxious to speak.

Janey answered on the second ring. "Hello?"

"Hi, honey, it's me," Barry said, indicating with a finger for Sanders to wait a minute.

The agent walked into the office and helped himself to a seat.

Janey teased, "I'm sorry, do I know you?"

"Hang on a second." Whitestone covered the mouthpiece with his palm and said to Sanders, "Give me a minute, would you?"

"Take your time," Sanders said, but he didn't move.

Back to Janey. "It's been a wild day. I've got Secret Service crawling around like maggots on a dead skunk."

"Oh, now isn't *that* a pleasant image," Janey said.

Whitestone glared at Sanders, whose face never moved from its humorless Secret Service scowl. "Never seen such an obnoxious group in my life. They think they own the world."

"Their boss does own the world, doesn't he?"

"Nah, he just has the power to blow it up at his will."

"You've got an agent sitting there in your office, don't you?" Janey asked. Sometimes her powers of deduction amazed him.

"I sure do."

"Barry, you should be ashamed."

Whitestone laughed. "I was just calling to check in. Everybody okay?"

"Disturbing case, eh?"

"What are you talking about?"

"I don't hear from you all day, and then your first question is, 'everybody okay?'. That means something's eating at you."

"You're good," Barry said. "It's the missing kids from the airplane. I just hate to see the families suffering the way they are."

"So, you're still no closer?"

"It's like the earth swallowed them whole. Not a trace."

"That's such a shame," Janey said. "We're all just fine. Well, I'm fine. Tyler is anxiously awaiting the opportunity to tell you about his D in algebra." In the background, he heard his son shout, "Mom!"

"Terrific. Do we need to talk to his teacher?"

"You need to talk to the guy in your office, Chief Whitestone. Finish up there and come home."

Barry smiled. "Yes, dear. It'll be a while yet."

"I'll be here."

Whitestone hung up the phone and looked at Sanders. "It doesn't bother you to hear me call you a maggot?"

"You didn't call me a maggot," Sanders corrected. "You compared me to one. There's a difference." His face twitched, in what might have been a derisive smile. "Can we get down to business now? Eagle will be moving about town tomorrow."

"Eagle's the president, right?"

"That's right."

Barry scowled as he leaned back in his chair. "You know, I'm not sure that I know him well enough to do the interspecies thing."

"That's our code name for him," Sanders said.

Whitestone smiled. "Irony isn't your long suit, is it, Sanders?" The vacant expression he got in return said it all. "It's another name for humor. You might want to try it. I hear it's good for the skin."

"Can we get back to the issue, please?"

"Okay," Whitestone said. "Vulture will be moving about town tomorrow afternoon."

"Eagle."

Jesus, he bites every time, Barry thought.

"And I'm going to need every officer you've got to help with traffic and crowd control."

Barry shrugged. "Okay. Let's see the plans."

Agent Sanders unfolded a map of Eagle Feather and laid it out on the chief's desk. It was an amazingly detailed rendition of the town, clearly shot recently from overhead, presumably from a satellite. On it, he could see every building and every geographic highlight. He also saw that every street was marked with bold black lines.

"These are the crowd control checkpoints," Sanders explained, pointing to the black marks. There were over a dozen of them. "You'll need to assign at least two of your men at each of these locations," he explained. "And here, here and here . . ." he indicated points with his pen ". . . is where we expect the most pressure from the crowds, so I'll need at least three of your people at each of those."

Barry scowled again. "How many people do you think I have?"

"Thirty-two," Sanders said, nailing the number on the head. "And I'll need them all."

"You can't have them all," Barry countered.

"Actually, I can. Shall we turn this into a pissing contest?"

"Protecting Turtle Dove from harm is not my only priority."

"It's Eagle. And you have one potential murder investigation and the search for two dead boys. The rest is routine crap than can be put off until anytime."

Suddenly, it all came back to Whitestone just how much he disliked this man. "Seems to me you've been working pretty hard at doing my job."

"Well, someone has to." Sanders crossed his legs and folded his arms. "Does it really have to be a war, Chief? At the end of the day, we're going to work together, so why don't we make it as pleasant as possible?"

Whitestone wanted to tell the agent to jam it, if only to obliterate that smirk, but fact was, the man had a point. Like it or not, the president of the United States was destined to be a repeat customer for at least the next two winters, so now was as good a time as any to get used to the inconvenience.

Barry conceded the point with a perfunctory nod. "Okay," he said. "Tell me what you need."

TWENTY MINUTES LATER, they were done. The Secret Service would do most of the heavy lifting, with Barry's troops mostly providing the impression of force. Sanders made it clear that he wanted firearms to be out and visible, in hopes of countering the notion that such a little burg would be a pushover.

Whitestone summed it up: "So, the preparations kick off tomorrow, and Sparrow makes his big speech the day after."

"That's it," Sanders said, the tiny shadow of a smile invading his government-issue mask. "And it's Eagle."

"Oh, yeah." Whitestone grinned. "I keep forgetting that."

A knock drew both their heads around to Whitestone's office door, where James Alexander stood, waiting to be recognized.

"I'm not interrupting the part where you two shoot each other, am I?" James asked.

"We checked our weapons at the door," Sanders said.

Whitestone checked his watch. "James, enter this in the station log. At precisely 7:03 on Friday, February 27, Special Agent in Charge Ed Sanders made a lighthearted comment."

"For God's sake, don't write it down where my boss can find it,"

Sanders said. He stood. "I believe my work here is done. Good night, gentlemen."

James Alexander slid into Sanders's chair. "I thought I'd catch you up on Maurice Hertzberger," he said.

"Still dead?"

"Very. Turns out he died of a heart attack, just like we thought." Barry smiled.

"But I told the medical examiner to go over him one more time." The chief raised an eyebrow.

"The guy was a trucker," James went on. "Last seen at a truck stop outside of Grand Junction, where he apparently hooked up with an overly talkative stranger. They left together."

"A queer thing?"

James shook his head. "I don't think so. I think it was a favor thing. The stranger—who either called himself Teddy or Tommy, depending on who you talk to—needed a ride out this way, and he'd apparently been bumming off anyone who would listen to him. Maurice was the guy."

"What do we know about Tommy/Teddy?" Whitestone asked.

"Only a description. He's a heavyset guy—roly-poly, they said. Not obese like Hertzberger."

"Well, that certainly narrows it down."

"Let me finish." James referred to his notes, to make sure he got the details right. "A waitress at the truck stop—Patricia—noticed that Mr. Chubby had thin hands."

"Thin hands?"

"That's what she said. Apparently, he wore a bulky sweater trying to hide it, but Patricia told me that his wrists looked bony, like a guy who worked out a lot. His face was thin, too, she said, but he wore a beard to cover it up."

"And because of this, you've sent the coroner back to work on a case he wanted to close?"

James pondered the characterization for a moment, then nodded. "Look at it: you've got a guy in a disguise who hooks a ride on a snowy night—the very night that said driver wakes up dead. Sounds suspicious to me."

Whitestone considered that. "You know, James, sometimes I think you wish you were on a much larger police department."

"Nah, we've got cold and boredom. What more could a cop ask for? Anyway, I asked Doc Cooper if a heart attack could be stimulated with drugs, and he said yes. And then I asked him if he searched for any of those drugs in his blood and tissue tests and he said no."

"What about the moonshine?"

"He hasn't gotten to that yet. Not a detailed analysis, anyway."

Whitestone smiled. "With Doc Cooper, you never know. I wouldn't put it past him to start with a sip test. When do you expect results?"

"Couple of days."

"Good. So that means you have nothing better to do than help the Secret Service tomorrow."

James groaned. "Traffic detail?"

"For everybody."

"What about the kids—O'Toole and Jamieson? You going to call the parents?"

The mood in the room turned dark. "Not tonight. They don't need to know tonight."

DAY FIVE

22

SHERRY PEEKED THROUGH the curtain at the gathering crowd.

"It's huge!" Larry exclaimed, his voice an excited whisper. "My God, there must be nine hundred people out there. Standing room only."

"Half of them are media," Sherry observed.

"And this is a problem?"

"They're not here to listen to my seminar. They're here to watch me fall apart in front of everybody. They're waiting to see the lady with the reputation for strength come unzipped when the pressure is on."

"This lady would be you?" Larry asked, scowling. "Since when did you start referring to yourself in the third person?"

"Not now, okay, Larry?"

"It's an opportunity to shine like you've never shone before. If you step out there and give your message of strength and independence, in spite of the week's hardships, my God, you'll be the poster child for grieving mothers everywhere."

Sherry nodded because it was the easiest way to get him to shut up. He wasn't the one with it all on the line out there. He wasn't the one who'd absorb the criticism, the public battery. He got to sit safely backstage while she was forced into performing despite the aching in her heart.

To people on the outside—to her critics and her fans—it all

looked so easy, so glamorous. They had no idea how hard she'd worked and how much pain she'd endured to become who she was. And now the bill had come due. She'd talked the talk all the way to fame and fortune. Now it was time to walk the walk and the pathway seemed impossibly narrow. And unspeakably lonely.

Sherry was in a box. If she demurred from the stage in deference to Scotty's missing status, she'd be pilloried for violating her own message of strength through all adversity. On the other hand, if she went ahead on the adage that the show must always go on, then she'd be crucified as a coldhearted bitch. No matter what she did, the press and her fans would be watching every twitch of her mouth, every movement of her hands for some sign of her underlying motivations.

God forbid that she cry. To cry was to show weakness. According to her own teachings, tears were the one frailty that no woman could afford. Something had happened over the course of the past generation; the roles had reversed. Nowadays, it seemed that men of power sought out opportunities to shed tears in the media, to show their softer, more human side. When a presidential candidate showed up on an afternoon talk show, for example—an audience of women— you could pretty much guarantee that his eyes would well up during some reference to his family. The tears would show that he was strong enough to show his feelings. For a woman to do the same thing merely perpetuated the stereotype of the weepy female.

Such was the collateral damage of the women's movement, she supposed.

"Look at it this way," Larry said, confusing her silence for indecision. "Canceling the engagement won't do anything to find Scott sooner. Going ahead might even take your mind off your worry for a while."

"I'm not canceling anything, Larry," Sherry said, not bothering to look at him. Let them think what they like. She had a job to do. "Go on out there and introduce me."

BRANDON HAD CHOSEN a seat that no one else wanted, in the back of the room, his view of the stage partially obstructed by a pillar. He'd paid full price to be here, but he still felt oddly like an intruder. Truth be told, he'd heard so much about his ex-wife's seminars over the years that he was kind of curious what she had to say that was so inspiring. Maybe if he'd read one of her books he'd have a clearer understanding, but hell would freeze over first.

The public address system popped and Brandon looked up to see Larry Chinn on the stage. "Good morning, ladies and gentlemen," he said. He waited for people to settle into their chairs and quiet down. "Welcome to Your Hour of Towering Power, with Dr. Sherry Carrigan O'Toole." The room erupted in applause, which Larry accepted with a blush and a little wave of his hand. "I'm Larry Chinn, Dr. Sherry's personal assistant, and before we begin, I'd like to remind you of some of the ground rules, especially those of you in the back with the media."

As one, the room turned to gape at the television cameras, as if they'd somehow missed them before.

"Dr. Sherry doesn't like to be interrupted with flash photography, and we'll ask you to honor her wishes along those lines," Larry said. "I know many of you have questions regarding your personal circumstances, but I'm going to ask everyone to keep their questions to themselves until the very end of the presentation, at which point she'll answer as many of them as she can in the remaining time available. At the end of the presentation, Dr. Sherry will be signing books in the back of the room. Stand up and wave, Jocelyn."

A freckled twenty-something stood amid a forest of hardcover books and gave a shy little wave.

"That's Jocelyn," Larry explained. "She's our bookseller today, and she'll be happy to give you as many copies of Sherry's books as you can afford. I know some of you brought books from home to be signed, but because of the size of the crowd, I'm afraid we'll have to limit signatures to books that are purchased here today . . ."

Brandon rolled his eyes as he listened. Did people really value Sherry's handwriting so much that they would pay out real money for a copy of a book they already owned?

"With those logistics out of the way, now it's the moment you've been waiting for. Ladies and gentlemen, I give you Doctor Sherry Carrigan O'Toole!" He announced her name in a manner that reminded Brandon of boxing matches, the syllables overpronounced and building to a crescendo with, "O'Tooooole!"

Only Brandon remained in his seat as the crowd leaped to a standing ovation. Larry stepped to the side and ushered Sherry on with a grand sweep of his arm. When she appeared from the wings, she glided across the stage, accepted a kiss on the cheek from Larry, then stood there, her hands at her sides, absorbing the love of the crowd.

"Thank you," Sherry said. "Thank you very much." But the applause rolled on and on. "Please, be seated. Thank you so much."

Jesus, Brandon thought, *she's a rock star.*

The clapping and the whistles continued for the better part of a minute before it all finally died out and people settled back into their seats.

"You're very kind," Sherry said, her voice amplified by a tiny microphone clipped to the collar of her suit. Her smile looked tired, Brandon noticed, but it was beautiful, nonetheless. More beautiful than the day they'd met. "It's always wonderful to see smiling faces," she said. "But on a day like today, after a week like this one, it's particularly heartwarming to know that I have the love and support of so many wonderful people."

That triggered another standing O, which Sherry acknowledged with pained nods and blown kisses. When they were seated again, it was time for the show.

"Life doesn't always deal you the hand you want," she said. "I know this through my practice, of course, but this week has given me a close-up taste of my own medicine. . . ."

Up there, on the stage, Sherry was an entirely different person than the one Brandon knew. Up there, she was polished and professional. He understood, finally, how people could assume that she had all the answers. How was it, he wondered, that someone fraught with so many insecurities and so much anger could come off in a crowd as something so entirely different?

She was playing a role up there, just as assuredly as any actress in a play. On the stage, reading from the script that she had written herself, she was a sage giver of advice because that was what she had declared herself to be. Up there, she was cool and collected, every argument logically constructed, every controversial point delivered as the natural, inevitable conclusion to its antecedent.

"Cue up your television cameras, gentlemen," she said, twenty minutes into her talk. She'd already covered the way that men oppress women, touching on all the hot-button clichés of the male-female competition for space on the planet. "Make sure I'm in focus, because I'm coming to the part that you most like to misquote.

"According to the male population of this country, our role as women is to sacrifice. We're supposed to sacrifice our bodies to our husbands, our careers to our children and our equality to the world."

Some in the audience clapped, but others stirred uncomfortably.

"They don't just come out and say it, of course. It's not in-your-face quite like that, but it's part of the common Zeitgeist. Watch television on Mother's Day, and you'll get a glimpse of just how expendable we women really are. 'Good mothers' "—she said this with finger quotes in the air—"sacrifice themselves so that their families can thrive. I want to know why we can't thrive right along with them. Think of the maternal archetype in the war-torn ruins who gives up her share of meager rations so that her children might have more." She paused for a moment for the audience to see the image. "She essentially kills herself so that her kids can be left to fend for themselves. Why am I supposed to find this inspirational? Why can't we both have half-rations, go to bed a little hungry and then wake up alive together?"

The crowd chuckled.

"When was the last time you saw a scene where Daddy is cowering in the basement starving himself? Oh, that's right, he's out on the front lines, because he's *strong*. He's *smart*. He's the *warrior*. Have you ever heard such bullshit in all your lives?"

The chuckles turned to laughter.

"That's the technical, psycho-medical term for it, too. *Shitticus bullicus*, in Latin. I see it every day, people. Every single day. Only here in America, it's not about bread in wartime. It's about work in prosperous times. Mommy guilt. That hole we burn through our guts every single day when we swing through day care for our kids. You know what I'm talking about, don't you?"

Oh, yeah, they certainly did.

"Think about the abuse we have to endure from the old men on Capitol Hill and the windbags on AM radio. God forbid we remove unwanted pregnancies from our own wombs, but once we deliver the little darlings to the world, we're supposed to abdicate everything smart or exciting or challenging to the warrior spouse. And we're supposed to pretend that this makes sense."

Brandon noted how thoroughly she owned the crowd right now.

Sherry raised her voice louder and louder, just to be heard. "Do you remember what the technical, psych-med term is?"

The audience answered as one: "Bullshit."

"Ah, yes. *Shitticus bullicus.* Listen to me closely now, because I'm going to commit social heresy. Are you ready? Here it is: selflessness and self-actualization are mutually exclusive." That line seemed to settle the audience down some. "What's wrong? You seem shocked. There's nothing new here, men have known it for years. Self-actualizing is about achieving goals, and I can think of precious few intelligent human beings whose lifetime goals extend no further than fruit juice and Band-Aids.

"And before the hypersensitive among you start seizing on the floor, I am not bad-mouthing motherhood. Did you hear that? Motherhood is good. So is childhood. I'm just sick and tired of having to counsel brilliant, wealthy, successful women who continue to buy into the *shitticus bullicus.* Success is a cause for celebration; it should not require the use of antidepressants because darling little Charlie ate a nutritionally balanced meal in day care while his friends with stay-at-home moms got to rot their teeth on handmade peanut butter and jelly sandwiches. I mean, my God, can we possibly build a stronger emotional cage for ourselves?

"Soccer games and school Halloween parties are delightful diversions, folks, but so is closing a multimillion-dollar business deal. You can have both."

Brandon watched the performance, his belly boiling. Yes, you could indeed have both, he thought, but how the hell would she know? It all sounded so terribly *reasonable* when he heard it coming from the stage, so carefully balanced for dramatic effect, but the fact of the matter was, Sherry was never interested in both; she was interested in Sherry. When a publisher dangled a pile of money where she could see it, her beloved husband and son transformed into mere roadblocks.

Brandon stood and stepped out from behind his pillar, and just like that, Sherry broke character. Her recognition was instant, and her discomfort shined like a beacon from her face. The audience locked in on her line of sight and soon they were all staring at him. This was his chance. Finally, he had the opportunity to expose the *real* Sherry Carrigan O'Toole; not the one on the poster or the book jacket or the stage, but the vindictive bitch who not only wanted it all, but felt compelled to take it from him. He wanted to tell the entire room, the entire *world*, how her evil little prank had inflicted so much pain on so many people.

The moment grew uncomfortable as Sherry's eyes darted to the wings, bringing Larry just barely into view. The audience didn't know what to make of the silence, but the murmurs grew quickly as they waited for someone to say something.

And God, did he have something to say. Sherry valued her image and reputation above all other things in the world, and this was his one golden opportunity to hurt her more deeply than she ever dared imagine. But the words wouldn't come. What was the point? This was her stadium, not his. Finally, he looked down to the lady sitting next to him, a Gen-Xer with lips pursed so tightly that he could barely see them. "Excuse me," he said, and he made his way toward the exit.

BRANDON HAD COME TO THINK of the seat at the end of the bar as his own. Back home, his regular watering hole was the Conservatory Bar in the lobby of the Reston Hyatt, where Luis Martinez, champion of all bartenders, never let him down. Here at the Whiteout Saloon, Joe had become his best friend, knowing when to make small talk, and knowing when to just keep the liquor coming.

The place was crowded for eleven in the morning, a dozen people or so, mostly men or women who looked like men. Beer seemed to be the drink of choice, but Brandon was sticking with scotch for the time being. It got him where he wanted to be and kept him there longer.

On the television, speed skaters tore across the ice like greyhounds chasing a fox, their bodies low and sleek and looking positively ridiculous. For Brandon's money, skating only made sense if you had a stick in your hand, chasing a puck. The thought of a pickup hockey game sat very nicely with him, as a matter of fact. It'd feel good to slam a few people.

"Not giving up hope yet, are you, Mr. O'Toole?" Joe asked.

Brandon didn't realize he was so transparent. "I'm not giving up anything, Joe. I just had a bad morning."

Joe leaned in closer, his forearm resting on the bar. "For what it's worth, I think he's gonna end up being just fine."

Brandon felt himself moved by the tenderness of the old man's delivery. He toasted him. "From your lips to God's ear, buddy."

Something in Joe's face changed as he watched the back of the room. Brandon caught it in the mirror behind the bar: Barry Whitestone stood in the doorway, hands on his hips, clearly looking for somebody.

Brandon hissed, "Shit." As he spun in his seat to face the newcomer, he caught a peripheral glimpse of Joe making himself scarce. Brandon just glared at the chief, waiting to catch his eye. He didn't wave, he didn't call out. It made no sense to beckon trouble when trouble was already hunting you down.

Finally, their eyes met, and the rest of it was just a formality. Whitestone's scowl never so much as twitched as he waded through the tables to join Brandon. "We need to talk," he said when he arrived.

"You here to convince me my boy is dead, Chief?" He said it a little too loudly, making Whitestone uncomfortable.

"Why don't we talk someplace a little more private?"

Brandon twisted in his stool, surveying the room. He knew he'd had too many just from the way his head spun separately from his body. "For what you've got to say, this is as good a place as any. Probably a lot safer for you, too."

Whitestone didn't rise to the threat. "I wish there was another way, Brandon, I really do. I wish we had more time, and I wish the weather was better, and I wish we had more manpower. But wishing doesn't make anything so. I'm sorry."

"That's a lot of words for a simple message. You're turning your back on my son."

"I'm not turning my back. I'm facing realities."

Brandon scoffed. "I've seen the barricades going up on the corners, Chief. I know what your realities are. What's one little plane crash when the president of the United States has autographs to sign?"

"That's not fair," Whitestone said.

Brandon turned his back on him. "You don't want to get me started on fairness, Chief. Go on, you've done your job. Consider your news broken."

Whitestone didn't know what to say. Brandon sensed him standing there for a good half minute. Finally, the chief asked, "You want me to tell your wife, or are you going to take care of that?"

"Go on about your business, Chief," Brandon said again. "I'll take care of it all." He watched in the mirror as Whitestone made his way back to the door.

Joe gave Brandon ten minutes to compose himself before wandering back. "You're not giving up," he said. It was a statement, not a question.

"No."

"What are you going to do?"

"I don't know, but I'm not letting them do this."

Joe smiled. He reached across the bar and squeezed Brandon's hand. "Give 'em hell, kid."

23

BRANDON HEARD THE CAR slide to a halt outside the chalet, but opted against meeting them at the door. Sherry was on a tear, no doubt about that. He could hear her bitching all the way up the walk.

". . . could he do that to me? Why was he even there, Larry?" The door opened, and she stormed into the foyer. Brandon stood from his chair in front of the massive front window.

"I let myself in," he said.

Sherry nearly jumped out of her skin. Then, instantly, her wits were about her again. "You bastard!" she growled.

Larry moved past her like an overly protective house cat to confront the visitor. "How dare you break in here. Get out right now." He started to reach for Brandon's sleeve.

"Be careful, Larry. Think orthopedic surgery."

Larry froze. "Are you threatening me?"

"Grab my arm and find out."

Larry made a gallant effort at holding Brandon's gaze, but it just wasn't in him. "You have no right to be here."

Brandon felt himself blush. "I've got no fight with you, Larry," he said. It was as close to an apology as he intended to get. "In fact, I never thanked you for all your help the other night when I was trying to get through to Her Highness here." Turning his attention toward Sherry, he said, "I talked with Chief Whitestone a while ago. They're abandoning their search for Scott."

Sherry brought her hands to her mouth, her eyes wide. "Oh, my God. He's dead?" She sat heavily on the step leading from the foyer to the living room. Larry sat next to her, his arm around her shoulder.

Brandon held out his hand to her. "We need to talk," he said.

Sherry kept her hands at her mouth, her expression unchanged.

"Let's walk her into the living room," Brandon said to Larry, who continued to pull her close to his side.

"She needs a minute," Larry said.

"We all need a minute," Brandon said dismissively. "Everybody but Scott, who doesn't have a minute. Come on, Sherry, we need to talk."

"It's not my fault," Sherry whined through her fingers, her eyes focused someplace else. Then she looked at Brandon. "It's not my fault."

"Nothing ever is," Brandon said, and he gently but firmly grasped her arm. He was surprised to see that Larry was helping him.

"Let's go to the living room, Sherry," Larry coaxed, and she rose to her feet.

Her show of emotion caught Brandon off guard. It wasn't like her to waste tears on so small an audience. Any minute now, he expected a Scarlett O'Hara swoon. When they had her seated on the sofa, Brandon shifted his eyes to Larry, who instantly got the point.

"I'll make myself busy upstairs," he said.

Brandon thanked him with a nod, but Sherry reached out after him. "No, Larry, please stay with me."

"Not on your life. I don't belong within twenty miles of this conversation." He headed for the stairs.

When they were alone, Sherry asked, "Did they find the bodies?"

"He's not dead."

The statement confused her. "But you just said—"

"I said that they're giving up the search. They've written him off, but I think he's still alive. I'm sure of it, in fact. But if we let them presume otherwise, it becomes self-fulfilling."

"You're not making sense. If you know something they don't—"

"It's not like that," Brandon said. "I've told them, but they don't want to listen." He paused. He knew he was talking in circles. "It's a feeling, okay? If Scott were dead, I'd know it. It's hard to explain. But I want you to help me change their minds."

She waited for him to elaborate.

"I saw the crowd you drew today."

"You were a bastard to show up like that."

He let it go. "I saw all the press. You're a damn celebrity, Sherry. The press will listen to you. You can make these bozos stay with the search."

"Because you have a *feeling?* I'll look like an idiot."

"It's only been five days," Brandon argued. "He's trained for winter survival. He can make it this long."

"But they're the experts, Brandon. They know what—"

Brandon blew up. "They're going to let him die! Jesus, Sherry, he's our *son!*"

Sherry gave a bitter little laugh. "Oh, so now he's *our* son? I thought the whole world revolved around Team Bachelor."

Brandon felt like he'd been slapped. His face showed it.

Sherry couldn't believe she'd just said that. "I'm sorry, Brandon. I didn't mean that."

"The hell you didn't. My God, Sherry, you shut yourself out of his life."

"Bullshit." Sherry spat. She was sorry as hell that she'd fired the first shot in this round of battle, but she wasn't about to let him lay any more of this off on her. "You couldn't handle my success."

Good God Almighty, it always came back around to Sherry, didn't it? "I'm not doing this," he said. "Not again. Not today."

"You think I don't know what poison you fill his head with every day? I just spent a week with him, Brandon. He hates me. My own son hates me. How do you think that makes me feel?"

"I bet it makes you feel like shit," he said. "And if it doesn't, it should. And for the record, I don't fill his head with poison. Actually, you rarely come up in conversation." He intended those words to hurt, and they found their mark. "What would we talk about? Whether your check came with a note? Hell, you don't even sign your own checks anymore. We're just another auto-pay from the bank."

"You designed the settlement agreement, Brandon, not I."

"And you jumped at it! That's how anxious you were to be rid of us."

"*You*, Brandon," Sherry corrected, thrusting a finger toward him. "I was anxious to be rid of *you*, not Scotty."

"He hasn't called himself Scotty in three years."

His words seemed to break her momentum. He'd already told her that, hadn't he? Did he have any idea how much it hurt to be shut out from your only child's life? Didn't he realize that she was the *hero* in this family war? She could have dragged the divorce out forever, but what would that have accomplished? It wouldn't have been right to shuttle Scotty—*Scott*—from one house to the other. This was Brandon's favorite kind of argument, though; the kind at which he truly excelled. She'd never known anyone who so quickly claimed the moral high ground for himself and demonized anyone who opposed him.

"Fine," she said. It just wasn't the time for this. "You're right. You're the best parent in the world, and I'm the worst. Congratulations. All I can say is, this is one bizarre approach to getting people to do you a favor."

A puff of air escaped Brandon's lungs when she said this, and in that instant, Sherry didn't understand what she'd said wrong. "You think I'm asking you for a favor? A *favor*? What would that be?"

"You want me to put my reputation on the line because you have a *feeling*. Despite what all the experts say. What would you call it?"

"I call it trying to save a boy's life," he said. "Two boys' lives, actually. If you're doing anybody a favor, it's them." How could two people see the world so differently?

Again, loaded with all his righteous emotion, it sounded so simple. But it wasn't at all simple. If Sherry called a press conference, sure, people would come, but what would she say? No matter what Brandon thought, she loved her son as much as he did; she was just more of a realist. Did he think for a moment that she wouldn't want people scouring the countryside looking for Scotty—*Scott*—if she thought it would do any good? Did he think that the police department and the Civil Air Patrol would just randomly abandon a search effort if there was still a glimmer of hope? Sherry was a psychologist, for God's sake. A professional. If she pulled together a special news conference to criticize local officials and then rambled on about feelings and intuitions, she'd look like a fool. She'd *be* a fool to do it.

Brandon helped himself to the chair in front of the panoramic window. "Sherry?"

She broke her concentration to look at him.

"Okay, it's a favor, then," he said. "And I'll concede any point you want, sign any papers you want. I'll beg, if you want me to." He fought hard to control the flood of emotion, and Sherry brought her hand to her mouth as she watched him age ten years before her eyes. "We were such a total disaster, you and I," he went on. "But out of all the misery and the fighting, we produced one miracle."

His voice caught in his throat and Sherry took a step forward to comfort him. He held her off with a raised hand. "Maybe you're right," he said. "Maybe I am jealous. You have your fame and your career and your things. But that boy is it for me. He's my entire life."

Sherry looked down to give him a moment. She'd never seen him like this. Even in the worst of times, he'd always been a rock—stubborn, passionate, angry as hell, but always solid and strong. The sight of him crumbling took her breath away. His pain, she saw, was physical, and somewhere in her soul, buried under years and years of hatred, something stirred in her that was akin to affection. She sat on the coffee table opposite him.

"He's out there, Sherry," he whispered. "He's alive. And without us on his side, he's got nobody."

She nodded, her throat suddenly thick. "Okay."

24

THROUGH EVERY STEP OF HIS ORDEAL, Scott had planned to sleep all day. When the opportunity finally arrived, though, he could only make it to 1:30 in the afternoon. Isaac had lent him a bedroom on the second floor, just at the top of the stairs. He'd even put on sheets and a luscious down quilt. It should have been good for a week of sleep.

Ultimately, it was the smell of food—bacon again—that lifted him from his cocoon and brought him back to consciousness. He dressed as quickly as his battered body would permit, and headed out for another meal. It simply wasn't possible for him to eat enough.

Outside his bedroom door, the narrow log-railed balcony offered him a view of most of the first floor, with the living room directly below and to the right, and the rustic eat-in kitchen on the left, the front door directly across.

The kitchen appliances, such as they were, looked as old as the cabin itself. A thin blue flame rose from a front burner. Next to it, safely off the fire, sat a cast-iron skillet with strips of bacon floating in a pond of grease.

Isaac was nowhere to be seen. "Hello?" he called, but there was no response. "Isaac?"

Nothing.

The skin on the back of his neck pulled tight as he remembered the half-million-dollar contract on his host's life.

"Isaac, are you here?"

Still, no response.

Shit. In the kitchen now, Scott turned a complete circle, looking for . . . something. Anything. But there were no signs of a struggle, no broken windows, no open doors. He called out one more time, just for the hell of it.

What was he supposed to do now? Should he look outside? Find a place to hide? Maybe he should—

There was a crack in the wall to the right of the stove, running vertically, from the floor nearly to the ceiling. Curious, he moved in for a closer look and saw that it actually was a door, so carefully camouflaged as a wall that he never would have found it if it were closed all the way.

Using two fingers, he pulled the door open a little more. "Isaac?" Clearly, Scott was alone. He stepped inside.

What he saw made him gasp. It was a room he was never supposed to see. It looked like a home office, he supposed, with one major addition—a vault. It looked like something out of a bank, actually, and it, too, was propped open. Inside, Scott counted a dozen different guns, from pistols to rifles to machine guns. If this were a movie, they'd all be stacked vertically, on display, but in here, they just lay on shelves inside the vault, some of their muzzles pointing toward him, and others pointing away.

"Holy shit," he breathed as he fingered the weapons. What had he stumbled into? Would the government really let an ex-criminal have this much firepower just to protect himself?

On the shelf above the guns, he found what appeared to be some kind of foam rubber suit, thick and squishy. Except for the light emitted through the open door, the room was dark. "Isaac?" he whispered. "Are you here?"

Scott found the light switch on the wall. The overhead fluorescents confirmed his first impression of a home office. A desk occupied one corner, and next to it stood a heavy-duty locked file cabinet, four drawers high. The desk was clean, not so much as a pencil in sight.

Feeling like a burglar, he carefully opened the center desk drawer, just to see. There in the front, under a couple of papers that didn't interest him, Scott found a telephone.

"Well, I'll be damned," he whispered to the room. It looked like an older model cell phone, about as big as his hand, but with an unusually stubby antenna. He'd heard of satellite phones, but this was the first one he'd ever seen up close. More secure than cell phones, and capable of calling from anywhere, they were more than adequate for calling the police.

Scott picked it up and hit the power button. The LCD display showed a full battery but no signal. Not surprising, really, given that he was indoors. To make a call, he'd have to be outside. Later.

So, why did Isaac lie to him? And what else did he lie about? He turned off the phone and put it back where he'd found it.

Feeling more and more like a felon, he searched the other drawers, too, but found nothing interesting—just more papers he didn't have time to read, some pencils and a stack of Post-its.

So, who was this Isaac guy, really?

Turning back to explore the gun vault more carefully, a glint from something on the floor caught his attention. It looked like a door pull, flat on the floor, just below a wall-mounted flashlight charger. Scowling, he stooped for a closer look. It wasn't *just* a door pull, as it turned out. It was a door pull between two slide bolts. Shifting his eyes to the left, he could just barely make out the flush hinges in the floor.

"It's a trap door," Scott told the room.

Every fiber in his being told him that it was time to turn off the lights, put everything back the way he'd found it, and get out of this place, but even as the thoughts flowed through his brain, he knew there wasn't a chance he'd do it. A trap door, for God's sake! It was like something out of a movie.

The otherwise dull surface of the floor had been worn shiny over time from the action of the bolts, and Scott noted how easily they slid as he shoved them back. With that done, he wrapped his fist around the pull and lifted. The door was heavier than he'd expected, making him shift to grab the edge with his other hand as he pulled. The door was every bit of three inches thick, and it surprised him when it flopped all the way open, until its face was flush with the floor. Inside the edge of the door panel itself, Scott noted the presence of two more bolts, the actuators for which were on the trap side of the door. Given the stoutness of the receivers on the jamb, someone had thought of this hole in the floor as a refuge—a place to go, maybe, when people are trying to kill you.

A metal-rung ladder led from the edge of the door down into the darkness.

"So, Mrs. O'Toole, did you raise any idiots?" Scott mused aloud as he swung his legs over the side of the opening and placed his feet on the third rung down. "Only Scott, I'm afraid. He just couldn't leave well enough alone."

Balancing himself with a hand flat on the floor, he pulled a flashlight from the charger on the wall and pressed the button, nearly blinding himself with the burst of high intensity light. With each rung he descended, he confirmed to himself his own stupidity.

You don't know who this guy is, you don't know what pisses him off, and you do know that he's heavily armed. Are you out of your friggin' mind?

Yes to all of the above, but he still had to see.

It wasn't a room after all; it was a *tunnel.* And a cold one at that. A gentle, constant breeze raised goose pimples on his flesh. The base of the ladder marked the beginning, and as he stood there, shining his light straight ahead, it seemed to stretch forever, the ceiling only slightly higher than he was tall. Fifty yards ahead, the tunnel took a hard turn to the left. Fifty *yards.* How long could the thing be? And where could it possibly go?

"You're an idiot," Scott sang softly as he inched forward, oddly comforted by the company of his own voice. The tunnel was a crudely constructed thing, unpaved and unlit, and pitched steeply downhill. Tree roots extended into the passageway like so many arthritic fingers, twisted and gnarled, but not so far as to impede passage. If this were an Indiana Jones movie, he'd have had to fight massive cobwebs every step of the way, but here, there was none of that. He wondered if the relative cleanliness spoke more to a lack of spiders or to frequent use.

Twisting the lens of the MagLite, Scott expanded the light beam to its widest circle, concentric rings of light that brought life to a hundred new shadows. The silence of the place was absolute, in effect amplifying the tympani tattoo pounding in his ears. The light beam jumped with each beat of his heart.

Sometimes, you just get a feeling that you're not alone. You can't quite put your finger on it, and ninety-nine times out of a hundred it turns out to be your imagination, but right now, Scott knew that something was terribly wrong. Was it a sound he'd heard? Something he'd seen?

It's all in your head, pussy-boy, he told himself. Still, he couldn't help but think what a perfect lair this would make for a pack of wolves, or maybe a hibernating bear. With that thought, the air grew suddenly colder.

He reached the end of the first section of the tunnel, and pivoted the light beam to examine the sharp turn to the left. This leg was longer than the first, probably twice as long, but if he wasn't mistaken, the darkness seemed lighter down there. Sure enough, when he thumbed off the flashlight, he clearly saw a tiny pinprick of daylight. If it were possible, this section seemed even steeper than the first.

"What the hell does he do in here?" he asked no one.

Scott moved forward, the treacherous angle cramping his battered leg muscles. One degree steeper, and a flight of steps would have been mandatory. The tangle of roots made it three times more difficult.

Maybe a third of the way down this second corridor, a noise to his left made him jump, and as he whirled with his light, something slammed down hard on his wrist, smashing the MagLite to the ground. Scott didn't even have time to react before something hard and fast plowed itself into his gut, driving the air from his lungs and sending his diaphragm into a violent spasm. His mind registered only pain as he fell backward against the tunnel wall and then in a heap on the floor.

Gasping for air that wouldn't come, Scott tried to roll himself into a protective ball, but his attacker wouldn't let him. He imagined a giant fist grabbing a handful of his hair as his head snapped back hard, and a brilliant white light dug like a stiletto into his eyes.

A voice from behind the light hissed, "Say one word and I'll blow your head off."

THE PRESIDENT'S DECISION to go shopping in downtown Eagle Feather created a nightmare for Barry Whitestone. What was supposed to have been a quick fire-hall speech to dedicate a new ladder truck bought in part with federal funds had turned into a four-hour affair that snarled everything.

Main Street and its feeders were closed to both vehicular and pedestrian traffic. Anyone who had pressing business elsewhere was just plain out of luck. Even air traffic was directed away from the main approach to the airport while POTUS popped in and out of the trendy boutiques. The newspapers and television networks would show smiling merchants shaking hands with the leader of the free world, but word had already reached Barry from all directions that those same merchants were losing revenue by the bushel basket. Five minutes of presidential publicity didn't pay anybody's mortgage.

For his part, Barry was exploiting his rank. Never one to shy away from grunt work, this kind of traffic detail had always driven him over the edge, and now that he had the eagles on his collar, he didn't have to do it anymore. Instead, he drove his Humvee from checkpoint to checkpoint, making sure that his troops were managing okay. After all, this was only the beginning. The president's main event wasn't scheduled until tomorrow. Given the predictions for postcard weather, those crowds were likely to be huge, and Barry didn't want his people to burn through their bullshit tolerance too early.

Parking his truck with two wheels on the sidewalk, Barry climbed out of the Humvee at the intersection of Aspen and Ponderosa streets and walked to the sawhorse currently manned by Jesse Tingle.

"Next time, I'm voting for the guy whose favorite pastime is golf," Jesse said as his boss approached.

Barry smiled. "Aren't you supposed to be partnered with James?"

Jesse gestured with his head toward the department Explorer parked a little ways down Ponderosa. "You mean Supersleuth? He's sitting in the car down there solving the world's great mysteries."

Barry cocked his head, gave a confused look.

"Maurice Hertzberger," Jesse clarified. "Actually, he asked me if I minded being alone here for a while and I told him to go ahead. Off and on, he's been on the phone for an hour."

Barry set his hands on his hips and sighed. Sooner or later, shit like this happened with every hungry young buck who joined the department. Early on, the lure of the resort environment was intoxicating; but as time went on and reality sank in, they came to realize that small town policing is a daily grind of boredom. Barry didn't mind James taking such a strong lead on the Hertzberger investigation—he admired the commitment—but it wasn't right to jam your partner with a brain-numbing assignment while you sat in a warm car doing real police work.

James lowered the truck's window as he saw Barry approaching. "I got a call from an FBI buddy of mine," he said.

"Hey, James, this isn't where you're supposed to be right now."

Deputy Alexander gave a brusque, disinterested nod. "Yeah, I know. Listen to this—"

"James, Jesse is standing out here all by himself. That's not how this works."

"I know," James said. "Honest to God, Chief, I know, but you've got to listen to this." He was like a little boy with a secret, and until he got it off his chest, nothing else was going to get done.

"Is there a short version?" Barry asked.

James shook his head. "Not really, no."

"Then I might as well be warm." He walked around to the passenger side. Just before climbing in, he caught Jesse Tingle's frustrated glare and acknowledged it with a sheepish grin. He slid into the passenger seat and closed the door. "Shoot."

James riffled backward through what looked like a dozen pages of notes, stopping when he found the page he wanted. He could barely contain his grin. "What does the name Agostini mean to you?"

"Oh, God," Barry groaned. "Please don't turn this into a trivia game."

"Okay, okay. Giovanni Agostini—otherwise known as Johnny Big Nose—"

Barry snapped his fingers. "He was a mob informer, right?"

"Exactly. His testimony broke up the Paroni family and sent a bunch of goombahs to jail for like a thousand years."

"New York, right?"

"Chicago."

"I meant Chicago. What about him?"

"Well, ever since he testified against his buddies, he's been a protected witness, living wherever the hell he is with a huge price on his head. Hit men from all over the world are hunting for this guy, but no one can find him. His father, on the other hand, Giuseppe Agostini, has lived for years just outside of Concordia, Kansas."

"Was he a mobster, too?"

"No, a plumber. Bear with me. You know we found about a million fingerprints in Hertzberger's motel room after he turned up dead. That's no surprise, of course, because, well, it's a motel room. About a million people have slept there. Just for grins, though, I ran some prints on the booze bottle we found, on the off chance that we might find something interesting." He paused, waiting out a rise from Barry.

"Will you get on with it?"

James's smirk turned to a grin. "Okay, the FBI computer found a match between some latent prints on the bottle and other prints from Giuseppe Agostini's house. They can't tell me who the prints belong to, but they can tell me that they're the same." He paused. "Did I mention that the old man was found murdered?"

"The plumber?"

"Right. Well, the retired plumber. In Concordia. He was murdered after being tortured. Tied up, burned with cigarettes, that sort of thing."

Barry winced. "Lovely. So, the fingerprints link Hertzberger to the plumber. The informer's father."

"Right. Now, stick with me here, because this is where it gets confusing."

"God help me."

"According to my FBI buddy, Giuseppe had terminal cancer when he was killed. Given Johnny Big Nose's high profile, and the fact that there's such a huge contract out on his head, the Bureau assumes that Giuseppe was tortured to reveal the whereabouts of his son."

Barry still didn't get it. "What does the cancer have to do with anything?"

"Isn't it obvious? Some hit man figured that with the old man sick, the son might come by to pay his last respects. You know, say good-bye to the old guy. By all accounts, father and son were pretty tight."

Barry tried to piece it together. "You're not suggesting that Maurice Hertzberger was a hit man."

James shook his head. "Different prints. I'm just suggesting that he might have been connected with the hit man. Or, better still, that the hit man might have killed him."

"By giving him a heart attack?"

"We still don't have the tox report back from Cooper."

The chief turned it over in his head. "I don't know, James. I mean, it's certainly an interesting development, but does it make sense to you that a guy who'd torture one guy to death would gently poison another? That doesn't seem right to me."

"Different measures for different needs, maybe. My first thought was, maybe Hertzberger was really Johnny Big Nose, but that's not looking so promising."

"His fingerprints should tell that story, I'd think," Barry said.

"You're right. Or, you would be if they still had Giovanni Agostini's fingerprints on file."

"Where are they?"

James shrugged. "I don't think anybody bothered to look for them until I asked to check it out. Turns out that Big Nose wields a pretty good computer. He must have gotten into the files and erased them. Anyway, I sent a post mortem photo of Maurice to the Bureau and they sent me a mug shot of Giovanni. No way are they the same guy. By process of elimination, then, the killer who did the plumber also did the truck driver."

Barry winced again. He didn't like that conclusion at all. "Have you been able to link them in any other way?"

"Not yet, but—"

"I think you're jumping too early, James. Maybe they just had a common friend."

James looked at his boss as if he'd grown a new head. "Come on, Barry. Two people who just happened to turn up dead? That's a strong link."

"People die every day, James," Barry said. This was where experience paid dividends. There wasn't a cop on the streets in any city on earth who hadn't learned the hard way the evils of jumping to conclusions before all the evidence was in. "You continue to assume that there was something wrong with the hooch in the bottle, but you haven't given me evidence yet. You convince me that Hertzberger was murdered, and I'll agree that we know what the killer's fingers look like."

25

THE LIGHT IN SCOTT'S EYES hurt almost as much as the grinding pain in his belly. He'd never been hit that hard by anything, and despite his attacker's warning to be quiet, he could not stop gasping for air.

"Who the hell are you?" the man growled from behind the light.

Honest to God, Scott wanted to answer him, but his voice refused to work.

"Answer me, goddammit."

"I . . . can't . . . breathe." Scott's words came out as a harsh, gasping whisper.

The man growled, "Aw, shit, sit up." Before Scott could do anything to help or resist, he felt himself being lifted by his shirt collar and placed against the tunnel wall. Next, he felt a hand grabbing the front of his pants at the belt line and pulling them away. "Just breathe normally," the man said. "You got the wind knocked out of you."

Scott shoved the man's hand away from his pants. "Get away from me, you pervert."

"I'm just trying to help you get your breath," the man said. He repositioned himself and his light so that he was no longer blinding Scott. A flash of gold, and Scott could see an FBI badge six inches in front of his nose. "Special Agent Jerry Price, FBI," the man said. "Now, who are you?"

Scott's head swam with possibilities. "Scott O'Toole. And I think you broke one of my ribs."

"It'll heal. I want you to tell me—" He paused. "Wait a second. Scott O'Toole." He said the name as if he were tasting it. "The plane crash?"

Scott nodded.

"Holy shit. What are you doing here?"

"Mostly getting the shit kicked out of me," Scott said.

"Where does this tunnel go?"

Scott hesitated. Suppose this guy was the killer Isaac had been waiting for? "Where do you think it goes?" he hedged.

"You don't want to toy with me, young man."

"I don't even want to know you." Scott found himself surprised by his own bravado. If only this guy knew how totally petrified he was.

"Look, kid. Scott. If I'm not mistaken, this tunnel leads to an old bootlegger's cabin, where a man named Thomas Powell lives. He's a very dangerous man. A killer. I need to know—"

Scott heard a soft *thump,* and then Agent Price's eyes grew huge. His jaw dropped, and for just a second, Scott wondered if he were trying to make funny faces. But there was fear in the man's eyes.

Instinctively, Scott reached out for him. "Are you—"

Before he could finish the question, Agent Price's left eye exploded from his body, spraying the boy with a mist of hot gore. Scott screamed as the man collapsed forward onto him. The flashlight tumbled, and just like that, he was again bathed in total darkness. A horrible hot wetness flooded Scott's shirt, hot as piss, and he knew without seeing that he was absorbing the man's brains and blood.

He didn't even hear himself screaming—that panicked, endless scream that was normally reserved for only his worst nightmares. The blood. The horror.

"Scott!"

The boy's head whipped to the left at the sound of his name.

"Shut up, for Christ's sake. You're not hit, he is." It was Isaac. Scott couldn't see a thing, but he could hear the voice. Scott's hand found the flashlight at his side and he picked it up. "No, don't!"

But it was too late. Scott hit the switch, and there was Isaac coming at him, an odd-looking weapon cradled in his arms. The man yelled as his free hand raced to his face to pull off some kind of mask. In the instant that he saw it, Scott recognized the mask as night vision goggles.

"Jesus, Isaac, what did you do?"

"Get that thing out of my eyes," he commanded, and the light moved to his feet. "I saved your life is what I did. This is the asshole they sent to kill us."

"Us?" This was a new twist. Isaac had forgotten to mention that they were coming after Scott as well. Why would they do that?

"What, you think they're gonna whack me and just leave you as a witness?"

"But he had a badge," Scott said. "He showed it to me. It was FBI."

Isaac slung his rifle over his shoulder by its strap, then lifted Price's body with one hand while he snatched the light from Scott with the other. He shined it on the man's face. "Look at that. Perfect. Behind the ear and out the eye." Scott looked away, then returned his gaze as Isaac repositioned the beam to show a hole in the man's coat. "That was to get him to sit up a little straighter," Isaac explained. "I didn't want to get you with the same bullet."

Scott felt light-headed and his stomach churned. As he groaned against an urge to vomit, Isaac lashed out and grabbed him. "Look, Scott, I didn't want this, okay? I didn't start it, but I'm not going to wait for you to come apart. This man is dead, and if he wasn't, you would be."

"But he had a *badge*," Scott repeated. "FBI."

Isaac grabbed Scott's cheeks in his fingers, smearing the blood. "Look at me. You want a badge? I can get you a dozen of them. What'll it be? FBI? DEA? Hell, I can get you a New York City police department badge if you want one. You can pick 'em up by the dozen in novelty stores."

Scott wanted to understand, he really did, but all of this was too much. Jesus, a man's brains were on his shirt!

"Don't you see?" Isaac said. He let the body fall to the dirt floor.

"The badge is how he gathers information from people. That's how he figures out where I'm staying. He says he's an FBI agent and people tell him everything he wants to know."

Scott nodded absently because it was the thing to do. Jesus, the blood.

Isaac interpreted the nod as assent. "Okay, then. Let's get this guy buried."

"*What?*"

"You heard me."

"We need to call somebody," Scott protested. "We can't just—"

"I don't have a phone, Scott! We've been over this once before."

"What about—" he started to ask about the satellite phone, but stopped short. That was the second time on the same lie.

"What about what?"

"Nothing." Scott needed to be very careful now. "Please get the light off him."

"He's a hired murderer, Scott!" This time, Isaac yelled, and it startled the hell out of the boy. "For chrissake, will you try to wrap your mind around that? He's a professional killer hired to kill me for a suitcase full of cash. I got him first. Big fucking deal."

Scott just stared.

"Look at me, kid. If I had a phone, I wouldn't use it anyway. He's vermin, a yard pest. Not worth the price of the call. You don't report his death to the police, you just throw a damn party." He shined his light again on the corpse. "God, what a mess. Go on back to the house and get me a garbage bag out of the closet next to the stove. Keep him from gooping up the floors."

Gooping the floors? Jesus. Scott just stared.

"Today, kid. Now."

Scott moved as if his body belonged to someone else, his arms and legs performing without commands from his head. His mind was in a thousand different places right now. Flashlight in hand, he sleep-walked back to the ladder and up into the house. The bags were right where Isaac had said they'd be, and by the time Scott returned with one clutched in his hand, Isaac had already turned the sharp corner in the tunnel, and was on the final leg of the trip back to the trap door.

When they joined up again, Isaac unceremoniously yanked the bag over the dead man's ruined head, twisted it tightly at the neck, then pulled it over a second time. When that was done he separated the two front corners of the bag, drew them tighter still around the base of Price's skull and tied a double knot under his chin. The efficiency of it all sent a chill through Scott; it was as if Isaac had done this a thousand times before. Watching the man work, he saw not the slightest trace of revulsion. Not the slightest trace of emotion.

"Come on," Isaac said when he was done. "Help me get him up the ladder."

"You mean touch him?" Scott gasped.

Isaac shook his head with disgust. "Je-sus Christ. Get out of the way, then. I'll do it myself." He started to heft the body into a fireman's carry, then paused long enough to unsling his weapon. "Here," he said, handing it to Scott, "carry this."

In the eerie light of the flashlights, the gun felt exotic; lighter than he'd expected, and invisible in the darkness. He was staring at it when Isaac brushed past him, the dead visitor doubled over his right shoulder.

When he was halfway up the ladder, Isaac said, "Come on, Scott. And don't touch the trigger. I don't remember if I put the safety on or not."

Just like that, the gun felt fifty times more dangerous. Like a bomb, maybe, or a beehive; a terrible thing that was ready to hurt him at any moment.

When Isaac cleared the entryway, it was Scott's turn. He had some difficulty navigating the ladder with the weapon in his hands, but he did all right. By the time his head poked through the opening in the floor, the dead man's feet were disappearing into the kitchen as Isaac dragged him across the polished wood.

In the kitchen now, in the light, Scott could finally see the gun he carried. It looked like something you'd see Arnold Schwarzenegger use in a movie, barely bigger than a pistol, but made twice as long by the fat silencer on its snout.

Isaac arrived at the front door and pulled it open. "Let's move now, Scott. Grab a coat and come help."

Scott told himself, *Run! Run fast! Get out of here!* But where would he go? Running away made no sense unless you knew where you were running to.

Shoot him. Shoot Isaac. All of this was terribly wrong. The world had somehow shifted, knocking him down the rabbit hole where Alice and the Mad Hatter lived.

"Scott!"

Shoot him now, while you've got the gun. Why? Why did he feel so strongly that he needed to kill this man? Why did he feel as if it were the one last chance he'd have to save himself from the fate met by Agent Price, at the hands of the same nut case?

"Scott!" Isaac reappeared in the doorway, his face looking oddly parental. He raised his eyebrows and nodded to the weapon in the boy's hands, the muzzle of which was pointed directly at him. "You planning to shoot me?"

Scott jumped, startled that he could so accurately read his thoughts. Then he understood. "Oh. No, sorry." He pivoted the muzzle away.

Isaac smiled and nodded. He looked so ordinary with his navy blue jacket with its forest green shoulder patches. He could be anybody's neighborhood dad, maybe an insurance salesman. The last thing in the world he looked like was a killer. "Put the gun on the table and get your coat," he said. "I need you outside." He started out the door again, then paused to pluck a big fur hat off the shelf over the coatrack—something right out of *Doctor Zhivago.* "Don't forget your hat. It's cold out here." And then he was gone.

Moving with mechanical stiffness, Scott did exactly as he was told. Even if he'd had the balls to shoot the man, why would he have done it? Because he lied about a telephone? As Isaac had said, if he'd wanted Scott to die, he'd be dead already. Sometimes you find solace in the oddest thoughts.

The coats hung from hooks just inside the front door, and as Scott lifted his to put it on, he caught the first glimpse of his face in the mirror. He saw the blood smears and he quickly looked away. His wet shirt and jeans stuck to him.

"Scott!"

"I'm coming!" He hurried out onto the wooden porch that led to the work yard separating the main house from some squatty outbuildings across the way. He froze. There in the middle of the work yard lay another body— a man in a winter coat, his arms and legs splayed oddly in the crimson snow. Isaac stood over the man, Price once again slung over his shoulder, waiting for Scott's reaction. "There were two of them," Isaac explained. "I thought I'd heard movement outside when you were still in bed. I was waiting for this one."

"Jesus," Scott breathed.

"Don't think so." Isaac smiled. "Satan maybe, but definitely not Jesus. Now, come and help me before they start attracting varmints."

THEY DIDN'T BURY THE BODIES so much as they dumped them into a hole between the outbuildings. Isaac called it a dry well, whatever that was. Scott said nothing, and he made a point to look away as the corpses disappeared over the edge of the well. He didn't want to see them as they impacted the bottom. The dull, fleshy *thump* was bad enough.

For his part, Isaac was downright chatty, talking about his strategy for stalking his prey, but Scott wanted none of it. He just kept replaying the image of that exploding eye.

After the bodies were deposited, Isaac covered the top of the hole with planks that might have been siding from one of the outbuildings, then together they shoveled snow to cover the planks. "That should keep the stink down," Isaac said. "Wolves can sometimes be a problem out here."

Scott remained silent. He'd just buried two dead men. First he was going to jail, and then he was going to Hell.

26

IT ALL TOOK A SURPRISINGLY LONG TIME. By the time Scott was done with his shower—he'd nearly scrubbed the flesh off his face, but he still swore he could feel the blood spatters—it was almost six o'clock and dark outside.

Oddly enough, the nerves didn't hit him until he was drying his hair. As he lowered the towel, the mirror greeted him with an image of a gaunt, pale ghost of the Scott O'Toole he used to know. Now, the wispy goatee and the blue hair looked stupid to him. They were the trappings of a kid trying to look like a man—an innocent boy who fancied himself a rock star. On a conspirator in a murder—a future prison inmate—they were embarrassing. Until a week ago, he'd never seen a dead body; now he'd seen three and had come *this close* to becoming one himself.

He slumped to the floor and sat there for the longest time, his whole body trembling as the room spun. What was happening? Who was this guy Isaac, and what was this place, with its tunnels and its vaults and its guns? Isaac assured him that the danger had passed, but who was this animal who could do such unspeakable things, yet feel no emotion?

A knock on the bathroom door startled him. "Scott? Are you okay?" It was Isaac.

Scott cleared his throat and tried to sound strong. "Yeah, I'm fine."

"I put some clean clothes for you on your bed. When you're ready, get dressed and meet me in the living room. We need to talk."

Yeah, no shit, Sherlock, Scott didn't say. The shivering still hadn't settled down when he rose unsteadily to his feet, wrapped the towel around his waist and padded down the hallway to his bedroom.

Five minutes later, he was on his way downstairs. He didn't know what had happened to the first set of clothes and he didn't care. What mattered was, he wore a clean shirt and a new pair of jeans, though they fit no better than the others. There were no socks, though, and he couldn't find his boots.

"I'm going to need a new wardrobe at the end of this visit," Isaac said from below as he saw his houseguest on the stairs.

Scott wasn't in the mood to be amused.

Isaac gestured to a chair near the fire. "Have a seat. I think I have some explaining to do."

Scott lowered himself into the chair, drew his legs up under him. He folded his arms to keep his shaking hands a secret. The heat of the fire felt great.

Isaac poured himself some bourbon from a bottle on the table next to his chair and offered some to Scott, who declined with a quick shake of his head. Isaac capped the bottle and settled into his own chair.

"Scott O'Toole," he began, "you are the king of bad timing. When I put myself in your position, I think I'd be terrified. You've seen horrific things and you don't know what to make of them. You don't know what to believe. If I were in your position, I think I'd probably want to run away, as fast and as far as I could, not worrying about who's right and who's wrong."

Something in Isaac's tone unnerved Scott even more, and as he listened, he worked hard to keep his expression completely impassive.

"Thing is, my friend, I can't afford to let you run away. Believe me when I say that I don't like this any more than you do, but you're in a position to do some very serious harm to me."

"But the killers are dead," Scott said.

"Two killers are dead," Isaac corrected. "There will be more. What did our friend in the tunnel say to you this afternoon before he . . . died?"

Scott cocked his head. "Why did you dig a tunnel under your house?"

Isaac chuckled as he sipped his drink. "You'd make a good lawyer one day, Scott. Always answer a question with a question. I didn't dig the tunnel. It's been there for over sixty years—it's as old as the cabin. You know what a bootlegger is?"

"A moonshiner?"

"Close. Back during Prohibition, this place was a vacation lodge for bootleggers, a place to get away from it all. Rumor has it that Al Capone visited here once, but old Al is a little like George Washington; if you believe the plaques on the walls, they slept everywhere. Anyway, that tunnel was their escape route, in the event that the law came looking for them."

Scott nodded. That made sense, actually.

"Now, what did your dead friend tell you in the tunnel?"

"Nothing," Scott said, even as he remembered the question about Thomas Powell, a very dangerous man.

"You just run into a man in the middle of a dark tunnel and you say nothing?"

"He kicked me in the stomach," Scott said. "Mostly, I was coughing and sputtering for air. Where did you get all the guns? And if all these killers are after you, how come you don't have marshals or SWAT team guys here shooting it out for you?"

Isaac's eyes narrowed as he took another sip. "This is why you're so dangerous. You think too much."

Scott felt himself blush. He hated it when people accused him of being smart.

"I wasn't a hundred percent truthful with you," Isaac confessed.

"So, you're not in the witness protection program?"

"Oh, I am. At least I'm supposed to be." He saw the confusion on Scott's face and smiled. Taking his drink with him, he stood and walked to the fire. "I don't know what you think witness protection is like, but I can tell you it wasn't what I was expecting. It's like another damn prison, moving all the time, checking in and out with marshals who'd just as soon shoot you as help you. That wasn't for me."

"So, you escaped," Scott said.

"I ditched the program," Isaac corrected. "I just did it without telling the right people first."

"So, that guy *was* FBI," Scott gasped.

Isaac sighed. "No, he *was* a hired gun sent to kill me for his reward bounty."

"So, why don't you just tell the police and set everything straight? I mean, you're not *required* to be in the witness protection program, are you?"

Isaac rubbed the back of his neck and sighed again. Clearly, this was all more complicated than he was willing or able to synopsize. He sat back down in his chair, this time on the very front edge, his elbows resting on his knees. "I used to kill people for a living, Scott. I was one of those people I shot today, only a damn sight better at it. I killed people for Uncle Sam for a while till they got tired of that sort of thing, and then I went out on my own."

"Freelance," Scott offered.

Isaac grinned. "Watch a lot of movies, do you? Yeah, I went free-lance, working mostly for the Mob. One family would hire me to take out somebody in another family."

"Anybody famous?"

"I already said that names don't matter. Anyway, my former business, as violent and nasty as it was, ran primarily on trust. I won't go into the details, but suffice it to say, somebody along the line betrayed my trust, and I ended up with about fifty feds at my door one morning."

"You were arrested?"

"Very. Very arrested and very pissed. The U.S. attorney wanted to throw me in a cage forever, but that didn't suit my needs at all. In fact, they offered me what they thought was a sweetheart deal: if I ratted out all the Mob connections I worked for, they'd keep me out of the general population in prison and make me eligible for parole after twenty-five years. I said, 'I don't think so,' and countered with a deal more to my tastes: I'd testify only if they dropped all the charges against me and put me into the protection program."

Scott scowled. "That's it? It was that easy?"

A proud, sly grin began to grow on Isaac's face. "Well, not quite. My trump card was the work I did for the feds. I told them that if I so much as saw the outside of a prison, I'd name all those names as well. I guess that scared them."

"Would you have done it?" Scott asked. "Named the names, I mean?"

Isaac's grin disappeared. "Here's some advice, kid. Or maybe a warning, you decide. Don't ever cross me. I play for keeps."

Scott felt a chill, despite the heat of the fire. He took a moment to process it all. "So, why'd you leave the program?" he asked. "I mean, you got everything you asked for."

"You tell me," Isaac said, leaning back into his chair. "You're a smart guy. Put yourself in my position. You've made this deal with the government, and they've gotten their convictions."

Scott saw it right away. "There was no reason to keep you alive."

"Worse than that," Isaac said. "There was damn good reason to make me dead. I'd made their case, skirted jail and signed my own death warrant all at the same time. I used to do this shit, remember. I know how they work. There I was, under their thumb twenty-four hours a day. They knew where I slept and when I slept, what I had for breakfast, who I fucked—oh, sorry."

Scott grinned, embarrassed.

"I was a sitting duck. So I bolted."

For Scott, it all kept coming back to Agent Price. "So, how do you know that guy in the tunnel was a hit man, when the FBI is after you, too?"

Isaac shook his head. "But they're not. They have no reason to be. Not anymore. Remember again, I know these guys. They know that if I was going to rat them out, I'd have done it by now. I have *proven* to them, through my actions, that everything's fine so long as they leave me alone."

"Do they know how to find you?"

"No. At least, I don't think so. Well, maybe now that the Mob does, I suppose."

"How did *they* find you?"

Isaac regarded Scott long and hard before answering. "Do you remember me telling you that I did something stupid?"

Scott nodded.

"Well, what I did was, I let myself be predictable. My father is sick, dying of cancer. For all these years, I haven't been able to contact him, but when I found out, I had to see him. It's the one place they'd expect me to go, and I went there. I figure they must have tracked me down."

The whole thing made Scott's head spin. It all made sense, though; it all had the ring of truth, as his father would say. Having feared this man just a few moments ago, he now found himself almost admiring him. It was smart, the way Isaac turned the tables on the people sent to arrest him, and then again on the people who had no reason to keep him alive. Isaac knew enough to be very dangerous to the feds, and they had all the opportunity in the world to set their fears to rest. With what Isaac knew about the CIA or whatever, they almost *had* to kill him.

It was in many ways similar—

A shot of adrenaline launched Scott's heart into overdrive. He felt the panic building in his gut as he looked up at his host.

"You see my dilemma," Isaac said.

Scott felt his face flush as his eyes grew huge. "Are you—" He couldn't bring himself to ask the question.

"Relax," he said. "I'm not in the killing business anymore."

"But the silencer. The night scope . . ."

Isaac gave an innocent shrug. "Toys. I do like my toys. And my hunting isn't always sportsmanlike. I can drop a deer at two hundred yards in the dead of night."

Scott's heart continued to race. Isaac had laid out the logic for him to see. Nobody even knew Scott was here. Why keep him alive when he didn't have to?

"I said relax, Scott," Isaac repeated. "Even at the height of my career, I wasn't in the business of killing kids. Never. It's not right."

The words were exactly what Scott wanted to hear, but the soft tone of Isaac's voice didn't quite match the hardness of his eyes.

"It's all about seeing the world from the other person's viewpoint, kid. That's the secret to everything there is. And after hearing what you've heard, if I were you, I'd run out of here like a rabbit on fire. But you can see how I can't let that happen."

Scott shifted in his chair. "S-So, what are you going to do?"

"It's a problem, isn't it? The rooms here don't lock from the outside, and even if they did, there'd be nothing to keep you from climbing out a window. I could tie you up, but let's face it, that would be just a damn unpleasant way to spend the next few days."

Scott nodded. Damn unpleasant. Well put.

Isaac smiled and tented his fingers. "I stole your shoes and socks," he said.

Scott's jaw dropped. "What?"

Isaac pointed to Scott's bare feet, tucked under his butt in search of warmth. "I got the idea when I was getting rid of the bloody clothes," he explained. "It's ten degrees out there, with snow on the ground. I figure you won't be going anywhere." His grin got wider.

Scott felt the cool wash of relief. "That's it?"

"It's not that I don't trust you," Isaac explained, almost apologetically. "It's that I *can't* trust you. I can't afford to. This seemed like a reasonable compromise."

Scott nodded enthusiastically. "Yeah. Yeah, that's a fine compromise."

"Now that the weather is finally breaking, I'll head off tomorrow to places unknown. The next day or the day after, I'll drop a dime on you and let people know where you are. That sound simple enough?"

Scott nodded. This wasn't at all where he thought the conversation was going.

"Good." Isaac slapped his thighs as he rose from the chair. "What do you say I fix us some dinner?"

BARRY WHITESTONE SPENT EVERY February praying for an early summer. For some reason, summer tourists were just easier to deal with. He guessed that it had something to do with the lower median income of the summer crowds, who were far more likely to be carrying well-worn backpacks than carting thousand-dollar skis on the roofs of their $50,000 SUVs. A man could endure only so many whiny rich New Yorkers.

Plus, during the summer, the president of the United States vacationed elsewhere—places far away, where he could be a thorn in the side of some other town's police chief. Barry glanced at his watch and smiled. If everything went according to plan—and with Special Agent in Charge Sanders at the helm, things *always* went according to plan—in less than twenty-four hours, at 7:00 tomorrow night, Air Force One would be wheels-up and on its way out of his hair.

Twenty-three hours, seventeen minutes and nine seconds, for those who keep score. For today, though, work was finished. Time for Barry to be home with his wife and his kids for a dinner that only had to be heated once. Pushing the lock button in the knob, he stepped out into the squad room and closed the door behind him.

"Good night, people," he said to the few occupied chairs. In a department the size of Eagle Feather, there was no knife and gun club to keep a strong patrolling presence in the wee hours.

" 'Night, Chief," somebody said.

Janey had said something about ham and canned pineapple for dinner, but he was hoping she'd intercept the brain waves he'd been transmitting for her to cook up tacos instead. She often teased him that his tastes in food hadn't matured since he was in the fourth grade.

He was almost to the exit when the door opened and a breathless James Alexander hurried inside. "Oh, thank God you're still here," he said.

Barry held up both hands to stop him. "You just think I'm here. Think of me as a 3-D projection."

"We need to talk, Barry."

"Is this about Hertzberger?"

Alexander's eyebrows danced. "Sure is."

"Tell me tomorrow." Barry tried to scoot past, but James cut him off. "James, your boss wants to go home and see his family. Do I need to review the chain of command with you again?"

"According to the FBI, Giovanni Agostini's last known where-abouts were in the Utah-Idaho-Wyoming area."

The words froze Barry in his tracks. "He's the squealer, right?"

"Right. The dead father's son."

"Why is this important?"

"Because it closes the loop. A direct link from the dead plumber to Maurice. And remember the prints that linked Giuseppe's house to the moonshine bottle? Well, we picked up some matching latents in the cab of Hertzberger's truck. Passenger side."

"The skinny fat guy."

James's eyebrows danced again. "On a whim, I asked a buddy of mine in Denver to dust around the truck stop where our man picked up his hitchhiker." He smiled.

"They found the prints there, too?"

"A thumb and a partial forefinger. Not enough for court, but enough to put our hitcher in all the places. It means we have a murderer on the loose in our fair community."

"Cooper's tox screen?"

James's smile grew larger. "Positive for a drug I can't pronounce. Simulates heart attacks."

Barry's whole body sagged, as if someone opened an air valve. "Goddammit."

Pulling his keys from his pocket, he turned on his heel and led the way back toward his office.

DAY SIX

27

THE DAMN EYE KEPT EXPLODING.

The sickening image returned every time Scott closed his eyes, that horrible jet of gore. Lying there in the darkness of his bedroom, he kept rubbing the spots on his face where the brains had hit him.

All that evening, Scott and Isaac had tried to pretend that nothing had changed, that everything was fine; but nothing was. Not a single thing was even close to fine, and while Scott could put on the act in the presence of his host, now that he was all alone in his bed, and the clock inched past midnight, all he could concentrate on was the wrongness of it all.

Murder was murder, no matter how you cut it. He kept thinking about that eye. And the dead man in the yard whom he'd never even seen in life. Movies and television make this business of dying so routine, so uneventful, but the reality was anything but. Those guys were somebody's sons, and maybe even somebody's father. Probably somebody's husbands or boyfriends, and now they were gone. Just like that, their bodies dumped into a pit. It wasn't right.

He kept dissecting Isaac's explanation, trying to make it all add up, but it was just too much—the witness protection, the double cross on the government, the squealing mobsters. All of it made sense at its face, so why couldn't he just relax?

It was the lies. Not just about the phone—though that was a big one—but about his sick father, too. Why would somebody follow him all the way out here when they could have shot him on the spot in the father's house?

Then there was the sheer number of weapons, the night scope, the silencer, the vault. The tunnel. This place out in the middle of nowhere. All of that took money. So, there's the big question: where does an allegedly retired professional killer get that kind of money?

There was no coherence to the thoughts. They flashed as images through Scott's mind: shelves stacked with weapons, the vault door, the weird foam rubber vest. He saw the phone—

The vest was a fat suit. The thought came to him out of nowhere. He'd seen something like it on a television show that took him behind the scenes of a movie shoot, where skinny actors were donning fat suits in the makeup department. The vest was a disguise of some sort!

Okay, so what? That was consistent with his story, wasn't it? A man hunted by the Mob and chased by cops probably would want a disguise, wouldn't he? That'd go with the business of visiting his sick dad. Maybe disguises were as common to men on the run as cell phones were to salesmen.

So, what about the telephone? Why lie about that—twice? Just an excuse, maybe, to keep from calling the police? What was it that Isaac had said? The secret to everything was to look at the situation from the position of the other guy. So, here's this reclusive ex-killer who suddenly finds himself with a houseguest. Is he going to tell the truth? No, of course not. Certainly not under these circumstances.

It all checked out. No matter how many times Scott ran Isaac's explanations through his head, it always checked out. Why, then, was he so convinced that the man had something big and important to hide? Why did Scott continue to feel that he was in jeopardy?

If Isaac wanted to kill him, he'd have done it by now. Nobody knew Scott was even there, so they'd certainly never come looking for him. And if they did, they'd just find his body at the bottom of the dry well with the others. What difference would one more body make?

Thomas Powell is a very dangerous man.

The warning from the FBI agent/hired killer reverberated

through Scott's brain. And then he thought of the look in Isaac's eyes when Scott told him that the man hadn't said anything to him in the tunnel. Why had he lied like that? And why had the lie come so instinctively? At the time, it seemed like dangerous information to pass along, but now it seemed more like a stupid thing to hold back.

Don't ever cross me. I play for keeps.

Isaac had said to consider that a warning. A warning from a killer. Suddenly, Scott had the urge to come clean, to correct the record for Isaac. Maybe if he cleared his conscience, he'd be able to relax. If Isaac was telling him the truth about his plans, then all he had to do was hang out for a few days, and it would all end. Isaac would disappear, and sooner or later, Scott would be rescued.

So, why hadn't Isaac left already? It was a gorgeous day today. Yesterday, his excuse had been the storm. So, why was he still here tonight? Scott knew he was close to unraveling the mystery and his stomach tightened. If Isaac truly was a hunted man, why wasn't he off on the run?

Answer: He had something left to do—a solid, affirmative reason to stay. There was no way for Scott to know what that reason might be, but it certainly tickled his imagination. What would a hired gun need to stick around for?

Scott bolted upright in his bed, his heart hammering, his eyes wide in the shadowy darkness. Suddenly, he understood. All the guns, all the paranoia. Isaac DeHaven—or maybe Thomas Powell, a very dangerous man—wasn't retired after all. He was here to do another job.

It was the answer that made sense. Isaac had another person to kill, and for whatever reason, the timing mattered. Maybe he had to meet somebody first, or maybe the victim had to be in a specific place. Who could say?

The more he thought about it, the more it made sense. Isaac wasn't in the business of killing just anybody—the fact that Scott still breathed was testament to that. No, his customers hired him to kill specific people, maybe at specific times.

Who might the next poor bastard be? Scott wondered. Whoever it was, he surely didn't know it was coming. Scott thought of the phone in the drawer. He needed to get the hell out of here—to get help, not only for himself, but for that next victim. Maybe some of those Secret Service guys he'd been tripping over all last week could—

Just like that, Scott knew who the next target was. He remembered the posters all over SkyTop announcing the big Founder's Day celebration in Eagle Feather. Holy shit, it was the Super Bowl and World Series of murder all wrapped together: the president of the United States.

STAYING THERE WAS NO LONGER AN OPTION. Scott needed to leave, right by-God now. Jesus, this was huge. He didn't understand the game that Isaac was playing by keeping him alive, but suddenly, he knew as certainly as he'd ever known anything that his hours were numbered.

You've got to look at it from the other guy's point of view. Scott knew what Isaac looked like, he knew where he lived, and maybe he even knew his real name. There was no rational reason for Isaac to keep him alive.

Scott dressed quickly and silently, the coldness of the floor reminding him of his first problem: no shoes, no socks. Such a brilliant move when you thought about it. No shoes, no escape: a prison as secure as anything ever built with bars. But there had to be a solution. There had to be. He'd come this far on his wits, beating the odds; he'd be damned if he was going to let it end with a bullet through his own eye.

In all of this house, with its hidden panels and all the toys, there had to be something that could double for shoes.

Moving to his bedroom door, Scott pushed against the door with one hand while he turned the knob with the other, a trick that he'd learned from home experience would keep the latch from making noise as it opened.

Walking on tiptoe, he glided to the mezzanine railing and peered over the side. Light from one lamp in the living room cast a yellow glow over everything, the only glimmer that separated the house from total darkness. Under different circumstances, Scott might have been amused by the fact that a hired killer needed a night light. He stood there for a long moment, watching for signs of movement from below. If Isaac saw him, he was dead for sure.

ISAAC KNEW THAT IT WAS all out of his hands. As he sat in the darkness of his room, he reassembled his pistol as he considered his options—more accurately, as he considered the lack of them. It was a useful skill, disassembling and reassembling his weapon in the dark. Of no practical use in the real world—if he needed to clean his gun, he'd turn the light on—he nonetheless liked the notion of being at one with his firearm. There was something intimate about the connection between man and machine, nearly as intimate as the act for which the machine was employed.

Sometimes, the mixture of truth and deception that defined Isaac's life was a disturbing, confusing thing. Truly, he was not in the business of killing children. Most of his targets had been old men who likely would have been dead soon anyway. He couldn't remember a single one much under the age of forty. It wasn't in his nature to judge the justice of his victims' deaths. A customer had deemed their deaths to be worthy of his fee, and that was all the rationalization he needed. The rest was just mechanics and logistics. He planned, he acquired his target and he pulled the trigger. A simpler world would be hard to find.

Problem was, his heart actually went out to this kid. He had a lot of balls to set out on his own from a plane crash and wander through the woods to this tiny spot on his map. Isaac wasn't sure that he could have done that himself. Took a lot of courage to pull it off, and if there was one quality in a person—especially a young person—that Isaac admired above all others, it was courage. So, when he hobbled Scott by taking away his shoes, he'd done it with his heart in the right place. At the time, it seemed like a reasonable solution to both of their problems. He only needed one more day. One lousy day. Then it would all be taken care of.

He never would have made the phone call, of course, but at least the kid would have had shelter and enough food to keep him alive for a while. Sooner or later, Scott would have had to make some choices that might have gotten him into trouble, but hey, that truly wasn't Isaac's problem.

He'd convinced himself at the time that it made sense to keep Scott alive, but now that he thought about it, he knew that it could never work. The kid was too smart. And he'd lied to him. Isaac had heard the dickhead in the tunnel ask about Thomas Powell (and just how the hell did he come up with *that?* He hadn't heard that name in years!), and the fact that Scott didn't answer about it truthfully told Isaac something that he frankly didn't want to know. It all came down to the fact that the kid was too goddamn smart for his own good. Certainly too smart for Isaac's good.

His was a business of details. Every job carried its risks, and on every job, something went wrong. Call it Murphy's Law or just plain bad luck, but that's the way it was. One or two things *always* went wrong. Since Isaac was a professional, though, his plans allowed for a certain number of mistakes. That's why he always carried an extra weapon and extra ammunition, an extra driver's license and pass-port—all of them packaged for easy disposal if it came to that. It was the nature of his business to be extremely careful, and to capitalize on the mistakes of those who were not.

But it was unconscionable to allow so huge a complication as a witness to go uncorrected. It's why he had to kill the truck driver. And it was why the boy had to die.

In the darkness, his fingers found the ammunition clip, and with his thumb, he verified that he'd loaded hollow points. With luck, Scott would be sound asleep when it happened, and he wouldn't know a thing. Isaac would blast him three times in half that many seconds, and the hollow points would do the rest, expanding to twice their size as they shredded the boy's vitals. Guaranteed death, no suffering.

Scott was a nice kid. Isaac owed him that much.

NOTHING MOVED BUT THE WIND OUTSIDE. With the fire and the wood stoves banked down for the night, the place was downright cold; cold enough to see your breath, Scott thought, even though he in fact could not.

He made it down the stairs to the main level without a sound, and walked quickly to the front door, where he plucked his coat from its peg and put it on. There he paused. He was being foolish. No hat, no gloves, no shoes, he wouldn't make it two miles. More than that, he didn't even know where he was going.

He needed to find something for his feet. That was nonnegotiable. But what? The place was as clean as a model home—not a piece of paper out of place, let alone a pair of shoes. So, what was he going to do? For a second, he thought about cutting up the cotton cloth on the kitchen table and wrapping the strips around his feet like the pictures he'd seen of George Washington's troops at Valley Forge, but he dismissed that as senseless. He needed something to insulate against the wet and the cold.

His eyes moved to the hidden door that led to the secret room and its secret tunnel. No doubt, that's where Isaac put his stuff. Probably in the safe. On the off chance that Isaac had left it unlocked, he pulled on the handle, but of course nothing moved.

Dammit. The phone was in there, too—his backup plan. If he could somehow get inside the little room, he could duck outside long enough to make a call on the satellite phone and then return to bed to await his rescue. He could be in and out in just a few minutes and Isaac would never be the wiser until a SWAT team swooped down on him.

The hinges.

He heard himself gasp. Could it really be that simple? He knew for a fact that the door opened outward, so didn't that mean, by definition, that the hinges were on the outside? The living room light was only moderately helpful this far away, so he had to feel his way with his hands.

"Yes!" he whispered. Not only were the hinges on the outside of the door, but the pins had already worked themselves partially out. If he could pull them the rest of the way, he wouldn't even need the latch to open the door. It was a trick he'd learned at camp one summer after he and his roommate found themselves locked into their room by pennies crammed into the doorjamb.

Scott pulled on the pins with his fingers, but they wouldn't budge. He needed a screwdriver or a chisel, something to slide under the head of the hinge pin that he could then whack to get it to slide.

A butter knife would do just fine, thank you very much, and here in the kitchen, there was a whole drawerful.

The real trick was to be quiet. With the handle of the knife clutched in his left fist, he tucked the blade under the top ridge of the pin and used the heel of his right hand as his hammer. He didn't hit so much as he tapped, gentle yet firm strokes that he hoped would break the pins loose. The first one turned out to be easier than he'd expected. He felt it budge on the third or fourth stroke, and on the very next, he felt it sliding free.

Yes!

Only one more to go. He stuffed the first pin into his pocket, for lack of a better place to put it, and stooped for a better angle on the second. He'd just settled the blade into place when he heard a door open somewhere behind him. Crouched in the shadow of the kitchen's center island, Scott craned his neck to see Isaac, dressed in his nightclothes, walking out of his bedroom and across the living room toward the stairs.

Scott felt the panic boil in his belly. If he was coming for a midnight snack, Scott was totally screwed.

His heart hammered as he watched Isaac scan the room as if sensing that something was amiss. Scott would have sworn that he looked directly at him, and he was ready to bolt, but then the man looked away and up the stairs. Isaac was disturbed by whatever was on his mind, and Scott didn't like it one bit.

Then, Isaac started to climb to the second floor. *Oh, shit!* Scott's mind screamed. *He's going to find my bed empty!*

When he saw the gun in Isaac's hand, his fear turned to horror.

28

BRANDON SAT IN THE DARKENED LIVING ROOM, staring out the
towering windows at the ghostly outline of the trees below. In his
right hand, he swirled ice cubes in his scotch, waiting for the temperature to get just right inside the glass. It was his fourth, so his lips and
tongue were well calibrated by now. He heard a door open, and as he
shifted his eyes upward, he caught the reflection of a door opening
on the second floor, beyond the railing to the loft. A shapely silhouette in a quilted bathrobe filled the lighted space, and he watched as
she glided toward the steps, and on down to the first floor.

"I thought you were sleeping in Scotty's room," Sherry said softly,
her voice barely a whisper. "Scott's room, I meant."

"That was my plan," Brandon said. "But between the trophies on
the wall and the monsters in my head, I thought I'd sit here and get
drunk instead."

"Is it working?"

"Oh, yeah. Nice scotch, by the way. The Macallan, twenty years
old."

"It's not mine. Mark Olshaker's a great fan of the single malt."

Brandon's eyebrows arched. "The publisher? This is his house? I
never thought to ask." This afternoon's confrontation had led to an
uneasy truce between the two of them.

Sherry nodded. "Uh-huh. He opens it up to his more profitable
authors."

"Nice perk. And what's with all the dead animals on the wall? Are those the disguised heads of the less profitable authors?"

Sherry laughed. "Hunting's his other passion. Behind skiing." In the awkward silence that followed, Sherry helped herself to a spot on the sofa next to him, close but not touching, and wrapped herself in the blanket that had been tossed on the back. "I just got off the phone with Audrey," she said. "She twisted enough arms to pull a press conference together tomorrow afternoon around three. After the president is done with his dog and pony show."

Brandon checked his watch. "It's after midnight."

Sherry gave a little shrug. "She's her most persuasive when people are too tired to fight back." Another awkward pause. "Did I hear you on the phone with Chief Whitestone?"

In the dark, she could see his shadow nod. He said, "I want to hate that son of a bitch, but I can't. He's a good man in a bad spot. I look at things from his perspective and I realize I'd probably make the same decisions as his." He paused for a long sip on his drink. "I just wish I could make somebody understand that he's still alive out there."

Sherry let the comment hang there, unsure whether to pursue it. "Tell me why," she said finally. "Tell me about this feeling you have."

Brandon shook his head. He knew that no one but he could possibly understand. "It's a certainty, not a feeling. That's the best I can do. I just know, beyond all doubt, that Scott isn't dead. Yet."

Sherry heard the frustration in his voice, took a deep breath as she considered it. "It's not beyond the realm of reason, you know." What little light there was glinted off Brandon's eyes as he turned toward her. "Psychologists know that there are levels of communication between people that defy rational analysis. I can't count the number of studies I've read over the years where siblings or parents and children are separated by half a world, yet when one is in trouble, the others somehow know it. Usually, it's more of a feeling than a certainty, but it's all part of a continuum."

Brandon looked at her for a long moment. "So, you're saying you believe me?"

"I've always believed that you believed," she hedged. "I'm skeptical about a lot of things, Brandon, but too often, the evidence bears out exactly what you're saying. I think it's what the power of prayer is all about."

"Believe this, too," Brandon said. "Your saying that means a lot to me."

A minute later, Sherry said, "I *am* sick with worry, you know."

"I know you are. Too many people are watching for you to show it." Brandon chuckled. "I personally prove one of your primary points, you know." He had her attention. "I'm living proof of what happens when you allow your kid to become your primary focus. Over these past six years, I've allowed Scott to *become* my life—or, mine to become his—and look at me now."

"You're a good dad, Brandon."

His eyes glinted again.

Sherry laughed in spite of herself. "Don't gape at me like that," she said. "You know you're a good dad. Scott knows you're a good dad. Just as he knows that I'm a crappy mom."

"Oh, Sherry—"

"Don't patronize. I know what I know. I'm not a totally bad mother, mind you; I just suck as a mom. There is a difference."

Brandon nodded in the darkness. Yes, there was a difference, and he knew exactly what she meant.

For the longest time, they sat there together, staring out the frosted window at the vast expanse of the mountains, each reveling in the first civil words they'd shared in over half a decade.

"Larry's panicking, you know," she said. "I told him you were staying here in Scott's room and he freaked."

"What's wrong with me staying here?"

"Not a thing. He's just afraid we might try to get back together."

Brandon still didn't get it.

"He said that he's very happy with us quietly hating each other. He's afraid that if we reconcile, it's only a matter of time before the cold war goes hot again, and then he'll have to endure the fallout."

Brandon smiled. "He's probably got a point."

But maybe he didn't, Sherry thought. Sitting here in the dark, wrapped in her heavy wool blanket, Sherry tried to imagine what it would be like to reconcile, to be a family again. The images came easily. It wouldn't be the same family structure that she'd rejected all those years ago, that was for sure. She could afford housekeepers now, and someone to do the cooking. A new house with Brandon would be the household of adults. Even Scotty was grown now, though only God knew how he'd shot up so fast.

Sherry Carrigan O'Toole was nobody's sentimental sap. She knew the damage that had been done over the years, but sitting here in the quiet, next to Brandon, watching his shadow, she could again see the man with whom she'd fallen in love, nearly at first sight. Somehow, the heat of their crisis here in Utah had smoothed the edges of her anger, and as that poisonous emotion eroded away, she found herself facing a hole in her heart. All the success in the world wouldn't fill the other side of the bed every night.

These thoughts were silly, she told herself—the stuff of desperate battlefield romances. Still, where flames once flourished, surely there was a chance of a lingering spark. Maybe if they took it slowly. It wasn't as if they had nothing in common—

"It won't happen, you know," Brandon said.

"Huh? I'm sorry?" She could see his scowl, even in the darkness.

"I hope you told Larry to relax. There won't be a reconciliation."

Sherry scoffed, as if it were the most preposterous thing she'd ever heard. "Of course not."

"It'd be nice not to be at each other's throats all the time, but to get back together . . ." Brandon leaned forward, as if trying to get a better look at her face in the shine of the moon. "I hope I haven't signaled otherwise."

Sherry laughed a little too hard. "I don't care what you've signaled," she said. "I'm too smart to make the same mistake twice."

Brandon let the comment hang for a moment, trying to read it. "Good," he said, finally. Placing his empty glass on the coffee table, he pulled himself out of the sofa and stood. "Thanks for the press conference, Sherry."

She waved him off. "I'm just glad to help."

"Well, I know you're not completely comfortable with it, and I wanted you to know—"

"Really, it's nothing."

Brandon felt uneasy, confused by the change in the atmosphere. "Okay, then," he said. "I'm going to try to get some sleep." He paused. "Are you okay?"

"Good night, Brandon."

When she was alone again, Sherry lay down on her side, her head resting on the warmth of the pillow where Brandon had been sitting. Pulling the blanket tight around her shoulders, she stared out at the vastness of the night. The tears came from nowhere. Once they started to flow, she was powerless to stop them.

FOR WHAT SEEMED LIKE MINUTES, but couldn't possibly have been more than a few seconds, Scott stared at the pistol dangling from Isaac's hand.

I'm dead, he thought. *He's going to kill me!*

Just like that, all options evaporated. This was no longer about whether he should stay or leave, it wasn't about shoes. It was about getting the hell out of there. In the flash of an instant, his mind calculated the options. He had what, thirty seconds? Probably less. That's the time it would take for Isaac to enter Scott's room and discover that he was no longer there. Then the chase would be on. If he dashed for the front door, he'd have to run through wide open spaces, and Isaac would be able to drop him with a single shot. The very thought of it turned his stomach.

That left only one option, and before he'd even made a conscious decision to use the tunnel, he was already on his way. He had one hinge pin to go, and a whole life to lose.

YEARS OF EXPERIENCE had proven to Isaac that speed mattered in these things. From time to time, particularly in his dealings with organized crime, his clients specifically ordered a torturous death, but they were rare. Fact was, Isaac took no more pleasure out of his victims' pain than a dentist did from his patients'. The job was a messy one, and a certain amount of pain was inevitable, but except in the most unusual circumstances—and for the highest prices—he liked to keep things fast and simple. Certainly, that was what he intended for the boy.

He reached the top of the stairs and started down the hallway. Isaac had assigned Scott the second door down on the right for no real reason, other than the fact that it was the largest of what he imagined once were guest rooms. Isaac had acquired the place fully furnished, and hadn't entertained a single guest since. Until yesterday.

He paused at the bedroom door, gathering himself for what arguably was the most disturbing hit of his career. But waiting made nothing easier for anyone. He turned the knob and glided silently into the darkness.

His own shadow, cast by the dim lamplight from below, blocked part of the bed, where nothing moved as he entered. Among the shades of black and gray, he clearly made out the pillow, and what he thought was the outline of the sleeping boy under the covers.

It was important to Isaac that the boy not awaken to understand his fate, that he be taken in his sleep. Rather than risk getting too close, then, he fired from just inside the door.

IN THE SILENCE OF THE DARK CABIN, the pistol shots sounded like hand grenades. There were three of them altogether, fired quickly, just as the pin cleared the bottom hinge.

Stealth meant nothing anymore. From here on out, it was all about speed and distance.

With the hinges free, he jammed the knife blade into the thin crack where the side of the door met the jamb and he pulled hard, trying to pry them apart. The knife bent from the effort, and with no time to switch it out for a new one, he just flipped it around and pried in the other direction.

If the door panel had been made of stouter stuff, it never would have worked, but as it was, Scott pried it out just far enough that he could slip his fingers behind. From there, it was just a matter of pulling it open. He never even saw the alarm sensor. Nothing fancy, just a stupid buzzer like you could buy in any RadioShack. But God, the noise. Imagine ripping the skin off a live cat.

Two seconds later, the living room erupted in a sunburst of light.

•   •   •

"WELL, I'LL BE DAMNED," Isaac muttered. He thought he'd seen it in the glare of the muzzle flashes, but it wasn't till he turned on the bedroom light that he saw it was true. The kid had bolted on him. There was a hint of admiration in the thought. And a renewed commitment to kill him before he could do any damage to his plan.

Isaac sifted all the available options in the span of two heartbeats. Every shoe in the house was locked in the closet in Isaac's room, so that part of the plan hadn't been violated. That meant the boy was wandering the countryside with feet that would soon freeze to uselessness.

Funny, he thought. He'd had a sense that something was different in the living room when he'd crossed through it just a moment ago, and at the time he couldn't quite put his finger on it. Now he knew what it was: Scott's coat was missing from its spot on the peg. But the door was still locked, from the inside. That meant he was still in the house somewhere.

The goddamned tunnel.

But he'd have noticed if that door had been opened. Certainly, the alarm—

To Isaac's ear the shriek of the alarm seemed even louder than the gunshots.

He pivoted on his heel and made the hallway in two quick strides, slapping the wall switch as he passed and bringing daylight to the cabin in the middle of the night. He stepped onto the mezzanine balcony just in time to see his prey slipping into the secret room. He reacted instinctively, snapping the pistol up to firing position and taking aim with both eyes.

SCOTT YELLED AT THE SOUND of the gunshot, a scream devoid of thought or intent, erupting from his throat as he dove onto the floor of the secret room. Two more shots followed in rapid succession, each of them punching holes through the wood paneling. He heard Isaac's voice yelling something, but he didn't care. He didn't have time to listen. Seconds made all the difference now.

Moving with speed that he didn't know he could muster, Scott threw open the trap door, slamming it loudly against the floor.

Behind him, he could hear the sound of approaching footsteps. Isaac was running. And from the sound of it, he was fast.

Scott hesitated for a second, long enough to yank open the desk drawer and snatch the satellite phone. He stuffed it into his coat pocket and dashed to the hole in the floor. The ladder's iron rungs bent his feet painfully at the arches as he balanced there, trying to grab the hatch door to close it down on top of him. That's when he saw the MagLites sitting in their chargers, just inches out of reach.

Scott made the decision in an instant. In that kind of darkness, he'd never have a chance. In one fluid motion, he heaved himself out of the hole. For one long moment, he felt suspended in the air, like Michael Jordan slam-dunking a basketball. He grabbed a flashlight from the charger with his left hand, even as his right stayed closed around the handle of the hatch. On his way back down, he saw Isaac in the kitchen, braced for his next shot.

ISAAC COULD HAVE KICKED himself for even taking the shots from the mezzanine. His target was just a flash of fabric, really, as Scott dove for cover behind the wall. He'd tried his best to judge where the boy would land, but he knew it was useless even as he pulled the trigger. Even the best shot in the world couldn't hit a hidden target.

He was halfway down the stairs when he heard the tunnel hatch slam open, and he knew that the timing would be tight. He charged across the living room toward the kitchen, his weapon up and poised for a clear shot. Seconds counted.

Then the most amazing thing happened. Scott O'Toole jumped *out* of the opening in the floor, high into the air to snatch a light from its charger. It was the mistake that would cost the boy his life.

Isaac slid to a halt, braced himself, and took his shot.

THE MOMENTUM OF SCOTT'S FALL raised the heavy trap door just in time to take the bullet that would have killed him. He pulled the hatch up and over, the final slam nearly tearing his shoulder from its socket as he desperately hung on. He just dangled there, one-handed, his feet bicycling in the air. Somewhere down below, the MagLite clattered to the ground. With his free hand, Scott searched for the sliding bolt that would lock the hatch shut from the inside. It had to be there. Hell, he'd seen it just a few hours before, but in the impenetrable pitch blackness, it was all by feel.

There! There it was! He'd just wrapped his hand around the knob when he felt himself rising. Isaac was pulling the door open, lifting him right along with it.

IT WAS ONE OF THE MOST athletic moves that Isaac had ever seen, and it caught him totally by surprise. The hatch swung up from the floor the instant he pulled the trigger. But for the wooden barrier, the bullet would have torn through Scott's face.

"God*damm*it!" That kid was the luckiest son of a bitch on the planet.

He hurried to the hatch and tried to lift it. It moved, but barely, as if it weighed a couple of hundred pounds. Then he realized that it actually did. The kid had hung on! Isaac knew how small that handle on the other side was. It must have hurt like hell to do that. His admiration continued to bloom. Now, it would be an honor to kill him.

Isaac took a wide stance, the elbow of his gun hand braced against his thigh as he grabbed the handle on his side of the hatch and heaved with everything he had. On his worst day, he could outlift a sixteen-year-old boy.

SCOTT FELT HIMSELF coming right out of the hole.

"No!" he yelled. Jesus, the seam of light at the opening was three inches wide. Six inches.

Still hanging by one hand, he pulled his knees to his chest and gathered up his whole body. When he was nearly upside down, he planted his feet against the ceiling and pushed with everything he had. Yelling against the effort, he felt his attacker's grip break, and the hatch slammed shut again.

"Dammit!" the voice yelled from above.

And then he heard more shooting. Only this time, the noise of the bullets impacting the wood panel trumped the noise of the gunshots themselves.

Dangling again in midair, Scott's left hand found the slide bolts and he rammed them home, driving them a good six inches into the floor joists overhead. He'd bought himself some time. He didn't know how much, but somehow he knew it wouldn't be enough.

Disoriented in the blackness, he reached out with his feet to find the ladder rungs. They weren't exactly where he'd remembered them, but they were close. He gripped the cold metal rod with his toes to steady himself, then grabbed on with his hands.

On the ground now, he stooped to his hands and knees and searched through the darkness for the flashlight. It took too long but he found it, and the light reassured him.

A plan would be nice, he told himself, but for the time being, running seemed like a good substitute. A whole unexplained, frigid world lay beyond the tunnel, and he had to find it before Isaac made his next move. As it was, if Scott didn't hurry, all the killer would have to do was park himself at the end and wait.

With the flashlight beam opened to its widest spread, he started down the tunnel. His rational side told him that nothing had changed about the place since he was last here, but the irrational side wasn't impressed. Somehow, the shadows seemed spookier, the dark spots deadlier.

As the adrenaline ebbed, Scott found himself keenly aware of how cold he was. As his bare feet darted in and out of his peripheral vision, he saw how frighteningly red they looked. Every step was like running on broken glass. The lectures of his old buddy Sven returned: When hands or feet or noses were red, they hurt and they were healthy. As the tissues froze, though, the skin would turn white, and the whiter they got, the less pain there would be. When the pain went away entirely, the frostbite would be so deep that amputation would likely be required.

"Only a fool would be outdoors without proper foot protection," Sven had said.

Yeah, well, let's you and I trade places for a while, Scott thought.

At the end of the first section of tunnel, he made the hard left and started down the steeper slope. God*damn* the rocks hurt. His hands had begun to sting as well, that burning, tingling sensation that made you think you'd been playing in a nettle patch all day. The tunnel went on and on, it seemed, an impossible tangle of rocks and roots. It seemed so much longer at night, without the shining pupil of light gleaming back at him.

As he passed the spot where Agent Price had died, he tried to keep the light away from the crimson smears. From that point on, everything was unexplored territory. It was rockier here, and steeper still, but he pressed on, as quickly as he could—which wasn't nearly quickly enough.

Finally, he was out, his freedom marked by the unrestrained wind and the agony in his feet as they propelled him through the snow. He thought of those pictures he'd seen of the medieval torture devices where they'd enclose their prisoners' feet in boots lined with nails. He'd never felt anything so agonizing—so inescapable.

I can't do this, he thought.

"No, you *have* to. You *have to,* goddammit." As if saying it aloud made it more convincing.

But the temperature took his breath away. He'd never been in trouble this deep.

Stumbling to a deadfall, he sat with his feet out of the snow, retracted as far as he could get them into the legs of his pants, and he set about the business of making the satellite phone work. Finding the power button was easy. A luminous green dial jumped to life, giving him data on signal strength and volume. Truly, it appeared to be no more complicated than a cell phone. Between the cold and his fear, the boy's hands shook so badly as to be nearly useless as he dialed 9-1-1 and pressed send, only to be rewarded with a shrill error tone. What the hell . . . ? He tried it again, with the same result.

"Come on, work, dammit," he growled. But it wasn't going to. Okay, he had a better idea. He tried a new number, this one from memory, starting with the 703 area code for Virginia.

29

THE NIGHT WOULDN'T END. Brandon lay in Scott's bed in the chalet, staring at the silhouettes of roaring beasts on the wall, the razor-tipped weaponry crossed and mounted below. He lay under the covers, but he hadn't straightened the mess his son had left on the bed. That was Scott's job. He could pick it up himself when he got back.

He came here hoping to be comforted by these artifacts from his son, but instead found mostly torment. They haunted him. For the first time since this whole ordeal began, he felt a genuine sense of danger, of impending doom.

Something was wrong, and try as he might to ascribe it to his overactive imagination, he couldn't make it stick. His heart raced and breath eluded him. Perhaps this was what people meant when they talked about panic attacks. It was as if he'd run a race and now there wasn't enough air in the room to compensate. He was losing it.

When he first heard the phone, he didn't know what to make of it. There was a distant quality to it, as if it belonged in another world. It took two rings for him to recognize the sound for what it was, and a third to realize that it was coming from the other end of the house, all the way across the giant foyer, near the door.

Who in the world could possibly be calling him at this hour?

Whitestone! With that thought, he bolted out of bed and dashed across the living room, clipping his shin on the coffee table as he made a run for the foyer.

"What's wrong?" Sherry shouted sleepily from the sofa, but then she got it, too.

Five rings. He slid across the polished marble tiles in the entry-way, and jammed his hands into both coat pockets at the same time. He couldn't remember where he'd put the damn thing. It rang a sixth time before he finally found it and snapped it open.

"Yeah? Hello?"

"Dad!"

Brandon's heart leaped out of his chest. "Scott!" In the living room, he heard Sherry knock something over as she scrambled to her feet. "Oh, my God, Scott, is it really you?"

"Is it him?" Sherry yelled. "Is it really Scotty?"

Brandon held up his hand to silence her, then plugged a finger into his other ear. The signal seemed scratchy, filled with the kind of background noise you'd expect from a call placed from Borneo. "If this is some kind of prank, I swear to God—"

"No, it's really me," the voice said, and Brandon recognized it right away as the real thing. Nothing he'd ever heard had sounded so sweet as his son's voice; not the grandest symphony nor the sweetest love song. Breathless, his eyes huge, he nodded a confirmation to Sherry, then staggered to the steps to sit before he fell down. "Jesus, son, where are you? Are you all right?"

"No!" Scott said, his voice a harsh whisper. "No, he's trying to kill me. And then he's going to kill the president. I'm freezing to death and he's going to kill me!"

Brandon grabbed the stair rail to steady himself against the spinning room.

SCOTT COULDN'T KEEP a decent signal for all the trees. He didn't know if he was being heard at all. "Can you hear me?"

". . . trying to do what? Who?"

"His name is Isaac," Scott said. "Or maybe Thomas. I'm not sure." Suddenly, in the head rush and the freezing cold, Scott's mind wouldn't cough up last names. "You've got to help me, Dad."

"How, son? How can I help you?" He could hear the panic clearly, even through the terrible connection. "Hello?"

"I'm here, can you hear me?" He was talking louder than he should, but he couldn't bear the thought of losing the connection. "Send help. There's a hunting cabin in the woods somewhere. I don't know exactly where, but it's along a river. A bootlegger's cabin. That's where he is. But you've got to hurry."

On the other end of the line, in the chalet, Brandon's free ear hurt, he was pressing his finger so hard. He heard, "cabin . . . woods . . . exactly where . . . bootleggers . . . he is . . . hurry."

"Tell me where you are," Brandon said, shouting to be heard over the static.

Scott couldn't afford to speak any louder. He couldn't afford to speak as loudly as he was. "I don't know!" he hissed, his exasperation growing. "But Isaac, or Thomas, or whatever his name is, is trying to kill me."

His dad couldn't hear him anymore. Or, if he could, then he wasn't responding. Scott stepped back into the snow to change the position of the antenna, breaking into tears at the terrible pain that consumed him from his toes to his groin. "Dad, please. Can you hear me?"

"Yes!" Brandon's voice cheered. "Yes, I can hear you now. Whatever you just did, that was good. Now, tell me where you are."

The sound of an approaching engine paralyzed Scott. At first, he thought it was a motorcycle, but a second later, he recognized it as a snowmobile, revved high, and coming in fast.

"Shit, he's here!" Scott whispered. His time was up. As he'd feared, Isaac knew exactly where to find his prey. "Oh, God, he's gonna kill me."

"Who?" Brandon shouted. "*Who's* going to kill you? What are you talking about?"

Scott was out of time. Good signal or not, he had to scramble for a hiding place. But where could he possibly go? He turned to head for the woods, and on his first step, he tripped, losing his grip on both the phone and the MagLite as he sprawled face-first into the snow.

This was never going to work. He was doomed.

• • •

"SCOTT! ANSWER ME!" Brandon shouted. "Please, son, speak up, I can't hear you!"

Sherry stood at his arm, straining to hear. "What is it?" she asked. "What's wrong?"

"I don't know, dammit. I think he said something about somebody trying to kill him."

Sherry recoiled at the thought. "*Kill* him! That can't be right."

"Scott, are you there?" To Sherry: "Him and the president."

"*What?*"

"Scott!"

WITH THE NIGHT VISION GOGGLES IN PLACE, the whole world glowed an iridescent green. And despite the darkness, the glare of the snow was bright enough to hurt Isaac's eyes. Scott O'Toole had executed a gutsy escape, but when all was said and done, it would prove useless, effectively trading the quick and painless for the fearful and extended. The net result would be the same: within just a couple of minutes, the boy would be dead. A half hour after that, Isaac would be back in bed and asleep, girding himself for the task that lay ahead.

It had been a mistake to load hollow points. He'd screwed up, and he was man enough to admit it. The irony! The intent had been to make it easy on the kid. Now, as a result, he was racing through the snow in the middle of the night to finish a job that should have taken only a few seconds. If he'd loaded armor piercing rounds, or even steel jackets, it all would have ended in the warmth of the cabin. How many times did he have to learn the same lesson? In his business, compassion was the greatest liability.

He navigated the path at full throttle, easing off only when the side slope became too treacherous. He knew this trail thoroughly, and he'd traveled it most recently six nights ago, after the truck driver dropped him off. Besides the driveway, which Isaac used only occasionally for trips into town, the trail was the quickest route to the main road, which lay four miles to the east, over six little humps of ridges, just on the other side of Old Man Pembroke's place.

He slowed to a crawl as he approached the mouth of the escape tunnel, scanning the scenery as he went. On a normal day, the tunnel entrance looked merely like a gap between a couple of giant rocks—a cave of sorts, but with a steel gate set into the stone to keep out bears and their ilk, not to mention the kind of visitors he'd had to repel this afternoon.

Isaac came to a stop in front of the opening, shifted the snowmobile into neutral and throttled it down to a low idle before dismounting and unslinging his rifle. This time, he was taking no chances. The H&K MP5 rifle with its integrated suppressor had long become his preferred weapon for close-in work. Barely larger than a pistol when the stock was collapsed, it extended to be a thirty-inch carbine capable of taking down targets at considerable distances.

He was done underestimating the boy now. No more shortcuts. Isaac moved as he'd learned many years ago in his SEAL Team training, the weapon pressed tight against his shoulder, his knees bent, and his finger just outside the trigger guard. The weapon became an extension of his arm, the sights an extension of his eyes. If he saw it, he could shoot it, but out here, you had to be careful. Firing lanes were elusive, and no matter what kind of ammunition you'd chosen, impact with a tree trunk deflected the aim.

The boy would be hiding; it was the only weapon available to him. As in any game of hide-and-seek, victory went to the one who was most patient. Isaac moved at an impossibly slow pace, continuously scanning all compass points as he walked like a fencer, always taking care not to tangle his feet.

The footprints in the snow made the whole game ridiculously unfair. Slightly more difficult to see in the flat green light of the night scope, they nonetheless led from the mouth of the tunnel, up an adjacent hill, where they became more difficult to follow. Difficult, but far from impossible.

Isaac knew that Scott had taken the satellite phone, so it only made sense that the boy would want to find the higher ground, and sure enough, that's just where the footprints led. And there, up ahead, the light of the phone's display might as well have been a lighthouse beacon. It was almost too easy.

The boy had chosen a deadfall as his hiding place—as logical a spot as any—and as Isaac climbed through the tangles of branches and tree trunks, he yet again found himself admiring the kid's guts. He couldn't imagine making this climb barefooted.

Thirty feet away now, Isaac quickened his pace. Stealth was irrelevant now. If Scott jumped up and bolted, he'd shoot him on the run. If he continued to try to hide, he'd shoot him where he lay. Now, it all came down to a seventy-five-cent bullet.

"Hey, Scott," he taunted from fifteen feet away. "Why don't you just stand up and make this easy?" But of course, the boy didn't move from his spot in the corner of the log. Isaac sighed. "Well, what the hell," he said, and he closed the distance in five seconds.

Only, there was no one there.

Down the hill and through the trees, the grinding roar of the snowmobile motor ripped the night into a thousand pieces.

Isaac whirled at the sound, firing at the blur of movement. The gun bucked against his shoulder and the action clacked, but even in the stillness of the night, the gunshot was merely a whisper.

SCOTT HAD THE THROTTLE TWISTED all the way to full before his butt had even hit the seat, and as he engaged the clutch, he was gone like a NASA launch, accelerating through a cloud of exhaust and snow and noise. For the next thirty seconds, it was all about speed. Speed meant survival, it was really that simple. As he struggled to maintain control of the vehicle, he wondered where all the shooting was. He'd expected to be making this escape in the proverbial hail of bullets.

He got his answer when the snowmobile's windscreen shattered, followed a half second later by the *tink* of a bullet punching a hole somewhere else on the machine. Another buzzed past his ear, and he crouched as low as he could and twisted the throttle to its limits and beyond. All around him, tree trunks sprayed high velocity chunks of bark. There for a second, it seemed as if every tree were exploding, and the vehicle itself vibrated from two more hits somewhere.

But he raced on, the treads on the snowmobile kicking up a rooster tail of powder.

Scott had no idea how fast he was going—it didn't matter—but thirty seconds after the whole thing began, after he knew that he was safely concealed by the shelter of the next hill, he didn't let off a bit. He didn't need to. Maybe his eyes had just become adjusted to such things these past few days, but with the glimmering moon overhead, filtered through the trees, the trail laid itself out perfectly for him. After a minute or two, he even found the switch for the vehicle's headlight.

He didn't know where the trail went, but that, too, didn't matter; all trails went *somewhere.*

As he powered toward the crest of the next hill, Scott realized that he had won. He'd beaten the odds again. On this night, Scott O'Toole was invincible. And in spite of the agonizing cold, and the fear that pounded in his temples, right at that particular moment, he knew without a doubt that he was the luckiest teenager on the planet.

ISAAC LOWERED THE WEAPON from his shoulder and looked at it as if it had let him down. Even with the action set to full-automatic, the bastard had still gotten away.

"He set me up," Isaac mused aloud, genuinely amazed that he'd taken the boy's bait. "He knew I'd go for the obvious and he doubled back on me."

A buzzing sound, not unlike that of an angry insect caught his ear, and he cocked his head curiously as he stared down at the telephone. The line was open!

Scowling, Isaac brought the phone to his ear. "Scott!" someone yelled. "Scott, are you there?"

"Who is this?" Isaac asked.

"Oh, thank God!" the voice exclaimed. "Is that you, Scott?" Then, as if to someone else, he said, "It doesn't sound like Scott."

"Who are you?" Isaac asked again. "Are you his father?"

"Yes, I'm Brandon O'Toole, Scott's father. Is he there?"

"I'm afraid your son is dead," Isaac said. "And I'm the man who killed him."

He disconnected the line, then opened it again for one more call.

30

It wasn't just his hands and feet anymore.

As Scott tore through the wilderness, the wind lashed at his face and his ears as well, making them feel brittle as glass. Tears flowed from the onslaught, only to freeze on his face. If he didn't find shelter soon, his escape would mean nothing, merely an opportunity to die somewhere else in the vast wilderness. Even the invincible, it turned out, could freeze to death. For a while, he tried backing off the throttle to cut down on the wind, but then he worried about the additional exposure time, and then he sped up again.

He found himself longing for the times when a mere plane crash seemed like a huge problem.

Speed, time and distance had no meaning for him anymore, all of it measured in slices of forever. A crushing fatigue overtook him without warning, leaving him dizzy and slightly disoriented. For a moment there, as he contemplated what life would be like without fingers and toes, it seemed as if the woods were moving past him at a rate much faster than the snowmobile was moving forward. Sven's warnings about death by exposure tried to infiltrate his thoughts, but he pushed them away, wishing that he'd never attended that goddamn gloomy class.

When he first saw the glimmer of light ahead through the trees, he assumed it to be a hallucination, and sure enough, when he blinked his eyes, it was gone. A few seconds later, though, it returned, only to blink away again, and Scott realized that the trees and hills were playing hide-and-seek with him. On one sighting, it would be on his left, and then as he steered his way down the trail, it would reappear on his right, only to disappear again among the trees.

At first, he thought the light was moving—maybe another vehicle—but as he got closer, he realized that with the twists and turns in the trail, he was the one moving relative to the light, not the other way around.

Scott smiled, in spite of his agony. It was a house, that much he could tell. And the trail led right to it. Elated, he tossed his head back and cheered, "Invincible!"

He was going to make it, after all. He'd step inside, tell the owner what had happened, and wait for the police to come and rescue him.

He thought of Isaac again. Surely he knew where the trail led, and just as surely, he'd be along soon to settle all accounts. Okay, then, new plan: He'd alert the owner to the danger ahead, and they could drive together to safety. It couldn't be any simpler.

Scott slowed to barely moving as he navigated the last turn, finding himself at a T-intersection with what looked to be a driveway.

The snow here was churned and broken, two tire tracks clearly visible, leading to an old pickup truck parked in a doorless garage. Scott pulled to a stop as close to the front door as he could manage, peeled his numb fingers from the handlebars and dismounted. It wasn't like walking on broken glass anymore. It was like walking on fire.

The door opened as he raised his fist to knock, revealing a short disheveled old man who smelled of stale sweat and alcohol. His stringy yellow hair hadn't been washed or combed in days. "Come in," the man said. "You look like hell."

Scott more stumbled than stepped into the little house. It smelled like a concentrated version of the old man, and was furnished in Salvation Army rejects. He could see the whole place in a single glance. "Thank you," he said.

"Take the chair by the fire. Get yourself warm. You're lucky if you ain't frostbit."

Scott did him one better, limping to a spot ten inches in front of the fire. The intensity of the heat was nearly as agonizing as the cold.

"Thank you so much," Scott said again. "But we can't stay here. There's a man chasing me—"

"I know," said the old man, drawing a curious look from Scott. "You're Scott O'Toole. I've been expecting you."

That's when Scott saw the gun in his hand.

BRANDON SAT ON THE SOFA, his arm around Sherry, watching Barry Whitestone hang up the telephone. He didn't like the look on the chief's face. "What?"

The chief cocked his head curiously. "The call traced to Waco, Texas."

"That's ridiculous!" Sherry blurted. Brandon agreed.

"I asked them to recheck twice. That's where it came from."

"Do you have a name?" Brandon asked.

"That'll take a little longer," Whitestone said. As much to himself as to anyone else, he added, "That just can't be right." He looked to Brandon. "Tell me again what he said."

Brandon started at the beginning and plowed through it all for the fourth time. "It's not going to change, Barry," he said at the end.

James Alexander had been the last to arrive, and had been listening quietly from the foyer. When he cleared his throat, all heads turned to face him. "That business about the president," he said. "I think we need to get the Secret Service involved."

Whitestone sighed. As much as he hated the notion of prolonging his exposure to those sons of bitches, once someone breathed the word *assassination* it all became a new ball game. He nodded and made it so. To Brandon, he said, "We need to shift this meeting to our office."

Brandon nodded. "I'm coming with you."

"Suppose he calls back?" Whitestone asked.

"He called on the cell phone. I'll have it with me."

Whitestone wasn't in the mood to argue. "We'll see just how many people one little police station can hold. James, make your phone call."

Alexander tossed off a two-fingered salute and headed for the phone. He hadn't taken two steps when he stopped. "Wait!" he exclaimed, launching everyone out of their chairs. "Waco? I know what that's about." He thought for a moment to recover the name. "Terrastar. You familiar with it?"

"Sounds like a software company," Sherry said.

"It's a satellite phone company," James corrected. "One of those little portable jobs, works anywhere. I have one of them on my boat. The phone bills all originate in Waco, Texas. That's the local number for them."

"No matter where you are?" Whitestone asked.

Alexander nodded. "Right. Think about it. The whole concept works on shooting a beam to a satellite instead of a cell antenna. No matter where you are, the satellite thinks that Waco is home."

The room fell silent for ten seconds as they all contemplated this.

"So, Scott is still local," Whitestone said. "And I'd bet real money that he's still alive."

Sherry sat up straight, wiping her eyes. This sounded like something she needed to hear.

Whitestone explained, "It doesn't track for me that he's dead. From everything said, it seems we're working with a professional killer. Wouldn't make sense for him to taunt you like that."

"But why would he say it if it wasn't true?" Sherry asked.

"I'm guessing frustration. Anger." He turned to Brandon. "That's one resourceful kid you've got."

Brandon smiled. "What did I tell you?"

SCOTT STARED AT THE PISTOL, his mouth agape. "W-What are you doing?" Tears pressed behind his eyes as his hope for rescue evaporated. "Who *are* you?"

"Wayne Pembroke is my name," the old man said. The pistol looked like something out of an old cowboy movie, and it seemed to take everything Pembroke had just to keep it pointed at him. "Mr. Clavan called me a few minutes ago. Told me to keep an eye out for you. Said you stole his snowmobile and was headin' this way. Said if I saw you, to keep an eye on you till he got here. Shouldn't be more than a few minutes."

"I didn't steal anything!" Scott protested. *Jesus, how many names does this guy have?* "He's trying to kill me, and I got away."

Pembroke laughed, as if that were the most ridiculous story he'd ever heard.

Scott rose tentatively back to his feet, prompting the old man to cock the pistol. "Stay back," Pembroke said.

"Look at me, for God's sake!" Scott proclaimed. "I'm barefoot. I got no gloves, no hat. Do I look like somebody who's out to steal a snowmobile?" In spite of the danger, he found himself laughing at the absurdity of it all. "Wouldn't you at least think I'd bring *shoes?*"

Pembroke's face darkened as his eyes dropped to the boy's feet, and then back up to his eyes. He looked half-sold.

"I was in a plane that crashed," Scott explained, wishing for all the world that he had a story that was less outrageous. "Maybe you heard about me on the news? The author's kid who was lost in a plane crash in the snowstorm?"

"Ain't had no TV here since ninteen and ninety-seven," Pembroke said.

Scott limped a couple of steps closer. "Just trust me, okay? I'm telling the truth. I hiked through the woods and I stumbled upon Isaac DeHaven's house. His ranch. The bootlegger's place."

"Isaac who?"

Scott instinctively checked out the window, expecting to see headlights in the driveway. "DeHaven. The guy you call Clavan. Some guys came to the house this afternoon, and they thought his name was Powell. The guy's got like a thousand names."

It all seemed too much for the old man. "You're talking crazy," he said.

"He's a killer, okay?" Scott blurted. His voice rose an octave. "Clavan—whatever you want to call him—he's a killer. And he's planning to kill the president."

"Of the United States?" Pembroke scoffed. "He's staying here on vacation."

Scott gave him an expectant look, waiting for him to put it together for himself. He rapped his own forehead with his knuckles. "Hel-lo. That's the point. The president of the United States is here. The killer is here."

"Clavan is always here," Pembroke said. "He *lives* here."

"I watched him kill two people today, Mr. Pembroke. Saw it with my own eyes. He made up some story about the witness protection program, but I guess he knew that I saw through it, so now he's coming after me."

"This is crazy," Pembroke said. But his face showed a crack in his commitment.

"It *sounds* crazy, I know," Scott granted. "But I'm telling you, every word of it is the truth."

"If he's a professional killer, then how come you're still alive?"

"Because I never was where he thought I was going to be. Christ, he shot at me—" Scott paused, suddenly struck with an inspiration. "Come with me," he said. "I want to show you something." He headed for the door.

"Where are you going?"

"Outside. I want to show you."

Pembroke raised the revolver a little higher. "You just sit down like I told you in the beginning."

"There are bullet holes in the snowmobile," Scott explained. "He shot at me when I was leaving—"

"Of course he did. You was stealin' it."

"I wasn't stealing—" Scott let out a roar of frustration. "He was going to *kill* me for stealing a damn snowmobile? Does that make sense to you? If he was so attached to the machine, why would he shoot it full of holes? Come here, I'll show you."

Scott watched as the wheels turned in Pembroke's head. He was coming around.

"He's trying to kill me," the boy said softly. "And after he's done it, he can't afford to keep you alive, either." That piqued the old man's interest. "You'd be a witness. In his line of work, witnesses are bad. That's why he's after *me*."

Bingo. Scott actually saw his argument strike home.

"So," Scott pressed, "all we have to do is call the police—"

"No!" Pembroke said it so suddenly, with such force, that Scott jumped. "No cops."

"But he's—"

"No cops!" Clearly, this was nonnegotiable. "I've done some business with Clavan over the years, mostly taking care of equipment for him—that snowmobile, in fact. I don't need no cops snoopin' around here and findin' that out."

"So, what do you suggest?"

Pembroke gave him a hard look. "My instinct is to throw you back like a fish that's too small to eat," he said. "I don't need none of this shit, okay? My instincts say if I shoot you myself, nobody'll be the wiser, and won't nobody be on my back." He paused, his gray eyes narrowing. "But they also say that if I was Clavan, I'd think that you probably told me all of this, and if it's true, then you're right, he'd have no choice but to kill me, too."

The old man took a deep breath and scowled. "Goddammit," he growled. "What size shoe do you wear?"

"Excuse me?"

"Shoes, boy!" Pembroke roared. "What size do you wear?"

"Um, ten. I think."

The old man eased the hammer of the revolver down and gestured with his head toward a dark corner of the living room. "Check in that pile over there, and you should find some eleven and a half boots. Put 'em on and meet me outside."

"Where are we going?"

"Outta here."

EVEN AT THREE-THIRTY in the morning, Agent Sanders wore a suit and a crisply starched shirt. Every hair was in place. It was as if he'd never lain down. Barry Whitestone was lucky he didn't have his badge on upside down.

"We've confirmed that the Waco telephone number is, indeed, a Terrastar number," Sanders said.

Whitestone turned to James Alexander. "I thought *we* did that."

"Well, I've confirmed it. The number traces to a man named Cranston Burkhammer of Toledo, Ohio. We've got Toledo police rousting him right now."

"In *Ohio?*" Brandon said. "He's not going to be the same guy."

"You a detective in your spare time, Mr. O'Toole?" Sanders said.

As if it were possible, he was even more condescending early in the morning.

"No, I'm a rocket scientist," Brandon said. "But it doesn't take one of me to know that Burkhaldter, or whatever the hell his name is, can't be in Ohio if I just talked to Scott on his phone from Utah."

"You're assuming that the call was made locally."

"Scott said he walked to the cabin. He sure as hell didn't walk to Toledo." Brandon looked over at Whitestone, who seemed to be enjoying the back-and-forth.

Sanders paused for a second, seemingly low on steam. Finally, he said, "When the president of the United States is involved, you cover every available base."

"Does he know about all this?" Alexander asked. "The president, I mean?"

Sanders shook his head. "No, and I don't intend for him to. He doesn't consult me on foreign policy, and I don't burden him with the details of my job." He turned to Brandon. "I'm terribly sorry for your loss," he said, his voice leaden with forced sympathy.

Brandon shot a look to Whitestone.

"Uh, Sanders," Barry said, "we're not ready to call that case closed yet. Just because a fruitcake says something doesn't mean it's true."

Sanders nodded. "Of course. Well, I hope everything turns out perfectly for you all, then. What I need to know is, how sincere was your son when he talked about this assassination threat?"

Brandon could count on one hand the people in the world whom he genuinely disliked after only one meeting. Agent Sanders was one of them. "Well, he sounded damned serious about someone trying to kill *him*," he said. "Neither of us had a whole lot of time to assess the seriousness of the threat to the president."

Sanders stewed for a moment. "I don't understand how your son could still be alive—even when he spoke to you—if a professional killer was after him."

"What a ghoul," Sherry said, her first words since arriving at the police station. "You sound disappointed."

Sanders scowled. "Hardly disappointed," he said. "Just confused."

"He's a resourceful boy," Brandon said.

Whitestone added, "And damned lucky."

Brandon was tired of talking about the president's problems. The president had all the power and authority of the most powerful nation on the planet to take care of him. For Scott, it was just a couple of exhausted small-town policemen.

"I've got a question," James Alexander said. "What about the other kid? Cody Jamieson?"

All eyes turned to Brandon, who blushed and looked away. "I never thought to ask," he said.

31

BUT FOR THE RUST, Pembroke's Ford pickup would have been a collection of steel panels. The engine roared like a tugboat, and from the way the lifters rattled, you'd have thought he put dice in there.

"It's about forty mile into town," the old man yelled over the noise. "A little place called Eagle Feather."

"Eagle Feather!" Scott exclaimed. "That's where I started out."

"Well, I ain't takin' you all the way in. I don't want to be no part of this nohow, you understand?"

Yeah, he understood. "Where do I go when you drop me off?"

"Why don't you just go home?"

"We're staying up in SkyTop."

Pembroke snorted out a laugh. "Well, I sure as hell ain't takin' you up there. If you just stick to Main Street, you'll see the police station up and on the left. Don't look like much, but trust me, they got jail cells you don't want no part of."

That sounded like the voice of experience, but Scott didn't pursue it. "I don't suppose you could crank the heater up, could you?"

"This is all she wrote," Pembroke yelled. "By the time we get to town, she should just about be warming up. I'm afraid it's a little tough on her, keeping up with all the breezes blow through here."

When he didn't hear a response, the old man turned to see if his passenger was all right.

Scott was lost someplace in his head, staring at a spot in the dark that only he could see.

THE PUNCH TO HIS SHOULDER nearly knocked him out the door.

"Hey, wake up!" Pembroke yelled. "We got trouble."

The words sliced through Scott's guts like a hot knife. He shook his head and blinked his eyes to wake up his brain. "What?" But Scott already saw it in the beam of light from the mirror that exposed the terror in Pembroke's eyes. Scott whirled in his seat to see the vehicle behind them, racing to catch up.

"Thirty seconds ago, he wasn't even there," the old man said.

Now he was only a hundred yards away and closing fast.

"Speed up!" Scott yelled.

"I got it on the floor as it is!"

"Maybe it's not him," Scott offered, and even without looking, he could sense the old man's glare. He felt something tap his thigh, and he looked down to see Pembroke's horse pistol, turned backward, butt facing him.

"Take it," Pembroke shouted. "Slow him down."

"*Shoot* him?"

"That, or throw it at him. I thought you said he was gonna kill you."

"Yeah, but . . ." Actually, he didn't have an argument. Behind them, the racing vehicle already had nearly halved the distance.

"That window there opens," Pembroke said, indicating the sliding panel in the middle of the rear windshield. "Open it up and pop off a shot. See if it don't get him to back off."

"Suppose I hit him?"

"Then I guess we all drive slower. Ever shoot a pistol before?"

"No. Well, a flare gun. Killed a wolf with it."

Pembroke craned his neck to look at Scott, flashed a yellow smile. "You'll have to tell me about that someday," he said. "Well, that bastard's gonna kick like a mad mule, so hang on tight. Pull the hammer all the way back."

That much, Scott knew. He thumbed the hammer back.

"All the way," the old man said. "Four clicks."

Scott was one shy. He pulled it all the way.

"Now stick it out the window and shoot it."

With the back window open, the temperature in the cab instantly dropped to unbearable. The approaching vehicle was only fifty yards back now, probably less. With the high beams in his eyes, all he could see was light. He held the gun with both hands, just as he'd seen on television cop shows, but the weapon was completely lost in the glare.

"Shoot!" Pembroke yelled.

"The light is blinding me!"

"Well, shoot the light, then! Jesus, shoot something!"

Scott hesitated. "But what if—"

Before he could form the question, a burst of automatic weapons fire ripped through the flatbed of the pickup. No gunshots, just the *tink tink tink* of bullets finding their mark.

Pembroke initiated a series of S-turns, taking up the entire roadway as they topped the crest of a hill. "Goddammit, boy, shoot! He's trying to drive and shoot at the same time. He won't be able to hit nothing."

Scott pulled the trigger. The blast and the muzzle flash were more what he would have expected from a cannon. He felt the recoil all the way into his shoulders. Isaac's vehicle slowed and swerved. Scott cocked and fired again. And again. Each time, the distance between the vehicles grew.

"Take it easy, Sundance!" Pembroke yelled. "After six, we're outta business, and he knows it. Settle into your seat for a bit and let me drive."

The shootout was more relaxing. Running downhill now, at speeds that made the whole truck vibrate, the S-curves of the road seemed somehow to be at odds with the S-curves Pembroke was driving. Scott watched him for a moment, amazed by the old man's athleticism as he yanked the steering wheel violently from one side to the next.

"He's not right on our tail anymore," Scott offered. "I can't even see him. I don't think you have to take the whole road anymore."

"I'm not trying to take the whole road," Pembroke barked. "I'm tryin' to settle her down. The steering linkage ain't as tight as it used to be."

What, in 1960? Scott didn't say. He just settled into his seat, the pistol gripped in his right hand, and his left braced against the dashboard. Funny, after surviving a plane crash, a twenty-four-hour hike in a blizzard, an attack by wolves and a couple of shootouts, it never occurred to him that he might die by sailing off the side of a mountain in a truck.

"How much further?" Scott asked.

"Five, ten mile, I'd guess. I figure by the time we get to the outskirts, if Clavan is the killer you say, he won't want to risk getting caught in town and he'll break off the chase." Pembroke's dim headlights revealed a hairpin turn up ahead, doubling around, and heading back uphill.

Scott saw in an instant that they were going too fast. "You see that?" he shouted.

Pembroke kicked out the clutch and downshifted. The ancient truck lurched and the engine screamed, but with a hundred yards to go, they were still way too fast.

"Slow down!" Scott yelled. "We're gonna wreck!"

The old man stood on the brake and cranked the wheel as if he were turning an aircraft carrier. The tires skidded and the back end fishtailed, first into a snowbank and then, on the rebound, into the side of the mountain. The left rear fender sent out a spray of sparks as it dragged along the rocks. But Old Man Pembroke hung on, never losing his concentration or his grip as the truck stayed on the road to complete the curve.

Scott couldn't believe it. He whipped around in his seat, surveying the damage—or the lack of it—and let out a war whoop. "You did it! Holy shit, I thought for sure we were gonna go flying, but you did it! All right, Mr. Pembroke!"

The old man tried to look annoyed by the outburst, but smiled in spite of himself. "Before you get too carried away, start looking through that window again." Ahead of them stretched a long, narrow bridge.

"Why, do you see him?" Scott spun in the seat.

"No, not yet, but he'll be there. After we get to the other side of this bridge, it's almost all uphill."

The engine screamed from the effort. For ten full minutes, which seemed like five full hours, the ancient pickup lumbered up the hillside, barely able to get out of its own way.

"See that sign up there?" Pembroke called, pointing to a rectangular plaque that read SCENIC OVERLOOK ½ MILE. "That's the halfway point on this hill."

Scott nodded, relieved. "Well, I still don't see any sign of Isaac's truck."

ISAAC DeHAVEN, a.k.a. Kevin Clavan, had broken off his chase nearly twenty minutes ago. That was stupid, driving at fatal speeds while shooting and being shot at, left-handed, no less. Amateur stuff; movie stuff. You never let your target have a level playing field, let alone let him have the advantage, but that's exactly what he had done. Surprised the shit out of him, too, when the kid took a shot at him. All things considered, given the mistakes he'd made back there, Isaac was lucky to be alive. He tried to tell himself it was because he was pissed, but that didn't make it any better. He was a professional, for God's sake. He couldn't afford to get pissed.

That was then; this was now, and finally, he had his advantage. As in all hunting, the secret to Isaac's line of work was to know two things very, very well: your prey and your terrain, and in this case, he was preparing for a turkey shoot.

The road to Eagle Feather traced the outline of the Arroyo Gorge, some geological formation in which Isaac had exactly zero interest, beyond the fact that on busy tourist days, traffic would back up for miles as cars pulled in and out of the scenic overlooks that faced each other on opposite sides. The view was indeed spectacular on a clear day, but at this hour, it was just a black stain against the night. Knowing that Pembroke would have to drive past the wide-open overlook, Isaac had set up shop in the pullover on the near side.

On a good day, with clean roads, the circuit from overlook to overlook would take fifteen minutes. With conditions the way they were, and given the condition of Pembroke's rattletrap piece of shit, he figured a minimum of twenty-five. At the fifteen-minute mark, just to be on the safe side, Isaac took his night goggles and his rifle and walked to the far side of his Suburban, there to wait for his prey to cross into the open.

He left the MP5 on the front seat and unlimbered the latest addition to his arsenal—a Heckler & Koch PSG-1, the most accurate semiautomatic sniper rifle in the world. At nearly eighteen pounds, it was heavier than his previous long-range guns, but the trade-off in performance was more than worth the compromise. The shot he'd have to make here would be a bitch, well over a thousand yards, but the road on the opposite side was very steep, and the opening fairly wide, so Isaac figured he'd have a solid ten to fifteen seconds to pump in as many rounds as it would take.

After twenty-five minutes, he was having a hard time keeping warm. He stomped his feet and marched in place to keep the blood circulating.

Headlights approaching from behind startled him. It was three in the morning, for Christ's sake, too late for tourists and too early for truckers to be making their rounds. He saw it from less than a quarter mile away, and he barely had time to sweep the goggles off his head and stash the rifle behind the right front tire before the approaching car's headlights swept over him. Isaac winced against the glare, concerned that the car seemed to be slowing.

His concern deepened when the blue-and-white light bar jumped to life on the vehicle's roof.

SCOTT DIDN'T UNDERSTAND why Pembroke had pulled the truck to a stop. "What are you doing?" he asked.

"Any signs of him yet?"

"Nothing but empty road," Scott said. "Come on, let's go."

Pembroke shook his head and wiped his nose with the palm of his hand. "I don't like it," he said.

Scott couldn't believe what he was hearing. "Don't like what? Jesus, let's go!"

"I don't think so."

A new fear gripped Scott's insides. Maybe Pembroke was chang-
ing his mind. Maybe he wasn't going to help him out after all.

"There's a big clearing up here," the old man said, scowling into
the night. "We go through that, and we'll be wide open for a good
long time. Fifteen, twenty seconds, maybe more."

"So?" Scott's voice strained with incredulity. "Isaac's nowhere to
be seen."

Pembroke pointed at the boy with a gnarled forefinger. "That,
young man, *is* the problem. Where the hell is he? He's had plenty of
time to catch up. So, I'm thinkin' he's not behind us at all no more.
I'm thinkin' he's on the other side of the Arroyo Gorge waiting for us
to cross so he can take us out."

"Is there another way?"

Pembroke's whole face pinched together as it folded into a hard
scowl. "Nope. 'Fraid not." He opened his door.

"Where are you going?"

"The overlook's just up there a bit. I'm gonna go take me a
look."

Scott opened his door, too. "I'm coming with you."

"Stay put," the old man said, waving him off. "Keep them feet
warm while you can. And keep an eye out the back window in case
I'm wrong."

Before Scott could object, Pembroke was off, disappearing into
the darkness beyond the headlights.

"HOWDY," SAID THE COP, as he stepped around the front of his
cruiser.

"Evening, officer," Isaac said. He moved quickly to meet the cop
before he had a chance to see the rifle he'd stashed. He extended his
hand. "Kevin Clavan," he said.

The cop eyed him suspiciously, then gave in and shook hands.
"Officer Tingle," he said. "Something wrong with your vehicle?" he
asked.

Isaac seemed surprised by the question. "What? Oh, no. Only
with my bladder. Too small for my own good. When you gotta go, you
gotta go."

He didn't like the look the cop gave him when he said, "Uh-huh. Could I see your license and your registration, please?"

"Um, yeah, sure," Isaac said, reaching for his wallet. As he tossed a look over his shoulder, he noted that the clearing was still empty.

SCOTT THOUGHT FOR A MOMENT that Pembroke was dancing a jig as he reappeared in the wash of the headlights, then he realized that the old man was merely jogging back to the truck.

"He got pulled over by a cop!" the old man announced as he pulled open his door and climbed in. "Sure enough, he's over there, but I see flashing lights on the other side." He laughed, but the sound was more of a high-pitched wheeze. "Well, that'll sure as hell put him on edge."

"So, what do we do now?"

Pembroke ground the transmission into first gear and popped the clutch. "We wave at him as we drive on by."

AS HE SEARCHED HIS WALLET for his driver's license, Isaac riffled through his options. Killing a cop was a mistake. It was always a mistake, no matter how small the jurisdiction. Politicians were nothing compared to the ire raised by offing a cop. On the other hand, the kid knew too much; and, by extension, so did the old man who sold him out. Plus, professionalism be damned, Isaac was plain-ass pissed off, and he wasn't going to be able to live with himself if he let them just get away.

Now, if he could get this cop to move along before Pembroke's truck appeared in the overlook, then everything might work out just fine.

"Sometime tonight would be nice," said Officer Tingle.

Isaac forced a chuckle. "I guess my fingers are a little slow tonight," he said.

"I can hold a light for you, if you'd like."

Isaac shook his head. "No. No, that's okay. I know it's here somewhere."

Nearly a mile away, he saw headlights enter the clearing, and he dropped his wallet into the snow. "Goddammit." He bent down to retrieve it.

And came up with his rifle braced against his hip.

Jesse Tingle jumped as if he'd been zapped with a cattle prod. He didn't even reach for his weapon to defend himself. Instead, he raised his hands to his face and yelled, "Jesus!"

Isaac fired a single round dead into the center of his chest and turned away, not even bothering to watch his victim sprawl backward into the snow. He knew the cop was wearing a Kevlar vest, just as he knew that it wouldn't even slow down the armor-piercing bullets he'd loaded.

Moving fast now, Isaac hurried back to his chosen sniper's nest along the guardrail and slipped the night goggles back into place. Dammit, the pickup was already halfway through the clearing, leaving maybe five seconds to make his kill, and nearly two of those seconds would be lost to the flight time of the bullets. It wasn't supposed to be this difficult!

Settling the rifle into his shoulder, he rested the forestock on the guardrail post, acquired his target and started squeezing the trigger. By the time the fifth round left the barrel, the first one had nearly reached its target.

PEMBROKE WAS STILL LAUGHING. He couldn't get over the irony of it all. "There he is!" he shouted, pointing past Scott to the flashing lights a mile away. "Can you see anything?"

"Just the lights," Scott said, squinting through the fogged window. He rolled it down halfway for a better view. "Looks like two people just talking." As he watched, the man on the right bent down, and when he stood again, the man on the left flew backward onto the ground.

"Oh, shit!" Scott yelled. "Oh, shit, he just shot the cop! Move! C'mon, we gotta move!" The booming report reached them a few seconds later.

For the first time, he saw genuine fear in the old man's face. "She won't go no faster!"

Scott continued to watch out the window. From this distance, in the dark, cut only by the lights from the police car, it was tough to make out any real detail, but he could see enough. "I think he's getting ready to fire."

Up ahead, the clearing was giving way to a protective wall of trees. "We only need a couple more seconds," Pembroke said.

They didn't have it. Scott watched as a thin tongue of flame danced in the dark.

"Shit!" he yelled. Without a conscious thought, Scott pulled hard on the door handle and rolled to his right, out of the door and onto the snow-packed shoulder. As he tumbled and rolled, he heard the bullets hit. It was the sound of marbles hitting the bottom of a galvanized trash can, a terrible metallic pounding, punctuated by exploding glass and flying sheet metal. The heavy booms of the gunshots arrived later. The entire assault lasted all of five seconds, and then it was over, the pickup barely moving to the cover of the trees. Scott clawed his way to his feet and scrambled to catch up, jumping on the passenger side running board and hoisting himself back through the open door.

"Mr. Pembroke, are you all right?" The inside of the cab had been torn to shreds, the vinyl upholstery and the windshield—what was left of it—spattered with blood. "Oh, God."

"I been better," Pembroke said. He tried to laugh again, and the result was a bloody spray. "I think I was hit."

Scott was horrified. What was he supposed to do now? God, he was going to bleed to death if he didn't do *something*. As the truck slowed more and more, it finally shuddered and stalled out. "I think you might be right," Scott said. He reached across the old man's lap and set the parking brake. "I need to drive now."

As Scott grabbed Pembroke under his arms to pull him over to the passenger side, the old man howled with agony. "No! Don't! Lord Jesus, don't do that!"

But he had to. It was that or just sit there in the driver's seat and die. Every place he touched was slick with blood. "I'm sorry, Mr. Pembroke," he said as he pulled again. "It'll be just another few seconds." Pembroke screamed and he cussed, but he didn't fight the boy.

Scott was careful not to touch him or hurt him any more as he climbed over him into the driver's seat. He was shocked when the motor caught on the first try.

32

PEMBROKE WAS IN AGONY, moaning endlessly, his rattling lungs producing sounds unlike anything Scott had ever heard. Propelled by fear and rage, the boy drove like a madman, his foot all the way to the floor, the sloppy steering careening him from one shoulder to the other. If a car had been coming in the opposite direction, they'd all have died.

As smoke poured from the damaged motor, the smell of burning rubber combined with the stench of spilled blood and shit to form a mixture that turned his stomach. Every time he dared a glance at the passenger seat, the old man's skin looked grayer, even as the crimson pools grew larger on the seat.

"Hang in there, Mr. Pembroke," Scott yelled. The smoke scratched his throat, making him cough. "We'll get help for you. Just don't die, okay? Please don't die."

The sign read, Eagle Feather 1 Mile.

"All right!" Scott cheered. "Did you see that? We're almost there. We made it, okay? We made it!" He cheered again, but not Pembroke. The old man wasn't making any sound anymore. "Mr. Pembroke? Come on, stay awake for me. Mr. Pembroke!" The man didn't move.

Scott leaned over to his passenger. "Come on, Mr. Pembroke, wake up! Please wake up." Grabbing a fistful of the old man's jacket, Scott pulled him closer, until Pembroke sat upright. Then the bleeding man came the rest of the way, sliding sideways and then onto the floor, his head faceup on Scott's lap, one eye closed and the other staring into nothing, dead. "Oh, Mr. Pembroke," Scott moaned.

When he returned his eyes to the road, there was no time left to miss the tree.

BRANDON HAD DOZED OFF, his feet propped up on somebody's desk. Sherry sat at another desk, her eyes closed, head resting on her folded arms. At this point, the police station was merely a place to be, a place not to be alone. A twisted, fitful dream had taken Brandon to Scott's funeral, and he woke up terrified, burdened with a terrible sense of dread. At the front of the big room, Whitestone and Alexander were still locked in a discussion with Sanders. None of it interested Brandon anymore.

"What's wrong?" Sherry asked sleepily. Her head was still on the desk, but now her eyes were open.

"I thought you were asleep," he said.

"Ditto." She sat up straight. "Are you all right?"

Brandon tried to smile, but the best he could manage was a smirk. "Not really. Are you sure you don't want to go back to the chalet? You've got the press conference tomorrow." He checked his watch. "Make that later today."

"No," she said, "I want to be here. Do I look as bad as you do?"

"You couldn't possibly look as bad as I feel," Brandon said.

"I keep watching them," Sherry said, nodding to the Jamiesons.

They had arrived at the station about a half hour ago, summoned by a phone call from Chief Whitestone. Hearing the news that Scott was still alive, they'd arrived full of hope. "I'm sure that your son would have said something if Cody was in danger," Annie Jamieson had said.

Sherry could feel their agony as they spoke. "I'm sure you're right," she'd replied. "I'm sure they're both going to be just fine."

Since then, the old couple had just sat there, holding hands tightly and saying nothing to anyone.

"They make me sad," Sherry said to Brandon.

In the back of the squad room, a door labeled Communications opened quickly, and out stepped a woman whom Brandon had never seen before. A tiny boom microphone lined her cheek, coming from a plug in her left ear. She carried the connection for the thing in her hand. "Hey, Chief?" she called from across the room.

Whitestone looked up from his discussion with the others. "What is it, Mattie?"

"I can't find Jesse Tingle."

Whitestone scowled. "Can't *find* him? Was he lost?"

"I mean, I can't raise him on the radio. About forty-five minutes ago, he called in that he was making a stop out on the main road, but I haven't heard a thing from him since."

The chief's face showed concern, but not worry. "You've tried alternate channels?"

"Every one of them," Mattie said.

"What kind of stop was it?"

"He never said, exactly, but he didn't seem upset by it. It's not like him to just disappear off the air."

"Probably holed up taking a nap," said Agent Sanders, earning himself a withering glare from Whitestone.

"Is that what you and your agents do in your spare time?" Whitestone shot back. In the background, the buzzer sounded from the front door. James Alexander rose from his chair to answer it.

Sensing the opening salvo of another turf war between Whitestone and Sanders, Brandon headed for the coffeepot in Whitestone's office. "Want any?" he asked Sherry.

She shook her head no and closed her eyes again.

This was Brandon's fifth cup since he'd arrived this morning, and even before he poured it, he knew that he'd regret it soon. Maybe with enough cream and sugar . . .

His back was turned to the inner door when it opened, but just from the suddenness of the sound, he knew that something was wrong.

"Okay, okay, slow down," Alexander was saying. "Just take a seat and start at the beginning."

"There's a dead man in a car down the street—"

Brandon recognized the voice the instant he heard it. He whirled around. It was too good to be true, he knew—too miraculous—but please God, let it be.

"—he's been shot, and I wrecked the truck. We have to—"

They made eye contact the instant Brandon stepped out of Whitestone's office into the squad room. The boy seemed two inches taller and fifteen pounds lighter than the last time he'd seen him. He was bloody and his clothes were torn to shreds. He walked like his body hurt, listing a bit to one side, and on top of it all sat an unruly mop of blue hair. Brandon had never seen a sight so beautiful. "Oh, my God," he breathed, and at that instant, the rest of the people in the room understood.

Scott seemed bewildered. "Dad?" His features melted and he started to cry. "Dad!"

Brandon sprinted across the room, knocking over a chair and pushing Sanders out of the way as he hurried to hold his baby boy again. He folded Scott into a crushing bear hug. "Oh, my God," Brandon sobbed. "You're safe. Jesus, I've been so worried, thank God you're safe . . ."

They sank to the floor, just the two of them, and for the next little while, strapping Scott O'Toole was eight years old again, afraid of the dark and of the monsters in his closet, his feelings hurt by the bullies in school. He hugged his father back, embarrassed by his tears, but unwilling to stop them, grateful to finally be back in the embrace of the one man in the world who, with a single word or a well-placed joke, could make the worst calamities right again.

Whitestone and the others gave them space, unsure what they should do, while in the back of the room, Sherry Carrigan O'Toole stood with her fingers pressed against her lips, her face wet with tears, watching the reunion of Team Bachelor.

Never in her life had she felt so alone.

SCOTT FELT SHERRY'S PRESENCE before he saw her. He looked up from the crook of his father's neck, and there she was, standing so far away, watching without moving. He gently pushed himself away from Brandon, who didn't want to let go at first, and he struggled back to his feet. Everything ached. Every joint screamed. But he was safe again.

"Hi, Mom," he said. He couldn't tell if she was angry or sad or merely frightened. Her face was red and her lip quivered, and it occurred to him at that moment that he'd never seen his mother cry before. He held his arms out in front, open, beckoning, and she hurried past the desks and the staffers to embrace him in a hug the likes of which he'd never felt from her.

"Thank God you're safe," she said. Her voice was a raspy whisper. "Oh, my God, I've been so worried."

Scott hugged her back. "I've been kind of worried myself," he said.

Sherry cupped the back of his head in her hand. "I am so sorry," she said.

"For what?"

She pulled away from him just far enough that she could frame his face with her palms. "For *everything*," she whispered.

And he understood. She hugged him again, but this time he embraced her with only one arm, offering the other to his dad. Brandon didn't hesitate, and for a long moment, there in the police station in Eagle Feather, Utah, they were a family again. It felt odd, at first, Scott thought, in a weird, imbalanced way. But then he allowed himself the fantasy, if only for a minute or two, of what life might have been if a thousand things had gone differently.

Finally, it was official. He was alive.

"Excuse me," someone said. It was a tentative sound, a stranger's voice. Scott looked up to see an older couple watching them, standing so closely together that they might have been one person. "I'm Arthur Jamieson," the man said. "Cody's father. I was wondering . . ."

The expression on Scott's face was enough, it seemed. The woman at Arthur's arm seemed to shrink at a single glance, and she covered her face with her hands. Scott felt his mouth working to form words, but he didn't know what to say. Several cops moved quickly to help the old couple into chairs.

Scott looked to his dad. "Cody didn't make it," he said. Somehow, the words came more easily when speaking to his father. "He was killed in the crash."

"They know," Brandon said softly.

Watching the Jamiesons surrender to their grief triggered something deep inside of Scott. It came from a dark, terrible place, and once the gate was open, there was no holding it back. The emotion came without warning, pouring out in long, choking sobs and his parents were on him in an instant, trying to console him, to comfort him. But how could they? What could they possibly say that might dim the memories of white snow churned red by wolves? Of a new friend disembowled and lifeless? What could anybody do to make the agonized shrieks of Cody and Mr. Pembroke echo less loudly in his head?

What could they possibly do to bring the dead back to life?

"It's so unfair," Scott sobbed.

His parents said nothing. They just held him and rocked him until he was ready.

33

"FOR CRYING OUT LOUD, SANDERS," Brandon growled. "Give him some room. He's exhausted."

"He can sleep tomorrow," Sanders replied. "Right now, I need to know what he knows. Give it to me again, kid."

"His name is Scott," Sherry said, but Sanders's only response was a bored glare.

It looked like what it was, essentially—a jailhouse interview, with Scott on one side of a conference table, flanked by his parents, and Agent Sanders and James Alexander on the other side. Scott was so tired he couldn't remember what he'd already told them, so he started from the beginning. He told them about Isaac's witness protection story and about the two men who came to kill him. He told about dumping the bodies into the dry well, and, finally, about the chase that ended here in the police station. So far, the only portion of the outlandish tale that had been verified was the part about Mr. Pembroke and the dead police officer, Jesse Tingle. Barry Whitestone was out breaking the news to Jesse's mother.

"If the FBI were running some kind of a covert operation up here, I'd know about it," Sanders said. "It would have been in the security brief."

"Isaac said they were bogus," Scott said.

"Might've been bounty hunters," James suggested.

Sanders looked at Scott. "Or a figment of a young imagination."

Scott fired a panicked look to his father, then said to Sanders, "You think I'm *lying* about this? You think I'd make this stuff up?"

"I've never seen anything shot up like that truck was," James said. "I want to know how you got out of there."

"I jumped," Scott said, rubbing the bruises he had to show for it.

"Out of a moving car?"

"The truck was barely moving," Scott explained. "I yelled to Mr. Pembroke, but . . ." His voice trailed off.

"Tell me what he said about the president," Sanders said.

"I already did."

"Again."

Brandon had had enough. "For God's sake, Sanders, show some respect for what he's been through."

"Why do we keep talking?" Scott wanted to know. "Shouldn't you guys be raiding Isaac's house?"

"That'll happen in time," James assured.

"But he'll be gone!"

"From what you tell me, he's gone already. Either way, it'll take some time to muster the troops and get the paperwork done."

"Paperwork?" Sherry asked, aghast.

"We're trying to find a magistrate to approve the warrant."

"Can we talk about this assassination plan, please?" Sanders said. "You're worrying about horses that have already left the barn. I've got a healthy thoroughbred to protect. So, Scott, tell me. Where did this assassination plot come from?"

"Think about it," Scott said. "Why else would he stick around after the shootings this morning? Whether those people he killed at the house were cops or mobsters, *somebody's* trying to get him, so I figured that unless he had another job to do first, he'd take off. Then I remembered that the president is in town, so I put two and two together."

"Two and two," Sanders repeated, musing. "So, you never actually *heard* this DeHaven guy say he was going to kill anybody."

"I *watched* him kill people. He didn't have to tell me anything."

"But he never *said* he was going to kill the president."

That question slowed Scott down. "No," he said after a moment's reflection. "But who else?"

"I don't understand you, Sanders," Brandon said. "If it looks like a duck and walks like a duck—"

"You don't understand the way the Service works," Sanders said. "I'm not trying to badger the boy. It's just that we're expecting about five thousand people in the square tomorrow, and if the threat were more direct, I might be able to convince Eagle to change his plans and let us make ourselves more visible. Like any politician, he doesn't like to be surrounded by bodyguards. I don't think he'll go for it based on this." He rested his forearms on the table and leaned closer to Scott. "You're sure he didn't make a direct threat?"

"I can say he did, if that makes your job easier," Scott offered.

Sanders held the eye contact for a moment longer than was necessary, then sat up straight again. "No, that's fine. Last thing I want you to do is lie." He shifted his gaze to Brandon. "You guys gonna be around for a while?"

Brandon looked first to Scott and then to Sherry. "We're going back to the chalet. If you need us, you can reach us there."

They all stood. "Thank you very much," James said, shaking Brandon's hand. Then it was Sherry's turn, with Scott saved for last. "Glad to finally meet you, Scott. We've all been thinking about you a lot these past few days."

Scott smiled. "It's good to be back."

"You sure you don't want him checked out by a doctor?" James asked the parents.

Scott pleaded with his eyes. "No," Brandon said, "I think we'll save the poking and prodding for later."

James said, "Suit yourself," and he started to follow Sanders out the conference room door.

"Oh, James," Brandon said, prompting the cop to turn around. "Try not to need us, okay? Not for another couple of days, anyway."

IT COULDN'T POSSIBLY have been six hours. Six minutes, maybe, but six *hours?* No way. Yet, that's what the clock on the nightstand said, and the sunlight streaming through the massive windows verified it. It was all Scott could do to stay conscious in the shower when they got home. After that he'd collapsed in the king-size bed, and that was the end of it.

Now, seemingly seconds later, it was eleven in the morning, and he thought he'd heard his name.

"Over here, Scott," the voice said again. It was his father's, and it sounded delightful.

Wincing against the intrusion, the boy rolled over and burrowed deeper under the covers. "Leave me alone," he groaned.

"We can't do that," said another voice.

Something about the tone shot fear through Scott, and he sat up abruptly. God, he hurt. Through his barely open eyes, he saw a cluster of silhouettes in his doorway. "Who are you?"

"Chief Whitestone, Eagle Feather police," the voice said. "We met earlier this morning. You probably remember Agent Sanders."

Yeah, sure, he remembered, and after vigorously rubbing his eyes, he could see them all.

"I'm sorry, son," Brandon said. "This really can't wait."

Scott adjusted himself against the headboard, and pulled the covers up protectively. "What is it?"

"Mind if we sit down?" Whitestone asked, even as he helped himself to a corner of the bed. "We raided the Flintlock Ranch about two hours ago, and found everything just the way you'd described it, from the bodies in the well to the tunnel in the secret room. What we didn't find was your friend DeHaven."

Scott looked at Sanders. "I told you he'd get away."

"We also found the vault you'd described," Barry went on, "wide open and stripped of everything. Looks like he took his arsenal and nothing else but a few clothes."

"Get to the point, Chief," Brandon prompted.

"A quick check of the fingerprints in the cabin show that your Isaac DeHaven can be tied to several other murders over the course of many years, some as recent as a few days ago."

"No shit," Scott scoffed.

"I mean in addition to the ones you've witnessed. We do indeed believe that your Isaac DeHaven is a professional killer."

Scott smiled, in spite of himself, proud to have figured it out.

Sanders stepped forward to take over the narrative. "Just because we can match the fingerprints doesn't mean necessarily that we can trace them. We can put DeHaven at the scene of the other murders, but we still don't have any idea who we might be looking for. We simply don't know what he looks like."

A sense of dread had begun to bloom in Scott's stomach. When he saw the grimness of his father's expression, the size of the knot doubled.

"They need your help," Brandon said.

Scott's eyebrows joined in the middle.

"It's simple," Sanders said. "You *do* know what he looks like. All we want you to do is watch the crowds this afternoon—"

"He'll kill me!" Scott blurted.

"You won't be alone," Whitestone said. "At least one of my officers will be with you the whole time. If you see DeHaven in the crowd—"

Sherry walked into the room in the middle of the pitch. "Absolutely not," she said.

"He'll be perfectly safe," Sanders assured.

Sherry shook her head vehemently. She was dressed for her press conference—recently recast as her victory conference—and looked stunning. "No, perfectly safe is what he'll be if he stays as far away from that madman as possible."

"Relatively perfectly safe, then," Sanders said. His annoyance with the interruption was palpable.

Sherry turned to her ex-husband. "Tell them, Brandon."

Yeah, Scott thought. *Tell them, Brandon.*

The boy's father cleared his throat and shifted uncomfortably. "I said the same thing initially. But I'm afraid there's a darker side to all of this."

"That's right," Whitestone said. "These murders that DeHaven has been linked to. It appears that a good portion of them were carried out solely to eliminate witnesses."

Scott's stomach-knot quadrupled in size.

"What are you saying?" Sherry gasped, but her expression showed that she already knew.

Whitestone looked straight at Scott as he said, "Son, this might be the best and only chance for you to find peace of mind. Ever. As you know, we have every reason to believe that DeHaven will be lurking in that crowd somewhere this afternoon. If you see him, or if we get him on our own, then he's out of business and the good guys have won. If not . . ." He trailed off.

"I'll never sleep soundly again," Scott said, finishing the thought for him.

Whitestone sighed and nodded. "I'm afraid that's the way we see it, yes."

Scott turned that horrible thought over in his mind. He'd seen the coldness with which DeHaven dispatched his enemies, and that was without the frustration of a score to settle. Jesus, he'd never be able to relax. Every stranger passing him on the street, every waiter in a restaurant . . .

You don't ever want to cross me, kid.

The words echoed through his head. When he looked up, they were all staring at him, waiting for his answer. "This really sucks," he said, finally.

"Yes, it does," Whitestone agreed. "Righteously."

They shook on it, and it was done.

34

Scott felt like somebody's mannequin.

He stood in the middle of the police station's squad room, his arms outstretched as James Alexander fitted him with a Kevlar vest. The place was packed with police officers now, apparently representing a number of jurisdictions, judging from the various styles of uniforms. The one thing they all had in common was a black stripe across their badges, in deference to Jesse Tingle.

"I'm really sorry about your friend," Scott said to James. "I feel kind of responsible."

"Thanks for the thought," James said, drawing the Velcro tight under the boy's armpits, "but you're not the least bit responsible. Jesse died doing his job, and it was a job he'd have cheerfully laid down his life for."

Scott looked at his dad and got a sad smile in return.

James stepped back to admire his work. "Okay, that looks about right. You'll wear that under a coat."

"That'll stop a rifle bullet?" Brandon asked.

"It's what we all wear," James said. It was an artful dodge that neither of them pursued.

"What about his head?" Brandon said. "Don't you have a helmet or something to protect his head?"

Scott was horrified. "I'm not wearing a helmet, Dad. People will think I'm a retard."

"I'm thinking about your safety, son. Besides, you've got to cover that blue hair with *something.*"

"I'll wear a hat, then. A ski cap. But I'm not wearing a helmet." All he could think of were those kids in his elementary school who wore modified football helmets to keep from hurting themselves.

James explained, "We're playing the odds, here, Mr. O'Toole. First of all, even the vest is overkill. Merely a precaution. That said, most killers go for the body because it's a higher-probability kill shot—a bigger target. Chances are, to even better his chances, a killer will be using hollow points or devastators, which are designed to open up and slow down on impact. Without a vest, it's almost a guaranteed kill shot. With the vest, it's nothing more than a bruise. Okay, a really big bruise, but one you can walk away from. Finally, by keeping the vest under his outer garment, we make the body that much more attractive a target. Does that make sense?"

As the cop made his little speech, Scott felt his skin contracting under the vest as it reacted to the thought of being pierced with a bullet.

"I want to go with him," Brandon said.

James laughed. "I never suspected otherwise." He handed another vest to Brandon. "This one's yours, just in case. I figure, after all you've been through this past week, I won't be able to squeeze a piece of paper between you two. I'm a little surprised Mrs. O'Toole isn't here."

Brandon removed his jacket and slipped the vest over his head, mimicking what he'd seen done to his son just moments before. "Here's some life-saving advice for you, James: never let my ex-wife hear you refer to her as Mrs. anything. She's *Doctor* O'Toole, and proud of it." He and Scott were the only ones who found the comment funny. "But she won't be joining us," Brandon concluded. "She'll be somewhere around City Hall, doing a press conference."

And what a battle that had been. When the decision had been made for Scott to help on this crazy mission, Sherry had wanted to cancel the press conference to stay with her son. "He's the one they'll want to talk to, anyway," she'd said, back in Scott's bedroom. "I'm staying with him every step of the way."

"No, you're not," Sanders said. "I'm willing to let one of you come along with him—like I've even got a choice—but not both. And with all due respect, Dr. O'Toole, I don't need a celebrity face drawing attention to what we're doing. Please don't argue, because it's not negotiable. The boy gets to decide whether he goes in the first place, but after that, everything else is up to me." There was absolutely no room for argument.

"So, what am I supposed to do?" Sherry asked, her dignity bruised. The dismissive shrug she got from Sanders didn't help.

"Do the press conference," Brandon urged, drawing a confused look from his ex. "Tell them that Scott isn't ready to face the cameras yet, and that you're there to answer their questions. Somebody's got to do it, and God knows I don't want it to be me. Do it for your fans. They must be worried sick for you. Let them know how everything turned out."

Sherry clearly wasn't comfortable being on the stage alone. "But this isn't about me," she said.

Brandon smiled. "You know, I don't think I've ever heard you say that before." A week ago, those words would have started a war. Now, they were just gentle teasing and Sherry smiled, too. "What else are you going to do? Just pace around the chalet? Go and face your public."

Looking back on it now, Brandon felt pity for her—not the spiteful pity that he'd vocalized so many times in the past, but the genuine article. Here she was trying to work her way back into her son's life as quickly as possible, and at a moment of crisis, she was being shut out by the Secret Service. It had to be a tough pill. If nothing else worthwhile came out of the nightmare of the past week, maybe Brandon and Sherry had finally found the knob that would allow them to dial down the acrimony between them.

"Do you think they'll let me play my guitar if I go on the *Today* show?" Scott asked, squirming under his vest in an effort to make it more comfortable.

The randomness of the question made Brandon laugh. "Well, I guess that's just something we'll have to negotiate when the time comes."

"Ladies and gentlemen, may I have your attention, please?" It was Chief Whitestone. He stood atop a desk, his hair nearly brushing the ceiling tiles. The room fell quiet. Scott found a desk chair to sit in. "Thank you, folks. As you all know, we've got a big crowd forming up out there, and if I estimate correctly, about half of them are cops."

For the next five minutes, Whitestone outlined in detail the events surrounding the president's speech. First, the mayor would talk, followed by the governor, who would then introduce the president. The officials gathered in the squad room right now had but one purpose: to be as visible as possible. "If anyone in that crowd so much as thinks an unfriendly thought, I want them to feel squirmy."

From there, the speech devolved into logistics and trivia. He talked about entrance points and exit points, and about all manner of official detail that couldn't keep Scott's attention. His mind drifted back over the days he'd endured. The image of Cody Jamieson's frozen corpse being torn to shreds haunted him. Cody deserved a better end than that. So did the two guys in the dry well, but at least their bodies were recovered.

A nudge to Scott's shoulder lurched him back to the present. An entire roomful of people stared at him.

"You slept through your introduction," Brandon said, his voice a loud stage whisper. People laughed. "The chief wants you to stand up."

Cringing at the redness that flooded his cheeks, Scott stood and gave a little wave.

"Now, if he can stay awake through this exercise, young Mr. O'Toole will try to spot our man in the crowd. Officer James Alexander—wave, James, so everyone can see you."

Alexander smirked. It was an ongoing joke between the chief and him. In a crowd this white, no one could possibly miss him.

"If Scott sees our man, he'll tell James, and James, in turn, will put the word out on the radio. We'll move in and get him. The rest of you just please keep an eye out for anything that strikes you as suspicious."

A murmur of assent rumbled through the crowd.

"One last point," Whitestone concluded, "and then we can get out of here and go to work. I don't want to sound patronizing, but I think this needs to be said: there's a big difference between vigilance and paranoia, okay? We have reason to believe that *one* man may be trying to kill the president of the United States this afternoon. One. That means, we'll have roughly five thousand other people out there who want nothing more than a distant view and maybe a handshake. I'd just as soon not send those hands back home broken."

SHERRY STOOD IN FRONT of the enormous window, watching the skiers below. Standing in the wash of sunlight on this cloudless day, she was uncomfortably warm, despite the thirty-degree reading on the digital thermometer. The glare off the snow was as beautiful as it was blinding.

The old anger was returning, grinding in her belly like a three-day fast. Intellectually, she knew it was unreasonable, but there was something about the reuniting of Team Bachelor that made her feel empty and angry. Of course she was thrilled that Scott had survived and was healthy, and that moment of warmth as she and Brandon both comforted him there in the police station was not lost on her. It was like a taste of the poisonous fruit.

For a while there, during the darkest hours, she'd felt that she'd rediscovered her love for Brandon, and that maybe, just *maybe* they might be able to start the process of mending as a couple; but now, as she looked back on it, she realized that they'd merely shared an emotional buoy in the midst of a raging storm. As the wind died and the skies cleared, she'd once again be left alone as Team Bachelor motored off again.

Hearing the brief summary of Scott's adventures, Sherry marveled at her son's nerve, his pluck. Given the same circumstances, Sherry knew that she'd have panicked on the first day and made some stupid fatal error. Her admiration for the young man whom she'd so recently found annoying and irresponsible now bordered on awe. She wondered when he'd grown up. How could she have spent so much time in the presence of a budding young man, yet have seen only an irresponsible boy? How could she have missed what Brandon had so plainly seen all along?

Thinking these things, watching the antics of the skiers through the window, Sherry Carrigan O'Toole caught a glimpse of the mistakes she'd made, and tasted for the first time the price she would have to pay. She'd squandered her one and only opportunity to witness the metamorphosis of boy to man. The years lost would never return, and it was entirely possible that the threadlike bond that linked mother and son would never strengthen.

The realization took her breath away. In chasing what appeared to be the opportunity of a lifetime, she'd blown the opportunity to share a life; she'd abdicated it to a man she'd once thought so naïve, but now appeared to have it all. He alone would know the *real* story of Scott's adventure in the woods—the details that would dribble out a little at a time over the course of months and years. Sherry would learn only the headlines, just as she'd learned only the headlines for the past six years.

That anger brewing in her gut, she realized, wasn't anger at all. It was envy. A raging jealousy that she'd chosen a route that would leave her to be only an observer in Scott's life, the emotional equivalent of a benevolent aunt. It was so much easier when she could hate Brandon, but now she didn't even have that anymore. She had only loneliness.

"Okay," she said to the room. "The pity party's over." She pulled three tissues from the box on the end table and dabbed her eyes. The last thing she needed right now was a mascara emergency.

At least the press conference would be fun, she thought. And packed to the gills, thanks to all the news crews who would already be on hand for the president's Founder's Day gig. What had so recently been billed as a plea for patience in the face of overwhelming odds could now address wholesale triumph over those odds. She couldn't wait. She might not be able to do much else for Scotty, but at least she could help to make him famous.

Even though her appointment with the cameras didn't begin until 3:30, after the president had concluded his remarks, Larry was supposed to pick her up at 2:00 to deliver her to City Hall before the Secret Service shut down everything at 2:45. From then until the president was out of the area, no one would be allowed to enter or leave any building within a two-block radius of the bandstand in the square.

Now, if only Larry would get here. If there was one thing about Larry that consistently pissed her off, it was his total disregard for promptness. He'd sent a message through the front desk that he would pick her up and bring her to City Hall himself, but it was already after two. Honest to God, she couldn't count the number of times he'd raised her blood pressure over the years—

Finally, the doorbell rang.

"Well, it's about time," she said. Grabbing her coat off the back of the chair where she'd left it, she climbed the two stairs to the foyer and opened the door.

DOWNTOWN EAGLE FEATHER looked like the Fourth of July with vanilla frosting. Red, white and blue bunting draped the bandstand gazebo in the middle of the square, continuing the theme that stretched across the front of the speakers' scaffold that had temporarily replaced the steps of the public library. According to comments Scott had overheard, the president would announce his reelection bid at this speech, thus explaining the huge throngs of people. In the bandstand, a cluster of musicians played a piece that Scott recognized as a march, but he didn't know which one. To his ear, marches pretty much all sounded alike.

The Kevlar vest made him feel fat as he meandered through the crowd, James Alexander on his right, and his dad's hand perpetually on his left arm. Living as close to Washington, D.C. as he did, Scott found that he took for granted all things presidential. At home, POTUS was just another celebrity resident of the city. Out here, though, in the president's home state, Scott found himself genuinely impressed with all the pomp and plastic patriotism. Given the party atmosphere, it seemed impossible that anyone would try to take a shot at anybody.

"You're supposed to be watching faces," James admonished quietly, "not the decorations."

"How am I supposed to spot one person in all of this crowd?"

"I have no idea. But if he's here, you'll recognize him a hell of a lot sooner than I will."

It all felt so awkward. In school, eye contact was a thing to be avoided, particularly among the more aggressive ethnic groups. To lock gazes was to show disrespect and invite violence. The question, "What are you lookin' at?" was invariably followed by a fist. Yet, here he was, deliberately looking people in the eye. It surprised him that most looked away.

As the commencement time for the speech approached, the knots of people drew tighter and tighter, each of them pressing in for a spot closer to the action. For Scott and company, it made crowd wandering all but impossible. If Scott had said "excuse me" once, he'd said it a thousand times.

"This is hopeless," he said to his father. "There's no way I'm going to be able to find one face."

"Hey! Scott! Brandon!" They both turned as Larry Chinn shouldered his way through the crowd. As he approached, James Alexander drew protectively close, but Scott pushed past him and the two skiing buddies exchanged a huge hug. "God, am I glad to see you!" Larry exclaimed, tears in his eyes.

"Me, too," Scott said. "It got pretty hairy."

"You poor thing. But you're okay. That's the important thing. I've never heard your mother so excited. I'm so sorry to hear about Cody, though."

James Alexander conspicuously cleared his throat, breaking up the reunion. "The crowd, Scott. Watch the crowd."

Scott shot the cop an annoyed look, then said to Larry, "We can catch up later?"

"You bet we will." To Brandon, Larry said, "Have you seen Sherry? I got a message that a driver was picking her up to bring her to City Hall."

"Last I heard, that driver was you," Brandon said.

"Who told you that?"

"Can you folks do this another time?" James asked. "We've got work to do."

"She's at the house, Larry," Brandon said. He checked his watch. "And right about now, I'd say she's pissed as a wet hornet at you."

Larry pressed his hand to his forehead. "Why does she do this shit to me?" He spun on his heel and headed back into the crowd.

"Don't plan anything for tonight," he called over his shoulder. "I want to hear every detail."

Scott beamed, loving the attention. "Okay!" he shouted. "Come for dinner!" When he turned back, he caught the disapproving look in Brandon's eyes. "He's a nice guy, Dad. Good skier, too."

"Look at the crowd!" James insisted yet again.

"I've been looking at the crowd!" Scott shouted. "I keep telling you, I can't see the crowd. There are too many people!"

Brandon put a hand on Scott's shoulder to settle him down. "What about it, James? This is seeming a little pointless. Maybe if we could move to a better vantage point?"

James shook his head. "You heard the instructions, just like I did. We keep wandering and we keep looking."

But as the witching hour approached, and crowds continued to flood the square, the situation became unbearable. Suddenly, it was impossible for the threesome to keep together. Squirting between people was always possible, but as the human knots tightened, it definitely became a solo performance. To make it worse, Scott's feet were still sore as hell, as was every bony protuberance on his body. Soon, he was concentrating more on avoiding injury than spotting faces.

"This all hurts like hell," Scott announced to James. "I feel like I'm getting beaten up out here."

James finally conceded the point. Standing on tiptoe, he craned his neck to find a spot nearby that might afford a better view. "Come with me," he said, and he led the way to a brick retaining wall in front of a women's clothing store. A family of five had been standing there since Scott and the others had arrived in the square, having staked out this prime viewing location no doubt hours in advance. "Excuse me," James said to the father, "but I'm afraid you're going to have to get down off that wall."

The father gave a pleasant if annoyed smile. "I talked with another officer earlier, and he said this place would be just fine. We've been here since noon."

"I'm sorry, sir," James said, remaining very stern. "The rules have changed. Now you're going to have to get down."

"But we've been here since noon," said the mother, as if maybe James hadn't heard her husband the first time.

"I understand that, ma'am, and I'm just as sorry as I can be for the confusion, but that doesn't change a thing. Now, if you don't mind—"

"But the other good spots are already taken!" the father protested. Fingers of red had begun to scale the sides of his neck.

This time, James said nothing. He merely planted his hands on his Sam Browne belt, and shifted his stance to one leg.

Furious, the father said, "Would it have killed you to let us know this three hours ago?" He jumped to the ground, then assisted his family off the wall.

James said, "Thank you very much for your cooperation." With the wall cleared, James climbed into the spot himself and motioned for Scott to join him.

The displaced father went ballistic. "What is this?" he yelled. "You kick me and my family off so you can watch from there yourself?"

"This is official business," James assured him.

The other man thrust a finger toward Scott. "He's not official business."

Scott felt like every set of eyes was looking at him, and he finally found himself happy to be wearing the vest—for reasons that had nothing to do with Isaac DeHaven.

James Alexander climbed off the wall and confronted the aggrieved father eye-to-eye. "Let's understand something," he said, barely loud enough for Scott to hear. "He *is* official, if only because I say he is. Now, is this going to be a problem, *sir?*"

If ever in the history of mankind there was a question asked for which there clearly was a right and wrong answer, this was it. The father backed down, turned and ushered his family into the crowd.

When James turned back toward the wall, he actually looked a little embarrassed.

"Have you considered State Department work, James?" Brandon asked. "We can never have too many diplomats in the world."

James gave him a look that was closer to a snarl than a smile and climbed back on the wall to stand next to Scott.

"Remember," he said. "Watch the crowd, not the show."

Scott hadn't been noticing the band much, but when they stopped playing abruptly in the middle of yet another march, the silence startled him. He looked that way in time to see the conductor raise his baton. Two seconds later, two dozen loudspeakers throughout the square announced, "Ladies and gentlemen, the president of the United States."

On cue, the band played ruffles and flourishes, followed immediately by the familiar strains of "Hail to the Chief." As the music played, Scott watched, oddly mesmerized, as the president and first lady entered from the right and wandered across the stage, huge smiles on their faces as they waved to the packed square. Other familiar faces trailed them, though Scott couldn't quite place where he'd seen them. One might well have been a senator, he thought, and the others, by process of elimination, must have been the mayor of Eagle Feather and the governor of Utah.

The president stopped short of the podium, and stood at the edge of the stage until the music stopped, at which point the crowd erupted in cheers and enthusiastic applause that was nonetheless muted by gloved hands. About five steps behind and to the president's right, Scott recognized the face of Agent Sanders. At the far edge of stage left, barely visible to the crowd, he could see Chief Whitestone standing in an uncomfortable posture that told Scott he didn't know what to do with his hands.

"The *crowd*, Scott," James whispered.

It took more concentration than he would have thought, trying to recognize one face. At least from up here, he could see the proverbial forest and not just the trees. And what a huge forest of humanity it was, splashes of brilliant colors against a sparkling white backdrop. Above the crowd hung a misty cloud of condensed breath, and somehow, through all of that, Scott was supposed to find one—

Something on the near side caught his eye and his back stiffened.

"See something?" James asked, alerted by the body language.

Below and in front, Brandon came to full alert. "What is it, Scott?"

He didn't answer because he didn't really know. It was a flash of something familiar in the midst of so much that was strange, over there just this side of the bandstand. "There!" he said, pointing. "That hat. The fur hat."

"Where? I don't see it."

Scott didn't either, anymore. But it had been there. The plush fur hat that looked like something out of a Russian movie. Following one person in this crowd was like trying to follow one drop of water in a rushing stream. Then, he saw it again. "There! See it? The big fur hat."

James craned his neck, but still saw nothing.

"Does he have something?" Whitestone's voice asked over the radio.

From all the way at the back of the stage, he'd read their movements for what they were. James brought his portable radio to his lips and keyed the mike. "Stand by, Chief. I don't know yet." Then, to Scott: "Say something, son."

"Give me a second," Scott snapped. How could he be sure? A hat was a hat, after all. How could he tell one from the other? Then he saw a flash of green, and he remembered Isaac's coat. Navy blue ski jacket with green shoulders. "Holy, shit! That's him! That's Isaac!"

"Where?" James insisted.

"There! Right there!" How could he make it any plainer? "The fur hat. Blue and green jacket."

James said into his radio, "The boy sees him, Chief. Fur hat, blue and green coat." With those words, he'd just described no fewer than three dozen people in the crowd. "I still don't see him, Scott."

Aw, screw it. "Follow me," Scott said, and before anyone could stop him, he'd jumped off the wall and was running into the crowd.

"Move in!" James shouted into his radio. "Follow the boy and move in."

Scott didn't care about excuse me's anymore. He plowed head-long into the crowd, doing his best to avoid people, but pushing anyone who got in his way. Problem was, through the sea of bodies and heads he couldn't see a damned thing. All the more reason to move quickly. Get to the spot where he'd seen DeHaven before the killer had a chance to move on.

Everywhere, throughout the square, dozens of police officers and Secret Service agents moved in for the capture, and within seconds, the assembled crowd knew that something was terribly wrong. The concerned murmur turned to pandemonium as officers converged on a spot none of them had seen.

Up on the stage, Sanders spoke two words into his wrist mike, and seconds later, Secret Service agents swarmed onto the stage from all directions, first surrounding the president, and then whisking him to safety in the wings. One agent, in an image that would make the front page of virtually every newspaper in the Western world, ostentatiously brandished a submachine gun, and then the panic was complete.

"Scott! Wait!" Brandon shouted over the noise. "Wait for the others!"

But Scott couldn't stop. He was the only one who knew what he was looking for: the hat and the jacket. And now, he was trying to find them in the midst of panic. Where did he go? Where the *hell* did he go?

Oh, shit! There! The killer was running. Isaac knew he'd screwed up, and now he was getting the hell out. "Isaac!" Scott shouted. "Stop!"

But the other man had no intention of stopping. He joined the surge of running spectators, trying his best to blend in with the others.

Then he disappeared entirely. *Poof,* just like that, he was gone. Scott slowed to a jog, then stopped altogether, his arms outstretched, baffled.

"Where?" James said when he caught up, his weapon drawn. "Where is he?"

"I don't know!" Scott said. "He was right here." He emphasized the words with a chopping motion of his hand. "Right. Here."

"Well, where is he now?"

Scott heard the frustration in Alexander's voice, and as law enforcement officials converged from all over the universe, he felt a sense of desperation himself.

"Where!" James shouted.

"I don't know, okay?" Scott shouted back. "I don't fucking know!"

He felt a reassuring hand on his shoulder. "Scott . . . ," Brandon said, his voice soothing.

Scott shook himself free from his grasp. Suddenly, he was the center of a large crowd. There was enough firepower to start the Battle of Utah. "I saw him!" Scott insisted. "He was right here, and then he slipped into the crowd and he was gone!"

"I believe you, son," Brandon said.

"They don't!" Scott said, making a sweeping motion at the winded, twitchy cops. "It was Isaac DeHaven. He was wearing a fur cap and a blue-and-green ski jacket, okay? When everybody panicked and started to run, I guess he saw it and he took off. Then he disappeared." As he scanned the crowd, he saw a lot of skepticism. "I am not making this up!"

"Hey!" someone yelled from off to Scott's right. Everyone turned to see a cop holding a blue-and-green ski jacket in one hand, a fur cap in the other.

35

BACK AT THE POLICE STATION, Barry Whitestone tried to help Scott remove his Kevlar vest, but the boy yanked himself away. "I can do it myself," he snapped.

"Nobody's blaming you," Whitestone said.

"The hell you're not. You think I ran him off."

Brandon put a hand on his son's shoulder. "Take it easy, Scott."

"Officer Alexander thinks I made the whole thing up."

Whitestone scoffed, "He thinks no such thing."

Scott deepened his voice and mocked, "Maybe you were mistaken." He pulled the vest over his head and slammed it onto the table nearest him. In his own voice, he said, "I'm not the one who set off the panic, you know. I'm not the one who pulled out all the artillery and started shouting."

"You were supposed to stay put and let us do the chasing," Whitestone said gently.

"I tried! I kept pointing, but Officer Alexander just kept saying, 'Where? Where?' If I hadn't chased, him, he'd have gotten away."

An eavesdropping cop Scott didn't recognize said, "And the difference is . . . ?"

"Screw you!"

Brandon stepped in and slipped his arm around the boy. "Okay, Scott, that's enough. You've got nothing to apologize for. Without you, they wouldn't have anything. They wouldn't know what the guy looks like, they wouldn't have DNA samples of his hair, and the president of the United States would likely be dead. No matter what else happened, you accomplished that much."

Scott didn't want to talk about it anymore. The words of Agent Sanders, the dickhead from the Secret Service, still echoed in his head: if there'd been a real threat to the president, he would have heard it in his security briefing. As if the Secret Service automatically knows everything. Seemed to Scott that it was the ones they *didn't* know about that always bit them in the ass. Sorta by definition.

God, it was so *easy* for these jerks. While they were all pissed off about their *alleged* assassin, Scott was the only one who had to worry about the *real* one tracking him down for the rest of his life.

"I wouldn't worry about the guy," Whitestone said, somehow reading his mind. "If he's out there, we'll get him. Bacteria couldn't squeeze through the blocks we've set up."

Yeah, right. Don't worry. This from the man who woke Scott up just this morning by telling him to worry.

In the background, a cell phone chirped, and as one, everyone checked their belts and pockets.

"Hey, Dad," Scott said. "Your coat's ringing." Brandon had left his coat draped over a desk chair, and sure enough, his pocket was chirping. While Brandon fished out the phone, Scott stepped away from the others, trying to be alone in the crowd. All he wanted was to go home.

"Hey, Scott," Brandon said, calling him back. "It's your mom. She wants to talk to you."

Oh, now that was *exactly* what he needed—another count-your-blessings lecture. He paused for a second before launching a great sigh and taking the phone. "Hi, Mom."

But it was Isaac's voice that said, "Keep a poker face, kid. It's all that's keeping your mama alive."

Scott felt the blood drain from his head. He turned away so the others couldn't see. "What are you—"

"Hush, Scott. Poker face, remember? Smile and say, 'Oh, pretty good.'"

For a second, Scott didn't get it. Then he did. "Oh, pretty good," he said. They were faking a conversation here.

"Nicely done," Isaac said with a laugh. "Almost casual. You're a natural. Say, 'Thank you.' "

"Thank you."

"Outstanding."

Scott dared a glance behind him, but his dad seemed to have zoned into a conversation that Whitestone was having with the cop who'd busted his chops.

"Take a look at your watch," Isaac instructed. "Mine shows four twenty-three." So did Scott's. "Five thirty-eight is the number you need to remember. Tattoo it on your brain. That's one hour and fifteen minutes from now. At five thirty-nine I put a bullet through your mother's head. Laugh."

His mind racing, Scott did a serviceable impression of a chuckle. "Why?"

This time it was Isaac's turn to laugh. "It's what I do, kid. You can save her, though. All you have to do is follow directions. You know where the Widow Maker lift is on SkyTop?"

Scott nodded and shot another nervous look toward his dad. "Yeah."

"Be there by five oh-eight. That's forty-five minutes from now. Look for your skis in the rack outside the main lodge, between the dining room and the ski school bell. Got it?"

Across the room, Brandon finally did lock onto his son's gaze, and he didn't like what he saw. He started walking that way.

"Yeah, I got it," Scott said. Then he whispered, "Make it fast, my dad is coming."

"Makes it more interesting, doesn't it? You've got to be quite the actor now. I have faith in you."

"Something wrong, Scott?" Brandon asked.

Scott pivoted the mouthpiece away from his chin and did his best to look confused. "No, why?"

"You look disturbed."

"No, I'm fine."

In his ear, Isaac said, "I recognize that voice."

Scott covered the mouthpiece with his thumb. "Can you give me a minute, Dad?" He gestured for Brandon to mind his own business.

Brandon arched his eyebrows. "Secrets?"

The boy answered with an impatient glare.

Even more curious and maybe a little hurt, Brandon hesitated, then walked back toward the cluster of cops.

"Okay, we're alone again."

"And the clock is still ticking," Isaac said. His voice was so smooth, so calculating, that Scott had to stifle a chill. "Come alone, kid. If I see you with company, I'll kill her. In fact, I don't even want you talking to anyone. If this phone is busy when I call, she's dead. Tell me you love me, too."

This whole thing made Scott want to throw up. "I love you, too."

"Tick-tock." The line went dead.

For a moment, he just held the phone to his face, his mind suddenly and inexplicably empty. He had a thousand things to do, all at the same time, and now he couldn't grasp a single one. Christ, forty-five minutes wasn't enough time to get to Widow Maker—forty-two minutes now. Not nearly enough. If there was any traffic at all, he was screwed.

SkyTop wasn't like most ski resorts, where the lodge was at the bottom and all the slopes rose above it. At SkyTop, the lodge sat on top of the slope called Prospector, from which the entire world fell away, branching off dozens of times with chutes and trails that led to all of the other chutes and trails. At SkyTop, maps were mandatory. Cody Jamieson had told him that six or seven people got seriously lost every week. To get to the top of the Widow Maker lift, Scott would have to drive to the lodge, ski halfway down Prospector before veering off to the right and following a treacherous trail through the woods to Bald Eagle Glade, and then on down to the bottom, where he'd then catch the chair to Widow Maker.

He'd never make it. And Isaac knew that.

"Are you okay?" Brandon asked.

"Huh? Oh, yeah, I'm fine. I need the keys to the Jeep."

"What for?" Brandon could read the boy like a newspaper.

"I just want to get my water bottle," Scott said, surprised at how easily the lie came.

"It's unlocked."

"I locked it."

"When?"

"As I got out, okay?" He heard the edge in his own voice, and he quickly tried to cover. "What is it with everybody? You think I make stuff up, too?"

Brandon recoiled. "What is wrong with you?"

"Can I just have the keys, please?"

Brandon didn't like it; Scott saw it written in his dad's features. But he also knew that his status as a teenager bought him a little deference for emotional outbursts. Scowling, Brandon dug the keys out of his pocket and handed them over. "How about you dial it down a little?"

Scott took the keys and tried to look repentent as he walked toward the door. God, he'd just killed a whole minute. He was reaching for the handle when Brandon called after him, "You've still got my phone, kiddo."

Scott pretended not to hear. He just stormed out of the squad room, through the airlock and out into the icy air. He wanted to run. He *needed* to run, but he knew that he dared not. Dad was too curious as it was.

Don't cross me, kid. The admonition still stirred his gut.

The Cherokee sat where they'd left it, angled up on a snow bank that once had been a parking space. It was unlocked. As Scott climbed into the driver's seat, cranked the ignition and slipped the transmission into reverse, he tried not to think about the riddled corpse and blood spatters that had soiled the last vehicle he'd driven. He tried not to think about any of the blood he'd seen in the last week. All the gallons of it. Instead, he thought about the impossible task that lay ahead.

He had to hurry, but he also had to be careful. If he drove off the road, it was all over. He couldn't let that happen.

It never even occurred to him that in a little over an hour, he'd probably be dead himself.

"THEY'VE GOT HIM!"

The suddenness of the outburst drew all heads around to behold Mattie Simms, the dispatcher, standing in the doorway to her cubicle, the ever-present headset still dangling from her ear. "They've got the killer! James Alexander just called it in. He was still here in town, and James has him in custody. ETA one minute." Mattie could not have looked happier if she'd just won the lottery.

The room erupted in noise as over a dozen police officers surged toward the front windows to get the first glimpse of the prisoner in custody. Blissfully absent, Brandon noted, was Agent Sanders of the Secret Service, whose precious cargo was probably over Kansas by now, winging his way back to Washington on Air Force One.

Scott had only been out of the room for five minutes, but still, Brandon wondered where he'd wandered off to. After all he'd been through, Scott would want to witness the arrest, if only to set his mind finally at ease. Brandon tried to make his way to the front of the crowd to catch a glimpse through the window, but the knot of people was too tight. In the distance, the sound of an approaching siren cut through the chatter.

"There he is!" someone yelled, and the crowd shifted from the window to the area just inside the door.

"All right, people, back up!" Whitestone yelled. "Make a hole." At first, no one moved, but then the chief started moving them. Three seconds later, an aisle had opened.

Through the weaving crop of heads, Brandon could just barely see James Alexander helping someone out of his Explorer and on up the sidewalk to the front doors, which opened for them, as if by magic. James looked deadly serious until he crossed the threshold, at which point a grin spread from ear to ear.

Brandon smiled back at him, relieved that the ordeal was finally over. Seeing James was easy; his head towered above the crowd. It took a bit longer to see his prisoner, but at the very first glance, Brandon knew that someone had made a terrible mistake. The guy looked like he'd been snatched from a homeless shelter; not a bit like the description Scott had given. Woefully underdressed in just flannel shirtsleeves and blue jeans, he was about twenty years too old and half a liter too drunk. More than that, Brandon expected to see a certain look in the eyes of a professional killer. It's one of those things he couldn't describe up front, but would know when he saw it. He didn't see it here. James's prisoner looked scared to death.

"I didn't do nothin'!" the prisoner insisted as his captor dragged him down the center aisle.

Brandon shot a glance toward Whitestone and saw that he wasn't buying it, either.

"What have you got?" the chief asked.

James clearly didn't like the disapproving tone. "I was canvassing Snowbird Avenue and one of the shop owners turned me on to this guy. Said there was a man freezing to death in the alley. I went down there and found this guy trying to make himself invisible. The first thing he said when he saw me was, 'I didn't try to kill nobody.' This before I even asked."

"I *didn't!*" the old man insisted. From the emphasis, Brandon knew that he'd said it many times before.

Whitestone scowled. "What's your name?"

"Seyford," the man said. His fear was turning to anger. "Frederick Seyford, and you have no right to hold me here."

The chief smiled. On a different face, it might have looked patronizing, but on Whitestone, it just looked pleasant. "If I ask Officer Alexander here to take off your cuffs, are you going to cause a problem?"

"*I* haven't caused a problem all damn day!"

Whitestone nodded to James Alexander, who looked none too pleased as he fished the key out of his pocket.

"What'd you put 'em on so tight for, anyway?" Seyford growled.

Between his addiction to cop shows and the endless hours he'd logged here at the police station, Brandon had learned enough about procedures to know that you don't unshackle a man you believe to be a killer. *Where the hell is Scott?*

"Have a seat, Mr. Seyford," Whitestone offered, nodding to a wooden chair as he helped himself to the adjacent desk. "Tell me why your first words to Officer Alexander were about not assaulting any-one."

"Because I didn't assault nobody. I saw them people coming toward me with their guns out, so I figured it musta had something to do with the president bein' there."

"What made you think they were coming after you?"

"It wasn't like it was no secret," the old drunk scoffed. "Everybody was lookin' right at me."

"And why do you think, out of all the people in that crowd, that people would be suspecting you of something?"

Embarrassment flashed across the old man's eyes. "I figured it was the clothes. Too good to be true. From the very beginning I shoulda known."

The comment drew a look of curiosity from Whitestone, and sparked a flash of terror in Brandon. Scott had been gone too long.

Seyford explained, "Some guy gave me them clothes, plus a hundred bucks. He said all I had to do was walk through the crowd wearing them, and I could keep everything."

Whitestone scowled. "Somebody just gave you clothes to wear."

It started to come together for Brandon. He remembered Scott on the phone. The unnerved look.

"Tell me what this guy looked like," Whitestone pressed.

Ten words into it, Brandon recognized the description of the man Scott called Isaac. "Oh, shit," he breathed. The comment brought heads around, and the abruptness of his move to the front windows made people move out of his way. Instinctively, he knew what he was going to find, and his first glance confirmed it: the Cherokee was gone.

He whipped around to face the assembled stares. "He's got Scott again."

36

4:41.

God help him, he was never going to make it in time. All the way up the mountain, with his headlights flashing and his horn blaring, people refused to get out of his way. One guy actually made a point of slowing down and driving in the middle of the road just to piss him off. Prick.

Finally, he was able to get past the traffic, fishtailing his way to the mouth of the sprawling parking lot, and then on down the endless rows of cars. The thought fleetingly darted through his mind that whoever hadn't moved their car in the past three or four days would have a hell of a time moving it at all before spring. Between what had fallen from the sky and what had been piled on by other drivers digging out, the diehards were hopelessly buried.

The parking lot was crawling with day-trippers on their way back to their vehicles. Most walked like exhausted Frankenstein's monsters, their gait altered by the stiffness of their leg muscles and the unyielding rigidity of their ski boots. They walked with their skis and poles slung over their shoulders, the younger set mostly with snowboards under their arms. Their faces were flushed with exhilaration, and no doubt numb from the cold. If they didn't heed his blaring horn and get the hell out of his way, they all stood a good chance of becoming human bowling pins.

The architects had designed SkyTop to be the crown jewel of the Wasatch, catering to the tastes of the rich, while making them feel attached to the rugged outdoorsmen who'd built the place out of forests every bit as thick as the one Scott had survived. A grand lodge needed a grand entryway, and at SkyTop, that meant a long island of manicured landscaping, lined on either side by towering firs. They wanted visitors to be awed by the place, gazing down a half-mile-long corridor of trees, free of any vehicles, save for the occasional horse-drawn sleigh. They called it the Grand Mall. Today, for Scott, it was the SkyTop Raceway.

To hell with the pedestrians and the wandering cars. Scott hit the curb at twenty-five-miles an hour, nearly cutting himself in half with the seatbelt before stomping on the gas and heading toward the intricate archway of antlers that marked the entrance to the main lodge. He gunned it, throwing snow everywhere as he struggled to navigate something even close to a straight line in snowpack that extended above the bottom of his doors. God only knew what lay under the snow, but whatever the objects were, they were big, heaving the vehicle on all axes at once. The floorboards vibrated and banged as the undercarriage slammed against unseen protrusions.

Finally, he hit something particularly hard and entirely unforgiving, bringing him to an abrupt halt. He stomped on the accelerator, but it was usless; he wasn't going anywhere.

"Dammit!" He shifted the automatic transmission into low and tried easing his way out. No chance.

The roar of the motor nearly drowned out the chirp of the cell phone in his pocket. He felt his heart rate quadruple as he ripped the glove off his right hand with his teeth and fished through his pants pocket for the tiny sliver of phone. He nearly dropped it as he yanked it out and pulled it open. "Yeah? Hello?" As he spoke, he pulled his glove back on.

"Scott! What the hell is going on?" It was his dad.

If the phone is busy, she's dead. Isaac's warning rang clear. Scott didn't know what to do, what to say. So he slapped the phone closed.

The Jeep wasn't going to move, and every second he spent there trying to make the impossible happen was a second not spent on getting his ass on up to Widow Maker. "Screw it," he said, and he threw open the door and stepped out.

"You there! Just what in blazes do you think you're doing?"

Scott turned to see a middle-aged bald guy wading through the snow toward him. Scott didn't even bother to answer. Instead, he turned away and started his long run to the lodge.

"Hey, you can't park there!"

Stop me, Scott didn't say.

The phone chirped again in his hand. Shit. *Shit!* What was he supposed to do now? If he ignored the phone, his dad would just keep calling. He knew this. Dad was like that. And as long as the phone was ringing, then no one else could get through.

Dammit!

Without slowing his slow-motion run through hip-deep snow, he snapped open the phone. "Hello?"

"Dammit, Scott, talk to me," his father said.

"I can't."

"Excuse me?"

"Trust me, Dad, okay? I can't. I have to keep the line clear."

"For what?"

Okay, so what was he supposed to say now? What lie could he possibly cobble together that would make any sense at all?

"Is something wrong with your mother? Does DeHaven have her?"

Man, talk about putting two and two together! "Dad, I've got to do this, and I've got to do it alone. He'll kill her."

"Tell me where, Scott! Just tell me where you are!"

Suddenly, the frigid air seemed too thin. Scott's breath escaped him in a rush. He wanted to tell everything. He wanted just to stop and let everything take its course. To hell with Isaac DeHaven. To hell with his mom and everybody else in the world. Right now, he'd sell them all out just for the chance to lie down and forget. But he knew that tomorrow would be different. Tomorrow, he'd blame himself for everything that would happen and he'd never be able to live with it.

"Dammit, Scott, talk to me! Has that bastard threatened you?"

"He said I've got to come alone," Scott confessed. "If he sees anyone else, he'll kill her."

"He'll kill her anyway, son. And you, too, if you're there."

"I can think of something."

"What?"

"Something. I don't know yet."

The desperation in his father's voice jumped right out of the phone. "Please, Scott. Please tell me where you're going, and then we can figure out something on this end, too."

"You don't understand."

"I *do* understand, son. I don't want to lose you. Not again. Now please tell me."

Up ahead, about fifty yards away, the antler arch loomed high over everything. Beyond that, Scott saw the bustling population of late-afternoon skiers. He didn't want to do this. He didn't want to tell. But he owed his father *something*, didn't he?

Finally, he told him.

"Okay, Scott," Brandon said. "Don't do anything, okay? We'll be right there."

"And you've got to stay off this phone," Scott warned. "He'll start shooting if he gets a busy signal. I've only got about twenty minutes left."

"Twenty minutes," Brandon repeated, and for the first time, Scott got the impression that others were listening to their conversation. "We can be there in twenty minutes."

No way, Scott thought. "I love you, Dad," he said. And then he hung up.

"I LOVE YOU, TOO," Brandon said, but he was too late to beat the click of a dead line. He looked up at the rest of the room, the telephone receiver still clutched in his hand, and already, the assembled troops were mobilizing.

Somehow, Whitestone seemed to know exactly what to do. In the space of ten seconds, he issued a flurry of commands. "Charlotte!" he yelled. "Take Mr. Seyford to a cell until we can get this sorted out. James, you come with me."

"Us," Brandon corrected. "I'm going with you."

Whitestone knew better than to argue. Together, the three of them charged out of the station and on to Whitestone's Humvee. The chief had the siren yelping before he even dropped the transmission into gear. Cranking the wheel hard, he stomped on the gas, and three seconds later, they were at the end of Main Street, on their way to the top of the mountain.

"I don't understand," James said, over the cacophony of the siren and the roaring engine. "I thought you talked to Mrs. O'Toole on the phone."

"*Doctor* O'Toole," Brandon corrected. He'd done it so many times that the rejoinder had become a reflex. "And I did. I don't understand either. Maybe she had a gun to her head. If so, she should have taken the bullet."

Whitestone and James both shot glances over their shoulders.

"What?" Brandon said. "You think he's going to keep her alive after Scott gets up there?"

The cops didn't know what to say, but Brandon understood from their expressions that they knew he was right.

"Do we have a game plan?" Brandon asked.

"To stop him," Whitestone said, and as the words passed his lips, he knew how empty they sounded. "To stop Scott. Before he gets in too deep."

"If DeHaven hears the siren, he'll start shooting for sure," Brandon said.

"I don't think that'll be a factor for a few miles."

Brandon turned in his seat to see the parade of cop cars falling in line behind them, on their way up the hill. Eight, maybe ten of them, with enough fire power between them to hold off a military assault. "Do you think your buddies behind us have thought about that?"

"They will," James assured, and he reached for the microphone.

The road up to SkyTop was packed with cars either on the way in or the way out, and as Brandon watched the gridlock open up under the assault of the sirens, he couldn't help but think of Charlton Heston's big scene parting the Red Sea.

Still, something bugged Brandon; something about the brazenness of what Isaac had Scott doing. If this killer was as bright as everyone seemed to think he was, then he wouldn't back himself into a corner like this. It was one thing to scare a boy into coming alone, but it was another thing entirely for DeHaven to put his future in a boy's hands. What made him think that he could trust Scott with such a secret? And what was his way out if things went south?

He thought about mentioning these concerns to Chief Whitestone, but then decided against it. The last thing in the world he wanted to do was get Whitestone and James thinking too much.

SCOTT FOUND THE SKIS exactly where Isaac had promised, near the ski school bell. His orange and green Rossignol parabolics rested against the wooden rack, clipped together by their brakes, standing straight as an exclamation point. His poles drooped over the shovels, and on the ground, propped in the snow, lay his Technica boots, still in their carrying tree. He felt oddly indignant that his killer hadn't even bothered to throw on a lock.

He propped himself against the rack as he yanked off his gloves and dropped them in the snow, freeing his fingers to work on his shoelaces. Every muscle, every appendage felt swollen and beaten from the travails of the last week. With the added adrenaline rush, he could barely get his fingers to negotiate the knots. With one shoe off, he planted his sock-clad foot into the snow to hold his weight while he worked on the other boot. Did Isaac know how much this would hurt? Did he know how raw the skin of Scott's feet were, and plant the skis out here on purpose, just to be cruel?

But the worst was yet to come. His ski boots were stiff from the cold, and that meant pushing hard. He bit on his lower lip to keep from yelling out as his socks pulled tight against his ravaged toes and heels. It seemed to take forever, but once his feet were set in their vices, it was just a matter of stepping into his bindings and his boards were on. He had no idea what time it was as he pulled on his gloves, but he decided that it didn't matter. It was late; balls-out, God-help-anyone-who-got-in-his-way late.

The sun had begun to sink toward the treetops as Scott pushed off and headed down Prospector. Below him, hundreds of beginners crisscrossed the gentle slope, their legs locked in petrified snow-plow positions, taking up nearly the entire width of the slope with each traverse. Scott dug his poles into the snow to push off, and skated from one ski to the other to build speed. It was time to show these jerk-offs how it was done.

He was doing an easy twenty, twenty-five miles an hour when he passed his first cluster of beginners poised at the top of the only remotely challenging section that Prospector offered. They stood in a line at the top, shoulder-to-shoulder, waiting for one of them to grow the first set of testicles. Ahead and below, the snow was littered with panicky novices who had gone before them.

"Coming through!" Scott yelled at the line as he approached, and in the time it took them to turn around to see, he'd already blasted through the logjam, taking air as he sailed down the little ridge, heading for the carnage field. As people screamed at him to slow down, he found himself amused by the threats to report him to the ski patrol. *Let them come,* he thought.

As long as none of the fallen skiers moved, no one would get hurt. Scott had already plotted his course, knowing instinctively which was the best compromise for speed and safety; but if someone stood up, or even moved, the resulting collision would be fierce. Maybe deadly.

Up ahead on the right, maybe seventy yards away, he saw the crossover trail to Widow Maker. He swung wide to the left, then oh-so-slightly edged the inside of his left ski to make the sweeping right-hand loop that would allow him to speed onto the trail without slowing.

Barely wide enough to accommodate three abreast, the tiny trail afforded a breathtaking view. With the view, though, came a precipitous drop. If you didn't know what you were doing, and went a little too far left, you could very easily end up leaving a face-print in a tree. On a busy day, the crossover could be a train wreck of scattered skiers.

But today, thank God, the trail was clear for as far as Scott could see. He dared a look at his watch. 4:48.

"Shit!" That asshole had to be kidding. There was no way he could make this trip in the allotted time. It was impossible.

The crossover would dump him into the middle of Bald Eagle Glade. An ass-kicker in its own right, the trail served as the primary link between some of the less expensive condos and the Widow Maker lift. Last time he did this slope, he was with Cody Jamieson. It had been dark then, except for the moon, and he'd had a few beers on board.

Scott shot out of the crossover chute like a bullet, again taking air, but this time nearly overbalancing backward as he caught a glimpse of somebody else barreling down the hill, showing at least as much skill as he. They missed each other by inches, triggering a guffaw and an obscene gesture from the other guy. After Scott recovered his balance, he lowered himself into a tuck. Down below, the area around the lift line looked like Disney World on a holiday. People swarmed everywhere—sixty, eighty of them in the line ahead of him.

This wasn't going to work. Scott had exactly three minutes to get on that lift.

The trees thinned toward the bottom of the slope, then cleared out completely as he closed at full speed toward the lift line. Hotdogging was a common sight around here, and the ethos of cool required that no one officially notice the teenage antics. Something about the look in Scott's eyes, though, or maybe the sheer momentum of his approach, made people start to scatter as he closed to within fifty yards. At the last possible moment—actually, about ten yards past the last possible moment—Scott rocked his knees and engaged his edges hard, launching a rooster tail of snow in a high arc that sprayed everyone with a fine mist of dry powder.

Separately and together, the crowd protested mightily, barking at him to be careful and asking him just who the hell he thought he was. Scott didn't bother to engage them. Instead, he skied around them, easily ducking under the crowd-control ropes and on to the front of the line, where he nudged a mother and her young son out of the way to commandeer the next available chair.

Okay, it was more like a push.

He damn near started a riot. Skiers surged forward as one, shouting obscenities and reaching out for him as he slid out of reach on the far side of the chair. A few feet away, a bear of a lift attendant stormed out of his shack to see what was going on. He waded into the crowd and in an instant, he received dozens of essentially identical versions of Scott's transgressions.

"Stop him!" someone yelled, but by now, Scott's chair was already twenty feet down the line and at least that many feet off the sloping ground.

"You there!" the attendant yelled. "You're in big trouble, kid!"

Scott couldn't help but laugh. He wanted to yell, *You have no idea!,* but he thought better of it.

"All of you back off!" the attendant yelled, this time to the crowd. "I'm not stopping the lift. We'll have people waiting for him up at the top."

"Wait till I catch him," said someone else, but now the chatter was barely audible to Scott.

So, they'd have people waiting for him at the top. That could be interesting. Actually, it could be scary as hell, but these were worries for another time. For the present, he had to think about how Isaac was going to track him. He'd set such a precise time limit, Scott could only assume that he was somehow monitoring his progress. Maybe he was watching him from the woods. With binoculars, maybe.

Or a rifle scope.

IT TOOK FOREVER, Brandon thought, to move everyone into their places. "This is too many people," he protested to Whitestone. "If DeHaven sees us—"

Whitestone's glare shut him up.

James Alexander had produced a rifle from somewhere, a lever-action .30-30 that looked like something from John Wayne's saddle. Now, as they crouched on the front stoop to Sherry's chalet, the big cop jacked a round into the chamber.

"With luck, we'll have surprise on our side," James whispered.

"What about Sherry?" Brandon pressed. "It'll take only one shot—"

"I'm very good," James said softly. "If I can see it I can hit it. And that's the order, right, Chief?"

Whitestone seemed uncomfortable as he nodded. "You see him, you kill him."

Something still didn't sit right with Brandon. Why would DeHaven hole up in Sherry's chalet like this? Didn't it make more sense to be out in the open, where he could—

"Go! Go! Go!" Whitestone whispered urgently into his portable radio, and a second later, a dozen police officers stormed the place, crashing the front door, and streaming in with guns leading the way.

Whitestone's orders were clear and unyielding: Brandon was to stay outside, out of the way, until he got an all-clear from the chief himself. Crouched as he was, behind a concrete planter, he found himself awed by the courage it took for these barely armed and barely armored cops to engage in the work of a SWAT team without any of the special equipment he'd seen on television.

He heard shouting from the inside, all of it urgent with emotion, but mostly unintelligible to Brandon, who found himself shivering in anticipation of the gunshot that would mean a life had ended.

After two minutes of cringing and waiting, Brandon finally saw movement at the front door. Chief Whitestone stood in the opening and waved him in. The instant he saw Barry's face, he knew something was terribly wrong.

"It's not Scott," Whitestone said quickly. "There's no sign of him or your wife."

"What does that mean?"

Whitestone didn't answer. Instead, he ushered Brandon into the foyer and pushed the door closed to reveal a bloody mess in the corner. At first, all Brandon saw was the crimson smear extending up the wall nearly to the ceiling. Then, his brain and his eyes started working together, and he was able to make out a contorted figure on the floor—a man on his side, his legs oddly splayed.

"James Alexander said you know this man," Whitestone said.

Brandon recoiled. "I do?"

James appeared over Whitestone's shoulder. As Brandon's mind struggled to find traction, he incongruously noted that the big cop no longer held his cowboy rifle; that he'd left it on the credenza in the front hall. "He's the man who approached you in the crowd," James said. "The man Scott seemed so pleased to see."

A gasp escaped Brandon's throat. "Oh, no," he said. He moved a step forward and squinted for a closer peek. It was Larry Chinn, all right, barely recognizable with so much tissue and bone erupted from his head. "He's my wife's assistant," Brandon explained. And then he put it together. "When I last talked with him, he said he was coming here to pick Sherry up. He must've walked in on them."

"That was three hours ago," James observed.

Brandon tried to make sense of it. Why would DeHaven tell Scott to come here after he'd shot somebody? Why would he hang around—

"Goddammit!" he spat. "Scott lied to me. He knew I'd keep pressing him till he gave me an answer, so he just made this up. He's never been here."

"Well, that's just great," Whitestone growled. "That's just freaking great. So now we have no idea where they are."

"And we've given them time," James added.

"Excuse me, Chief?" The voice came from an officer whom Brandon had not yet met, but remembered from the police station.

Whitestone turned.

"We're looking for a green Jeep Cherokee, right? A rental?"

Brandon's ears perked up as Whitestone nodded.

"Well, the folks over at SkyTop Lodge are throwing a fit because a car matching that description just tore up their landscaping."

Instantly, the mood in the room changed. Whitestone gathered his troops around him and together they started spitballing a plan.

Brandon wanted none of it. He'd already seen one of their plans in action—very spirited, very well-meaning, but ultimately too damn slow as they tried to cover all the angles and protect themselves from harm. He no longer had time to do things their way—the slow way. They were too interested in seeking *justice,* anyway. Brandon would settle for simple revenge.

"I'm going to step outside," he said to the chief, but no one seemed to care. Just as well, he thought. When you were planning to steal a police car, it was always best to do it while everyone was distracted.

On his way to the door, he stopped by the credenza and gently lifted James Alexander's rifle. He slid the butt under his jacket and kept the barrel tucked in close to his leg as he glided quickly out the door.

37

SHERRY SAT IN THE SNOW, her back against the tree where her ankle was chained and her knees hugged to her chest, trying to stay warm. Never in her life had she witnessed such cruelty.

Never in her life had she felt so miserable. She'd set up her own son, for God's sake—her only child. How could she have done such a thing?

Her answer brought as much shame as the betrayal itself: she'd been frightened. She wanted it to be more than that, but that's all there was. She was scared.

The intruder—this man who called himself Isaac—had promised to carve deep trenches into her face if she didn't comply. "Think of the nerve damage," he said. "Who will want to listen to a lecturer who drools and slurs her words like somebody's stroked-out grandmother?"

He *smiled* while he said these things.

Sherry had invited him into her chalet, thinking that he was her driver. She just turned back for her briefcase in the foyer when he stepped inside and closed the door. "Excuse me," Sherry said, aghast that a driver would be so presumptuous. "Just what do you think—?" The instant she saw the gun with its enormous silencer, she understood. Only then did she recognize him as the man Scotty had described.

That first look he gave her—his knowing little smirk—told her in an instant that screaming for help was out of the question. "Who are you?" she gasped.

"I think you know," he said. "Some loose ends need tying between your son and me. He's quite resourceful, you know. You should be very proud."

Sherry remained silent, her hands clasped over her mouth, her eyes wide.

"Now we'll find out if he's loyal, too." He swept his free hand toward the great room. "Now, if you don't mind, I think we should watch some television." He smiled politely, and waited patiently for her to respond. She never took her eyes off the gun as she moved toward the three steps from the foyer to the great room. "Please, Dr. O'Toole, watch where you're going. You don't want to fall."

"A-Are you going to shoot me?" Sherry squeaked.

"That's up to you."

For the longest time, they just sat and watched television. Isaac flipped through the channels, obviously searching for something in particular. After he reached a local news station, he smiled and settled himself into a chair. "There we go," he said. "This should be quite an interesting show."

"What do you want from me?" Sherry asked.

Isaac smiled. But for the gun pointed at her chest, it would have reassured her. As it was, the juxtaposition of easy calm and impending violence chilled her blood. "I want only compliance," he replied. "When I ask you to do something—and that will come soon enough—I merely want you to do as I ask, and to do it well." Then he spoke of carving up her face and severing nerves.

They sat in silence, just the two of them, watching live coverage of an event that she came to recognize as the president's Founder's Day speech. This was a big deal in Eagle Feather, and the local news stations were treating it as such, offering what looked to Sherry like a pregame show. Reporters stood in the town square, taking turns speculating whether or not this would in fact be the day when Utah's favorite son declared his candidacy for reelection.

"It should get interesting very soon," Isaac said. When Sherry merely scowled, he clarified his point: "They all think I'm down there. They're looking for me." The smile turned to a laugh. "Come on, Doc, don't you get it? It's funny. They're all at the last place I'd be, while I'm at the first place they should be watching. It's really very funny."

"Scott said you're a hit man," Sherry said, her scowl creasing deeper into her forehead.

Isaac gestured with his gun, as if she hadn't seen it. "And so I am. I just don't do politicians. Certainly not presidents. Life's too short."

Sherry still didn't understand. "Then what are you doing here?"

"Here in Utah, or here in your house?"

"In Utah, I guess." She didn't want to hear the answer to the second part.

Isaac shrugged. "I live here. For the past three, almost four years."

Sherry cocked her head to the side. "You *live* here? That's it?"

"Even hired gunmen have to live somewhere, Dr. O'Toole."

It still didn't all add up. "So, how did Scott . . . ?" She didn't know how to form the question.

"Pure coincidence, I suppose." In his best Humphrey Bogart, he added, " 'Of all the gin joints in all the towns in all the world.' "

"But why . . . ?"

"He saw some things he shouldn't have," Isaac answered. He sounded nearly apologetic. "And then he royally pissed me off."

At that moment, the doorbell rang.

"Who is that?" Isaac hissed.

Sherry shook her head. "I-I don't know," she said. When she heard the key in the door, though, she figured it out.

The knob turned and Larry Chinn burst into the foyer. "Honest to God, Sherry, do you know what time it is? We can't—Oh, my God." He saw the gun.

"Don't shoot him," Sherry said quickly. "That's Larry Chinn. He's my assistant."

Larry looked scared to death. He raised his hands as if he were confronting Billy the Kid.

"Close the door for me, will you, Larry?" Isaac said.

For a long moment, Larry didn't move, and then he moved

quickly. It was as if it took a while for the words to reach him. He spun on his heel and pushed the door closed. "Please don't shoot me," he begged, again reaching for the sky.

Isaac said nothing. His gun hissed, and Larry's head blew apart, sending him sprawling backward into the corner.

Sherry screamed, and instinctively covered her head for protection.

Isaac calmly sat down next to her again. "Relax, Doc. If I'd wanted to shoot you, we wouldn't be talking right now."

"My God, what did you do?" Sherry screamed. She stood to run over to Larry, but Isaac grabbed her wrist.

"He's dead. Let him bleed in peace. Now, please sit down."

Sherry had never felt such fear. It doubled as nausea, a deep ache in the pit of her stomach that grew and spread like spilled acid. Larry was dead! Just like that, shot down like some animal, even as he was pleading for his life.

Her head reeled with the shock of it all. Fully aware only of the danger, the specific events of the next minutes—or maybe hours— felt to her as if they were lived by someone else and told in graphic detail. The textbooks called it disassociation, but she knew it now as a living nightmare.

She knew that they'd watched television for a long time, and she knew that something frightening had happened at the square, but she wasn't remotely sure of what that might have been. She remembered only the image of people running, and of the newscasters becoming very agitated as the crowd in the square surged madly in all directions at once.

Through it all, Isaac DeHaven, murderer of her dearest friend, laughed heartily, encouraging the people on the screen. "That's it, go get 'em. Track that bastard down and tear him apart."

And then it was time to go. Isaac had checked his watch and scowled, as if displeased by the lateness of the hour. He instructed her to bring her warmest coat, and then he led her to a pickup truck she'd never seen. Together, they drove past the main lodge at SkyTop, and on around the back, through the woods to a road so narrow that it ultimately disappeared, at which point they started walking. And walking. When she asked where they were going, he responded only with another command to keep up the pace.

Finally, they stopped. Sherry had no idea where they were, but clearly it was the place that he'd been looking for. He marched Sherry into the middle of a steep slope, on which ninety percent of the trees had been felled but not yet removed. It looked a lot like a ski slope under construction, but narrower and steeper than most she'd seen.

It was there, out in the middle of nowhere—at the final destination that they'd walked so long to reach—that Isaac handed her the phone and told her the number to call. He said it was the number of Brandon's cell phone (a number which she herself didn't know), and he told her merely to ask if everyone was okay, and then to ask to speak to Scott. Isaac would take care of everything else.

"Don't forget about your friend, Sherry," Isaac said, hovering the odd-looking phone in front of her face. "And don't forget about the scars. Pain can be a terrible thing to endure."

When the call was finished, Sherry felt a little proud of herself. But Isaac insulted her by producing a set of leg irons.

"This is the unfortunate part, Doc," Isaac said. He instructed her to sit in the snow and present him with a leg. For a brief moment, she feared that he might try to rape her, but the thought evaporated when she thought of the logistics—of the snow and the cold. Instead, he fastened one cuff to her ankle, tightly enough to hurt her Achilles tendon through the leather of her boot. That done, he attached the other cuff to the base of a sturdy young tree.

"That should do it," he said with a nod. "Try to keep warm."

And then he headed back into the trees.

"Wait!" Sherry cried. "You can't just leave me here! What am I supposed to do?"

Isaac smiled at a joke Sherry didn't understand. "Just keep doing what you're doing now," he said. Then he turned and kept walking.

That had been a long time ago. How long, she didn't know, because she'd left her watch back in the chalet, but easily the hour and fifteen minutes that the killer had mandated for Scott to come and get her. Between the fear and the cold, Sherry could not stop shivering.

What had she done?

She had made that phone call without so much as a word of protest. It was the fear, she told herself. Anyone would have done the same thing after what she'd been through, after seeing what she'd seen. This man killed without thought and without conscience. How could she *not* have made the phone call?

She'd set up her own son.

Sherry tried to tell herself that she'd had no way of knowing the terrible purpose of her call. Isaac had never mentioned anything about it ultimately being a trap for Scotty, after all, but merely that she should ask Brandon to let her speak to him. The rest was up to the killer. She couldn't have known any better. Really, she couldn't. Not until it was too late.

Maybe Scott wouldn't come. Maybe he would see through the trap and tell the police exactly what was going on. Maybe he would just chicken out and leave her here to be dealt with by Isaac the killer. That would be the best and the worst solutions all wrapped into one. She would die, yet Scotty would live.

But she would die.

The thought terrified her.

No, Scotty would come, and he'd come alone. He'd somehow figure that he could outsmart this man one more time. He would do it to protect her.

To protect the mother who first walked away from him in favor of barrels full of money, and now had set him up to be murdered.

"My God, what have I done?" she gasped.

SCOTT NEARLY DROPPED his ski poles as he fished for the ringing cell phone in the front pocket of his jeans. The pocket had seemed like the best place for it while he was standing, but now, in a chair lift a hundred feet above the skiers below, it frankly seemed a little stupid. He finally ended up jamming the shafts of his ski poles under his thigh and holding his gloves in his armpit. He got the phone out and opened it on the fifth ring.

"Yeah, this is Scott." As he spoke, his left glove tumbled out the slot in the back of the chair and sailed to the ground. *Shit.*

"You made it," Isaac said. "I'm proud of you."

"Yeah, well, it wasn't easy. Next time get me a lift ticket."

Isaac chuckled. "Yeah, next time. I knew you'd figure a way. I've got confidence in you, kid."

"That's why you want to kill me?"

"That's why you're a danger to me. And I never said I was going to kill you. Your mother either, so long as you do as I say."

"You're going to kill us, no matter what," Scott said.

Isaac made a clucking sound with his tongue. "You really are too cynical for so young a man. Truth is, I haven't decided yet. Every time I decide to either let you live or make you die, you end up getting the upper hand on me. I like you, Scott. I really do. You've got pluck."

"I'm running low on battery power here. What are you telling me?" The strength in his voice startled him.

Isaac sighed on the other end. "That I've had a change of heart. You've taken the best that I could throw at you, and yet you keep coming back for more. How can I kill you now?"

Scott let go a nervous laugh. "With a single bullet from very far away. I saw what you did to Mr. Pembroke and his truck."

"History, Scott. Ancient history. This is the present, and times have changed. You've got a reprieve, kid. Enjoy it."

"Until you change your mind again, right?"

"That's up to you; up to what you say to whom. You leave me alone, forget everything you saw, and you get to be an old man."

"Who can never relax because I don't know when you're coming."

Isaac laughed. "Let's not forget who walked into whose house, okay? From where I sit, your nerves are my best weapon. They'll keep you honest. It's like I told you about the feds and me. The more time goes by, the more evidence they have that they can trust me. Just prove your trustworthiness every day, kid, and you and I will never have problems again."

"So what's with all this running around?" Scott asked.

"It buys time for me to get away. I needed to get you alone so we could negotiate. If you brought a bunch of cops with you, it would have gotten complicated. I need you apart from the others. That's how I get the time I need to get away. Think of it as an investment in trust. Do you know where Orphan's Holler is?"

Scott scowled. He knew he'd seen the sign. "It's a ski trail, right?" But why hadn't he skied it?

"More like a future trail," Isaac corrected. "Runs off Widow Maker. To the right."

Scott nodded. "Yeah, okay, I remember."

"That's where you need to be in ten minutes. It's a haul, so you'll have to hurry."

"What do you care how long it takes me to get there?"

"That's the way I know you haven't stopped for help along the way." Isaac's tone turned suddenly very serious. "I'm letting you off the hook here. Try not to screw it up. Break my rules and I start shooting, understand?"

"No, I don't."

"Then I'll go ahead and shoot her now."

"No, wait!" Scott shouted, drawing a curious look from the skiers in the chair immediately in front of him. "I understand what you said, I just don't understand why you're doing it. Jesus, don't shoot anybody."

The phone was quiet after that, for long enough that Scott wondered if maybe they'd lost their connection. "What do I do after I get to Orphan's Holler?" Scott asked, spooked by the silence.

"I want you to ski down." Isaac's tone was friendly again. "It's a little treacherous, but an expert skier like yourself shouldn't have any trouble. The clock's still ticking."

38

IT WAS BRANDON'S RENTAL, all right, bottomed out on some bit of ornate shrubbery, in the middle of the Grand Mall. A resort security truck was parked next to the Cherokee, its yellow lights sweeping great circles in the darkening afternoon. Brandon tucked the Humvee in behind the rent-a-cop and stepped out into the snow.

The security officer looked alarmed at first, but then his face lit up when he recognized the badge on the door of the cop car. "Oh, man, that was fast," the guard said. "But this isn't where you want to be."

"Excuse me?"

"You're here for the fight, right? The kid who jumped the lift line?"

Brandon's heart lifted. "Yes, that's right," he bluffed. "A teenager, right? Blue hair?"

The guard shrugged. "I don't have a clue what color his hair is, but yeah, it's a kid. He pulled a couple of guests off a lift, then jumped on without a ticket."

"Right. And what lift was that?"

"Widow Maker." The kid's expression soured. "How come you're not in uniform?"

"Came in from off duty. What's the quickest way to get to Widow Maker?"

"You're driving, right?" The kid realized it was a ridiculous question as soon as he asked it. "Of course you are. Well, they're gonna be holding the kid up at the top, so the best way to get there would be around that fire road right over there."

Brandon watched and tried to keep track of the complicated instructions as the guard rattled them off. "Good thing you got that Humvee. A lot of them roads ain't even cleaned yet."

The guard was in the middle of a warning about the wildlife refuges along the way, but Brandon already had all the information he needed. He waded back to the Humvee and slid into the driver's seat. The engine roared as he fishtailed off the decorative island and back onto the hard-surface road.

He hadn't gone a tenth of a mile before he heard someone calling his name. It was the police radio. He'd blocked out the garbled transmissions that constantly flowed through the damned thing, but his name jumped right through the noise. "Brandon O'Toole, if you are on the air, you by God better answer up, do you hear me?" There was no missing the anger in Barry Whitestone's voice.

Brandon pulled the white microphone from its clip on the dash and keyed it. "Chief, this is Brandon O'Toole. Listen, I found Scott."

"You also found yourself a grand theft auto charge, pal," Whitestone shot back. "Wherever you are, you'd better pull my vehicle to the side of the road and wait for me, or I swear to God I will see your ass in prison."

Brandon nodded. Yeah, okay, that was fine. "I'll be at the top of the Widow Maker ski slope. That's where Scott's going. I need you to make a phone call and make sure that when he gets off that lift, they keep ahold of him. As long as he's in a crowd, I think he'll be okay."

"I guess you didn't hear me, O'Toole," Whitestone said. His words seemed measured for maximum effect. "I want you to pull over and park right now. You are not authorized to drive a police vehicle. And don't think we don't know what you took from Officer Alexander. Do you understand what I'm telling you?"

For some reason—probably for Brandon's protection—Whitestone didn't want to broadcast the fact that he'd taken a rifle as well. "I told you where I'll be, Chief," Brandon said. There really was no room for negotiation. More to the point, there was no desire. "Just make the phone call, okay?"

Whitestone launched a diatribe, more or less reprising what he'd already said, and Brandon returned the microphone to its clip. Either the chief was going to help at this point or he wasn't; no amount of coaxing or arguing from Brandon was going to change things. So, he decided to let the man rant, ignoring him even when Whitestone demanded that he pick up the damn radio and say something.

Brandon didn't have time to talk, anyway. He was on the fire road now, and the terrain was getting dicey. It took both hands and his full concentration just to keep the Humvee pointed in a straight line.

SCOTT'S FEET FELT NUMB from dangling for so long, weighted as they were by his boots and skis. He watched with a mix of dread and amusement as the chairs ahead of him discharged their passengers, two of whom made a beeline for the clutch of ski patrollers who were gathered there waiting for him. Scott knew just from their postures that they were ratting him out: a squared stance with an arm leveled right at him. One lady pointed so aggressively at him that he waved back.

He wished he had a plan for this. What could they do to him, really? Were ski patrollers empowered to detain him? Suppose he just skied past them. Could they tackle him and hold him down?

The questions were engaging, but purely academic, and he knew it. They would try to stop him, and he would get away. Somehow. Hopefully, without spilling blood.

Approaching the exit point, Scott raised the crossbar and butt-walked to the edge of his seat, reminded as he grabbed the steel arm-rest how much he missed his other glove. His reception committee had backed up to the end of the run-off ramp, giving him a chance to clear the chairs before they pounced on him. He made eye contact with the lift attendant who peered at him through the frosted glass of his little phone booth of a control shack and had to smile when the guy gave him the finger. Now *there* was cheerful service.

Scott stood at the top of the ramp and allowed his momentum to take him into the waiting crowd. On the off chance that they might fall for it, Scott stood evenly on both skis and pointed at the chair behind him. "That guy got into a fight with the lift attendant down at the bottom of the hill."

"Scott, what the hell are you doing?"

It was Tommy Paul, one of Cody Jamieson's ski patrol buddies—the one Scott had beaten by two lengths in the midnight snowmobile races. "Hey, Tommy," Scott said.

"Why are you causing all this trouble?"

If Scott read the signs right, Tommy wanted a reason to cut him a break. He turned instantly repentant. "Does it help to tell you I'm sorry? It hasn't been the best of weeks for me."

"Us, either. But that's not an excuse for fighting your way onto a lift."

Scott looked at his feet and nodded. "Yeah, I know," he said. "I just . . . Well, I don't know what happened. I guess I was in a hurry to get one last run in before it got too dark to ski. I got impatient. I'm really sorry." He looked up at the onlookers, some of whose faces he recognized from the lift. "I apologize to you guys, too. I got pissed off, and there's really no excuse other than that."

"Are you Scott O'Toole?" someone asked from the group. "The plane crash guy?"

Scott nodded, then cast his eyes down again. Jesus, this was taking a long time.

"You can't do this kind of shit, Scott," Tommy said. "Not even Cody would have let you get away with it."

Scott nodded some more. "I know. Does it help that this is the last run? I'm leaving for home tomorrow. This is it. One last run to the bottom, then I'll scoot over to the Prospector lift, and then I'm outta here. I promise."

Tommy Paul sighed, clearly at odds between what he wanted to do, and what the rules required him to do.

"Give him a break," somebody said. "It's not worth the trouble this late in the day."

Tommy allowed himself a bit of a smile. "Last run, right?" Tommy asked. "Swear to God?"

"Swear to God," Scott agreed. Then, as if to prove the point, he held up his bare right hand. "I lost my glove on the lift anyway."

Another sigh from Tommy. "Yeah, okay, fine," he said, finally. "Just take it easy and stay out of trouble. For one more run."

Scott beamed. "You got it." Before anybody had a chance to

change their minds, he did a quick kick turn and pushed off hard, pointing himself straight down the hill. As he squirted through the crowd, he caught movement out of the corner of his eye. The lift guy with the fast finger was leaning out of his shack, yelling something, with the telephone clutched in his hand.

Scott figured it didn't concern him.

WIDOW MAKER WAS ONE of the longest runs at SkyTop—every bit of four miles—and while it wasn't officially the most difficult run at the resort, it offered the largest variety of terrains, from relatively flat to nearly vertical, with some ass-kicking moguls. Get in the troughs of those bumps and the whole world disappeared. God help you if you fell and the guy behind you didn't see you. That'd be a good way to get your head sheared from your shoulders.

Ordinarily, the mogul field was Scott's favorite—an aggressive workout that, if you hit every turn just right, made you look great. But after a week of woodland survival, his legs betrayed him. His thighs knotted from the constant pumping, and his knees felt lubricated with sand. It took everything he had just to keep pushing from one turn to the next. Even his brain felt exhausted.

Why couldn't he remember the turn for Orphan's Holler? He knew he'd seen it—dozens of times in the days leading up to the accident—but now he couldn't pull it from his mind. What if he'd missed it? God, that would be a disaster. This was not the kind of hill that encouraged backtracking; not with its steep slope and massive bumps.

You haven't missed it, he told himself. If the sign had been there, he'd have seen it. He had to believe that. Still, the time had come to sacrifice a little speed in favor of control and attentiveness.

As crowded as the lift had been, the slope seemed fairly empty. Not deserted, by any means, but empty enough to give the sense of freedom that ultimately was the reason why people came all the way out here to ski. Overhead, the sky had begun to take on purple hues, signaling the approach of another frigid night. It almost looked peaceful.

But he knew better. The danger was very real, no matter how much Isaac tried to convince him otherwise. Scott's gut told him that Isaac's last phone call was a ruse—a mind game to trick him into letting down his guard. It was a good one, too; half of him even wanted to believe him.

There was the sign, up ahead. Now that he saw it, he remembered why it stood out so well in his memory: Orphan's Holler was the right-hand fork of a sharp left-hand turn in the slope. To go straight would require wings.

His calves, shins, knees and quads all screamed as he flexed hard against the front of his boots and jammed his edges into the snow. It took three harsh turns to bring him to a stop, and at that, what he saw nearly made his heart stop. Orphan's Holler was pitched at something steeper than forty-five degrees and the snow barely covered the obstacles underneath. Rocks and tree stumps and giant tufts of grass rose everywhere from the snowpack.

Scott stood there for every bit of a minute—a minute he didn't have—contemplating his next move. If he removed his skis, he'd sink to his hips in the snow; with the skis on, he'd stay closer to the surface, but wouldn't know what the obstacles were until he hit them. Which was safer?

Screw safety. Which was *faster?*

"Scott! Wait!"

He turned to see Tommy Paul catching up, spraying Scott with snow as he ground to a dusty hockey stop. Scott's stomach fell.

"Are you following me?" Scott demanded.

"Bet your ass. Just after you took off, we got a phone call from the cops saying that we're supposed to 'take you into custody.' " Tommy leaned on the last phrase to show that they weren't his words. "You really shit in your Wheaties down there on the lift line."

Scott felt the panic building. He didn't have time for this. "So, you're *arresting* me?"

"I have to, man. Got no choice."

"How?"

"Excuse me?"

"How are you going to take me into custody?"

Tommy's features knotted into a scowl. "Don't piss around with this, okay? I know you're all screwed up in the head with the crash and Cody and all, but I'm going to do my job. I came alone because we're friends, but if you want to make this a big deal, I can do that, too."

Scott's mind raced for a way out of this.

"Now, just ski down to the bottom with me, and we'll wait for the cops to come and do their thing—"

Scott didn't swing his ski pole all that hard, but when it caught Tommy on the bridge of his nose, the words froze in his head. Blood launched from his nostrils as he brought his hands reflexively to his face, and Scott hit him harder, this time across the ear, hard enough to bend the aluminum pole.

"Hey!" Tommy yelled. "What the hell—"

The third and fourth shots landed on the back of his head and knocked the ski patroller to the ground. With his feet still bound to his skis, he was virtually helpless, just trying his best to keep himself covered up while Scott waled away at him.

"I'm gonna break your goddamn neck!" Tommy shouted, and Scott knew that he meant every word of it. Tommy Paul was not a small man, and while Scott had suckered him, he wasn't going to put up with it for long. The flimsy aluminum ski poles might split skin, but there wasn't enough heft in them to keep anybody down who really wanted to get up.

Scott needed to make his way down Orphan's Holler, and he had to do it alone. Those were the only rules, and as uncomplicated as they seemed, they were turning out to be damn difficult to follow.

Tommy lay on his right side in the snow, his legs extended out straight. Scott saw the gap between Tommy's top leg—his left—and the snow, and in a sickening flash of inspiration, he knew how to stop him for good. Moving quickly, before his brain had a chance to think it through, Scott jumped as high as he could and brought the flats of both skis crashing down on the outside of Tommy's unprotected knee. He didn't so much hear the pop as he felt it.

Tommy's agonized howl made Scott want to vomit.

"I'm sorry!" he shouted over the scream. "Oh, Jesus, Tommy, I'm so sorry."

"My knee!" Tommy wailed. "Oh, goddamn, you broke my knee!"

Scott apologized again, but he knew the words were hollow. He only hoped the damage could be corrected.

He'd worry about it later. For the time being, he had a mission to finish.

THE HUMVEE WAS THE MOST amazing vehicle Brandon had ever driven. It was a tank, minus the tracks and the guns. What he couldn't dodge as he powered his way up the slope, he merely ran over.

In twenty minutes—a half hour at the most—it would be dark out here, and then everything would be different. It was hard enough making out the road in the late afternoon daylight. When darkness fell, it would flat-out be impossible.

Certainly, if it had been dark, he would have missed the slender, hand-lettered sign that read WIDOW MAKER LIFT, with an arrow pointing off to the left. Brandon took the turn a little too fast, but hung on through the skid to find himself facing the back end of the lift shack.

Another hand-lettered sign said SNOWMOBILES ONLY BEYOND THIS POINT. Brandon barely heard a crunch as he ran it over. A few saplings and two Christmas-tree-size firs stood between him and the unloading ramp for the lift, but they went down pretty easily, too. The noise of his approach turned the heads of everyone gathered, and when they saw him, they scattered.

Brandon zeroed in on one guy with a name tag on his jumpsuit and slid to a stop next to him.

The lift attendant's feet got tangled and he fell. "What in the hell are you doing?" he shouted.

"Where's Scott O'Toole? You were supposed to get a phone call—"

"Damn right we got a phone call. I just got a radio call, too. That son of a bitch attacked one of our ski patrollers and headed down Orphan's Holler. That slope's not even open—"

The attendant pointed down the hill as he spoke, giving Brandon all the information he needed. He tapped the horn twice, and pointed the Humvee down Widow Maker. Somewhere down there, he would find a wounded ski patroller.

And somewhere beyond that, he'd find his son.

39

ISAAC FIGURED THAT CUMULATIVELY, over the span of his career, he had spent over a year of his life sitting perfectly still over long stretches of time, hunting human beings. It was the most enjoyable part, really—luring the prey to the kill zone. Nine times out of ten, the kill itself was anticlimactic.

In his line of work, it always paid to assume that the hunted was smarter than the hunter. It was a lesson he thought he'd learned, but it was the one mistake he'd made repeatedly in hunting down Scott O'Toole. Isaac had never accepted the boy as a worthy adversary, and as a result, here Isaac was on the hillside, braced in the sitting pose he'd learned so many years ago in basic training, his heels braced, his knees bent, his elbows locked.

He'd thought long and hard about promising safe passage to the boy, and even now, he couldn't decide whether he'd done the right thing. Thinking back on the way the kid had talked about his mother, though, he'd decided not to trust Scott's sense of loyalty alone. So, he'd sweetened the pot with mercy.

This time, there'd be no dicking around. As soon as the kid showed himself cleanly in one of the many narrow firing lanes through the trees, Isaac would fire one shot to separate boy from brain. After that, Dr. Mom would be next, and then he'd be ready to move on to his next and last paying gig.

Isaac checked his watch and frowned. In about four minutes,

Scott O'Toole was going to be late, and for that, there'd be a price to pay. Pivoting at his waist, the gunman panned left with his rifle, settling the scope on Dr. Sherry Carrigan O'Toole. She was much closer than the range Isaac had selected for Scott, and he made the appropriate adjustments to the reticle.

THE HUMVEE'S ENGINE SCREAMED in first gear, yet Brandon still had to ride the brakes to keep his speed in the realm of sanity. Skiers dove out of the way as he twisted the siren knob to "yelp" and leaned on the horn to clear the slope. He worried some about the noise—about alerting that lunatic DeHaven that Scott was not alone—but the bottom line here was simple: If the time came when Brandon had to choose between Sherry's health and Scott's, Sherry was in trouble. And that was what was in play here, right? If Scott didn't come alone, DeHaven would kill Sherry.

The ride was a wild one, but manageable until he negotiated a dog leg to the left and found himself in the middle of a mogul field the likes of which he'd never seen. Great humps of snow stretched on forever, their bald, icy tops glowing orange with the reflected light of the low-hanging sun. He hit the first one way too fast, blasting it apart with his bumper and causing the Humvee's wheels to lose traction. He recovered and slowed down, but he still found himself airborne as much as he was on the ground. But for his seat belt, he would no doubt have been thrown through the roof by now. Next to him, James Alexander's rifle bounced from the seat onto the floor, causing Brandon to twitch and wince in anticipation of a shot that never came.

This was one long-ass hill; it seemed to go on forever. Thank God the crowds weren't thicker or he'd have killed someone for sure. As it was, he only scared the bejesus out of them.

Up ahead on the right, he finally saw a knot of skiers, all of them agitated, gathered around the base of a tree. When they saw the Humvee, they started jumping and waving their arms.

Brandon aimed the big vehicle in that direction, and nearly flipped over as he got sideways on the hill. Like a boatswain negotiating a roiling sea, Brandon lost sight of them in every trough. When he finally surfaced for the last time, there they all were, waving their arms and shouting as if he were their rescuer. On the ground among them, clearly in pain, he saw the face of the man he recognized from earlier in the week—the ski patrol guy (Tommy, he thought) who'd been so nice to relay some of the good times Scott had had in the days preceding the accident. Even from here, Brandon could see that something was not right about the guy's leg. It bent funny at the knee, and the ashen color around his eyes told Brandon that he was in agony.

He'd barely come to a stop when the face of a teenager appeared in his window, knocking on the glass. "It's his knee!" she yelled. "He needs an ambulance!"

Brandon nodded and hoped he'd remember to pass that information along to someone. For right now, all the injury meant to Brandon was that the ski tracks he saw ahead of him—the ones that disappeared under the rope across Orphan's Holler—belonged to Scott.

He was close. So, so close.

SCOTT DIDN'T LIKE IT. Not one bit. He churned Isaac's story through his head, but his mind kept returning to Mr. Pembroke, and the caution with which he approached that overlook during last night's escape. Scott remembered how the old man had *known* that a trap lay ahead.

Scott's instincts told him that Isaac's promises of a reprieve were bullshit. Mercy made no sense. Besides, a quick check of his watch showed that he was already two minutes past the deadline, and that fact alone changed everything. With the deadline expired, much of the urgency was gone.

In Scott's mind, it all boiled down to a few alternative scenarios: One, that Isaac had made good on his promise to kill Sherry, in which case promptness no longer mattered for anyone; two, that Isaac had been bluffing all along and had already left the area; or three, the most likely of them all, that Isaac would wait all day for Scott to show his face so he could shoot it.

No matter how Scott cut it, this was a time for him to tread very carefully.

He'd kicked off his skis fifty or sixty yards back, opting to walk the rest of the way. His skis didn't afford him enough control, not with all the hazards just under the surface of the snow. Walking, it turned out, was no picnic, either.

This was crazy. He was nuts to make this trek alone. He was three minutes late already, and if Isaac was willing to tolerate three minutes, why not fifteen or twenty? Long enough for Chief Whitestone and his friends to put together some kind of a posse, or whatever the hell they called them these days? Why should Scott risk everything on what was probably a bluff?

A few yards ahead, Orphan's Holler took a sharp turn to the left, and from that point, it seemed as if the world disappeared. Beyond the turn, Scott knew there'd be a huge, breathtaking drop—a future jewel in the SkyTop crown. As viewed from a sniper's nest, a person making his way down a slope like that would be a ripe target, he realized—a black spot against a stark white world.

Scott was thinking like his enemy now, and it made him proud. Not only had he smelled the trap, but now he felt certain that he'd found its location. Approaching the crest of the hill, he stooped to a deep crouch and did his best to line himself up with a stout evergreen tree, keeping it between himself and any view from below. As he got closer still, he lowered himself completely to his belly, and crawled the last ten feet to the base of the tree. His right hand, already brilliant red from the cold air, screamed at him as he pushed it through the snow.

The view from the base of the tree was just what he'd been expecting—a gorgeous panoramic view of the Wasatch. The terrain down below looked remarkably like the terrain he'd just completed, only much, much steeper. This would have been impossible with skis. The top of the slope was bad enough with all its obstacles, but down here, it was ridiculous. Huge logs protruded from the ground, as did the stumps from which they were separated, all of it covered with a layer of white powder.

Something moved. Down there, in the middle of the hill, just beyond one of the deadfalls, something shifted; a shadow, maybe. Trying to press himself into the very core of the tree, Scott raised himself a little higher, and sure enough, there was his mom. She sat in the middle of the slope, her knees drawn up for warmth. Something about her posture told him that she was somehow tied in place. The bait for Isaac's trap.

Scott checked his watch again. Five minutes late now and she still looked perfectly healthy to him. So, it had been a bluff, after all.

It was time to call in the cops. Retreating back to his belly, he rolled to his side just enough to access the cell phone again, preparing to do what he should have done an hour ago. It had just cleared his pocket when it rang.

Scott snatched it open quickly and brought it to his ear. "Yeah?"

"You're late," Isaac said.

"You didn't give me enough time. I got hung up and—"

"I told you I'd shoot her if you were a second late, and as it is, I gave you an extra five minutes."

Scott felt the blood drain from his head. Jesus, it wasn't a bluff, after all. "No, no, wait a second. I can be there in ten more minutes. I had to take my skis off. Fifteen minutes at the most." As he spoke, he pulled himself up again, just far enough to catch a glimpse of his mother.

"Can't do it, kid. Listen now, and remember it's your fault."

SHERRY WAS TERRIFIED. She'd been terrified from the very first moments when all of this started, and now, as more time passed, she sensed that it all was coming to a head—that very soon, someone was going to get hurt.

"Please, God, don't let it hurt too badly," she prayed.

Oh, but it did hurt badly. For an instant there, as she saw the impact against her coat and she tasted blood in her mouth, she'd have sworn that her right arm had ripped completely away from her body.

SCOTT YELLED AS HIS MOTHER flew back against the snow, and then, a second later, the sound of the shot rolled past him.

"I shot her, Scott," Isaac said. "Just as I told you I would. Why wouldn't you listen?"

"But I *did* listen!" Scott cried. "Jesus, what did you do?"

"I say something, I mean it, kid. How many times do you have to learn the same lesson?"

"But I said I needed more time, you didn't leave me enough."

"I left you all that you had," Isaac growled. "You didn't move fast enough. Now settle down and listen to me."

Scott strained to see past all the construction debris for a better look. Oh, God, oh God, the bastard had shot his mother!

"She's not dead, kid," Isaac said. "I got her in the shoulder. On purpose, I might add. With luck, it didn't even do much damage to the bone. So with that, you've got your ten minutes. At ten minutes and one second, I shoot the other shoulder. You decide how long it takes to get here." And the line went dead.

"Oh, shit," Scott breathed. "Oh shit oh shit oh shit." He had to think of something. And walking out there in the middle of the slope just to get himself killed wasn't even on his radar screen. There had to be a way to get in closer without being seen.

Scott scanned the mountains for some trace of the gunman, but he knew better. Isaac was good at what he did. He'd be well camouflaged and dug in. Invisible.

Scott knew all too well the acoustical tricks the forest could play, but he'd have sworn that the shot came from ahead and to the left, from the thickly wooded forest. The way his mother fell to the right on impact told him the same thing.

Thirty seconds had passed. Scott peeked around his tree again. A steep gulley marked the left-hand edge of Orphan's Holler, and down where his mother lay, that gulley sported thick undergrowth. Thick enough, perhaps, to serve as cover as he moved in closer.

It felt like a plan. He had no idea what he'd do once he got closer, but that was the next problem. With luck, Isaac would be concentrating too hard on the slope to notice.

Yeah, right. With luck.

It was time to move.

THE SOUND OF THE GUNSHOT registered as a searing pain in Brandon's chest. As he pressed the accelerator harder, all four wheels spun at once, initiating a spin that sent him careening into a dead fall.

Wood splintered and metal tore. A tire blew, and in that moment, he thought that maybe there'd been another gunshot.

"Oh, God," he prayed aloud, "don't let it be Scott."

Brandon tried to downshift, but the Humvee was already in its lowest gear. With the right rear tire gone and momentum lost, the vehicle foundered in the snow like a wounded animal, its racing engine shrieking a cry to the gods as it tried to move despite its mortal injury.

The ride down Orphan's Holler had been a doomed one from the beginning, a treacherous maze of insurmountable obstacles. Now, as he clambered out of the Humvee to continue his trek on foot, he caught a glimpse of Scott's skis in the snow.

Maybe he was still okay.

Maybe.

Brandon pulled the .30-30 across the floorboards into his hands, then took off in Scott's ragged trail. As he walked, he opened the breech just enough to verify that there was a round in the chamber.

There was.

FOUR MINUTES LEFT.

Scott crawled on his belly along the base of the gulley, surrounded on both sides by steep wooded walls. The wall on his right rose only five feet before giving way to the denuded Orphan's Holler. The steeper slope on his left rose much, much higher—as high as the mountain ridge—and he knew that those were the woods where Isaac lay in wait. Somewhere.

The boy moved as quickly as he could, in the kind of army crawl that he'd used as a kid playing war with his friends. The snow seemed heavier down here, wetter. Ice crystals tore at the exposed flesh of his right hand.

The cover was even better than he'd hoped. By staying low and moving quietly, he felt invisible.

He heard a *crack* at the same instant that he felt the vibration under his belly. In that instant, the gulley and its vegetation made sense to him. He was crawling along a creek bed, so pristine with its frosting of snow, even as water still ran swiftly underneath.

The ground popped again, and before he could react, the ice under his elbow gave way, initiating a chain reaction that progressed with frightening speed. Before Scott could scramble even a few feet, more of the ice gave way, and within a second, his face was underwater. His hands found the bottom of the creek bed, and then his feet, but by then he realized he was standing, and he quickly ducked back down into the freezing water.

Completely soaked now, and terrified of the noise he'd made, Scott scrambled for solid ground at the right-hand wall. He ran in a half-crouch to the base of a stout conifer, where he placed the thick tree trunk between him and where he thought Isaac to be.

The killer had to know where he was now. He'd have been deaf not to.

The trembling started immediately, uncontrollable muscle spasms that shook his whole body and turned his teeth into rows of castanets. Within seconds, the water on his coat and his pants refroze. When he moved his elbows, the icy film popped.

He had two minutes left. When he heard no gunshots, he pressed on, slipping and falling repeatedly on the snowy banks, trying desperately to stay away from the buried torrents of the creek.

One minute. He found another towering conifer and rested for just a moment before scaling the gulley wall to dare his first peek. He'd come a long way. There was his mom, right out in front of him at two o'clock, and about twenty yards away. She looked dead in the crimson-stained snow, and for a horrible, sickening moment, he wished that she were. That would free him to get the hell out of here.

Then her legs moved. It was a useless bicycling motion that made Scott wonder if she thought she was running away. Above the noise of his own staccato breathing, he heard her agonized moan.

Bile burned his throat. One way or another, it was going to end here. He looked around. Sherry lay among deadfalls and broken trees, but essentially out in the open, even as shelter lay a few yards away. If he could somehow dash out there and drag her into the shadow of one of those deadfalls, or even behind the tree she was shackled to, he could at least buy them some time. Maybe—

A familiar laugh broke the silence, slicing Scott's innards like a hot knife. He ducked back behind his tree. "Why, Scott O'Toole, is that you?" a familiar voice yelled. It wasn't nearly far enough away. "Glad to see you made it." He laughed again.

Think! Scott screamed at himself.

"You might as well show yourself now," Isaac said, his voice the very essence of reasonableness. "Save your mommy a lot of additional pain."

Scott dared another peek around the tree. They were screwed.

BRANDON FOUND A SPOT at the crest of a hill where the snow at the base of a fir tree was all churned. Scott had obviously spent some time here, and over there to the left, Brandon saw the boy's tracks leading off toward a gulley that appeared to run the length of the slope.

"Why, Scott O'Toole, is that you?" a voice boomed from out of the woods. Brandon ducked for cover, then peered out to see what was happening.

". . . Glad to see you made it."

For an instant, Brandon thought that the voice was talking to him, but then he realized the truth. Down there on the slope, he saw the smear of red snow, and in the middle of it, he could make out a splash of neon green—the color of Sherry's favorite ski jacket. That's when he understood everything.

". . . Save your mommy a lot of additional pain."

"Holy God," Brandon breathed. Something moved in the gulley to his left, and Brandon brought James Alexander's rifle to his shoulder. If that was DeHaven, he was dead.

"You want me to count to three, Scott?" the voice yelled. "I can do that if you'd like."

Brandon jumped as if jolted by electricity and instantly broke his aim. Jesus, he'd nearly shot his son. The voice was coming from a different place entirely. He shifted his eyes to the opposite slope, to the woods. Of course, that's where a sniper would stake his claim for the best shot.

"One . . ."

Brandon pressed the rifle against his shoulder and scanned the area of the voice with both eyes open. He had to be there some-where. . . .

"Two . . ."

There! A flash of light. Too bright to be a muzzle flash; more like a camera strobe. Light reflected off a sniperscope. That had to be it. He still couldn't see the shooter, but he knew just from the syntax of the count that they were coming up on—

"Three!"

Brandon pulled the trigger.

SCOTT JUMPED AT THE SOUND of the shot. It came from the wrong direction! Had Isaac moved his position? How could he have done it so fast? He jerked his head from behind his tree for another quick look at his mom, and nothing seemed to have changed. What—

Then another report boomed, this one from Isaac's hill, and it was answered a second later by another from behind.

Holy Christ, it was the Good Guys!

Scott moved totally by instinct, driven by fear and the distant knowledge that whoever had come to his rescue had bought him his only chance. He dashed out of his hiding place, into the open, his stride made awkward and lumbering by the stiff ski boots. He could see his mom right there, bleeding in the snow, just ten feet away. Another shot boomed from behind, answered right away by one from Isaac, which in turn was answered by another from his rescuer.

His foot slipped as he pulled to a stop in his mother's blood and he went down hard. A second later, he was on his knees, looking down at her. Sherry's eyes were open and alert, but her color was all wrong, her skin just a few shades darker than the snow. There was slack in her chain; might be enough to pull her to the base of that deadfall. It wasn't much, but it was something.

"I got you, Mom," he said, and she smiled.

He pulled her by her good arm, but she started yelling anyway.

BRANDON COULDN'T BELIEVE IT. What was Scott doing? Was he out of his mind?

He saw his son leave the safety of the gulley, and in the same instant, he saw Isaac DeHaven, dressed in white and black camouflage, stand and step out of his hiding place. Brandon aimed and he fired. DeHaven ducked back down. He worked the lever, ejected a casing and fired again. Brandon knew his bullets had to be coming close. For the time being, all he needed was to keep the man's head down; keep him from taking the easy shot at Scott.

Isaac's scope glinted again, and in an instant, a bullet passed close enough to Brandon's ear that the concussion rattled his brain. Brandon dropped to his knee and tucked the left side of his body behind the fir and took aim again.

Those seconds were all that Isaac needed. Brandon watched in horror as the gunman, listing awkwardly to his left, hoisted his own rifle with one hand and fired into Scott.

THEY'D MADE IT! The deadfall was a big one, maybe two feet in diameter. If they crouched down low enough, pressed themselves flat against the snow, maybe—

Isaac appeared from nowhere, charging out of the woods, his face spattered with blood, his gait a bizarre, halting thing. In that instant, Scott knew that his plan had been terribly flawed. The killer had the high ground. All the advantage. This whole charade of heroism meant nothing.

Scott saw the muzzle of Isaac's gun raise, even as the man kept running forward.

The pain registered in the boy's mind as a molten railroad spike through his chest.

BRANDON SHRIEKED AS HE SAW THE BULLET blast through his son. "No! Goddammit, no!"

As Isaac struggled to a halt to take another shot, Brandon brought the .30-30 to his shoulder one more time. This time, his shot found its mark for sure. DeHaven's rifle flew from his hands and the murderer backpedaled a few steps before landing heavily on his butt.

The bastard just sat there on the hillside, as if surveying the damage he'd wrought. He presented a perfect target. Blind with rage and sick with panic, Brandon jacked the empty casing into the snow and pulled the trigger one last time.

The hammer fell on an empty chamber.

COLD.

Noise.

Unspeakable pain.

Scott lay facedown in the snow, dimly aware that he was supposed to be dead now. And as he tried to move, he remembered why.

Isaac's bullet had entered just below his collar bone, shattering it, and blasted out through the middle of his shoulder blade. For all that, and for all the blood, the pain was different from what he'd always imagined a bullet wound would be. There was a certain numbness to it. A dull heaviness on his left side that grew sharp and bright only when he moved.

His mother lay on the ground near him, smeared with blood, but he couldn't tell which was hers and which was his own. She looked terrified. She looked as if she were dying.

Scott worried about his breathing. It was all wrong; it sounded noisier than usual. He was in trouble. Serious, serious trouble.

But he wasn't dead. Not yet, anyway. *Why?* he wondered.

He had to move. He had to get away, to confront Isaac, to end this, once and for all. As he dragged himself to his knees, he saw Isaac over there on the hill, not seventy-five feet away. He looked as bad as Scott felt, moving awkwardly in the deep snow, leaving a crimson trail behind him. What was he doing? He wasn't walking toward Scott, but rather toward a spot between them—toward the rifle that lay up against a deadfall, its stock in the snow, barrel pointed straight toward the sky.

Scott didn't understand, but he assumed that Isaac had somehow tossed it there. Maybe when he was hit.

Now, it was up for grabs, anybody's ball. And the one who got there first got to walk away.

Or maybe just got to die last.

Scott howled like a speared wolf as the mosaic of bone that was once his left side shifted and the fragments rubbed against each other. He tried to stand, but his legs wobbled. Like a newborn fawn, he tentatively raised himself to his feet, gathering his balance, trying not to notice the heavy drops of blood on the snow, the spreading stain on his coat. He nearly toppled over, but sheer will kept him upright—a harsh resolve fueled by the horror of falling on his ruined side.

The snow was so light here. A mere whisper of powder, despite its depth. As he stumbled forward, the flakes seemed to flee from his shins. He moved closer and closer to the rifle, and finally it was in his hands. He had the sense, though, that he'd won a one-man race; that Isaac was no longer playing.

This was a different weapon than the one he'd hefted in the escape tunnel. This one had weight and length. It looked like a killer's weapon. The weight of it in his right hand seemed to be pulling his left side apart, and as he braced the butt against his thigh, he wasn't at all sure that he'd stay conscious for much longer.

Isaac stood ten feet away, swaying like a drunk, seemingly mesmerized by the blood leaking out of his own body. When he noticed Scott watching him, he gave a wan smile. "I don't even know where the hole is," he said.

Scott's vision blurred and he shook his head to clear it. He could see the hole just fine. It looked to be low in his abdomen, on the right side.

"You're about to do a terrible thing, kid," Isaac said. "Killing a man is a terrible thing to live with."

"You do it," Scott croaked. It seemed as if he heard his own voice a few beats late, like watching a bad foreign film, where the lips and the audio don't match up. "You live with it just fine."

Isaac smiled. "You call this living? What do you say we declare this one a draw?"

Scott blinked heavily. His vision was fading, and he found himself locked on DeHaven's gaze, on the kindness that seemed to glimmer somewhere behind his eyes. Suddenly, the rifle in his hand weighed fifty pounds. No, seventy-five. It was slipping from his grasp.

"Go ahead and let it drop, kid. It doesn't have to be like this."

Over to his left—to his broken side—Scott saw movement that

startled him. A man bounded toward them through the snow, wildly waving his arms and shouting. The man looked familiar, but for the life of him, Scott couldn't make out the words.

"Gun."

That's what it was. He was saying, *Gun*. But what about it? *I've got a gun,* Scott thought.

Then he understood. "Dad," he whispered. His dad had shot Isaac. *Way to go.* What was he doing here? And what about the gun?

"Watch out!" Brandon yelled.

For what? *Gun.*

Isaac produced the pistol from nowhere—a pocket maybe—and Jesus, did he move fast. Scott saw it as a blur, a swift movement of the hand and a telltale shift in posture.

Scott pulled the trigger on his rifle. He heard the shot, but he also heard himself howling again. The recoil reverberated through his body, rattling the shattered bones in his shoulder. When he saw the sky, he knew that he was falling.

But he never felt the impact.

AUGUST

40

SCOTT HATED THE SCARS MORE THAN ANYTHING. According to the doctors, they never would tan correctly. In time, the withered look of the arm, the result of four months of immobilization, would bulk up and improve, but the damn scars would always be there, a road map of torn flesh to remind him of one terrible week in February.

He wasn't going to let it get to him, though. He'd spent his sophomore summer enjoying the swimming pool just as he always had. If a little scar tissue grossed people out, then that was their problem, not his. Piss on 'em all.

Today, though, had been too hot even for the pool. With three weeks left before the start of his junior year, he'd slept till noon this morning, then spent an hour watching the Cartoon Network—his one major holdout from childhood. Like it or not, he was hooked on *Dragonball Z.*

Scott's music was the real long-term casualty from his ordeal. At first it was because of the immobilized arm and the weakness that followed, but now he was past all of that. In fact, his physical therapist encouraged guitar riffs as a means to speed recovery—anything to get the fingers of his left hand moving.

Sitting now in the family room, Scott went through the motions of "Enter Sandman" from memory, with the amp turned way down. If it had been anyone else playing, it would have sounded okay, but

Scott was used to being better than okay. Much better. He knew that it would all come back, but he didn't know if he wanted to work that hard. The heavy metal that used to rock his soul seemed somehow trivial nowadays. The music in his head had turned sad.

The doorbell rang straight up at three o'clock. He considered ignoring it, but given the number of visitors they typically got during an average day—say, zero—curiosity got the best of him and he peeled himself away from the television.

The man in the suit startled him. It was one of those faces he knew he knew, but couldn't quite place. It reminded him of bad times, though.

"Hi," Scott said. He didn't bother to open the screen.

The man in the suit nodded his greeting. "You've got new hair," he said.

Scott shifted self-consciously and touched his hair. It wasn't the wild mop that it used to be. And it was dark blond.

"I don't know if you remember me or not," the visitor continued. "Special Agent Sanders, Secret Service."

"I remember you," Scott said. He wanted the man to leave.

"Can I come in?"

"No. What do you want?"

It wasn't the answer Sanders had been expecting. "Well, actually, I came to show you a picture."

"Of what?"

Sanders gave an exasperated sigh. "Please, Scott? It'll only take a minute." After a second or two of indecision, he added, "I promise."

Hesitantly, Scott opened the screen and stepped aside.

"Your dad home?" Sanders asked.

"He took my mom to physical therapy."

"How's she doing?"

"They say she'll be a hundred percent by Christmas. What do you want?"

Clearly, the agent had wanted this to go more smoothly. Sighing again, he reached into the inside pocket of his suit coat, and pulled out a single snapshot. He handed it to Scott. The picture showed a man and his wife and three children. It was a goofy picture, obviously posed at a summer place in the mountains somewhere, with the kids in funny poses, and the mother and father wearing Groucho Marx noses and mustaches.

"Who are they?" Scott asked.

"A friend of mine works for the marshal's service," Sanders explained, "and I called in a favor from him."

Scott's eyebrows knitted together and he shook his head. "I don't get it."

"The marshals run the witness protection program. You know what that is, right?"

Scott shot a look that said, "Give me a break."

"Of course you do. Well, this is the family you saved by killing Isaac DeHaven."

Scott felt his face flush. "What?"

Sanders smiled, and for the first time, Scott saw that there might actually be a nice man somewhere under that suit. "It's a long story, most of it classified, but the man in that picture testified against some bad men a few years ago."

"The Agostini family," Scott prompted. He hated the patronizing "bad men." What was he, eight?

"Exactly. Well, the story that DeHaven told you was actually this guy's story. Only difference was, DeHaven was the man gunning for him."

"For five hundred thousand dollars, right?"

Sanders's face lit up and then he laughed. "Five hundred thousand? Is that what he told you? Try two million. This was the contract of a lifetime. Kill the family and retire to wherever you want to go."

The very thought of it made Scott's head spin. "Holy cow."

"Indeed." He reached for the picture. "Sorry, I need this."

Scott pulled it away. "I never heard from anyone who those guys were. The ones we dumped in the well."

Sanders shook his head dismissively. "They're no one you need to worry about." He beckoned for the photo again.

"So, they weren't FBI?"

"They definitely were not FBI."

"So, who—"

"I need you to give me back the photo."

And with that, Scott realized that there would be no answer. He looked at the faces one more time before handing over the picture. "How do I show my dad?"

"Tell him about it. If he wants to see it, have him give me a call. Your mom, too, if she's interested." Sanders pulled a business card from his coat pocket and handed it over.

Scott studied the card, unsure what to say. "Isn't it kind of weird, you doing this?" Scott asked.

"Weird? How?"

"You're Secret Service. I thought you protected presidents and stuff. Why are you showing me witness protection pictures?"

Sanders smirked, obviously a little surprised that the kid had caught on. "Well, the marshals are grateful and they wanted you to know. They also figured that maybe you'd feel better dealing with a familiar face."

Scott nodded. That made sense, he supposed. "Thanks," he said, and Sanders let himself out. He watched the agent clear the front porch, then stepped out after him. "I'm fine, by the way," Scott said.

Sanders looked confused. "Excuse me?"

"I said I'm fine. You asked about my mom, but didn't ask about me. I'm fine."

The agent nodded. "Good. That's good to hear. I'm glad."

"But you knew that already, didn't you?" Scott pressed, and Sanders grew uncomfortable. "You guys have been watching us."

Sanders smiled. "I only watch presidents and stuff," he said. "The marshals protect other people. Take it up with them."

"You mean, if I see them?"

"Yeah, Scott," Sanders said, walking away. "Take it up with them if you see them."